Homestay Family Victoria BC Canada

# A TRIP OF FURTHER STUDIES IN CANADA

The Trip of Further Studies of a 14-year-old Suzhou Girl in Victoria BC Canada

Written by
**Novar**

加拿大 修学之旅

一位14岁苏州小娘鱼在加拿大维多利亚市100天的日日夜夜

著／秦艺雯
摄影／秦艺雯等

图书在版编目（CIP）数据

加拿大修学之旅 / 秦艺雯著. -- 苏州：苏州大学出版社，2015.3
ISBN 978-7-5672-1271-8

Ⅰ.①加… Ⅱ.①秦… Ⅲ.①日记－作品集－中国－当代 Ⅳ.①I267.5

中国版本图书馆CIP数据核字(2015)第059907号

## 加拿大修学之旅
秦艺雯 著

| 责任编辑 | 刘一霖　沈　琴 |
|---|---|
| 装帧设计 | 张　敏 |
| 出版发行 | 苏州大学出版社 |
| | （苏州市十梓街1号　邮编：215006） |
| | （网址：http://www.sudapress.com） |
| 排　　版 | 苏州鹏举文化传播有限公司 |
| 印　　刷 | 苏州市大元印务有限公司 |
| 开　　本 | 787mm×1092mm　1/16 |
| 印　　张 | 19 |
| 字　　数 | 324千 |
| 版印次 | 2015年3月第1版　2015年3月第1次印刷 |
| 书　　号 | ISBN 978-7-5672-1271-8 |
| 定　　价 | 60.00元 |

版权所有　翻印必究　印装差错　负责调换
苏州大学出版社营销部　电话：0512-65225020

**秦艺雯 / Novar**

　　秦艺雯，女，2001年8月出生，2013年9月就读于苏州工业园区星海实验中学（Suzhou Industrial Park Xinghai Experimental Middle School），2014年3—7月，赴加拿大维多利亚市海岸线社区中学（Shoreline Community Middle School）开展为期100天的修学旅行。这本日记是她在维多利亚市住家、海岸线社区中学生活、学习的原真记录。100天、2400小时，这位苏州"小娘鱼"以一个初一女孩的独特视角，于细微处入手，关注身边的小人物、小故事、小场景，记述了在维多利亚市的所见、所闻、所思、所感，既有在异国他乡的快乐与惆怅，更有成长经历中的收获和启迪。语言质朴清新，文字恬淡真切，思想纯洁阳光……她笔下的加拿大家庭生活、学校教育、人文社会，读来别有一番滋味。

　　Novar, a girl, born in August 2001, entered Suzhou Industrial Park Xinghai Experimental Middle School in September 2013. From March to July 2014, she went to Shoreline Community Middle School in Victoria for a 100-day trip for further studies. This journal is a true record of her homestay, life and study of the school. During these 100 days, the little Suzhou girl paid attention to small potatoes, little stories and scenes surrounded from the viewpoint of a fresh middle school student, and wrote her happiness and melancholies in foreign land with simple and fresh language, tranquil and sincere text, pure but active thinking…The homestay life, the school education, humanity and society in Canada described by her offer a different flavor in reading.

# 留心处处有芳香
# 用心时时有收获

  12月2日下午，初二（10）班邱老师到我办公室，给了一本封面清新淡雅的出版物样书，她说这是她班秦艺雯同学赴加拿大修学的日记。我立马兴奋起来，加拿大修学还能有如此美妙的"产品"。于是，这本书就成了我的周末"美餐"。我细细地阅读每一页，急切地想通过这本书，从另一个侧面，看看加拿大修学项目给孩子们身心成长带来了什么。

  在《加拿大修学之旅》中，我看到了一个满载关爱的小姑娘。她生活在一个充满关爱的家庭，父母不仅为她提供了可能提供的一切庇护，而且很重视对孩子的培养，总能恰到好处地给予孩子指点。他们的家庭很温馨，每天晚餐时，父母都会聆听孩子的"校园新闻报道"，并适时恰当地做出评论。这是一种很好的教育方式。他们不仅知道在孩子离家远行的前一天晚上，为孩子做她最喜欢吃的菜，而且知道"小鸟终会离巢"。锻炼孩子自主、自立、自信比无微不至的生活照顾更有价值。这一切给孩子留下深刻的"家的味道"，也为孩子的健康成长提供了强大动力。小姑娘就是带着对家人、同学、老师的依依不舍，带着对异国他乡的美好期待开启加拿大之旅的。

  在《加拿大修学之旅》中，我看到了一个满载收获归来的小姑娘。她学会用心去发现身边的美好。在加拿大坐公交车上学，她发现加拿大学生虽然上学穿着很随意，但坚决不破坏排队上车的规矩。在维多利亚海岸线社区中学，她发现加拿大的学校"走读"上课模式与中国整班集体授课模式的不同；发现"操场午餐"可以增进食欲；发现加拿大老师是多面手，能担任多门学科教学；发现美术老师下课还给学生发糖，体育课可以移师海边沙滩。和住家爸爸一起看电视，她发现住家爸爸热衷的《小丑鱼》就是在中国深受小朋友喜欢的《海底总动员》（翻译太神奇了）；和住家妈妈交流时，她发现了加拿大学生和中国学生在玩和作业上所花时间不同（其实这种不同背后体现的是价值观的差异），发现加拿大家长对孩子学习的要求与中国家长不同……总之，小姑娘是用苏州女孩特有的细腻，用心体验，敏锐观察，收获了满眼的芳香和满心的欢喜。她学会用行动感恩回报身边的人：她感激爸爸妈妈的悉心呵护和良苦用心，于是，她坚持写日记并及时将日记传给父母，让父母及时了解情况以消除担忧；她珍惜父母给的零花钱，买东西知道算算汇率；她感激住家爸爸妈妈提供的生活照顾和周末旅行，于是，她积极融入住家的生活，欣然接受住家爸爸妈妈的邀请，逛超市、看曲棍球比赛、看电视、侍弄花草，用不太熟练的动作"在住家掌勺做中国菜"；她学会用友好对待他人，于是，她教Mr. Kronker学习苏州话，和小伙伴分享食物，和同伴一起照顾小魔头Julie，真心祝福还不太熟悉的八年级毕业同学。她在这些过程中体验了生活的乐趣与美好，体验了成功的喜悦与快乐，体验了异国的真情和文化。

在《加拿大修学之旅》中，我看到了一个心智渐渐成熟的小姑娘。她懂得了"万事境由心生"，遇事"要以积极乐观的态度去面对"，所以，为了不影响加拿大修学之旅的质量，必须保持好的心情，事实上她也是这样做的。关键时候手机不见、放学后进不了家门、在加拿大生病等意外出现时，她都能正确面对，当然也都能化险为夷；她懂得通过观察手工课、校园早锻炼、社团活动、沙滩体育课以及教师教学方法等，比较加拿大与中国教育的不同，认识到国外的教学注重在学习中体验，在体验中学习。通过"出海观鲸鱼、第一次海钓"，体会蓝天碧海的魅力，认识到保护环境的重要性。她懂得了"父母的爱是相通的、家庭和朋友是快乐生活的源泉、珍惜自己所拥有的才是硬道理"。在即将离开住家回中国的时候她还想到要为他们做一些自己能够做到的事情，因为"有付出有回报才是美好"。

为期三个月的初一学生的加拿大修学之旅，是星海实验中学的国际理解教育内容之一，目的是锻炼学生的自理能力，增强学生的国际视野，促进学生的多元文化认知。秦艺雯同学用自己的处处留心、时时用心描绘了加拿大修学之旅的一路芳香、满满收获。我们为国际理解教育促进孩子成长而高兴，也感谢孩子们，你们的成长增强了学校推进国际理解教育的信心。

苏州工业园区星海实验中学校长<br/>陈丽霞

献给我的住家和亲爱的爸爸妈妈
以及关心关注我成长的家人、老师、朋友……

# 目录
## Contents

赴加前的最后一晚　1
飞往加拿大的途中　4
两重天　7
小顽童的一天　9
成为Shoreline的一员　12
海岸线社区中学一天全记录　15
一种全新的上学体验　18
A Wonderful Day　21
维多利亚市教育局第一堂课　24
和住家妈妈在一起的快乐时光　26
沙滩体育课　28
Downtown拜访刘老师的咖啡屋　30
"饿死鬼"和"撑死鬼"的午餐时光　34
Mr. Kronker学中文　36
在加拿大的第一次迟到　38
温哥华印象一　40
温哥华印象二　43
加拿大学生与中国学生的玩与作业　47
海岸线社区中学的手工课　51
野营之第一天　54
野营之第二天　57
野营之第三天　60
一起出发去捡垃圾　62
校园里疯狂的早锻炼　65

| | |
|---|---|
| 67 | 社团活动Sock Monkey |
| 69 | 一次惬意的郊游 |
| 72 | Beacon Hill Children's Farm |
| 77 | 在海岸线社区中学划龙舟 |
| 81 | 放学回家后的意外情况 |
| 84 | 探访原始森林 |
| 88 | 在住家掌勺做中国菜 |
| 92 | 点滴思考，些许感悟 |
| 96 | 找手机，现真情 |
| 99 | 木工课（专题写作） |
| 105 | 连续受伤的我 |
| 108 | 在Downtown的自助午餐 |
| 111 | 加拿大游行活动 |
| 115 | 愉快的饭后游湖时光 |
| 118 | 练习羽毛球 |
| 120 | 重游Beacon Hill Park |
| 124 | 维多利亚购物中心——Hill Side |
| 126 | 100天修学日中的平常一天 |
| 129 | 手工课程介绍 |
| 132 | 在加拿大生病的日子 |
| 136 | 筹备回国的小礼物 |
| 139 | 家庭和朋友是快乐生活的源泉 |
| 143 | 嘉年华的盛大场面 |
| 146 | 维多利亚的公共巴士 |
| 149 | 我难忘的住家 |
| 152 | 放暑假前奏 |
| 154 | 我们毕业啦！ |
| 161 | 出海观鲸鱼 |
| 165 | 第一次海钓 |
| 169 | 致谢 |
| 172 | 生活是无声的教育——班主任邱玉立老师寄语 |

# A TRIP OF FURTHER STUDIES IN CANADA

The Trip of Further Studies of a 14-year-old Suzhou Girl in Victoria BC Canada

| | |
|---|---|
| Last Night before Going to Canada | 175 |
| On the Way to Canada | 178 |
| A Day of the Naughty Girl | 181 |
| Be a Member of Shoreline | 184 |
| One Day in Shoreline Community Middle School | 187 |
| A Brand New Schooling Experience | 190 |
| A Wonderful Day | 193 |
| Happy Time with Homestay Mother | 196 |
| Sports Class on the Beach | 198 |
| Visiting Teacher Liu's Café in Downtown | 200 |
| Mr. Kronker Learning Chinese | 203 |
| Vancouver Impression I | 205 |
| Vancouver Impression II | 207 |
| Play and Homework of Canadian Students and Chinese Students | 210 |
| The First Day of Camping | 213 |
| The Second Day of Camping | 216 |
| The Third Day of Camping | 219 |
| Let's Go Picking Up Rubbish! | 221 |
| A Pleasant Excursion | 224 |
| Beacon Hill Children's Farm | 227 |
| Rowing Dragon Boat in Shoreline Community Middle School | 232 |
| Visiting Primitive Forest | 236 |
| Cooking Chinese in the Homestay Family | 240 |
| Some Thinking and Feelings | 243 |
| Carpenter Class (Process Writing) | 246 |
| Buffet Lunch in Downtown | 252 |
| Canadian Parade | 255 |
| Happy Time on Lake after Dinner | 259 |
| A Normal Day in 100-day Schooling Trip | 262 |
| Sick Days in Canada | 265 |
| Family and Friends Are the Sources of Happy Life | 269 |
| Public Buses in Victoria | 272 |
| The Unforgettable Homestay Family | 275 |
| We Have Graduated! | 278 |
| Going to Sea to Watch Whales | 285 |
| Sea Fishing for the First Time | 288 |
| Acknowledgments | 292 |

3月19日,星期三

# 赴加前的最后一晚

抵达浦东机场

与爸爸妈妈的合影

今天,是我去加拿大修学前的最后一天。此时,躺在温馨的小床上,我辗转反侧,想到即将要飘洋过海去加拿大三个月的时间,心中不免有些激动,但更多的是对爸爸妈妈的留恋,对学校老师和同学的不舍以及对这次加拿大之行的担心害怕。从小我就在爸爸妈妈的羽翼下无忧生活,在爸爸妈妈的呵护下快乐成长,这让我很恋家。我已习惯了家的味道和生活的节奏,而这次爸爸要把我送到加拿大去修学就是为了让我能更加自主、自立、自信,让我能够得到全方面的锻炼和提高。想到这,我睡意全无。

3月19日上午,待在家里整理行李。中午,妈妈带我去外婆家吃了中饭。晚上,当我收到陈金熠(初中的好朋友)带给我的班级留言本时,忍了一天的泪水终于不受控制,情不自禁地从眼眶里涌出来。那是一本班级同学给我的留言册。我细细

苏州工业园区2014年加拿大修学团全体成员合影

苏州工业园区星海实验中学合影

地、认真地、一遍又一遍地看着同学们给我写的一条条离别赠言与祝福:"记得带上相机,多拍点照片哦""去加拿大后不要饿了自己哦""好好Enjoy吧""期待一个全新的你""小米!加油"……

　　心中又是一阵酸楚:我将一个学期见不到我亲爱的老师和同学了,我唯一能做的就是把他们送给我的祝福收藏好并带到加拿大去。

　　晚上,妈妈给我做了一顿"最后的晚餐",都是我最喜欢吃的。哦,在接下来的三个多月里,我将再也吃不到爸爸妈妈做的晚餐了!我慢慢地咀嚼着、品味着,半个多小时的晚餐,似乎用了很久,多么希望时光可以停滞,我思索着。

Google地图截图

哎！我要去加拿大了，也许在别人看来这是再好不过的一件事了，可以脱离学校，可以远离繁重的作业，可以不再有爸爸妈妈的唠叨。但是在我看来，这是一件令人伤感的事情。未来的日子里，我将告别星海中学，还有学校老师、同学。更重要的是，在接下来的日子里，我将要脱离我的爸爸妈妈，在国外，在一个远离他们的地方生活和学习。我无法尝到爸爸妈妈做的营养早餐，也不能在晚餐时间跟爸爸妈妈聊起学校里的事情，更不能奢望爸爸妈妈辅导我做作业了……只能每天吃着面包、三明治，说着英语，过我并不习惯也不了解的国外生活了。

但我对这次的修学仍充满了期待，因为，这也是我的选择。因为我可以去了解他们的文化，可以和我的住家一起逛超市，可以在加拿大的学校里与外国学生们一同交流，也可以和加拿大人一同欢度他们的节日……总而言之，心情很复杂。一切的一切，不管是期待还是害怕，我都应该也一定会坚强地去面对。一想到明天我将坐着飞机远赴遥远的加拿大，我充满期待，我想我已经做好了准备面对接下来全新的加拿大生活。

加拿大，你等着，我来了！

3月20日，星期四

# 飞往加拿大的途中

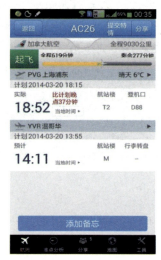

赴加航班信息

  今天，去加拿大修学的同学在星海学校门口会合，我们一起坐大巴车去上海浦东机场。经过两个半小时的颠簸，在杨老师的带领下，一行21人有说有笑来到了浦东机场，过安检、入关，一系列程序后，我们便来到所在的登机口，找了一个座位等候。很顺利我们按时登上了飞机，与两个同是星海的同学坐在一起，有些小庆幸。于是便开始了长达十几个小时的空中之旅。

  在飞机上，开始并不无聊，与同学随意地聊天，可等到吃完了晚餐（鸡肉饭）便开始有些犯困，不知不觉便睡着了。醒来后开始写日记，周围很少有人走动，旁边的同学在安静地看电视，没有多少噪音，但是脑袋就像是短路了一般，空无一物。正好飞机遇到气流，我思路全无，便合上电脑停止了写作，干脆戴上气垫枕再睡一觉，争取一觉到他乡。

  不知过了多久，我又醒来了。已经不知不觉过了四个多小时了，看了一下飞机的航程，居然才飞了三分之一左右。对！我要打起精神，向空姐要了一杯冰水，开始继续写日记。但刚写了一会，飞机又遇到了气流，不停地摇晃着，心里莫名地泛

飞机外云层上的朝阳

起一点小慌张，连卫生间都不敢去了。

写着写着，我忽然有些想爸爸妈妈了，毕竟这是我第一次远离爸妈。千山万水之外的他们，此刻定然也在牵挂着空中的女儿。我知道爸爸妈妈这次让我去加拿大，并不仅仅是让我开开眼界，了解一下国外的风土人情，更主要的是要让我学会自己照顾自己，而不是像小孩子那样，时时刻刻都要依赖爸爸妈妈。想到他们的良苦用心，当再一次的气流降临时，我不禁有些释然了。

十几个小时后，飞机终于抵达了温哥华，晚点了37分钟。我们一行赶着去拿行李，然后转机去维多利亚市。我和张欣悦落在了最后，被带队的杨老师给忽略了。我们像两只无头的苍蝇，在拿行李的地方瞎转，既要拿行李，又要找老师，鱼和熊掌这次必须兼得！正当我们与两个同样被落下的星湾同学在机场里徘徊时，突然发现了黄色外套的杨老师，我们立马冲了过去。可是杨老师仍然没有看见我们，还在专注地挑行李，似乎根本没有发现有人掉队了，直到我们走到她面前，她才惊讶地招呼我们。有点无语。

当我们在温哥华机场等候转机时，大家都拿出手机和爸爸妈妈打电话，我也不例外，但是左翻右翻就是找不到手机。我向杨老师求助，她帮我把书包又翻了一遍，仍然没有。只好去周围找一下，恰巧遇到一个咨询处的老外，向我们说了一大堆的英文，却没有一句是我们听得懂的。无奈中，我们又绕了一圈，还是没有找到，只好回到原来的座位上。正当我沮丧无绪的时候，我惊奇地发现手机就压在我的书包底下，真是有惊无险啊，看来下次不能再疏忽大意了。

顺利抵达维多利亚市后，我们来到教育局，各自分配好了住家。我与张涛暂时住在一起，因为我的住家全家去墨西哥度假了，要过几天回来，所以这几天教育局安排我暂住在张涛的住家。张涛的住家是一对年轻的夫妇。他们有一个2岁的女儿，叫Julie，很可爱，总是缠着我们，还让我们进她的房间玩游戏。房间里的玩具扔得满地都是。21:00才吃晚餐，是住家妈妈亲手做的pizza，很好吃。

3月21日，星期五

# 两重天

今天早上泡了一杯麦片当作早餐，然后就和张涛去拜访她同学Emily（茹云衣）的住家。

Emily的住家是菲律宾人，十分热情，家里有一个12岁的小女孩和一个日本来的交流生。

早上我们一起跳舞，那个小女孩虽然只有12岁，但是身手很灵活，每次跳舞的分数都是我的两倍之多。还有那个日本女孩，看上去大概16岁，非常友善，跳舞很棒，甚至比那个小女孩都要好。

很快玩到中午，Emily的住家招待我们吃午餐。这顿午餐很丰盛：有米饭、煎蛋、各种炒菜、火腿肠，还有一锅浓汤，这大概是我来到加拿大吃得最好的一顿了吧。再想想张涛的住家，一天到晚要么就是吃没有盐的东西，要么就是吃很甜的东西，要么就是吃超咸的火腿肉！哎，住家和住家的差别咋就那么大呢？！

《安德的游戏》截图

吃完了美味的午餐，Emily的住家爸爸带着那个日本女孩去参加一个聚会了。我们两个人原计划是骑自行车去，但是自行车不合时宜地坏了，我们只好待在家里看电影。我们看了《安德的游戏》和《波西杰克逊与神火之盗》，就这样度过了一个下午。之后我们便逛荡逛荡地回家了，回到了那个令人发慌的住家。

刚到住家门口就发生了一件小事故，我们两个突然不会用钥匙开门了。而住家的狗麦吉，在里面听到开门的声音，以为是陌生人，就狂叫起来。张涛在惊吓之中不知怎么搞的居然把

《波西杰克逊与神火之盗》截图

门打开了,麦吉就"呼"地从里面窜了出来,继续对着我们大吼大叫。这时,我们最忌惮的Julie突然冒了出来,原来他们一家要出去修浴帘。太好了,我们两个立马跑到房间里去享受这片刻的安宁。

然而,好景不长,不多时Julie就回来了,她又来到我俩的房间缠着我们去她的房间玩,我们两个立马一脸黑线,无奈之下只好陪她。Julie的爸爸仿佛看出我们的心思,立刻拦住Julie。Julie很不服气,又拗不过她爸爸,便大哭起来。她爸爸见我们两个一脸不安,让我们不要理会她,直接回到房间里去。Julie见我们走了,哭得愈发厉害了,她爸爸却无动于衷,不厌其烦地和她讲道理。但Julie就是不听,又一次来到我们房间,我见她哭得可怜便只好依她,但是仍然像上次一样,她又开始把所有的东西扔得遍地都是。我俩因为经历了上一次风雨,变得更加淡定从容。她爸爸进来让她不要再扔东西,她含糊答应了一下,然后等她爸爸一转身,她又继续肆无忌惮地扔。过了一会儿她妈妈进来对我们说她经常会这样做,然后将她叫出去,让我们到外面去玩,但是她的玩具总是到处都是!她拿出来一辆又一辆的小汽车,在沙发上自顾自玩了起来,口里还喃喃自语。我们便在沙发上看她玩,这倒也成为一种享受了。就这样等了半个多小时,才找到一个机会溜回房间。我们长出了一口气,哎,恼人、缠人的Julie。

晚上,同样是没有盐的西兰花和土豆泥还有两块超咸的火腿肉。想到下周一就要上学了,我的心突然间充满了期待。

3月22日,星期六

# 小顽童的一天

今天早上我大概6:30醒来的,脑袋有点晕,可能因为时差还没有完全调整过来吧。我和张涛跑到楼上去吃早餐,早餐只是一块半个拳头大的蓝莓味面包,味道不错,但意犹未尽没有吃饱,于是我就回到自己的房间里吃了一颗大白兔奶糖(从中国带来的)。

过了一会,住家的爸爸说今天早上带我们一起出去遛狗。听到这个消息很高兴!刚到加拿大也想熟悉一下周边的环境,于是我们兴高采烈地出发了。

维多利亚的早晨很冷,地上和车窗上都结了层薄薄的霜,白白的,很漂亮。我们迈开步伐,呼吸着新鲜的空气,在草坪上散步。来到维多利亚的海湾边,看来不止我们在遛狗,我们

Julie一家

Julie就像个小魔头,活泼好动,超级可爱!

的身后还有很多遛狗的人。麦吉(住家的狗)见到有好多比它大的狗,就乱叫起来。有的狗并不理睬,但是也有的狗对着麦吉大吼大叫。最后还是住家妈妈用手指着麦吉的鼻子,这才停歇了狗的争端。

  在回来的路上,Julie看到了几架滑滑梯和秋千,便吵着、嚷着、拽着把我们两个带到了那个迷你版的滑滑梯旁边,还非要我们爬上去,真是哭笑不得。那个滑滑梯实在太小,而且很幼稚。在Julie的一再要求之下,我们迫于无奈地上了滑滑梯。滑滑梯实在是太小了,我们坚决不滑。与其说是滑下来倒不如说是挤牙膏似的挤下来的!但是Julie不答应,又哭又闹,很任性。最后还是她妈妈把她叫下来,劝说了一翻这才放过我们。她可真行,眼泪说来就来,说走就走。没过一会,又屁颠屁颠地跑去秋千那儿,说要玩荡秋千。开始她妈妈帮她推着,可没多会又开始闹了起来,非要我们两个中间的一个推她玩。于是,张涛勇敢地接受挑战,跑过去推。推了很久,Julie丝毫没有想要停下来的意思,累得张涛直吐舌头。

  马上要回家了,她还是不愿意停下来,终于等来了她爸爸的一声"怒吼":"Julie, back home now!"在一阵阵高声吆喝下,Julie这才很不情愿地跟着我们回了家。

  想不到的是,回家后我们又迎来一个挑战。Julie把我拉到冰箱前,把所有的冰箱贴一个一个地摘下来放在我的手心里,然后又拿着这些冰箱贴一个一个地在我旁边绕来绕去,乐此不疲。过了一会儿他们家的麦吉也在我身边绕来绕去。正当我忐忐不安的时候张涛来了，Julie马上转移目标，把冰箱贴放在张涛头上。过了一会儿她似乎也觉得很无聊，就把冰箱贴放在冰箱上，我和张涛趁机"溜"回了卧室。

中午，我们吃了两块三明治和一碗怪怪的番茄汤。下午，住家爸爸把我们两个送到一个购物中心去买文具。到了目的地后，我们却没有发现文具店，于是我们询问了一个在逛街的中国姐姐，问到了商店。买好文具我们来到车站打算乘公交车去Uptown。在车站我们遇到一个中国人，但错误地把他当成了外国人。我们用"垃圾"一般的口语问了他一大堆东西，可惜他听不懂。后来他突然冒出来一句普通话！我们两个顿时无语，便和他一起上了公交车，在他的引导下来到了Uptown。我们莫名其妙地进入一个超市，买了一堆很昂贵的笔。后来居然错过了公交车，只好跑回原来与住家爸爸告别的那个地方等他来接我们。

回家后很疲惫，直接回房间休息了。下午住家出去办事，一直等到19:00才吃上晚饭。晚饭很简单，又是一碗黄油饭。这里补充说明一下，是黄油拌饭哦，想想都很腻嘴，很难吃唉。马马虎虎应付了一下肚子，草草地洗了一下，趴在床上写完了我的日记。

维多利亚湖湾

3月24日，星期一

# 成为Shoreline的一员

Shoreline中学Google截图

今天早上起来发现手机竟然关机了，闹铃自然也罢工了，害得我7:00才爬起来。急匆匆地快速洗漱完毕，喝了一杯麦片，带上住家准备好的午餐就匆忙上学去了。

我和张涛怀着激动的心情，走到住家告诉我们的公交车站。今天是我们第一天上学的日子呀，心中很期待。来到车站，看到路边有几个外国学生也在等车，一看他们的穿着就会惊讶一番。他们大多是：女孩披着头发，穿着长袖T恤，光脚踩着一双帆布鞋；而男孩嘛，就是一件T恤加中裤和一双运动鞋，比我们随意多了。大约等了5分钟，公交车准时来了。

有两个女孩并肩走上公交车，公交车的门口立刻响起一阵刺耳的喇叭声，其中一个女孩突然意识到了什么，马上跑到后面排队上车。想想在国内，有时候有人插队也很正常哦，但是不会像刚才那么自觉吧，这也许就是中国和加拿大的区别之一！

我们一路上还巧遇了同样乘公交车上学的茹云衣和金叶（她们是这次修学同行的星湾中学的同学，与我在加拿大上同一所学校）。一会儿之后，我们就来到了学校。这里的同学都很热情，我们刚到，他们就把我们围在中间，纷纷自我介绍，还有同学把我们领到校长室。校长热情地接待了我们，并且给我们每个人都发了一个笔袋，里面还有一面很大的加拿大国旗呢！

然后，校长让一个女孩带我们参观学校。那个女孩操一口流利的英语，她的语速和表达方式都很好，很容易让人听懂。参观介绍结束，我们就开始上课了。第一节课是英语课，老师是Mr. Kronker。这节课让我感触很大，用"震撼"二字也毫不为过，国外上课真的很悠闲。看上去学生们都不把老师放在眼里，有的翘着二郎腿，有的趴在桌上睡觉，还有的拿着手机在看电视，更有的插着耳机在听音乐！反正除了我们几个中国学生，没有看到哪个学生是在认真听课的。

下课铃一响，班级里轰然炸开，同学们作鸟兽散，没有一个人留在教室里，老师还打算叫住他们的，但是又能拦得住谁呢！他们像出膛的炮弹般跑出去，还没得到老师的允许，就好像已经发了疯似的。下一节课应该是生物课吧，我是这么认为的，反正我都没有听懂，基本上是在瞎猜。不过老师的一句话中总是能听懂几个单词的，我也只能以偏概全了。我觉得真的应该好好练一下口语了，因为我连老师上课在讲什么都听不清楚。

接下来，我们迎来了一个20分钟的休息时间。那位口才无敌好的女孩继续向我们介绍她们的学校。我们来到休息室，休息了20分钟，吃了一些面包，喝了一杯果汁。正打算扔垃圾的时候，她又滔滔不绝地把垃圾桶的一切信息都介绍给我们。她告诉我们要把垃圾进行分类，可回收的垃圾有：纸板、塑料、瓶子、报纸。还有就是不可回收的垃圾，包括：果皮、剩饭、生活垃圾等。然后，我们去了音乐房、电脑房、厨房等，还参观了各种器材。

下午，我们上了地理课和体育课。其中，体育课让我印象深刻。刚上课的时候老师让我们用8分钟的时间来活动身体，就是绕着体育馆跑圈再跑圈，然后才开始正式上课。体育课也就是玩游戏。老师拿出好多个球摆在地上让我们扔来扔去，刚开始不太熟悉规则，所以经常被扔到，我就像一只无头苍蝇在场地上转悠，好不容易挨到结束。

放学后，我的住家来接我了，住家妈妈有一个很好听的名字：Christina D. Lloyd-Jones（克丽丝汀娜·劳埃德·琼斯）。住家爸爸叫Randy Stuart（兰迪·斯图尔特）。住家妈妈把我带到家里，家里有个姐姐比我大2岁，叫Dannika Pauline（丹妮卡·波琳）。家里也有一只狗，叫库柏，虽然只有2岁，但是站起来时就到我的胸口。这个新住家比原来那个住家好多了，晚饭烧得特别好吃，还有饭后甜点。而且，她也不会来打扰你，大概21:30的时候他们就会睡觉。我在想，此时的Julie是否在缠着张涛玩游戏呢？

今天过得还算愉快，很期待明天再次见到我的新同学们。

Shoreline中学

3月25日,星期二

# 海岸线社区中学一天全记录

Shoreline中学教室全景图

今天我和茹云衣来到一个新的班级,我们分配到了一个柜子,Mr. B告诉我们密码,并且教我们怎样开锁。开这种锁很复杂,需要转两圈然后分别按顺时针、逆时针的顺序把密码填进去。我和茹云衣一开始搞晕了头,直到老师教了三四遍后,我们才渐渐弄懂。然后,老师让我们自己开一遍。我尝试了一下,没有成功。当我又一次不甘心地拧了拧锁,居然打开了!看来是我力气用得不够大的原因。紧接着茹云衣也顺利打开了,老师看我们都会了,便去上课了。我们也拿出了各自的书,去上第一节科学课。

今天的科学课内容是关于地球的内部构造。书本上都是大片大片有关地球的专有名词,我看不懂,更不清楚老师在讲什么,只好一边对着那本书胡乱猜想,一边拿着手机查阅重点的单词读音和意思。过了一会儿,老师拿出几团橡皮泥让我们做地球内部的模型，这个我倒是略微懂一些。就是按照地壳的颜色顺序把橡皮泥包起来，最后形成一个地球，再让老师把"地球"切成两瓣，就是今天讲的地球内部构造模型。我和茹云衣一起合作，不出多时就大功告成了。结果让老师一切，原本好好的模型，就变成扁的了，小小遗憾了一下。不过地球本来就是椭圆形的，我们自我安慰。最后，老师布置作业，这一节课就这样摸索着过去了。上午还有一节课是数学课，我回去开箱子，突然发现又打不开了，于是我就待在那里研究那把要命的锁，左转转右转转都打不开。这时，Mr. B出现了，他很轻松地帮我开了柜子，我忙感激地连声说"Thank you! Thank you!"

接下来是数学课，我来到数学教室。我们没有固定的教室，学校会提前把一周上课的教室印发给我们，我们按照要求到指定的教室上课，我把这种上课模式叫作"走读"。老师给了我一本练习册，并让我们四个人去图书馆登记。匆匆回来后，老师把我安排在一个女孩旁边，她很热情地帮我搞定了很多要做的东西，然后便开始正式上课。我发现这一堂课就是复习上一堂课的内容，依然很简单。做完后老师发给我和旁边一个女孩一副数字牌，其实就是用来检验我们对乘法的掌握情况的。我很明显地发现那个女孩的算术能力不太好，算乘法还要掰着指头数来数去，而我一看就知道答案了。

学校不允许在教室里用午餐，但是有几个地方可以选择：一是老师办公室边上有个小房间，二是图书馆（那里可以一边吃饭一边阅读），三是操场的草地上。我选择了图书馆，午餐是住家妈妈帮我准备的三明治，有点像汉堡，还有各种水果、小吃等。味道很好，我也小小地庆幸了一下。

下午则是一堂美术课，在课上竟然遇到了那个先前一直冲着我们说"你好！你好"的男孩。他又一次把我们拦住，冲我们说了一大堆不懂的东西，他不知所云，我们也莫名其妙。美术课老师让我们画一幅关于自己的家乡和爱好的画作，我们四个琢磨了好久才有了主意。我在画纸的左上角画了一面随风飘扬的五星红旗，旁边画了一支毛笔，红旗下面画了很多人，有做作业的我、看电视的妈妈、跑步的爸爸、购物的阿姨、种菜的奶奶、看报纸的爷爷等。老师走过来看到我的草稿,夸赞了我一下:"Perfect"。不过我还是蛮喜欢茹云衣的画的,她是横构图:有五星红旗,小桥、流水、人家,江南古村落和爸爸妈妈在骑自行车的剪影,很有中国风。就这样,一堂美术课在不知不觉中过去了。最后一堂是体育课。我们基本上就是不停地跳绳,运动量很大,出了很多汗,不过很舒畅。

放学后,住家妈妈把我接到她工作的单位办一点事儿,然后一起回家。晚餐只吃了一点面和米饭。一天的学习生活很丰富。

课间合影

我们八年级的课程表

3月27日，星期四

# 一种全新的上学体验

到海岸线社区中学（Shoreline Community Middle School）已经第四天了，每天都是步行上学。路上我会遇到一些同路的小伙伴，除了小朋友还有令我有些害怕的毛毛虫和大蚂蚁。当然也可以乘巴士，但是住家妈妈建议我还是步行好，可以锻炼身体，还可以一路饱览风景。早上用完一份简单的早餐，我就出门上学了。

上学路上大概需要15分钟，但实际上还是要多花上一点时间的，因为我的住家在海边哦！正因为在海边的缘故，所以上学的路基本上都是陡坡，就像在爬山一样，一会上坡，一会下坡，偶尔走快了还有些气喘吁吁。有得有失，一路上的风景很美：樱花树挺立着，怒放的样子好美好美；隐隐约约的远山能望到极致的远方；各种叫不出名字的大鸟在天空翱翔着、啼叫着，与人类一同享受着这晨光的沐浴……来这里的时候在百度上查到维多利亚市是一个气候温和、风景美丽、秀美宁静的花园城市，没想到现在每天能够沉浸其中，能够真切地体会到，看来住家妈妈的建议真不错！

8:00准时来到学校。这里可不提倡提前到校，提前到的话学校是不开门的！

今天第一节课是阅读课。英语老师竟然把他的宠物狗——Lucy带来了。要是在中国，把宠物带到学校是无法想象的。Lucy是一只很可爱的小黑狗，这一节阅读课基本上就是在闹着跟它玩，没人看书阅读。我们把一个绿球抛来抛去，Lucy好像特别热衷于这个绿球，球被抛到哪儿，它就跟到哪儿，乐此不

课间休息

疲。一节阅读课就在有趣的逗狗时光中过去了。上午的其他课都很无聊：数学课，什么都会，毫无新鲜感；科学课，专业名词很多，听都听不懂。

今天午餐我选择去操场。操场很大，还有许多加拿大本土的鹅（在Google地图上可以查到我们学校的操场，大片的绿地上散落着一些黑点，其实那些小黑点就是鹅），它们在草地上晒太阳，自由自在，非常悠闲。操场的四周满是蒲公英和怒放的小雏菊，看了忍不住会驻足停留。操场上视野很宽广，湛蓝的天空中飘着几朵白云，和地上大片的绿色搭配得非常和谐，让人心旷神怡，在这里用餐心情好，胃口大增。

下午第一节课是社会课，老师让我们做复活节面具。这一节课的时间是让我们查阅资料，要到下周才正式开始制作面具。我正打算打开手机上网查资料，却突然发现手机又一次不见了，我有点慌神。老师看我没有手机就给了一些基本参考书作帮助。借助参考书我初步确定了我的面具主题——做中国贵州少数民族的面具，而茹云衣决定做三星堆的面具，张涛和金叶则决定做京剧脸谱。因为手机的原因，心里老是不踏实，一下课我就飞跑到我的柜子边找手机。打开柜子，马上释然了，原来中午用餐后我忘在午餐包里了，真是虚惊一场啊！

下午还有一节美术课，这也许是我们在美术教室里上的最后一堂美术课，下周的美术课就会变成木工课了，我们这次要继续画上次未完成的家乡和自己喜好的画作。因为时间的原因老师竟然让我们在家画好后再交给她！唉，本来想要"逃掉"

这一劫，看来还是要老老实实把这幅画完成好啊。临走前，老师给了我们每人一块巧克力。每一次下课老师都会给我们一颗糖吃，不知道是什么意思？这也许又算是国外和中国教学的不同之处吧！我们上幼稚园或者小学的时候，老师一般会在表现好的同学头上贴小红花，现在想想还不如糖好吃。算了，不想了，吃了再说。

　　值得一提的还有体育课，我们临时换了一个瘦瘦的女老师，其实她也是一位数学老师，甚至还教过我们一堂科学课。一上课她就让我们绕着房间跑，跑在我边上的是一个叫Annie的同学，后面则是一个外国男生。跑着跑着，跑步的圈子变得越来越小，我有点发晕，正打算往外面跑的时候，"咣"的一声，我后面那个男生可能是转晕了，突然从我后面摔倒在我面前。我吓了一跳，下意识往后退了几步。而我边上的Annie显然也被吓到了，她不是向后退，而是向前倒下去，结果很悲剧：她直接就倒在了那个男生身上，其实也没有完全倒在那个男生身上，只不过她用手撑着地把那个男生又压在了地上，真是雪上加霜。当时我们都惊呆了，这样的姿势大概维持了几秒钟，他们俩才一个一个爬起来。那个男生倒没什么事，自顾自地玩去了，倒是Annie吓得脸色惨白。我们几个趁机在那边揶揄道："那个被压的倒没什么事，你怎么就被吓成这样了？！"我们还说一定要把这件事写在日记上。她沉默不语，回敬了几个白眼给我们。过了一会，这个事情好像还压在她心头一样，为了引开她的注意力，我们又开始无聊的跳绳，一直跳到脚抽筋。下课前几分钟老师又让我们练习蛙跳、高抬腿、俯卧撑，累得我气喘吁吁。这堂体育课把我中午摄入的卡路里都消耗殆尽了，累得我不想动了。

　　放学回家，我向住家妈妈说周末要去买蜡笔，因为要完成老师交代的美术作业，她一口答应了。大约晚上8:00的时候，住家爸爸突然拿了一盒蜡笔回来，对我说"5加元"。我的天哪，换成人民币的话，要30块钱一盒蜡笔呀，这么贵呀！晚上和妈妈视频了一下，然后洗澡、写日记、睡觉。

3月30日，星期日
# A Wonderful Day

我和我的住家

　　今天是周六，早上9:00住家带我们去遛狗，目的地是海边的一个森林沙滩（在海边树林里的小沙滩）。住家的狗——库柏和我一起坐在车后座，它是一只拉布拉多猎犬，全身披着黑色"夹克"，虽然只有两岁但已经长得很高大了。住家妈妈说拉布拉多个性温和、活泼，没有攻击性而且非常聪明，是加拿大的本地狗，跟哈士奇和金毛寻回猎犬并列三大无攻击性犬类，让我不必害怕它。

　　住家妈妈还告诉我，库柏是他们一家之前去野营的时候发现的，那时候的库柏又小又瘦，于是他们就收留了它，并且把它照顾得很好。他们还在自己家的大门上贴了库柏的照片，上面写着"拉布拉多——库柏，住在这里！"现在它俨然已经成为住家家庭成员中不可或缺的一分子了。库柏虽然很少叫，但是很热情，总喜欢跟在人后面。一路上它把头探出窗外，好像显示它很熟悉这条路，也最喜欢那个地方，嘴巴里还发出"嘤嘤"的叫唤声。

很快，我们就到了目的地。这里很美，典型的北美风景。我们爬了一小段山路，来到一个小沙滩边，这里有一片很清澈的湖泊。住家爸爸随手在地上捡了一根短树枝，把它远远地抛到湖里。库柏看到树枝马上就"腾"的一下冲到水里，开始朝着树枝游，不一会儿就把树枝叼了回来，然后放在身边，把身上的水甩干，一副很有成就感的样子。这使我想起了捕鱼的鸬鹚。住家爸爸趁这个时候悄悄地把它身边的树枝捡了回来，它立马不高兴了，跳了起来，打算抢回树枝，但是住家爸爸高举双手，它根本抢不到。随即又主裁判般的让它马上出现，它依然不甘心地跳了起来，但是跳了几下发现不奏效，只好又乖乖地坐下，如此反复。突然，住家爸爸假装又把树枝抛了出去，库柏以为树枝已经在湖里了，又一次猛冲到水里，逗得我们开心地大笑起来。过了一会儿，来散步的狗狗越来越多了，库柏与它们打闹成一团。还有一只狗叫巧克力，也是拉布拉多犬。它们两个在水里打闹。巧克力的主人扔了一根树枝出去。库柏以为是住家爸爸扔的，立马又冲了出去，巧克力也跟着冲进水里。两只狗就这样在水里嬉戏打闹。

过了一会儿，我们来到第二个沙滩玩了一会。因为要吃午餐了，我们便恋恋不舍地离开了这个美丽的森林沙滩。午餐是在麦当劳吃的，我发现国外的餐馆非常整洁，而且有很多自助的东西，例如番茄酱、吸管、杯子等。用完了午餐，我们去了一趟超市买了一些东西，然后回家接丹妮卡上学。

我们和库柏在丹妮卡的学校兜了一圈便去登山了。这里的山都是原生态的，没有台阶，甚至没有路径，要一步一步攀爬上去，虽然坡度不是很高，但依然爬得很累。好不容易爬到山顶，我们在山顶上拍了一张合影，突然发现我的照相机没有电了，于是只好用手机凑合，看来我未雨绸缪的功课还是做得不够啊!

我们在山顶上欣赏了整个维多利亚的全景,真的好漂亮。远远望去,维多利亚的一大半都浸在海里,还有一些小岛,整个城市绿意盎然,绿树丛中是各种颜色的房屋。天空和海水一样很蓝很蓝,水天一色,一簇簇白云点缀着湛蓝的天空,脑海中突然冒出"落霞与孤鹜齐飞,秋水共长天一色"两句诗来,王勃的诗句描写的大概也是这样的场景吧。

大约下午3:00时我们把丹妮卡接了回去,并在一个日食店买了一些吃的东西,然后就回家了。晚上,我自告奋勇展示了我的中国厨艺,做了蛋炒饭给住家爸爸妈妈吃。"手艺"生疏的缘故,本来以为做得很难吃,好像觉得没有在家里做的那份"功力"了,住家爸爸妈妈却大加赞赏,都吃了好几碗!这让我很意外,也很开心。看来,中国的美食文化真是博大精深、天下无敌。

晚餐后,我们看了一会儿《小丑鱼》,这是住家爸爸很喜欢的一部电影。但是我不怎么感兴趣,因为小时候已经看过了,在中国这部电影的名字叫《海底总动员》。同一部影片,国内外的名称却千差万别,谁能说出其中的奥妙呢?

晚上10:00,我准时上床睡觉。这个周末算下来,我一共看了6部电影,这真是一个惊人的数字。我想大概住家爸爸妈妈想让我尽快地熟悉语言环境。明天就是周一了,真的好期待再一次回到学校和同学们一起上课。

海边、森林、沙滩

4月2日，星期三

# 维多利亚市教育局第一堂课

今天下午最后一节体育课之前，当我们四个人正打算去体育教室的时候，突然发现了潘老师和杨老师（这次修学的带队老师）。潘老师戴上了一副酷酷的墨镜，而杨老师则摘掉了眼镜，难道她的近视突然好了？她们向我们走来，问我们怎么去教育局。其他三人都说要乘公交车去，而我则兴高采烈地说："住家会开着敞篷跑车把我送过去。"老师又问她们认不认得路，搞了半天只有一个路盲去过一次，但早就忘了怎么去的了。我兴奋地暗自窃喜，哈哈，我的住家真是太棒啦！

放学后，我跑到家里，匆忙吃了一点点心，就和住家妈妈出门了。住家妈妈把敞篷车的篷拉开，我坐在里面，别提多惬意了，这是我第一次坐敞篷车啊！好开心哦。库柏也待在车里面，东看看西瞧瞧。大约半个小时车程，我们到了教育局。本以为我是最后一个到的，没想到班级里只有稀稀拉拉几个人。杨老师也没有来，我们都怀疑她是不是迷路了。等待中，我们大声讨论着自己的住家，喜怒哀乐、酸甜苦辣，不一而足。

过了一会儿，杨老师来了，我们一群人拥簇上去，问她一些作业上的问题。因为大家争着抢着提问，所以就剩下不多的时间了。在接下来的半个小时内，我们就开始畅怀地聊天。主题都是关于自己的住家，有的庆幸不已，有的怨声载道。比如：郑知仪和顾立，一个说住家的宝宝很可爱，像洋娃娃一样，照顾他很有趣，而且连他的饮食起居、心爱的各种东西，都了解得一清二楚。而另一个呢，就一直在说住家老是让他干活，不停地干活，永无止境地干活，都不给他一点出去玩的时间！但是，实际上郑知仪也是一直在干活的，要自己做早餐，打扫卫生，帮住家烧饭，照顾小孩，并且还要逗小孩开心，摔倒了要扶他起来安慰他，哄他睡觉。而顾立呢？也就是打扫打扫卫生，其他似乎也没什么了。这样看来，郑知仪干的活可比顾立干的要多得多了。但是她很开心、很享受。所以我在想，其实我们对住家的各种夸赞或不满，都是源于我们看待住家的角度不同。如果你对这个住家一开始的印象好，那么你一定会对这个住家十分满意，而你在接下来的一段日子中，也会很享受这一段愉快的时光。但是如果你一开始就对住家存在一些意见的话，那么你将会一直觉得自己的住家没有别人的好，这也会对你的加拿大修学之行产生一定的影响。

万事境由心生。对事情的看法想法，都源于我们的内心，如果你对这件事情或东西很感兴趣，那么你将会快乐地接受它；相反的话，你将会对这个事情或东西产生自己的意见从而排斥它，这也许会导致你心情不好。我想，我们看待某一件事情，一定要以积极乐观的态度去面对。要面对的总是要面对的，何必去自添烦恼呢！就像台湾艺术家黄美廉说的："我只看我所有的，不看我没有的！"我想，我们要珍惜我们所有的，我们要努力创造我们向往的。

维多利亚市海景

4月3日,星期四

# 和住家妈妈在一起的快乐时光

今天,上完最后一节疯狂的体育课后,我疲惫地回到了家。看见住家爸爸和妈妈正躺在沙发上看电视。住家妈妈看了我一眼,说:"冰箱里有做好的三明治。"我谢过之后便冲到冰箱前,把三明治拿出来热了一下,又拿了一杯果汁,狼吞虎咽地大吃起来。知我饿者,住家妈妈也。啊!真是美味啊!住家妈妈做的三明治真是没得挑,有汉堡的味道,但是又不失三明治的风味。

吃好了点心我开始做作业。过了一会,住家妈妈过来问我要不要陪她去超市,我很爽快地答应了。库柏也想去,但是住家妈妈让它待在家里,于是它马上不开心了,表面上乖乖地坐在地上。但等我稍稍打开一条门缝,正打算出去的时候,它立马冲了出来,一直冲到住家妈妈的跑车旁边,对着住家妈妈直摇尾巴,好像是乞求带它去超市。住家妈妈没有办法,说了一句:"你只能留在车里哦!"库柏立刻心领神会,在它后座的老位置上坐好了。

不一会儿,我们就到了超市门口,住家妈妈把库柏留在车里,然后就带我走进超市。东挑挑西挑挑,买了一些零食和饮料,还问我要不要一些东西?我一看价格再算上汇率,就连连摇头。

满载而归回到家,住家妈妈又邀请我和她一起去种花。种花?我还从来没有种过花呢。于是我又点了点头,很高兴地答应了。跟着住家妈妈来到后花园,丹妮卡也在那边。住家妈妈帮我们弄好了小花盆、勺子,还有泥土和一堆花种。于是我们

住家后花园

住家餐厅

开工了。我东挑西选，终于挑出了一种，貌似是挺好看的花种。当我把一半花种倒在小花盆里的时候，我突然想起来，数量是不是太多了？于是便问住家妈妈，她说只要两三粒就可以了，我立马懵了！低头看了一看，"Oh, my god"，自己播的花种，大概最少也有二三十粒了吧！看来我对种花还是比较陌生的，于是我只好把花种重新放到花包里，好不容易种出来4盆。住家妈妈又给了我4个小花盆，于是我又开始新一轮的奋斗了。正当我把第四个小花盆填满土的时候，住家爸爸来叫我们吃饭了。

　　今天的晚餐好丰盛啊！有蔬菜沙拉、包菜、烤鸡腿和米饭。特别是烤鸡腿，又香又嫩，味道很足，比外面买的还要好吃。听住家爸爸介绍，做这个烤鸡腿要花1个小时左右的时间。今天，他还特意在鸡腿上多加了一层烧烤酱。看来住家爸爸和我爸爸一样，对家庭美食方面很有研究，烹饪手艺也不错，给个赞吧！

　　晚餐后住家开始看电影，我开始写我的日记。期待崭新的一天。

4月4日，星期五

# 沙滩体育课

今天下午的体育课，老师带着七、八年级的学生集体走路去海边，我们的学校就在海边。大概走了15分钟，我们来到一片密林之中。穿过密林映入眼帘的是一片沙滩。乍眼一望沙滩上面有很多很高很大的深色岩石，还堆满了各种稀奇古怪的贝壳。海水和天空一样都是湛蓝湛蓝的。海水之中还矗立着一座不知名的小岛，上面是一片繁茂的树林。沙滩的边上有一大片密林围着，保护着这一块风水宝地。此时，天上的海鸥，在蓝天和碧海之间飞翔，高亢的鸣叫着，悠闲地盘旋着……动静相宜，宛如画中。

一到沙滩，同学们就散开了：有的直接脱掉鞋子在沙滩上踩浪花；有的折了段小木棍在礁石缝隙下抓螃蟹；有的爬上树坐在弯弯的树干上吹海风；还有的仰面躺在岩石上晒太阳……我的心情也被迅速感染了，立刻朝沙滩飞奔过去。我踩着贝壳，迎着海水声，踏着海浪来到海边。这里静静地躺着很多颜色不同、形状各异的贝壳。我捡了一块白色的贝壳，把它放到海水里，看着它渐渐地被海水冲干净。这儿的海水好清澈啊！即使是站在一块很高的岩石上往下看，依然能够把水里的藻类植物和贝壳看得一清二楚。

玩了一会儿，我就回到沙滩，坐在岩石上用双手托着下巴眺望着这一片美景，开始遐想：大海那边的尽头是不是就是中国呢？往大海里扔一个漂流瓶，会不会漂到苏州呢？我在岩石上还发现很多小泡泡和一些不知名的藻类植物，看着有点像绿色的"爱心"。

沙滩体育课一景

　　正当我兴致勃勃地研究这些植物时，一只黄色的小虫突然从我旁边爬过，天生对虫子敏感的我立马"啊"的一声就跳开了，并拽着金叶跳下了岩石。跳下来的时候太用力了，脚上弄了一大滩泥沙，用树枝把鞋子弄干净后就去找张涛她们，发现她们正在沙滩上用树枝和石块写字，于是我们也加入了。我们写了"加拿大"三个字，而她们写的是"苏州"，最后又添了一个"Victoria"和一架飞机，意思是我们坐飞机越过大洋，千里迢迢来到加拿大维多利亚。这也算是留下了一个在维多利亚的"足迹"吧。临走的时候，我在沙滩上捡了几个漂亮的小石子，打算带回国留作纪念。

　　过了一会儿老师叫我们回去了，短暂的沙滩时光就这样过去了，我们又一次穿过那片密林回到了学校。一路上我们很纳闷，这也算是上课？在国内会不会算是逃课啊？还是集体逃课！哈哈。

　　回家后，休息了一会儿，住家爸爸就带着我和丹妮卡去她的学校，计划送她去打曲棍球。但丹妮卡的脚伤还没好，于是我们就只好取消原计划，去买了两张碟片，打算回家看电影。

4月5日，星期六

# Downtown
# 拜访刘老师的咖啡屋

刘老师和他的咖啡店

　　今天是周六，我和金叶一起去Downtown。在周五约好9:00在学校门口见面，8:45的时候，我们不约而同到达了学校。正好这时候有一班公交车，于是我们很顺利地就到达了Downtown。

　　因为对这里很不熟悉，我们只好沿着主干道瞎转。一开始我们认为只要一直沿着主干道走就不会迷路，但是不知不觉中，我们拐了一个弯。虽然仅仅是一个小弯，但是，对我们这两个顶级大"路痴"来说，真的是很难再回到原来那条路上了。真是差之毫厘谬以千里啊。于是我们开始左转右转，拐了好几个弯，误打误撞，才终于回到了主干道，一共费了半个多小时。这个时候已经10:30了，肚子开始"咕咕"地唱空城计了，我们打算在麦当劳解决午饭。金叶带了午饭，但是我没带，点了一份Hot Cake简单应付一下。接下来我们打算去找刘老师的咖啡店（刘老师是我们修学期间加拿大方面的联络人和负责人），听说他包的馄饨很好吃，而且第一次去吃还是免费的呢！

大概走了十几分钟吧，天空中突然飘下濛濛细雨。正好金叶打算买一把伞，于是我们便走进了一个最近的超市，这个超市很大而且很整洁、很安静。我们走到了卖伞的那一栏，金叶看中了一把，但是一看标价，14.99加元！换成人民币大概要85块，再加上税就要90块钱了。想想一把伞要90块，我们哪用得起呀。但是金叶又想了想，自己的那把伞已经坏掉了，而住家的那把伞"杀伤力"又太大，加拿大又是一个经常下雨的国家，没有一把质量好一点的伞怎么行呢，况且国外的东西质量都很好，拿回国内还能再用。她反复纠结好久，最后狠了狠心，手里拿了二十块钱，坚定地走向了收银台。

这时，一个老爷爷推着一辆小车正打算出去，他的轮子不小心压到了一个塑料桶，那个塑料桶上有很多个小挂钩，被他这样一压，小挂钩散落一地，还有很多小挂钩钻到了他的车底。他身体不便，只能待在车边，手又够不到车子底下。我见他一脸难堪，于是蹲下来帮他把车底的挂钩都捡了出来。那个老爷爷笑着轻轻地对我说了一句"Thank you"，我顿时感觉心里暖暖的。

买好伞后，我们又继续开始寻找刘老师的咖啡店。我们拿着他的名片，看到人就问路。这里的人都好热心，耐心地为我们指路。我们还遇到一位老奶奶，虽然不知道怎么走，但是帮我们到商场里拿了一张地图。就这样，我们拿着地图继续问……

只见风雨中，两个"路痴"合撑着一把小伞，用她们蹩脚的英语口语在问路……不知道过了多少条马路，转了多少个圈，正当我们两个疲惫不堪的时候，在一个转角处转了道弯，我们终于看到了刘老师咖啡店的标志。到了？到了！我们终于到了！！我们两个尖叫了一声，冲到刘老师的咖啡店门口，在他咖啡店前拍了好几张照片来表示我们到他咖啡店是多么的艰辛。

但刘老师好像没有认出我们,只好再自我介绍一番,并且讲述了一遍我们来到这里的"艰辛"历程。他听到我们两个"路痴"从9:30找他的咖啡店一直找到了12:00,瞪大了眼睛,惊讶得不敢相信。他看我们疲惫不堪的样子,就给我们每人一碗免费馄饨,而且还是双倍的量!兜了一上午,真的很饿了。刘老师的馄饨热乎乎的、香香的、鲜鲜的,实在是太好吃了,在国外待了那么久,第一次吃到这么好吃的馄饨,真是激动啊!没等我吃完一个,金叶就回过头来问我:"你吃了几个了啊?"我每次都回答她:"我没数啊,你关心这个干嘛啊?"她说:"如果等我吃完了你还在吃,那么我心里会不舒服的,我会很馋的。"好吧,这个想法真是奇怪啊。

刘老师包的小馄饨

说话间,我听到门口有人用中文讲:"刘老师好!"声音很熟,仔细一看,原来是我们的带队老师——杨老师和潘老师。他们看到我们在吃馄饨,于是也叫了一碗馄饨,并且让刘老师推荐他们一些有好东西吃的地方。用完馄饨,聊了一会之后我们两个便又出去逛了。

我们向刘老师打听巧克力店在哪里,他给我们指了一条最近的路,于是我们走了。但一会儿工夫突然又不知道自己在哪儿了。于是我们又看着地图回到了刘老师那里,不好意思地对他说一句:"刘老师,我们又迷路了……"

Downtown街景

刘、杨和潘,三个老师瞬间"石化"。刘老师又一次耐心地给我们讲解了一遍路。我们再次出发,终于找到了巧克力店。又一次感动地在店门口拍了好几张照,这才进去。里面琳琅满目的巧克力立刻迷花了我们的眼,服务员还给我们品尝了各种巧克力,香甜可口,入口即化,味道真是好。但是我一看那个标价就呆住了,9.99加元啊,换成人民币再加上税大概要60元唉!六十块钱买一块拳头大小的巧克力,谁会买啊?!想想,不就是买点巧克力酱把它们冻住吗,有必要那么贵吗!但是金叶对着那琳琅满目的巧克力,眼睛里满是星星,失去了免疫力,说:"我买哪一个好呢?"我在她旁边说道:"这个巧

巧克力店门口与巧克力熊合影

克力换成人民币要XXX,再加上税就要XXX,这要是在中国才XX啊,这里为何那么贵呢!"不过即使我这样说依然打消不了她这个吃货的念头,她还是买了一小块很便宜的巧克力,但是在我看来依然是很贵的。

　　从巧克力店出来,我们打算回到刘老师那儿。我问金叶:"你还记得回去的路吗?"她茫然地摇了摇头,就这样我们又度过了长达半个小时的迷路时光。等到我们终于看到刘老师的咖啡店时,我们两个又一次兴奋地大叫起来,不过我们还是在店门口调整好了心情才走进咖啡店。

　　当我们对三位老师说我们再次迷路的时候,他们对我们说应该多走走,让我们继续出去玩,不要老待在咖啡店里。于是我们就打算去唐人街。走到走廊的时候,金叶看见一个鸭子,问我"那是不是真的"。我看那鸭子动也不动,就随口说了一句"肯定是假的"。但是等我们回来的时候,看见一个老奶奶正在逗那只鸭子,我这才觉悟——鸭子原来是活的!于是我们也和那个老奶奶一样,拿着老奶奶给我们的薯片,喂给鸭子吃。看着它吧唧吧唧吃得欢快的样子,我奇怪地冒出个想法:国外的鸭子真的好幸福,还有薯片吃,要是在国内,这只鸭子会不会被拔光了毛摆在餐桌上了呀。

　　大概14:30的时候,我们两个实在是逛累了,于是打道回府。在Downtown的一天虽然很累,但是对这里的环境和路线倒是熟悉了很多,估计下次来不会再迷路了。

"假"?"真"!鸭子

4月7日，星期一

# "饿死鬼"和"撑死鬼"的午餐时光

我曾经的"六件套"

今天吃午饭的时候，我和金叶坐同一桌，张涛和茹云衣在另一桌。

我今天的午饭，从原来的"六件套"减为了"四件套"。再减去早午饭的时候吃掉的一块饼干，午饭就只剩下三样东西了：两块小小的三明治，一小盒苹果汁和一根香蕉。我把这三样东西一一拿出来，然后看着金叶拿出她的午饭。她今天又是米饭，只见那晶莹剔透的白米饭上，安静地躺着三块秀色可餐的火腿。金叶看着我那馋样，便慷慨地拿出一把干净的勺子，让我吃她的饭。我吃了半块火腿和一点米饭，就回去吃我的三明治了。住家爸爸做的三明治虽小，但还是很好吃的。过了一会儿，我吃完一块三明治，觉得很饱。这时旁边的金叶也吃完了米饭。我俩一个在那边说"好饱啊"，另一个却在旁边说"我还饿着呢"，于是我就把我剩下的一块三明治给了金叶。她有点不好意思，就拿了一盒酸奶和我交换。

过了一会儿，我们两个都吃完了午饭。我惬意地躺在椅子上吃着香蕉，喝着果汁。而旁边的金叶躺在椅子上，嘴里一边咕哝着："我还是好饿啊！"我瞬间一脸黑线。她的午饭，可是一盒饭加上一块三明治啊！那么丰盛的午饭，她竟然还吃不饱？更何况她还是一个瘦瘦的女孩。一看就是那种吃得很少的人，没想到吃了那么多还在说饿！

大概又过了3分钟，她实在熬不住了，从她的午餐包里拿出一包饼干打算吃，但犹豫了一下又放回了午餐包里，嘴里还自顾自地说："不行，这一包饼干我还要留着下午吃呢！现在刚吃完午饭就这么饿，下午一定会饿死的，我不能吃，我不能吃，这可是我的救命粮草啊！"

但是，秒针才转了一会儿，她又开始在旁边说饿了。

"我饿了，我饿了，我饿了……"只听见一声声哀嚎在我耳边萦绕着。

"下次一定要让住家为我准备两盒饭加六块火腿！"金叶叫完了就在我旁边说道。我仍是专心地吃着我的香蕉。

"我真是不知道你是怎么吃饱的？你才吃了一块三明治，就这么饱了吗？"金叶问道。

"吃饱了啊，而且我现在已经撑掉了。"我悠闲地啃着香蕉说道。

金叶再次熬不住了，她又把手伸到了午餐盒里，去拿她的那包救命粮草。可是拿出来后她又立马塞了回去。真是一个懂得为将来考虑的吃货啊！

这时，上课铃响了。金叶又跑到张涛和茹云衣的旁边，倾诉着自己有多么饿。茹云衣一脸淡定地对她说："你这个'五件套'的，对我这个'三件套'的人说你饿，你怎么不想想我会不会饿呢？我的午餐量少而且没有肉。每天都是三明治里面夹一片芝士。这就是我的主食。你明白吗？你明白我的苦和痛吗？"金叶立马回头对张涛倾诉，但是无论如何倾诉都不能让她吃饱啊，这也许就是吃货的苦吧！

4月8日，星期二

# Mr. Kronker学中文

认真工作的Mr. Kronker

　　今天下午的体育课，因为下雨的原因取消了，我们几个选择在Mr. Kronker（英语老师）的教室里做作业。

　　一开始，Mr. Kronker在旁边看电脑，我们在课桌前做作业。过了一会儿，Mr. Kronker听到我们在小声地用中文交谈，于是就起了好奇心，问我们说的是什么种类的中文。因为不会"普通话"的英语表述，所以只好告诉他我们说的是苏州话。Mr. Kronker一听就来了兴趣，让我们教他几句苏州话。

　　他说他想学苏州话的"你好"。在这个学校里基本上人人都会说"你好"，这一句话就像英文中的"hello"一样众人皆知。于是，茹云衣就说了一遍"倷好"。Mr. Kronker听了一遍，面孔扭曲地模仿了一下，我们四个差点没有听出来。"倷"字还好，但是"好"字嘛，这个就很难说好的了，Mr. Kronker把音调都读反了。于是茹云衣重复了一遍，Mr. Kronker就又模仿一遍，效果还是和原来一样没什么区别。茹云衣又一次不厌其烦地梳理一遍。这一回Mr. Kronker很认真地重复了三遍，虽然一遍比一遍好，但还是听不出来这一句的意思。说完了以后，他真心地说了一句："中文真的好难学啊！"

可是他说他还要学。我们就打算教他苏州话的"谢谢"，这个似乎容易些。仍然是茹云衣说了一遍，Mr. Kronker再重复一遍。反复了几次，我突然觉得茹云衣说的"谢谢"有点别扭。自己反复寻思了一番，原来茹云衣说的是错的，那不是"谢谢"的正宗苏州话。我说了一遍给他听，Mr. Kronker就又一次皱着眉头重复一遍，还别说，这一次他真是说准了。但是他说他不想再学苏州话了，他说他觉得苏州话太难了。我说还准备教他更有趣的苏州话呢，比如"倷是伲格先生，伲几个小娘鱼有空请倷来苏州白相"，哈哈，这个一定更难学哦。

Mr. Kronker知难而退，他又把兴趣转向城市的名字。第一个是"青岛"，这个词他倒是挺熟练地说了出来，而且说得很标准。然后一个就是"北京"。"北"没有问题，但是"京"，他总是说不准，总是读成"琼"。我们就在旁边笑，但是我心底里还是挺佩服他的，这个对我来说很难，但他依然锲而不舍地说了好几遍。

努力学习了好几遍，他又在网上搜了一些图片给我们看，都是关于苏州的。他说苏州真的好美丽，有那么多绿树、湖泊、园林……但是金叶在旁边一个劲地用中文说，这天怎么PS得那么蓝呀，这树怎么PS得这么绿呀，这景色怎么PS得这么美呀！我们几个站在旁边，也是一个劲地点头称是，看看那图片上的景色，再回想一下苏州的真实情况，真的难以把二者相提并论啊！不像国外，照片和实景拍出来都是差不多的，有时候照片甚至还没有实景好看。而我们的天空，似乎和我们真实生活的环境相差很远，来加拿大前的好多天苏州雾霾都很严重，连续一周都是重度污染的记录！唉，这就是我们保护环境不力的后果啊！

今天教了Mr. Kronker中文，突然觉得自己好有成就感，起码在中文这个方面强过别人了！

4月9日，星期三

# 在加拿大的第一次迟到

放学后，原计划15:00我从学校回家，但今天差不多14:55的时候我就准时回家了，因为下午我们要在维多利亚市教育局集中上课，所以住家妈妈让我在15:15到家。她在家里等我，然后送我去市教育局集中上学，一放学我就火速往家里赶。

回到家一看，屋子里空荡荡的，一个人也没有。我又敲了敲住家妈妈的房门，依然没有人搭理。我只好到厨房倒了一杯果汁，等住家妈妈回家。时间一分一秒地过去了。已经15:25了，但是住家妈妈还没有声息，按道理这个时候我应该已经在去往教育局的路上了。加拿大人应该很有时间观念的吧，如果晚了，也应该给我打个电话的呀！为什么这么晚了还没有消息呢？我越等越心急，于是就跑到客厅，用座机给住家妈妈打了一个电话。我问她什么时候到家？！她说她刚刚接到丹妮卡，应该很快就会到家的。我松了一口气，还好快到了，万一在路上还要很久才到家的话，那可如何是好？！

于是我趴在阳台上，像盯梢的侦探一般，看着住家妈妈什么时候回来。大概又过了十几分钟，我一看表已经15:40了，教育局的课16:00开始。这时，住家妈妈打来了一个电话，她说她忘记了我要去教育局上课这回事了，还说现在会以最快的速度到家，但是我肯定会迟到。我的心立马沉了下来，我最讨厌迟到了，我是一个喜欢走在时间前面的人，如果时间超过了我的预算，那我就会心急如焚。我开始有些急躁。为了节省时间，我先回到房间里，把东西整理了一遍，又把书包拿到了客厅里。然后给杨老师打了一个电话说明情况，告诉她我会迟到的事情，没想到杨老师很爽快地就答应了。

接着，我坐在沙发上盯着手表，看着秒针一圈一圈地转过，时间一点一点地流逝，看着时针一点一点地接近4，我焦急万分。这时住家妈妈又打来了一个电话，让我两分钟后在楼下等她，我立马冲出门，但是左看看右看看，就是没有看到住家妈妈的车。正当我打算回去的时候，我突然瞄见了一辆红色跑车，仔细一看，真的是住家妈妈来了，我好激动啊！立刻冲上车。住家妈妈一个劲儿地对我说"sorry"，我就一个劲地对她说"never mind"。她还说会以最快的速度把我送到教育局，但是一路上遇见的全是红灯，还有堵车，这决定了我会更晚到达。果然，我在16:38才到达教育局。

我以百米冲刺的速度冲到教室。这个时候课已经上了一大半了，杨老师刚要布置作业，正巧被我赶上了。布置完了作业，大概又过了5分钟吧，17点就到了，我们就要回家了。好好的一堂课，我就这样失去了。回家的时候，是住家爸爸来接我的，他开着一辆大卡车，那是因为住家妈妈的跑车坏了，或许是因为送我的缘故吧，我心里有一点愧疚。

晚饭我们就在外面吃，只有我和丹妮卡吃了一点。大人们都在忙着修车，我陪住家妈妈去买了一些修车用的东西，她还帮我买了一个下次去野营要用的手电筒。

一天就这样在紧张和忙碌中过去了，真的是又累又惊。

住家妈妈送的手电筒1号

4月10日，星期四

# 温哥华印象一

去往温哥华的海轮上

　　今天是星期四，放学到家后住家妈妈就让我整理一下行李，说是要一起去温哥华参加丹妮卡的曲棍球比赛。我很激动，一会儿就把箱子整理好了。住家妈妈过来一看，说只要拿旅行包就好，于是我又重新理了一遍。

　　大概17:00的时候，我们稍微用了一点晚饭，就是速成的意大利面。我本来不想吃因为不是很饿，但是住家爸爸说我们要22:00才能睡觉，其间吃不到什么东西，所以，要把自己吃到撑为止！

　　17:45，准时出发。住家爸爸和妈妈一起坐在前座，我和丹妮卡还有库柏坐在后面。库柏比我们还激动，张着大嘴巴往窗外看，压得我都不能动了。于是丹妮卡就使劲抱住库柏，把它往她那边拽，结果库柏就把口水流在了丹妮卡的手机上，丹妮卡"啊"的一叫，库柏睁着大眼睛看了她一眼，扭头又继续观赏风景。而丹妮卡则是拿起手机，在库柏的背上蹭了蹭，然后说了一句："物归原主，现在我的手机干净了。"我一脸惊讶。

很快我们就到了船港，住家妈妈指给我看我们将要乘的海轮，真的很大、很漂亮！蓝白相间的船体，一扇扇窗户在阳光下反射出一缕缕华丽的光芒。住家妈妈把车开到船里，也就是说这辆车会跟着我们一起到达温哥华。我依然是一脸惊奇，国外的一切，对我来说都充满着新鲜感，大海轮、超大停车场、大都市温哥华等。

走进船舱里，第一层是大型的购物区和一大块自助餐区。第二层则是座位，还有书桌、沙发、小圆桌、电视机等。船舱外面则是观赏海景的好地方。汽笛声一响，海轮缓缓开动了，住家妈妈就带着我走到船舱那儿去观赏风景。

住家妈妈耐心地给我介绍海面上的一座座岛屿，还有对面连绵起伏的雪山。其中有一座很小很小的岛，大概也就三四栋房子的面积吧，却异常美丽，在那仅有的一丁点土地上，满是绿树和鲜花，非常醒目。这里还是海鸟栖息的好去处，停了大概50只海鸟，还有很多海鸟在水面上游泳。再把目光转到旁边的一座大礁石上，那边有一只又大又肥的海狮，正眯着眼睛晒太阳浴呢，旁边还有几只小鸟，似乎在为它唱歌。好惬意的海狮啊！

不知不觉船驶进了两座大岛之间，这时太阳落山了，火红的太阳把两边的天都映红了。两座山都像披上了一件红色羽纱，朦朦胧胧的，上面还顶着一个"火球"，不停地给这羽纱增添光芒。远处的海鸥，一边鸣叫着，一边朝这边飞来，船在海上行，人在画中游，美丽的画面在我心中定格。我在家乡苏州的三山岛看过太湖夕阳落山的景色，也是非常美丽的。但这是我第一次在海轮上品味晚霞生辉！迎着舒服绵柔的海风，呼吸着新鲜的空气，背对着一片夕阳，我按下快门记录下了一张美丽的照片，心底留下了一份美好印记。

温哥华到维多利亚的海轮

  在21:00的时候,我们到达了温哥华。住家爸爸在一个加油站为我们买了一点小吃来充饥。随后住家妈妈就带着我们到了她朋友的一个闲置的宅子里,我们要在这里暂住两晚。刚一进门,库柏就煞有架势地对着旁边壁炉边的一只陶瓷狗瞪眼,引得我们哈哈大笑。晚上我和丹妮卡同睡一张床。这个时候已经是22:30了,丹妮卡懒得洗漱就直接倒在床上了,我稍微冲了冲。明天还要早起去看丹妮卡的比赛,今天一天脚走得有点累,眼睛看得有点疲劳,但心底是美好的。

4月12日,星期六

# 温哥华印象二

温哥华唐人街

　　今天丹妮卡早上的一场比赛比较早,匆忙起来后我们就去了比赛场地,看着她们热火朝天地打完比赛。本来,我们是要一起出去玩儿的,但是因为丹妮卡去了同学家,于是我和住家爸爸妈妈吃了午餐。餐后,住家妈妈去买了很多甜甜圈和小蛋糕,打算用来分给下午比赛的选手们,鼓舞士气。

　　中午,住家妈妈就开着跑车,带我来到了一个她从小长大的地方。那是一座极其美丽、富裕、繁华的大山。住家妈妈说那里是一座大公园,叫斯坦利公园(Stanley Park)。开进去就看到一条街,街上琳琅满目而且充满了中国气息。是一条唐人街!有很多商店的牌子都是用中文写的,旁边再加上一串英文小字。难得看到中文,心中猛然感到十分亲切。我们还路过了一座寺庙,住家妈妈估计没有见过中国的宗教场所,她居然还以为是一个超市呢!

燃烧着熊熊烈火的火炬筒

　　穿过这条街，就是居民住宅区。这里的房屋明显和维多利亚的不一样，都是高楼大厦，有十几层的、二十几层的、五六十层的，就像我们苏州的工业园区。玻璃的颜色也不一样，有透明的、白的、蓝的、紫的、黄的、绿的……各色各样，迷乱双眼。还有一座大厦的每一层玻璃上都写着一串英文，十分新奇。相比之下，维多利亚市区的房子都像一座座小别墅一样，分散着或者聚集在一起。

　　我们的跑车穿过一栋栋高楼大厦来到了一个码头，住家妈妈特意停下车，指给我看码头上的一个火炬筒，那是温哥华2010年冬奥会的标志。这是由四个很粗的铁管随意搭成的，上面点着熊熊烈火，好像不会熄灭一样。旁边很多人在围着它拍照，住家妈妈特意放慢了速度让我拍一张。目光越过火炬筒，我看到了一片山和一片海。我对住家妈妈说想要去拍照，于是她就带着我开到了半山腰。

　　果然，这边的景色更加美丽。参天大树高高地耸立着，一朵朵娇艳的小花在底下努力地绽放，对这美好的天气献出自己的一片微笑。远处的山上，顶着一片白云和一些雪。乍一看，云似雪，雪像云，二者交相融合，蓝天和碧海相映，这是多么美丽的画卷啊。再远眺大海，海上有潜艇，打出片片的水花；海轮发出"嘀嘀"的汽鸣；还有在海上盘旋、鸣叫的海鸥……

狮门大桥

图腾"面具鸟"

　　这一片大海上,还有一座美丽优雅的大桥,这是一座铁桥,全身上下刷着绿色的漆,与周围的绿树、雪山融合得天衣无缝。这座大桥有着优美的弧度,远远看去,就像一颗流星划过的背影,为这片大海增添了一个无比美丽的元素。我问了住家妈妈,这座桥的名字叫狮门大桥(Lions' Gate Bridge),是加拿大最长的桥。真威武!

　　下山后,住家爸爸又带我走进了斯坦利公园(Stanley Park)中间的一个公园。住家爸爸对我介绍说,这个公园西临英国湾,是北美地区最大的市内公园。公园人工景物极少,以红杉等针叶树木为主的原始森林是公园最知名的美景。一踏进那松软的草坪,我就看见六根大木头立在前面,每一根木头上都像画着好几个面具,一个一个对接起来,看上去像鸟或者是野兽。总之,我把这些木头叫作"面具鸟"木头。住家妈妈向我介绍说这是图腾,是加拿大的原始居民——印第安人留下来的,每一个图腾柱都代表着一个家族。我买的钥匙圈中也有一个是这种图案。告别图腾柱,住家爸爸带我走进了一个小礼品店。我看了一眼,品种有很多,如明信片、钥匙扣等。有的玩具上都画着图腾,我猜想这些图腾应该和中国的京剧脸谱一样,有着特殊的含义和悠久的历史吧。

　　因为时间关系,我们没能好好地饱览这座大公园,只是走马观花地看了一下,但是,即便如此,也让我对这座公园印象深刻。这里的小街、大厦、大海、绿树、鲜花、雪山、面具鸟、礼品店,或许只是惊鸿一瞥,但都是我的加拿大记忆夹里一片片最美丽的书签。

　　从斯坦利公园出来,我们开车去看丹妮卡下午的曲棍球比赛。比赛后因为丹妮卡明天还有比赛,而住家却有其他的事,所以住家爸爸妈妈要先把我带回维多利亚,然后再把丹妮卡托给她的朋友照看。住家妈妈非常不舍,看着她们母女拥抱告别的样子,我突然想起我离开中国,飞往加拿大的那一天和爸爸妈妈在浦东机场告别的场景,也是这样拥抱,并且还亲吻了他们的面颊。看到这里,我心中酸酸的,想起了在中国的爸爸妈妈,虽然我每天都和他们视频聊天,但是也只能说说话,见见面，总是摸不到的。有一句话说得好啊，"要珍惜现在拥有的，而不是去想自己未来能够拥有什么"。在中国的时候，我常常会和爸爸妈妈发些小脾气，或者是撒娇。现在想来，自己真的是太天真了，爸爸妈妈所做的一切，都是为我好，就像住家妈妈能够为丹妮卡花下血本，重新买一套守门员的盔甲一样。所以珍惜自己所拥有的，才是硬道理。还要珍惜爸爸妈妈对我们的爱和关怀，像我眼前所看到的一样，住家妈妈即使不给丹妮卡买新盔甲，她依然可以打完这场球赛，但是为了她能够舒服地、积极地面对比赛，还是给她添置了新盔甲。可见，父母之爱是相通的。

曲棍球比赛

4月14日，星期一

# 加拿大学生与中国学生的玩与作业

林间木凳一照

都说中国学生擅长背书考试，外国学生擅长创作发明。但是这并不是因为中国学生生来就脑袋聪明擅长考试，而外国学生擅长创作也并不是他们与生俱来的。

今天放学的时候，住家妈妈在家里。她给我准备了一盆蔬果点心和两根酸奶棒。然后她邀请我到花园里聊天。

住家妈妈问我今天晚上要不要去看丹妮卡打曲棍球比赛。我想一想，今天晚上我还要补前两天因为去温哥华而没有写的日记，而且还要做一些杨老师的数学作业，还要背英语第四单元的单词。又想了想，去看曲棍球比赛应该17:00就要出发，大概在21:00才能回来，我怕时间不够，于是我就拒绝了住家妈妈。

她听到我不去的原因是要写作业，非常不理解。于是就问我："你有很多作业吗？Shoreline应该是没有多少作业的呀！"

我就向她说了一下今天晚上我打算完成的作业和日记，又补充说："如果在中国，这个时候我们还没有放学呢，现在才16:00。"

住家妈妈很惊讶，她又问："那你们放学回家后做什么呢？"

我说："我们会做作业呀，一般要做到吃晚餐，晚餐后还要继续做。"

住家妈妈说："你们每天都有作业吗？"

为了让住家妈妈理解，我就举了一下每天作业的例子。

住家妈妈听了十分惊讶，她对我说："在丹妮卡七、八年级的时候，都没有作业的。"

这回该轮到我惊讶了，要说我们什么时候没有作业，那大概也就在幼儿园吧，连小学一年级都有一点点作业的。

再想一想Shoreline，我在那里上的是七年级。到Shoreline学习的日子也已经有快20天了，到现在为止，我一共也就做了两个作业（只是回家作业，不包括数学的课堂作业），第一个是为期三周的法语菜单，第二个是简单地冲洗一下牛奶壳子。特别是第一个，上面日期写着三个星期，还是可以合作的，我和同学合作也就仅仅做了三个小时而已！其中还包括把英文翻译成中文，把中文翻译成法文，再把法文翻译成英文，这些复杂的程序。而第二个作业，在我的印象里也就只用了几分钟而已。而在国内，一天的回家作业，也要花上2~3个小时，这就顶得上Shoreline20天的作业啊！哈哈！

聊着聊着，住家妈妈又和我聊到我在中国是怎样度周末的。我告诉住家妈妈，周末的时候我们除了有很多回家作业外，还要去上一些补习班。就像我，周五的晚上，放学后有一堂英语课，有时候来不及用晚餐就只能在车上将就一下。周六的早晨我需要为下午3个小时的数学课做预习准备，因为平常作业太多，得消化一下，否则下午的课就会生疏。然后下午休息一会儿就要去上数学课，回来后会稍微放松一下。等到周日，再花一天的时间把学校作业做完，或者周六晚上再做一点作业。

住家妈妈听完我的介绍后十分惊讶，她说："那你不累吗？"

我说："我累呀，但是累也要挺着呀！这样我们才能学习到知识呀！"

"哦，对！在我的印象里，中国人总是学习成绩很好，工作很努力，并且做什么事情，只要需要动脑力的都是很轻松的！"住家妈妈感慨道："原来都是这样培养出来的，在加拿大的孩子就只会玩。他们周末回来后，就是家庭时间，大家一起玩，吃一顿美味的晚餐，然后一起看电视，度过一个美好的夜晚。第二天睡个懒觉，起来后你可以和你的家人或朋友出去逛街，做一切你想做的事，好好放松一下。晚上继续是家庭时间。周日的早晨，也是玩乐时间，你可以做自己喜欢的事情，或者是邀请你的朋友到家里来。下午可以看电影或者和家里的人一起聊天。晚上你可做作业或者是度过自己的私人时间。"

我认认真真地听了一遍，心驰神往，再把两个国家小孩周末的时间比对一下，马上就可以发现区别所在。像我在苏州的话，美好的周末时间就是泡在作业堆里或者是补习班中。而现在，在加拿大就是泡在和住家幸福相处的家庭时间和玩乐之中。

住家妈妈又问我加拿大日的安排，我说我目前没有什么安排。于是她给我两个选择：第一个是和他们一起去乘船看烟火，第二个是可以邀请我朋友和他们的住家一起到我的住家来吃BBQ（Barbecue的缩写，也就是烧烤的意思）。我怕我朋友来了就光顾着说中文，令住家尴尬，于是就选择了看烟火。

聊着聊着，住家妈妈指着院子里一棵大树下的一个吊床，让我躺在那儿休息一下，享受这美妙的一刻。我开始爬不上去还摔了下来，最后还是住家妈妈帮忙我才上去的。躺在吊床上，任凭树上的花瓣飘落到我的面颊上，回想起我在中国的日子，现在肯定还处于最后一节自习课的时候，要不就是在狂做作业，要不就是在听老师讲课。总之不会像这样躺在吊床上，春风拂面，花瓣飘落，小蜂鸟在身边"叽啾"，头顶的大树帮我挡住刺眼的太阳，仅仅让温暖抚照在我的身上。我闭上眼睛，静静地享受着加拿大的慢生活，享受着这一片美丽的景色，享受着这难得的湛蓝天空，享受着这一片难得的清新空气，享受这珍贵的闲暇时光……

大树下、吊床上的我

4月15日，星期二

# 海岸线社区中学的手工课

在手工课上大家认真工作

### 动手能力得到考验

经过三个星期的面粉浸泡，我们的面具已经粘上两层报纸和一层面纸了。面粉已经干透了，所以整个面具就越发白了，而且经过太阳和时间的冲刷，整个面具变得硬邦邦的。

我和茹云衣兴奋地来到劳技教室，因为今天再也不用粘上那恶心的面粉了，我们将用颜料装饰我们想要画的面具。先把面具刷上一层底色。我做的是一个云南古老的判官面具，所以涂的底色是棕色。而茹云衣做的是古老的三星堆的青铜面具，所以她刷的底色是绿色。

我们一层一层地按着报纸和面纸的纹路刷。我刷了两遍，然后用吹风机把它吹干。再画上面具的眼睛、鼻子、嘴巴，还有各种装饰性的东西。这一次我换了一支很细的刷子，也许是这个刷子有点旧了，我蘸一点颜料它就会掉毛。这样，我画眼睛和鼻子的时候，就经常会有毛掉出来，把我的面具给搞坏。茹云衣同样也遇到了这样的问题，不过她的刷子质量比我好，所以没有我那么毛糙。于是我只能更加细心地，坐下来一点一点地刷。效果虽说是好那么一点，但是整体看上去依然不太好。于是我选择先易后难，放弃眼睛和鼻子，开始做面具的嘴巴。我先画左边的牙齿，但是忘了尺寸，在左边画了四颗牙，右边只有两颗，而且相当的不对称，没有办法，我就只好在右边又添了一颗尖牙齿，再把左边一颗牙齿变成尖的，就这样在修修补补中，画面终于协调些了。

### 耐心信心得到了提升

我慢慢地把整个面具吹干。然后问辅导老师，能不能给我换一把刷子？于是，她就把一根没有用过的刷子递给了我，并且嘱咐我说，用完以后一定要把它洗干净。我很高兴，兴冲冲地拿回去画了。

我的面具本来就是深色调的，于是我打算在白色的旁边刷上一层黑色，这样就可以把粗糙的地方掩盖掉。说是说得挺容易的，但是做起来真心难。在刷子上蘸的颜料不能多也不能少。还要在粗糙的地方一点一点、很小心地刷，如果刷多了白色部分就少了，那样面具表情就会显得呆板和奇怪。好不容易我把眉毛的部分修好了，我长出了一口气。又开始画鼻子，因为两条线之间空隙比较少，所以就更增加了难度，我只能用笔尖一点一点的蹭上去。好不容易画完了鼻子，这还没有结束呢！还有嘴巴。我先在每颗牙齿之间刷上一点黑色，要不然整个牙齿看上去就像一块白色的石头一样，很僵硬。然后开始刷嘴巴上端的一圈白色，这个部分是最考验我的耐心的。因为不仅要把黑色刷得很稳，还要把两端的黑色控制得宽度一样，这样才能使中间的白色不至于扭来扭去、弯弯曲曲、断断续续。我就这样拿着刷子在旁边一点一点地刷。这时旁边的茹云衣已经做好了,她就看着我刷。

看了一会儿,她问我:"你是什么星座的?"

"处女座啊,怎么了?"我说。

"哦,怪不得。都说处女座的人讲究完美,我在你的身上看到一个完美的例子!其实这个部分你粗粗糙糙也就够了,原图还没你这么精细呢,画那么仔细干什么?多耗费时间。"

我说:"我看着它不顺眼,所以我要这样做。再说了,你看它多丑啊!我非得把它改好,才罢休!"

于是茹云衣叹了一口气,说道:"那你怎么不看看我的?比你的丑多了,好伐?"

"那我好歹得对得起这个面具呀,耗了我那么久的时间,我才不要把它弄那么丑呢!"

终于下课铃响了,我的面具也完成了。下一节课就是做面具的简介了。听说还要上台做介绍,我一定要回去好好准备一下,这个面具可花了我三个星期的心血啊!

我和茹云衣的面具

4月19号，星期六

# 野营之第一天

住家爸爸、住家妈妈准备房车

今天起了一个大早，因为住家妈妈说吃完早餐，我们要开车去野营。想到能坐在篝火旁，周围全是树林，还有小鸟和松鼠在枝头跳跃，心情就十分愉快。很向往这一次野营，我的第一次野营。

这次野营，除了我、住家一家和库柏，还有丹妮卡的男朋友Tylie。想一想，国外可真开放啊，丹妮卡才大我两岁就有男朋友了，而且亲密无间。并且能邀请她的男朋友一起去野营，还征得了父母的同意。不可思议！

用完了一顿美味的早餐，住家妈妈开始整理东西。虽说她昨天已经整理了一天，但是毕竟要出去两天，要准备食物、锅碗瓢盆、生活用具、枕头被子，还有帐篷和挡雨的布。我倒是没有什么东西可理的，因为住家妈妈前天的时候就跟我说了，我早就已经整理好了一个小箱子和一个小背包。

大概10:00的时候，我们整装出发。住家爸爸一个人开着貌似很沉重的房车，住家妈妈则开跑车载着丹妮卡、Tylie、我还有库柏。大概半个小时后，我们就来到了野营场地。这是一片由群山组成的野营场地，山上栽满了树，有一条马路通到树林里，开进去满眼都是绿色。林间透着湛蓝的天空和明媚的阳光。枝头蹦跳的小鸟轻快地叫着，远处依稀可以看到几只松鼠，一会儿在草丛间窜来窜去，一会儿又跳到树桩上。袅袅炊烟从树林间冒出来，这是野营的人们做早餐的炊烟。整个画面清新自然，让人陶醉。

我们选好场地，就开始分工了。先是住家妈妈搭好了库柏的床。然后和住家爸爸把整理好的许多箱子拿出来，有手电筒的箱子，锅碗瓢盆的箱子，放衣服、放垃圾的筒子，放帐篷的箱子，还有放椅子的箱子。总之，大小不等，有十来个吧！而另一边，则是丹妮卡和她的男朋友在搭Tylie住的帐篷。因为房车的空间的确不大，只有三张床，所以她的男朋友不得不睡在外面。虽然说他睡在外面，但是他的帐篷可是比房车里的任何一张床都要大两倍！那是个六角形的帐篷，有几平方米的样子，里面还可以放很多东西。

目光转到天空，天空上飘下几滴小雨，渐渐地越来越多，住家爸爸立马从房车里取下几个蓝色的塑料布和住家妈妈一起遮盖东西。我看他们两个有点招架不住，于是就跑过去帮忙。好不容易颤颤巍巍地搭完了防雨塑料布（不知道怎么说，只好用这个先来代替一下，呵呵）。这时候大家忙得也都差不多了，住家妈妈让我和丹妮卡先熟悉一下周围环境，丹妮卡就带我去了一个非常重要的地方，就是洗手间。那是一个小木屋，走过去不远。房车里也有洗手间，但是毕竟空间小，很简陋，而且又没有水，根本用不了。想着去洗手间还要走一段路，心有不甘。

回来的时候，看到Tylie拿着斧头在砍柴。我和丹妮卡好奇心大起，立马奔过去。他砍得满头大汗，时不时还会劈空，要不就是砍得不均匀。于是丹妮卡就亲自上阵，挽起袖子，选了一个相对较小的斧头，对准那木头直砍，没想到砍到一半就劈

Tylie劈木头

不下去了。Tylie在旁边直笑,还过去抢过斧头,给丹妮卡做示范,虽然第一次还是劈空了,但是第二次完美地把木头劈成了两半,并且很均匀。丹妮卡看他劈得很轻松,又一次要求再试一次,这一次还卯足了劲,没想到把下面的木桩给砍断了。我们三个立即无语,因为这块木头着实难砍。Tylie又试了一下,无奈依然砍到一半就砍不下去了,竖着不行还尝试横着来,可惜木头的纹理不对,依然劈不断。最后住家爸爸亲自上阵,一下就把它劈断了,轻松无比。

　　木头准备好了,我们就开始生篝火。树林里很冷,用火烤手,很是温暖。过了一会儿,住家妈妈让我们打牌,Tylie推荐了两种玩牌的方法,用英文介绍的,我理解了大概的玩法。然后我们吃了一点面条汤,简单地用完了午饭。我有些累了,于是就到房车里休息。

　　晚上,大老远地跑去洗漱,再大老远跑回来。住家妈妈先让我上床睡觉,但这张床太小,高仅有20厘米,宽大概也就40厘米吧,和胶囊旅馆差不多。我爬着梯子上去,结果差点扭了腰伤了脚板。住家妈妈只好让丹妮卡委屈一下,看她能不能爬到床上?她在那扭来扭去扭了半天才上床,好不容易翻了个身,差点滚下来。于是住家妈妈就让我们两个睡了一张小床。晚上睡觉的时候,被子被她掀掉了一半,我只盖到了一点,很冷。早上醒来,腿都冻麻了,一个晚上基本没睡着。呜呜!

4月20号，星期日

# 野营之第二天

Tylie的大帐篷

  今天早上起来后，我和丹妮卡都在那儿埋怨，晚上睡觉睡得很冷，于是住家妈妈就让我们睡在他们昨晚睡的床上，让Tylie睡在我们昨晚睡的小床上，然后住家爸爸妈妈睡在Tylie的大帐篷里。

  早餐后就开始窝在火堆旁边取暖。住家妈妈说："大概10:30的时候，我们将去参加一个游戏。"

  时间过得飞快，10:30很快就到了，我们准时到达游戏场地。丹妮卡和Tylie被分在一组，我和住家妈妈则分在一组。大家各自起了奇怪的组名，我们的组名是Amazing team，丹妮卡和Tylie则叫Drink water，原因是Tylie的外套背后写着这两个英文大字。

我们玩的第一个游戏是将一个塑料小球弹到对方的杯子里，一共有6个，弹进哪个杯子，那个杯子就拿到一旁，双方谁先把对方的杯子弹完，谁就赢。因为我学过乒乓，所以打中了4个杯子，而住家妈妈只打中一个，还差一个的时候，对方竟然全打中了，于是我们输了。

第二个游戏是将一根两头拴有两个小球的绳子扔到远处的三根杆子上的任意一点，扔中每一根杆子，就能得到相应的分数。我们的对手就是丹妮卡和Tylie。我刚开始上手有点不适应，后来慢慢好了，住家妈妈本来就是高手，但是年轻的丹妮卡和Tylie则更是厉害。本来我们是可以高他们3分的，但是因为有一个球虽然拴住了那根杆子，但是绕了几圈后又被弹了回来。住家妈妈气得直咬牙，指着Tylie骂道："你竟然不让我？！我就不让你娶丹妮卡。"一个明明是赢了，却一脸无辜，另一个明明是输了却理直气壮。哈哈！然后玩了第三个游戏，我们仍然是毫无悬念地输了。0：3！Oh, my god！

带着些许遗憾，住家妈妈领着我回去吃点心、喝汤。路上我看到树林里有很多巧克力蛋，于是就问住家妈妈这些巧克力蛋的来由。她告诉我这是上帝特意洒在人间，给小孩子们作为复活节礼物的。如果你看到了巧克力蛋，就可以把它们捡起来。于是我毫不客气，把我们领地周围所有的巧克力蛋一下子都捡光了，大概有20来颗吧！手里捧得满满的，兴高采烈地去向住家妈妈报喜。她一脸惊愕地看着我说："你把所有巧克力蛋都抢光了，真厉害呀！"其实这些巧克力蛋放得都很明显，外面又有精致的包装，闪闪发光，再加上又没有多少小草为它们遮掩，自然是暴露在视线中。捡到了很多巧克力蛋，心情极好，也把刚才的三连败忘得一干二净。喝完了美味的汤就和住家妈妈跑过去拿礼品了，我随便挑了一个，竟然抽到了一张爆米花的卡，虽然搞不清这是什么，但是听住家妈妈介绍说这个卡很有用，下次可以带我去吃，里面的爆米花不止是金黄色的，还有棕色的、蓝色的、黄色的、粉色的、紫色的，各自代表了不同水果味的爆米花。于是，我们心满意足地回去，住家妈妈开始准备午餐了，是一个半手掌般大的小热狗。

傍晚的篝火

晚上篝火前和丹妮卡的合影

　　晚餐很丰盛，是所有野营队伍一起吃的，每一家都烧出一两个拿手菜，端过去一起分享。还有饭后甜点、苹果派、蓝莓蛋糕和不知名的小丸子。

　　满足地回到营地，大家又开始生起火来，在火堆旁边聊天。因为周围的光都被树林遮住了，树林里黑漆漆的。20:00的时候，整个树林黑了下来，说伸手不见五指也不为过。周围只能看到火光，于是住家妈妈拿了荧光棒，让我们带在身上，我戴了两个在手腕上，住家妈妈挂在衣服的扣子上，丹妮卡则是把它当成头箍戴在头上。住家爸爸又拿来了火腿肠，让我们烤着吃。他还借了我的手电筒，去搬了几根树枝，把树枝掰断后用来烤火腿肠。他直接把树枝用火烧干净，然后就把火腿肠插在上面，很原生态，但不知是否卫生？过了一会儿大家有些无聊，住家妈妈就把音箱拿出来放音乐。篝火旁，我们一起跟着音响哼唱，真美妙。

　　晚上睡得很沉，很舒服。今天又是美妙的一天啊！

4月21号,星期一

# 野营之第三天

回家的路上

　　第三天早上起来,住家妈妈开始整理东西,今天我们就要离开这片美丽的树林了。但是我发现自己的肚子很难受,有点恶心,头还有点晕,我就坐在木板凳上休息。住家妈妈理了一早上东西,才察觉到我不对劲,于是安排我在车子里休息。

　　回到家后,肚子还是很不舒服,头也更晕了,午饭都没有胃口吃。就倒在床上睡着了,估计是因为烧烤的东西吃不惯或者有点不卫生吧,于是我打算直接清清肠子,晚饭没有吃,早早就睡觉了。

　　第二天早上醒来,今天是要上学的。我察觉到身体有一些好转了,就打算去上学,但是等我走出房门发现还是不好,虽然肚子已经好多了,但呼吸还是不畅,老喘气,头依然是晕的，于是就只好跑过去对住家妈妈说，让她帮我请个假。她一口就答应了。她对我的生病满怀愧疚，生怕我吃坏了东西，给我泡了一杯药，我很感动，丝毫没有责备住家妈妈的意思。回房间后，打算好好休息一天，直接躺在床上了。今天住家妈妈也不用上班。为了不打扰我，她就在客厅里看电视，音量不是很大。我睡得很熟，一觉睡得很好。

午饭起来吃了一小碗面条。吃完后就发现肚子又有点难受，想想晚饭还是不要吃了吧，吃了估计又要难受了。因为马上就要期中考试了，我打算趁这个时间好好复习一下，于是拿起书本背了背单词，做了一点数学题目，脑袋依然晕得很，没见好转。第三天就这样难受地熬了过去，晚上倒是好多了，明天就可以去上学了。期待中……

回家途中一景

4月23日，星期三

# 一起出发去捡垃圾

按照平常，今天下午第一节课是Mr. Allen的课。就是前半节课用来阅读和做自己的事，后半节课做一个推理的题目。很难，到现在做了几次我都不知道是怎么做的。但是今天Mr. Allen只是把我们叫到教室，然后还神秘兮兮地拿来一个大袋子，手上还拿了几个很长的夹子，好像是用来捡垃圾的。当Mr. Allen拿出大袋子里的环保服的时候，大家都跑过去抢，还有捡垃圾的杆子。虽然我和茹云衣离Mr. Allen最近，但还是被一哄而上的外国同学抢掉了。Mr. Allen又给我们每人发了一个塑料手套，很结实，就像医生做手术时戴的那种。然后他宣布："今天我们要去捡垃圾。"我觉得很新奇，以为是在学校里捡垃圾，想想，不就是捡垃圾吗，而且在学校里捡也很容易呀！

大家整好了队伍，浩浩荡荡地出发了，20个人左右，再加上3名老师。我们的大队伍绕过操场，我和茹云衣对视一眼，心里咯噔一下，难道这是要出校门去吗？难道是说，我们要在大马路上捡垃圾吗？在星海学校的时候从没有去马路上捡过垃圾，虽然在学校里看到地上有垃圾也会捡起来，但不会像现在这样兴师动众。

果然，我们从侧面的门出了学校。到了人行道上，这时，我和茹云衣又开始犹豫了，到底是边走边捡，还是走到目的地后再捡呢？这时我看到马路上有一个小纸团，躲在草丛里，与这美妙的景象异常不符，于是就把它捡了起来。虽然不是很了解情况，但是好歹这美丽的景色总是不能破坏的，也许前面的人看到无动于衷，但是自己不仅代表了自己，还代表了我们的

温哥华街景

学校，往大的讲，我还代表了自己的祖国，总要给自己的国家争光啊！哈哈，这下搞大了。

走了一路，就像沿着我上学的路走一样，这一路还是很远的，而且都是一些上坡和下坡。我和茹云衣身体都不怎么舒服，一路上摇摇晃晃的，两只脚颠得不行。终于拐过一个弯，走了一段很平缓的路，稍微好多了，然后我们挑了一块草地坐下来休息。虽然我们的垃圾袋还不是很满，但是里面的东西却是各种各样：有餐巾纸、小纸团、可乐罐，还有很多烟头……望着天上的蓝天白云，周围的绿色大树，姹紫嫣红的郁金香花，还有天空中飞着的各色小鸟和趴在花朵上晒太阳的肥胖蜜蜂。我在想，也许我们捡掉的这一点点的垃圾，就足以使这美丽的环境更美。突然间，我觉得捡垃圾这项活动真是很有意义，而且也让人很有成就感呢！

休息片刻后，我们继续捡垃圾。前面有一大堆人在那说说笑笑，后面只有两个男生和三位老师。这时，眼尖的Mr. Allen看到旁边树丛里有一个啤酒瓶和两个纸杯。于是我们后面两位男生就冲进灌木丛，去捡那个纸杯和啤酒瓶。他们好不容易把东西都拿了出来，然后就塞进了垃圾袋里。

差不多两个小时后，我们回到了班级。大家坐在桌子上不想动了，感觉全身的血都流到脚趾头了，不过很有成就感，捡了那么多垃圾，还维护了维多利亚的环境。想想，这就是国外的教学，在学习中体验，在体验中学习。蛮好的！

4月24日，星期四

# 校园里疯狂的早锻炼

按平常来说每天的早晨都有早锻炼，而周四则是集体活动。因为前两周的星期四我不是因为有事出去了，就是因为复活节假期没有上学。而周四的早锻炼又是这几个星期才开始的，所以我根本不知道周四的早锻炼是什么样，也不知道包含哪些内容。但是听茹云衣说，周四的早锻炼是要累死人的！训练项目很多，比每天早锻炼的强度都要大。

随着上课铃的响起，今天的早锻炼开始了。首先，我们跟着老师，来到两个长凳旁边。这应该是第一项运动，用手撑在长凳上来支撑整个身体，脚踩地面，身体绷直，然后手臂弯曲，再绷直，再弯曲，就这样重复十遍。有一点像做俯卧撑的感觉，手臂很酸。紧接着我们要穿过一个走廊，但不是走过去，而是爬过去。先趴在地上，做好一个俯卧撑的预备姿势，然后，双腿绷直，平移着爬过去。这个项目虽然不是很累，但是做完后手臂更酸了。接下来迎接我们的是30个star jump，就是像星星一样跳，说着是容易，但是这30个还需要快速完成。随后，我们就出了一扇铁门，进行下一个项目，像螃蟹一样横行，绕过一栋教学楼。走到正门，门前有一排楼梯，我们在这里要做第五个运动项目，就是找第一阶台阶，双腿快速在台阶上擦过，要擦30个来回。我因为平衡力不是很好，所以总是踩空，很狼狈。

做完以后走进教学楼，再从第二层楼走到第一层楼。迎接我们的是10个仰卧起坐，我一开始没有听清楚，结果做了20个，很是吃力。这还没有完，还要找一个长凳，在上面快速蹬

狮门大桥前的合影

腿，要做20组，这个倒是很轻松。然后，双腿成弓字，走过半个走廊，最后拐进一间教室，快速趴在地上做10个标准俯卧撑。这真是要累死我！一个俯卧撑都做不下去的人，怎么办啊？看着旁边的茹云衣也在咬牙坚持做，于是我便狠了狠心，虽然还是压不下去，但是好歹手臂还是弯曲了，这已经是我的极限了。

让人意外的是做完以后还没有完！继续重复一遍刚才所做的所有项目。我简直无语，做得口干舌燥，汗流浃背。因为时间关系，第二遍的时候，我还差一个项目就做完时，下课铃就响了，国外很讲究时间观念，不会让你拖课做完这个项目的。于是，我就快速跑到自己的柜子旁，拿出水杯，咕噜咕噜地就直往下灌，可把我渴死了。

回忆刚才的课，这个早上过得真不容易呀。其实在国内我们也有体育课，但是绝对没有这么长时间、这么大的运动量的。大强度运动后，人虽然很累但感觉很舒畅，那些不敢想象的事情居然让我都顺利完成了，想想都觉得疯狂！

4月25日，星期五

# 社团活动Sock Monkey

今天周五是我们的第一次社团活动，我和茹云衣被分到了Sock Monkey。当初我们选的时候，不知道是什么活动，但觉得名字很有趣，于是就报名了。今天我才搞明白，原来就是用袜子做一个猴子。但还是挺有趣的，好歹还可以拿回去做纪念，这还是我做的第一个洋娃娃呢！听妈妈说，她小时候没有玩具，就经常自己缝。

这个社团的老师是教我们数学的，她就像一个"变形金钢"，既是数学老师，又是科学老师，还是体育老师，这不，现在还兼任我们Sock Monkey的辅导老师。上课后老师发给我们每人一双袜子，让我们用记号笔在袜子上按照黑板上的样子画好辅助线。今天我们所要做的就是猴子的脚，并且有时间的话还可以填冲好棉花。画好了线条，她做了一遍示范，然后又让我们每人拿了一根针线，线她已经帮我们穿好了，真是细心呐！

我之前在家里缝过豆沙包，所以还懂得一些。但是缝着缝着，我就乱套了，竟然缝错了，于是我就叫来老师。她倒是很干脆，快速地把错误的地方剪掉，然后再让我从后面一点重新开始。我缝得很细，基本上是一毫米一段，所以速度很慢。而旁边的茹云衣和我相比则是翻了一倍，她是一厘米一段。

我说："你就不怕待会儿填充棉花的时候会漏出来吗？"

她回答说："我也想缝得细啊，但是我可没有那耐心。"

等她快缝好时，我刚缝好了一只脚。这时已经有人缝完了，顿时感觉压力倍增。时间过得很快，还没等我缝完，下课

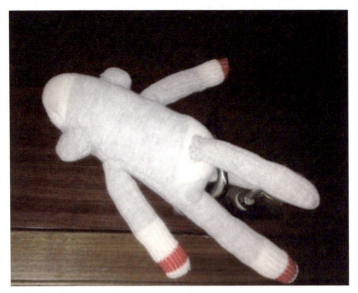

Sock Monkey

铃就响了。我们很好奇做完之后会是什么样？于是就问老师能否看看效果图。看了一下，好可爱呀！大大的嘴巴，又长又细的手脚，胸口还别着一颗红红的爱心。有点恋恋不舍，突然觉得缝娃娃这类事还挺好玩的嘛，还能锻炼自己的动手能力，要是在国内肯定是没有这机会的，老师和家长们都怕我们弄伤手指，又浪费太多宝贵时间。嗯，我很高兴能够选择这个社团活动。听妈妈说外婆和外公都是乡下很优秀的裁缝，到我这儿是女孩子的天性还是遗传因子的缘故呢？

4月26日，星期六

# 一次惬意的郊游

小溪边一景

上午9:00，我们在维多利亚市教育局集合，准备去郊游。

本以为自己到早了，但是一看，七八个同学都已经站在那儿有说有笑了，就跑过去加入队伍。之后陆陆续续有人来了，但还是少了几个。于是老师就一一给他们打电话。本来说是那四个人在一起的，结果搞了半天只有三个人，而且还是在9:20的时候才到的。刘老师和潘老师决定直接开车去接另外一个人。经过一番折腾，总算在10:10接到了最后一个人。而开到我们的目的地——金溪公园应该需要半个小时左右，这样我们游玩的时间就大大减少了。唉！不守时的家伙啊。

## 金溪公园

我们的校车晃晃荡荡地来到了金溪公园。这里就像一个大森林，全是树，还有几个木头桌椅。乍一看有点像我们上次野营的地方，仔细一看原来不是同一个地方，不过应该属同一座山脉。

我们踏着木桥来到了一块石头平台，旁边有一条清澈的小溪。水很浅，很清，水底都是鹅卵石，五颜六色。旁边还有很多大树，景色很美。刘老师说这里是三文鱼的摇篮，也是三文鱼的坟墓。因为每年七八月份的时候，三文鱼就会顶着水流，从这条小溪逆流而上，一直游到水浅，游不动为止，最后就死在这儿了。三文鱼死掉后，旁边就会有很多等待多时的棕熊，或者其他的野生动物来把三文鱼吃掉，所以在七八月份的时候，这边就会有一股很浓的鱼腥味。可惜的是，这条小溪我们玩到一半就不玩了，向另一个景点进军。

## 壁画城

昏昏沉沉地在车上睡了一觉，就到了壁画城。顾名思义，整个小镇的墙壁上都是壁画，各色各样，还看到了中国古代的壁画，还有奴隶们搬运木头和达官贵族们喝茶的壁画……转了一圈，饱览一番后就开始吃午饭了，刘老师特意买了香蕉和小蛋糕给我们吃。然后他推荐了一个冰激凌店，我虽然不打算买，但还是跟着大部队去了。冰激凌店在一个很美丽的小院子里，这个小院子里有很多熊，当然是假的啦。有的熊在钓鱼，有的熊在玩荡秋千，有的熊在当士兵把守大门，有的熊在旁边嬉戏，有的熊在爬栏杆……憨态可掬，十分可爱。出了小院子，我还在马路边看到一个木头长凳，上面还有几个熊爪印，超级可爱。

墙上的壁画

室内的壁画

## 图腾小镇

我们的下一个目标是图腾小镇。据刘老师介绍，这个小镇里的所有图腾都是以前加拿大的土著人创造的，都有特殊的意义。而据金叶所说，每一个图腾就代表一个家族。为了寻访不同的家族，我们便分散开来探索。我们先穿过马路，来到一个集市上，好像有人在叫卖，但是我们并没有去凑热闹。走着走着遇到一个阿姨推着一个铁球，貌似是用大小不同的自行车轮胎做成的。她看我们几个盯着那一个东西，就对我们说："想拍照吗？"我们欣然同意，三个人合影了一下。然后她又说你可以试着钻进去拍照。于是我一马当先，一脚跨进一个比较大的轮胎，慢慢将身体缩进去，再把另外一支脚抽进来，感觉还不错，挺好玩的，就是重心把握不好。大家玩够了后就和阿姨道别，前往下一个目的地。

我们找了一个咖啡厅休息。门口有两只小狗在晒太阳。一只小狗是黑白相间的，穿着亮黄色的小裙子，躺在一个大枕头上，看上去样子好滑稽。还有一只小狗，棕白相间，穿着橙色的小短裙，哈，小尾巴还在那摇啊摇。我忍不住摸了摸它们的头，它们还把小舌头吐出来，真的好可爱。

在咖啡厅小憩后，我们来到一家礼品店，店里东西很多，而且很可爱，又比较便宜。我们盯着那些琳琅满目的东西看了很久，我还买了一些小东西打算作为礼物送给国内的朋友。

集合后，刘老师就带着我们来到了一个购物中心。听介绍说这里的大鸡腿很好吃，我于是买了一个，果然味道不错。

图腾小镇的回忆

4月27日,星期日

# Beacon Hill Children's Farm

金叶在喂鹅

今天是周日,睡了个懒觉。用完美味的早餐后住家就带着我和张涛准备去Beacon Hill Children's Farm。

这是一个儿童农场,接下来学校还会组织来玩,但转念一想,先去熟悉一下环境也好。去Beacon Hill Children's Farm需要穿过一个大花园和一片绿草地。这里还有一条小溪穿过草地,两岸有柳树和不知名的类似桃花树一样的树。草地上还有很多懒洋洋的鸭子在晒太阳,看它们懒散的神情别提有多舒服了,还有很多鸭子三三两两躲在树荫下睡觉。有很多鸭子都是绿头鸭,还有一些鸭子灰灰的,就像一对鸳鸯一样。还有的鸭子成群结队地在小溪里游泳,过会儿都抖翅膀,过会儿啄会儿脖子,过会儿叼叼对方的尾巴,过会儿把头和身体埋在水下潜泳，场面十分和谐。

住家带着我们走进了Beacon Hill Children's Farm。公园面积不大，但是好玩的东西有很多。我们先走进一个木房子，房子里装饰得很漂亮。湖面有一棵小树枝上挂着很多千纸鹤，还有一些很精致的小鸟屋，里面有很多五颜六色的小鸟。有蓝色的，有黄色身体、橘色嘴巴的，像一只小鸡，还有白色的和棕色的，品种繁多，鸟窝里充满了"叽叽叽"的清脆鸟叫声。

看完鸟窝我们走到孔雀的活动场地，恰巧一只雄孔雀正在开屏。漂亮的孔雀毛展开成一个扇形，孔雀慢悠悠地转着身，让我们慢慢欣赏它美丽的羽毛，与此同时，它还忙着给旁边的雌孔雀们示爱。旁边坐着几只灰灰的雌孔雀，在那边抖抖羽毛，目不转睛地看着它，好像被它深深吸引住了。然而只有一只雌孔雀对它产生了爱慕，围着它团团转。看有一只雌孔雀走了出来，另外一只雄孔雀立马围上去，把自己的羽毛展开。同样是鲜艳夺目。你可以看到，两只雄孔雀纷纷展开自己的羽毛，旁边还有两只雌孔雀。之前我在上海的动物园里，也很难得看到这样的景象，最多是雄孔雀稍微展开一下羽毛就立马缩回去了。

孔雀开屏

看完了孔雀我们去了兔子的窝，有一股怪怪的臭味。兔子很大很可爱，而且它们的午饭也很丰富，有胡萝卜沙拉、包菜沙拉，还有水。一些兔子躲在它们的木头窝里不敢出来，或许是在睡午觉吧！

告别兔子我们还去拜访了羊驼和小马。羊驼是一黑一白的，也可以叫它草泥马，呆呆的，很可爱。小马则是一白、一棕和一个奶油色的，很神俊。饲养员还用梳子给它们梳毛呢！

看完小马，丹妮卡带着我走进了山羊的"天地"。这有母羊刚生出来的小羊。也许是因为怕它们在一起互相打斗，所以就把它们头上的角剪掉了，好可惜呀！这里的小羊最为可爱了，就像小孩子一样，在它们的领地里跳来跳去，和伙伴们玩耍，互相趴在对方的身上，或者是比谁跳得高，或者相互追逐着。看着有很多大人小孩和山羊们亲密接触，摸摸它们，还能抱抱它们，我也忍不住摸了一下身旁的一只棕色的小山羊。它抬头看了看我，然后就跑去和别的小羊玩了。我还看到有一对类似双胞胎的小羊在一起比赛谁跳得高，还会仰在对方的头上或背上，像两只小狗在打闹一样，有时还会"咩咩"直叫。

正看得出神，一只母羊走了过来扯扯我的衣角，然后把头对着我手上的热巧克力杯，好像是被巧克力的味道吸引住了，总想着把嘴凑过来，但是每次我就在它快碰到杯子的一刹那，把杯子往后一撤，让它无可奈何。可它倒没有流露出多少失望的神情，反而更加努力地把头往我的杯子上蹭，当然，它最终也没有得逞。

然后我和张涛去了羊房，里面大部分都是大羊，都在懒洋洋地睡觉，有的偶尔出来走动一下吃点东西，然后继续回去。我和张涛随便"抓"了一只羊拍了几张照。出来时，发现住家妈妈和丹妮卡在逗一只羊，我和张涛便凑了过去。这是一只奶牛色的小羊，很可爱，很有活力，好不容易被丹妮卡抱住，竭力想挣逃出来。

住家妈妈给我介绍了一个方法，让我坐在旁边的石头上，这样就会有羊过来。果然一只黄黄的母羊慢悠悠地走了过来，看了看我手中的热巧克力杯，有点馋的模样，看我没有给它的

可爱的小山羊

丹妮卡和山羊

意思,就识趣地走开了。趁这个时候我把巧克力喝完了。过了一会儿,之前那只母羊又来了,看样子对我手中的巧克力杯情有独钟。我仍是假装不给它,就让它稍微舔一舔,然后就拿开。于是它就开始撒娇,把头在我的牛仔裤上蹭,继而再用身体在我的牛仔裤上蹭。一番软磨硬泡没奏效后,才识趣地走开。

这时又有一只棕色的小羊从我背后过来了,看到我穿着桃红色的冲锋衣,就用嘴巴咬住冲锋衣不放。看来是喜欢这个颜色吧!我们笑着说它坏蛋,但它好像咬上瘾了,说什么也不肯放。"扑通",一个踉跄摔倒在地上,又坚强地爬起,走到我和张涛的脚边,然后轻巧地跳上我的腿。于是我就被压在了一只羊的脚下。它的脚还在我的腿上不停地踩,不停地蹬,感觉好有趣。因为时间关系,我们马上就要去下一个地方"喂鸟",于是就告别了小羊。

我们一行四人匆匆跑去喂鸟的草场地。住家妈妈给了我们每人一袋鸟食,让我们去喂鸟。这片场地很大,有多种类型的鸟类,乌鸦、海鸥,类似秃鹫一样的大鸟,还有鸭子和孔雀。

鸭子有的在岸上晒太阳，还有的在水里游泳，孔雀则是挺着脑袋，姿态优雅又很清高地漫步在桃树下，乌鸦则是毫无章法地到处乱飞。

　　喂鸟这件事倒也不容易。首先要找一只比较好相处的鸟或鸭子。一般来说鸭子比较好相处，但是你得要找到才行，因为有很多鸭子一看到人就跑。好不容易找到一只鸭子，在他们面前撒下一堆，它们就在那儿，用扁扁的嘴巴一个一个吃下去，还会发出"咕咕"的声音。看着它们的吃相，觉得好好玩。然后我转变目标，打算喂食两只鸽子。我先跟在鸽子身后，在它们面前抛下一堆鸟食，让它们先尝尝甜头，果然吃了食的鸽子明显放慢了脚步，于是我又撒了一把，它们立刻努力地啄食，到后来干脆转过身来对着我吃，但还是没用正眼瞧我。看来，食者，性也。我一看机会来了，趁它们光顾着吃时拍了张照。之后我打算去喂孔雀。孔雀很傲慢、很挑食，对于一些黄黄的、小米一样的东西，则是看也不看。于是我从袋里抓出一把瓜子，它看到瓜子就立马来了精神。孔雀的嘴巴尖尖的，啄到手心很痛，我立马松手。看看鸟食不多了，我又回过头去喂鸭子，抓了一点放在手里，它们马上用扁扁的嘴巴来啄，开始还好，后来觉得差点啄到我的肉了。

　　喂完了鸟，住家把我们送到一个Downtown的餐馆，还是老师推荐的呢，去尝试一下（Fish and chips）。味道还行。午饭后，我们逛了一会超市和商场后就心满意足地回家了。

4月29日，星期二

# 在海岸线社区中学划龙舟

划龙舟合影

13:00，我们准时在Mr. Allen的教室集合，因为我们将要去划龙舟。大家准时集合好后，我们便出发了。

我们需要步行到划龙舟的地方，其间要穿过一座大桥，还要过一个很长很长的林荫道，绕过半圈湖，才能到达目的地。细心的我在分岔路口发现了粉笔画的箭头，这些箭头指示着我们该走哪条路。看着这一个一个笔直的箭头，心中暖洋洋的。来到划龙舟的地方，用时大概半个小时，走到那儿的时候腿都有点发软了，感觉挺累的，都怪我平时没有加强体育锻炼。

接下来就是分队，七年级一队，八年级一队。八年级用的是大船，七年级用的是三驾小船。分好了队，我们就在旁边休息。看到旁边的人都在脱鞋脱袜子，在水泥地上乱跑，于是我们也跟着把鞋子拖掉。张涛说："他们脱鞋子肯定有他们的道理，万一待会儿脚湿了怎么办？先脱了吧！"于是我们四个人脱掉了鞋子和袜子，水泥地上很冷，而且踩着很不舒服，不是很平滑。后来我们跟着辅导老师走进了仓库，仓库里没有太阳的照射，显得更加阴冷，光滑是光滑了，但是很冷，就像走在薄冰上一样。换好了救生衣，出来拿了船桨。

一切就绪，大家在沙滩上集合。我和金叶刚走上沙滩，脚就像被刀割了一样。因为沙滩上并没有什么细沙，而是用较大的碎石子铺成的，走在上面就像在刀刃上行走一样，而且这些碎石子棱角分明，脚根本不敢移动。辅导老师看到我们两个的表情，于是对我们说："你们可以上去把鞋子穿上。"我们两个就像得到特赦似的，飞奔着跑向鞋子，走在水泥地上突然感觉没有那么难了。我们换好了鞋子，张涛她们却没有换，依然忍着，在碎石子地上艰难地行走。唉，是不是她的皮厚，还是她心理承受能力强大啊？！

我和金叶分在一组，正好互相有个照应。大家先是一起把船推进水里。船是用木头做的，别看不是很大，却十分沉重，搬着就像铁块一样。好不容易把船推进了水里。接下来就要一个一个上船了，我们是最后两个。还有一个在固定船，等我们两个上去后，再把船推到水里，然后一边推一边自己再跳上去，动作技术十分娴熟。调好方向，大家就开始划船。我没有划过船，所以不知道怎么握船桨，经过Mr. Allen一番指点后，渐渐领悟。坐在我们前面的是一个主力，他控制船的方向和速度，我跟着他的动作划船，因为他是主力的关系，所以后面的人可以休息，他却不能，必须一个劲地滑，一刻不能停。我因为要跟着他的速度，于是也跟着他一个劲地滑，从没有停过。划到手都快没有知觉了，我依然继续划，真没有想到划船这么辛苦啊！

划船的时候要把沉重的船桨正确地握在手里，右手抓住船桨的中心，左手则是握住船桨上面的一个把手，然后把船桨插进水里向后推。除了要领悟自己的动作和技巧外，还要跟上前面那个人的速度，动作节奏也要一致，这样才能划得又快又稳。我虽然和前面的人保持速度一致，但后面一个人总是打到我的船桨，貌似是节拍不合的缘故。

  这条河不是很深，但是水质很干净，往下可以望到水草。水里还有一股咸咸的味道。沿水的一侧是一片林荫道，很多绿树都垂下了自己的发丝，树底下还有几个长凳，供来往的行人休息。总之，在这么美的环境下划龙船，再累也无所谓。

  慢悠悠地划了一圈，形势突然变得严峻起来。周围的三条龙舟都在互相比赛，我们排在第二，第三条则远远地被甩在后面。前面一条船就是张涛她们的船，和我们也就一个船头的距离，但是总挡在我们前面不让过去，好不容易插到了她们的旁边，后面一个老师竟然把我们的船往后推借力把她们的船往前推。真是卑鄙呀！我们船上的所有船员都大叫起来抗议，结果她们倒来了个"恶人先告状"，居然拿水来泼我们。我因为坐在前面，帮后面的人挡了不少，水溅得我的裤子、袖子、眼镜、鼻子都是。于是我加快了划船速度，忘却了刚才的酸痛。终于经过了大家一番努力，最后两条船同时到达了岸边。

  上岸后，脱掉了救生衣，大家就齐心协力把船拖上岸，有人自告奋勇到水里去做支撑，看上去整个人就直接浸在水里了。把船抬到岸上这还简单，但是要把它抬到橡皮圈上，然后翻身，再继续抬到架子上，这就吃力了。架子很高，所以还要把手举起来，就像举哑铃一样，弄得我们手脚都很酸，但还有两条船等我们搬呢！

  一切弄完后，已经是15:30了，大家打算打道回府。有的人带了书包，就可以直接回家，但是我们四个还要回到学校，然后再回家。特别是我，回家还要再走上二十分钟，从这边走到学校就要半个小时，况且我现在已经是手软脚软、手酸脚酸了。

  好不容易，大家互相扶持回到了学校。我立即开启了补水模式：把自己水杯里的水一口喝干，喝得很爽。然后啃掉了一个苹果，这个苹果是中午我留下的，水分很足。接下来又吃了

龙舟架

三颗金叶免费提供的草莓。最后，又吃了两块苏打饼干，用来补充能量。但还觉得不够，又继续补水，喝了一杯本来中午喝的果汁。到家后，我又一口喝掉了一杯白开水，终于把丧失的水分都补回来了，觉得力气又慢慢回到了身上。然后进入复习模式，因为就要期中考试了，比较忙又只能一个人复习。突然有点想念学校的老师和同学了，他们现在肯定比我忙碌多了。

5月1日，星期四

# 放学回家后的意外情况

回家路上一景

今天下午放学后我马上就走回家了。因为住家离学校不远，又没有多少公交站，于是经常走着回去，路上大概需要花二十分钟。今天走得早，所以15:15就到家了。

走到家门口我拿出钥匙开门。平常回家的时候，有时住家妈妈在家，所以就不用我开门，有的时候也自己开门，但要转很多圈才能开出来。因为对国外开门的方法不怎么熟，也不怎么会开锁，所以以前我开门的时候经常需要花很久的时间。而今天，我拿出钥匙，现在剩两个孔，顺时针转一圈，下面一个孔再按逆时针转一圈，但是拧不开也打不开。想一想也很正常，因为之前开门的时候都要开上三五遍。于是我把钥匙拔了出来，继续第二遍，依然不成功，我有一些心急了。

我决定休息一下，然后再试了一遍，依然是打不开。焦急地转转把手，把手是能动了，可能是上面的锁还没有解开。于是我又去试着开上面的锁，钥匙插进去竟然还扭不动，而且左右都不行。我把钥匙往里推了一些，仍然不见效果，然后我又把门往里推了推，依然没有什么动静，只好再把钥匙拔出来。

　　又重复了好几遍，大门依然打不开。我怀疑住家妈妈会不会在花园里或者在房子里，于是就按了按门铃，没有人回应。实在忍不住了，我重重地敲了敲门，依然没有人应。看来房子里应该是没有人了，那我怎么办呀？！不甘心地又试了几次，门把虽然可以扭动了，但是门依然打不开。

　　打开手机看了看时间，已经过去15分钟了，我心急如焚。我的手机没有开通国际漫游，试了一下给住家妈妈打电话，没有打通。正握着手机愁眉不展时，正好看见Wi-Fi连上了。眼睛一亮，突然想到可以和爸爸妈妈打电话，因为可以利用网络手机，只要有网就不用花钱，也不需要什么国际漫游，正好爸爸妈妈那边刚刚早上起来。电话打通了，和爸爸讲述了一番情况。他就在电话那头教我怎样开门，我试了一遍，没有效果，又试了两遍依然没有效果，于是我们就打算视频聊天。我把摄像头对准钥匙孔，爸爸在视频那头教我怎样开门。左扭扭右扭扭，都没有动静，下面再扭一扭，依然没有动静，推推门把钥匙卡进去，再往外搬一些，还是没有用。这回我真是心急了，为什么这钥匙怎么开都开不了呢？之前也就试几次就开了，今天怎么回事呀！

　　于是爸爸给我提了个建议：让我从花园进去。想一想，花园外面有栏杆怎么进去呢？脑袋突然灵光一闪，住家妈妈之前好像走过一次花园的后门。虽然害怕后面的门也锁了，但还是抱着一线希望跑到后园。果然门锁了，但是在外面可以把锁打开。我顺利进入花园。爸爸在视频那头称赞花园很美的同时，我绕到了花园和房屋连通的那扇门，果然门也锁了，突然想起，早上还是住家妈妈让我亲手把门锁上的呢！我仍然抱着一线希望，拿着手中的钥匙插到钥匙孔里，心想这会不会是同一个钥匙呢，但是又想哪怕是同一个钥匙，我好像也打不开吧！

一边心中焦急,一边把钥匙插进钥匙孔,喀嚓一声,插进去了,于是抱着一线希望,我又按顺时针转了一圈,再拿出来,在下面一个逆时针转了一圈,扭了扭把手,哎,又没扭开。但是我依然不服输,因为前门是打不开了,我的希望就在这后门上了,我又试了一遍,抱着最后一丝希望,扭动了把手。咦!我转动了,会不会门开了?心中忐忑不安,往前用力一推,"吱呀"一声,门终于开了,我长出了一口气。

　　从后门踏进房子,心中感到特别有成就感,我把门打开了,看了看手机已经过去35分钟了。都快16:00了,平常到家最多也就15:30,今天算是最晚的了。今天的意外情况真是出乎意料啊!以后我还要多学学怎么开门。

　　往空荡荡的房子里探了探,果然没人在家,住家妈妈难道出去了吗?走到自己的房间,看到房门上贴了一张纸条,哦,原来住家妈妈去购物了,正想走进房间的时候,住家妈妈回来了。我向她讲述了一番刚才发生的事情,她有些抱歉,告诉我那个门本身就不是特别好,要等一会儿才能开。我这才释然。

　　晚上,住家的朋友过来吃饭,大家一起用了一顿很丰盛愉快的晚餐。回头想想今天发生的事情,还是心有余悸。

回家路上一景

5月2日，星期五

# 探访原始森林

今天，学校要组织我们五个交流生（四个中国学生和一个泰国学生）一起去踏青。我们四个中国女孩坐在老师的车上，另外一个则坐在一个老伯伯的车上，老伯伯是今天带领我们参观踏青的向导。

坐在车上心里不免有点激动，因为还不知道要去踏青的地方究竟是哪儿？只知道大概方位，就在我住家旁边的一条路上。

15分钟后，我们就到了目的地。这里是一片森林，向导老伯伯带我们走进去，还摘了一点树叶给我们。树叶非常新鲜，就像松针一样，但是没有松针那么硬、那么长，软软的，放在手里很舒服，而且它的气味特别清香，带着一股甜味，闻了以后觉得全身都很舒服。我一直攥在手里，手心都有一股甜甜的、香香的味道了。

走进树林，才发现树林里是那么的美妙。在中国的时候，很少有机会走进这样大的原始森林。只见一条小溪在远处轻轻地流淌，耳朵传来"哗哗"的流水声。放眼望去有很多树木高耸入云，近处有一些小石桥，远处还能听见清脆的鸟叫声，地上长着各种不知名的小草，间或有花开得满地都是。树林里踩出了一条曲折幽深的小径。说是小径，其实是一些枯黄的树叶和树枝铺成的，大概是百十年来，由不断的树叶累积而成的。走在上面，似乎比走在地毯上还要软。

老伯伯带着我们一边走，一边给我们介绍植物。这里的树木有的十分笔直，有的很坚硬，但是长得不高。老伯伯还对我

巨大的树桩

　　们介绍说，不同的树木都有不同的意思。像粗壮而长得很高的树木，虽然木质没有那么坚硬，但原始的人们最早发现了它们的用处。他们会把树皮弄下来，扭一圈，再把它们捆扎起来，用来做装饰，或者编衣服和帽子。所以这些高大的树木满山遍野都是。这种树的树叶还可以作为药材，对原始人类来说它们是十分重要的。再说一说那些木质坚硬，但长得不高的树吧。这些树普遍在2到3米之间，坚硬、笔直，但是生长极其缓慢。所以这种木材很珍贵，一般只用来造船或者搭建房子。

　　老伯伯又给我们介绍了一些不同种类的莓果，名字各有不同，样子也各有千秋，但还是有一些相似点的，比如果实都差不多大。这些莓果大概都要到7月份才会成熟，所以现在看到的就像草莓没有成熟之前，还只有一点点大。走着走着，老伯伯还发现一棵灵芝。这棵灵芝长在一棵断掉的树桩上，体型很大，足有一个人的脸那么大。老伯伯兴奋地站在旁边向我们介绍，但是并没有靠近那棵灵芝，说是怕把它碰坏了！

　　继续沿着小溪流前行，突然发现三只小狗在小溪里嬉戏，溅起朵朵水花，玩得不亦乐乎。小溪很浅，而且很干净，底下的鹅卵石五颜六色。如果你的视力够好，还能看到鹅卵石底下悠闲游弋着的小鱼儿。它们是灰色的，很机灵，在石缝间快速地游动着。跨过一个小桥，我们看到桥两边种着一些类似大包菜一样的东西，很大啊！一片叶子就像一片小芭蕉叶一样。老伯伯介绍说，这种植物以前是用来做菜的，味道很浓烈。说话间还摘了一点给我们闻，的确是有点冲鼻，但也不失清香，味道还有一点奇怪。走过桥发现对面还有更多这样的"包菜"。忽然感悟，以前的人真的好有智慧啊，竟然能发现这么多东西的独有价值，为他们的生存发展所用。接着我们又看到了几种不同的野生莓果，还发现了之前看到的一种树，就是一开始老伯伯给我们摘的叶子很香的那种植物。一开始遇见的那棵树树龄有点老了，而现在遇到的这棵，才刚刚抽出嫩枝来，叶梢上还有一些嫩绿色的小叶子。老伯伯又摘了几片叶子给我们，闻了闻，嫩绿的叶子的确比深绿的要好闻得多，更加清香。

穿过了树林，发现对面有一座古堡。老伯伯介绍说，这是一个拍电影的基地，曾经以古堡作为主题拍过一部电影。据说从前这座古堡是一个很富有的人和他的妻子住的，然后又传给了他们的儿子。这座古堡外型看上去十分大气，背靠森林，面临大海，古堡前是一片开阔的草坪，再往前眺望就是加拿大和美国的边界了，那里是一片皑皑雪山，配上湛蓝的天空，十分美艳。

踏着松软的草坪，老伯伯随手摘了一根草含在嘴里，吹出各种各样的声音，有高有低。于是我们几个也尝试了一下，一开始没有吹出来，但是突然一下子被我吹了出来，顿时感悟了技巧，原来要把叶子绷直并用两个手夹紧，然后要吹中间的部分。而且一定要靠准位置，如果靠得不准就会变音。老伯伯又教了我们另外一种方法，就是把它含在嘴里吹，这个有点困难，我怎么吹都把握不好，只是偶尔能吹出几个音。

伴随着口哨声和嬉笑声，我们又走进另一片丛林。老伯伯摘了一朵花，然后把它的花瓣按照不同的方向摆成一个圈，并向我发送出来，结果一些花瓣就落在我的身上。我们几个也兴致勃勃地学起来。看来大自然值得我们学习的和带给我们的乐趣还是有很多的，这些远是在课堂上学不到的。

我们又走近了一点，老伯伯发现了一些很尖锐的石头和贝壳的碎片。他对我们说，这一块地方是用来烤贝壳的，可以用这些尖锐的石头把树枝刮成木棒。说完他还亲自示范了一遍，果然，树皮很轻松地被刮掉了。

踏过草坪，我们走进另一片森林，进去满眼看到的就是之前见到的包菜一样的东西，一股浓烈的味道窜入鼻孔。我们还发现树干上有黏黏的东西，像胶水一样。老伯伯对我们说，这是从树干上渗出来的，还说这东西是可以吃的。抵挡不住好奇心，我用干净的木棒挑了一点，然后用手指蘸着伸进嘴里。开始还没有什么味道，可是过了一会儿，就觉得凉凉的，喉咙很舒服，再过了一会儿还有一些微微的苦味。这个东西不仅可以用来吃，还可以用来做照明。老伯伯拿出他之前制作的一个东西，就是在一个贝壳上斟满这些黏乎乎的东西，然后在上面点起火，马上像蜡烛一样燃烧起来。老伯伯说这东西还可以用来捕猎，吸引动物的注意力。

走过一段树林，我们发现有一棵树倒在地上，很粗壮的树干被劈成了两半。老伯伯说，这棵树起码有700年的历史。看了看它的年轮，真的能让人产生密集恐惧症。树干上还长了很多植物。绕过这个树干，我们还发现了一些蓝色的鸟蛋碎片。又过了一座小桥，我们发现很多树桩上长着菌类植物，有的是灰色底白色边，有的则是一圈颜色不同的花纹串起来的，还有的则是像小雨伞一样。我们还发现了一种小动物，就像没有壳的蜗牛一样，黏黏的，粗看它像是个小宝宝，但我还是不敢放在手里。过了一会儿，老伯伯还在树丛里发现了一只更大的，它像蜗牛一样爬行，爬过的地方还会留下一串黏液。

没壳的蜗牛

快到中午的时候，老伯伯带我们离开了这片美丽的原始森林。

下午的最后一节课是兴趣班。我和茹云衣继续做Sock Monkey。今天真是一个Wonderful Day。

5月3日，星期六

# 在住家掌勺做中国菜

今天是周六，我约了张涛一起到我的住家做客，顺便打算给住家做一顿中式午餐。一大早我绕了一大圈才遇到张涛，然后我们去超市采购了一些午餐需要的食材。

回到家已经是11:20了，我和张涛开始动手。我们要做的第一个菜是番茄炒蛋。拿好了一切所需要的东西，张涛负责切番茄，我负责打蛋，我们两个虽然都会做菜，但是都好久没有做了，有些生疏。我还差点忘了把锅加热。切好番茄，打好蛋，我们就开始了。这个菜由我来掌勺，我先把鸡蛋倒入锅中，住家的锅都是平底锅，铲子还是软铲，铲着软绵绵的，让我很不适应。不知道啥原因，这个锅不容易粘锅，所以我就把鸡蛋炒得很嫩。然后再把番茄倒入锅中，番茄很快变软了，说明菜也马上好了，加了一点盐，把火关小。因为我对这个厨房有一些不适应，怕烧出来的菜味道不好，于是就先尝尝，果然味道很淡，于是又加了一点盐，依然没有用。大概加了三四次，这才觉得刚刚适中，也许是这个盐和家里的不一样，也许是我太谨慎每次加得太少吧。

接下来的一道菜是青椒炒土豆丝。我把锅子和铲子都洗干净，这时张涛已经开始准备了：首先把土豆皮给削掉，因为没有找到削皮的东西，就只能用刀！当我们削了一小半的时候，住家妈妈来了，她帮我们找来了一个专门刮土豆皮的东西。很快，土豆皮这一关就过去了。然后就是要把土豆切成片，再切成丝，还要把它浸在水里，去掉一些淀粉。利用浸泡土豆的时间，我和张涛开始处理青椒。先把青椒一剖为二，然后把中间的瓤给去掉，再切成丝。回头一看，放土豆丝的那个碗，水面上已经浮起一层白白的东西了，看来国外的土豆含淀粉量真多啊！把水去掉，接下来就要开始炒了，因为土豆比较硬，所以我们先炒土豆。这个菜是由张涛来掌勺。

　　趁她在炒青椒土豆丝的时候，我开始准备下一个菜：蒜炒西兰花。西兰花就不打算切了，直接用手掰。还要把西兰花洗得很干净。我一点一点地洗，先把外面全洗掉，然后剥掉，再往里面一层洗，再剥掉，一层一层把西兰花整个都剥完了。然后就是切蒜，先把蒜外面的一层剥掉，然后用住家妈妈给我们的一个"神器"来挤压，可是我不是很会用这个东西，只能把它压扁，然后再用刀切。切完后，张涛的土豆丝也炒得差不多了，放了一些盐，觉得有点淡，又放了一些，这才够味道。但是，看似完美的背后总是有缺点的，因为张涛炒的时候不注意，有很多土豆都粘锅了，搞得锅上都是一层污垢，磨都磨不掉。于是，她又把这个洗锅的重任交给了我，自己去那边炒西兰花了。我拿着冷水不停地冲锅，还不停地用抹布在锅子的污垢处不断擦拭，但也只擦掉了一点，后来我还是用指甲给擦掉的。不过也幸亏张涛给我找到一块抹布，这才使我轻松一点。

　　蒜泥西兰花终于炒好了，虽然量很少，但很精致，然后我们开始点菜，只有三个菜，原计划是四个菜的。那还烧一个什么呢？想了半天，哦，原来是手撕包菜啊！又看了一下时间，已经12:35了，看来我们得抓紧了。张涛不会炒包菜，只能我一个人战斗。先把包菜一层一层剥开，然后用清水洗净，再用手撕的方法撕成小块。然后，从冰箱里拿了一根火腿肠，让张涛切成圆片，备用。又准备了小半碗水。炒菜马上开始。首先把锅烧热、倒油，然后把火腿肠往锅里爆炒一下，接着再把包菜放进去，等包菜变软一点，再用水淋上一圈，然后慢慢等待。等包菜变软了，最后拿酱油再淋一圈，用来调色和调味，再加一点盐，就大功告成了。

　　现在已经是12:45了，之前炒的菜有些凉了，所以稍微在微波炉里加热一下，就端去餐桌了。趁张涛把菜端到餐桌上的时候，我把先前煮好的米饭盛在盘子里端出去。饭做得也不错，水不多不少，香喷喷的。摆好餐盘，大家开始吃午饭了。

　　看到五颜六色的蔬菜，住家妈妈不停地大声叫好，还对我和张涛不停地说着"thank you"。平常不喜欢吃蔬菜的丹妮卡也吃了一大堆，但是她的男朋友不怎么喜欢吃蔬菜，好像是因为他对蔬菜有一点过敏，不能吃太多。我突然感到有点愧疚，因为不是很会烧肉，所以今天的菜基本上都是素的，除了火腿和鸡蛋。我把每个菜都尝了一点，发现自己的手艺还不错，这是我和张涛奋斗一个多小时的成果啊！住家妈妈高兴地对我们说，希望下次还能让我们做一顿，我们的心中顿时感到无比温暖。没想到外国人这么喜欢吃中国菜啊！下午和张涛一起去超市逛了一圈。因为之前复活节野营的时候赢得了一张爆米花的卡，可以消费15块钱，于是就用这些钱，买了一包爆米花，味道还不错。这个店的爆米花有很多种类，水果味、奶油味，各种颜色，我和张涛点了一份焦糖味的。边吃还边感叹道，在中国爆米花只有一种口味，那就是原味，不像国外创意新颖，连爆米花店都能开成连锁店。

爆米花店门口的我

然后我们还去了一家服装店,这里的衣服打折很疯狂,有三件衣服5块钱的,有买一赠二的,有买一件第二件5块的,各种各样的打折花样层出不穷。我没有多理会这些打折的活动,而是拿了一条没有什么活动的运动裤,面料很舒服,穿着很宽松。后来付钱时发现也就8块钱,本来以为要十几块的。这回折合成人民币,一件舒服的运动裤连50元都不到,真是难以想象啊!

逛了一会儿我们就各自回家了,今天走了很多路,感觉脚很酸,回到家后就"瘫"在床上,但还是很满足的,特别是给住家烧中国菜。听到住家一声声的赞扬,感觉很开心,没想到中国菜竟然这么受欢迎,看来我这个烧中国菜的菜鸟还要更加努力哦。我一定要多做些中国菜给住家吃,让他们感受一下中国菜的风味,我们可是有《舌尖上的中国》的哦。

5月4日，星期日

# 点滴思考，些许感悟

木桌上的思考

　　今天早上睡了一个懒觉，起来时发现已经8:50了。住家妈妈一大早就出去了，等我洗漱完毕她正好回来，问丹妮卡和我有没有吃早饭？听到还没有吃的时候，她就马上让丹妮卡做了一点早餐。简单地用完了早餐，回到房间休息了一会，又复习了数学，上午很快就过去了。

　　午饭用得很晚，就是三明治和几根芹菜。虽然很简单，却吃得很饱。午饭后觉得有点累，可能是由于昨天买菜、做饭、逛商场忙碌了一天，走路又太多了，所以打算回房间睡个午觉，哪知一觉就睡到了下午3:00多，起来的时候发现国外学校的作业还没有做，于是爬起来做。作业就是回答一个问题，也许对于外国学生来说很简单，但对我来说很难。因为需要看书,然后收集答案来回答问题。这是社会作业,我还把书带了回来,因为在学校里的时候看得不是很明白,回来打算查字典,把所有内容都搞懂后再回答问题。一看不知道,看了吓一跳,发现这本书上的东西,我基本都看不懂,连大意都搞不明白,还有很多地名,根本搞不清楚是哪儿,如幼发拉底河、底格里斯河、三角洲等。而且有一些专用名词,即使查到了中文,还要弄半天才能知道是什么意思。

内容虽然不多,但是一查下来生词却很多,都快查满一页纸了。内容大致搞懂了,不过还有点稀里糊涂。于是又把中文词解代到书里对照,把大概意思弄清楚就行了,因为翻译出来的不一定都是全对的。好不容易搞懂了,发现问题其实挺简单的,找了6个理由都写上去了,其实主要在书中找答案就行。又想了想,在国外周末的回家作业竟然只是回答一个可以在书上抄抄答案的问题,如果我看得懂书的话,也许只要花上10分钟就能做完了(包括看书的时间)。要是往常在国内的话,大概要做上4个小时,最少也要3个小时。这就是国外和中国的区别所在啊。

住家妈妈之前说过,孩子就要像一个孩子,在还小的时候,就要多玩,多长见识,在游玩中积累增长知识,而不是拼命地去读书。虽说书中自有黄金屋,但是小孩子所要掌握的知识,不是都在书中的,有很多都是要在生活中亲身体会才能掌握的。就像之前在原始森林里学习植物知识的时候,哪些植物可以吃,我们都是不知道的,都是自己放在嘴里含了含才知道,这种经历大概就叫实践出真知吧。中国古代有"神农尝百草"的神话故事,我想讲的也是这个意思。

我又联想起学校组织我们在大马路上捡垃圾的事情,更是难得。原先我在自己住的小区里都不会捡垃圾,看到垃圾也很少会把它捡起来,有的时候还会觉得有一点丢人,虽然大家口头上都挂着保护环境人人有责,但是又有谁能真正地做到看到垃圾马上把它捡起来呢?而在国外,学校竟然还带着我们去捡垃圾,看到地上有一个香烟头,就会捡起来,有塑料袋,就会不顾旁边的野草,把它捡起来。看到有易拉罐,也是直接用手把它抓起来。要说外国人不会随便扔垃圾，这倒也不算是真的，因为有的时候走在马路上，偶尔也会看到旁边有垃圾，但是，大家有保护环境的意识，更有爱护环境的行动，自然是不会轻易让垃圾出现在眼前了。学校组织我们去捡垃圾就是通过行动来教育我们爱护环境的重要性，这比简单的说教更让人印象深刻。

还有前一段时间划龙舟的事情，以前在中国划龙舟，只有在书上或电视里看到，而在国外，虽说龙舟是由中国创造出来的，但在国外尽然这样流行！国外的龙舟和中国的龙舟区别很大，都是像小船一样。先说我们大家一起合力把船推到水里的事情，当时老师把所有的同学都叫过来搬船，因为船较大。当把船搬出储藏室的时候要拐一个弯，船很长，所以需要大家的配合，后面的人不能心急，还要撑着船尾，前面的人也不能拐得太快，让后面的人吃不消。船头出来后，前面的人就不能动了，要等后面的人转个圈，才能继续向前行走。把船推入水中更是需要大家的积极配合，最后一个推船入水的人则更是要自告奋勇，因为他不仅要把船推入水中，还要趁那一瞬间跳入船中，他还是划龙舟的主力，还要控制船的方向和速度。等船入水后大家要齐心协力地划船，要不然船桨互相打在一起，船就不能往前行，而且还要掌握好所有人划船的速度，既要顾到前面的人，又要照顾到后面的人。你还不能因为酸痛而停下手中的工作，因为这样会连累别人，别人就要多出一份力来弥补你的时间。将船翻起来的时候，须更加小心谨慎，要照顾好队友，以防止对面的队友被船压到。

来加拿大已经有一段时间了，我也逐步感受到加拿大的教育和中国教育的区别，中国的教育不是不好，只不过是注重学生对知识的掌握而已，而加拿大则是注重全方面的发展。虽然在军事方面可能会弱于我们，但是在保护环境、团结协作等方面却高于我们。这也正是我们要向别的国家学习的地方。中国的学生在不落下自己学习的情况下，还要更加注重多方面的培养，这样才能让自己全面发展。在加拿大读书的日子里，我已经有过很多很多全新的尝试。这些尝试，也许在别人看来是好的，但是这背后有不少的付出和适应。而我也在努力地融入这个完全不同的学习环境。希望我回国后展现给大家的，是一个全方面发展的学生，而不是之前那个除了学习什么都不会的学生，或者说是只顾学习，不顾其他的孩子。

这次的加拿大之旅，不只是让我来学习、了解体验国外的生活的，希望能成为我生命中的一次全新的蜕变之旅。

游览布查德花园

5月5日，星期一

# 找手机，现真情

沙滩前的草地

今天最后一节体育课，老师带我们步行去了学校旁边的沙滩。这个沙滩风景很美，是在一片小树林后面。那里有沙石、贝壳堆积成的沙滩，还有蓝天碧海，海上还有一座小岛，离我们很近，上面有很多大树，还有许多在小憩的海鸥。之前老师也组织我们来过一次，第二次来到这儿，感受更加不同了，觉得这儿景色比之前更美了。阳光下，海面上波光粼粼，沙滩上黄沙灿灿，给身后的树林投下一大片阴凉。因为还要步行回去，我们只在沙滩上逗留了大概20分钟，就结伴陆陆续续回去了。

我和金叶开始闹着玩，先是她拉着我跑，然后我拉着她跑，跑跑停停，把张涛和茹云衣都甩在了后面。后来我们真跑起来了，我拉着她跑一段，跑累了，她继续拉着我跑。等到我俩都累了，再走一会儿，然后再跑。如此这样，竟然仅用了5分多钟，往常走这段路需要15分钟呢！

　　我们先回到学校，因为张涛和茹云衣还没有回来，于是我们就整理好了书包等她们过来，顺便坐在椅子上品尝金叶带来的曲奇饼干。一共有4片，本来是每人一片的，但是我们看她们还没来，于是就给她们30秒的时间，如果30秒内回来就给她们吃，如果还没回来，这剩下的两块我们就分掉！金叶刚数到30秒，我俩就把饼干给分了。刚把饼干放进嘴里，张涛和茹云衣就回来了。我们两个立马哈哈大笑，要是给她们35秒的时间，估计她们就能吃到饼干了。

　　放学后，我正打算拿出手机看一下时间，突然发现外套口袋里空空的，拉链半拉着。脑袋轰隆一下，不会又从口袋里掉出来了吧？已经掉过两次了，怎么又掉了啊？而且，自前两次以后，我天天都穿有拉链口袋的衣服。虽然说拉链拉得不牢，但是难不成这么小的口子，还能掉出来？我就像热锅上的蚂蚁一样，心急如焚，茹云衣让我去检查一下书包和柜子，看看刚才开柜子的时候有没有落在里面。我快速打开小柜子，里面除了一些书本，哪有什么手机的影子啊！书包里也是。金叶突然想到可能是我们刚才跑回来的时候，手机掉在路上了。于是金叶和茹云衣立马提出陪我去找手机，而张涛则是有事先离开了。

　　我们打算按照原来跑回来的路再走一遍，刚出门，天上就飘下了细雨。我找手机心切，自然顾不了那么多，戴上帽子就冲出去了。金叶撑了伞和茹云衣跟在我后面。我们一个看左边，一个看中间，一个看右边。走出了学校，手机依然踪影不见，这让我更加心焦。这时雨大了起来，于是茹云衣也拿出伞，我和金叶合撑一把伞后继续找。我心中十分感动，有这样的朋友真好。风雨中，我们三个人背着书包，在人行道上不停地搜索，依然是没有。转弯上天桥，天桥上空荡荡的，什么东西都没有。只有雨点打在马路上，激起朵朵水花，我们的鞋子都被雨水溅湿了。令我感动的是，金叶和茹云衣依然毫无怨言，帮我继续搜索着，还说一些搞笑的话逗我开心。我的心情慢慢静下来了，但还是很着急。走进了树林就要更加仔细搜索了，我们放慢了脚步，虽然跑回来时走的都是中间，但是两边的树丛，也不能放过。我想到我们跑过来的时候超过了几个人，所以我们并没有落在最后，这么说的话，如果我的手机掉在了地上，那么后面的人应该也会发现的，但是，跑回来却没有什么动静。这样一分析，手机一定是落在了沙滩上或是草丛里。沙滩的前面有一块草丛，正好是我们回来的必经之路。草间坠着一颗颗水珠，把鞋子都打湿了，我也视而不见。我紧张起来，如果草坪上没有？那么我的希望只能寄托在沙滩上了，万一沙滩上还没有怎么办？无限焦急中，我也只能静下心来寻找。突然，听到金叶"啊"的一声，发现我的手机了，就安静地躺在草丛里，上面都被雨水打湿了。擦干水珠开机，没想到还可以用，真的太感谢她了！开机的时候一看时间，已经15:37了，要是平常的话，她们这个时候肯定早就到家了，但是，她们因为陪我找手机，耽误了那么久的时间，还在风雨中，经受雨水的考验。有这样好的朋友，真是太知足了。

　　找到了手机，心情立马好了起来。大家一起撑着伞，在风雨中聊天，因为下雨的原因，这里的温度降低了不少，我们穿得都比较单薄，特别是下半身。大家又走了那么多路，才从海滩回来，又去了海滩，双脚不免有些酸痛。但是，金叶和茹云衣笑着说："我们帮你找到了手机，你要给我们付医药费哦，治腿哟！""买张狗皮膏药哦！"

　　雨不停地下着，洒下片片雨花。风雨中传来阵阵欢笑。雨声、笑声融合在一起。回家后，我沉默不语却思绪翻滚，今天朋友们帮我找手机的景象已深深地印在我的脑海里，并不停地回放。虽然裤子淋湿了，但她们毫无怨言；虽然脸蛋打湿了，但她们依然无怨无悔；虽然双脚走麻了，但她们毫不介意。有这样好的朋友，是一部手机所不能换来的。

　　今天，我收获了纯真的友谊，甘愿为朋友付出的友谊。

5月6日，星期二

# 木工课（专题写作）

木工课，做手电筒

### 画草图

在Shoreline的第三个星期我们开始了木工课的教程，教我们木工课的老师是一个很和蔼的中年人。我们叫他Mr. Mark。我们要做的第一步就是画草图。第一节课，老师在黑板上画了一个手电筒的草图，还发给我们每人一张格子纸。黑板上的草图画好后，我们按他的规定数格子画图。记得当时画草图的时候，还挺难的，因为老师在课堂上是用英语跟我们描述，有很多单词讲得不是很清楚，我们的课桌又离黑板太远，看不清他在黑板上写的厘米数。我只能半猜半蒙，再和边上的同学一起讨论后才画出来，下课后又跑到黑板跟前去确认了一下。就这一张手电筒的草图，一连画了两节课。接下来的几节课就是练习画三维图，倒是很简单、很轻松。

### 做胚胎

因为进度不同，所以Mr. Mark就给先做好的人发了一个木块，然后把我们集体带到一个工作坊里。工坊里面摆满了机器，他把我们带到钻孔的机器面前，自己先演示了一番。因为前面挤了太多人，所以我们都没怎么看清楚，最后还是看着前面的人做了以后，自己才做的呢！这个机器看上去很恐怖，当你把它打开的时候，马力就突然变得很强大，一根插在上面的铁钻高速旋转，要按着旁边的把手，慢慢地推，对准好位置以后，再往下推。第二次推的时候还要很用力，一连钻了三个孔，再去另外一个机器上钻第四个孔。这次要钻的是小孔，就没有刚才那个机器恐怖了，我也就放心大胆了很多。但是因为不是很会操作，还是同学帮忙才完成的呢！

把木块钻好并顺利通过老师的检查，我们就要进行下一步了，把木块多余的部分用切刀切掉。说着看着倒是挺简单，但真正做起来是很困难的。细的地方还好切，但一到粗的地方就很难切了。手根本使不上劲，还得用木块敲着下去，这还是我自己想出来的办法呢。切完了木块的边缘，就要切角了。大切刀被张涛占去了，所以我只能用小切刀。用木块敲了半天，也只切出一道小小的裂痕，回头再看看张涛，她已经切掉一个角了，看她那样子，即使是大切刀也依然很难切，明显是"咬牙切齿"嘛！等张涛用完大切刀，我马上借了过来，大切刀很重，但是切起来果然很带劲，一切就是一段，但切久了就使不上劲，切不下去了。于是我又继续用木头敲，大切刀配上木头，木块很快就"投降"了。

接下来的一节课，就是用来磨木块的。要把木块打磨光滑，包括里面。想把它磨光，也不是件容易的事，反反复复大概磨了两节课吧！然后就要换一种砂纸，再上油。先要用刷子蘸了油抹到木块上，等木块浑身上下都粘上油以后，再用另外一种红砂纸，把油磨掉，然后再上油，再磨掉，重复七八遍后，木头就变得异常光滑，就像打了蜡一样。有收获就有付出，为了使木块光滑，我可是花费了差不多两节课的时间啊！

## 焊电路

将木块打磨好，给老师检查后，老师给我配了一些电线和橡胶圈，让我先把它们组装起来，然后再焊接。来到焊接木头的房间，房间里只能容纳四个人，所以我就站在门外等，后来发现好多人在插队，还有一些人好像没有发现里面已经人满为患了，依然毫无顾忌地走了进去。我就这样在门外等啊等，好不容易等到里面有三个人了，马上就跑进去。

首先用钳子把老师给我们的电线两端的橡胶部分掐掉，我因为力气小，所以就叫了旁边一个女孩子帮我掐，然后用掐掉的一头与一根铁丝连接并套上橡皮圈。再掐掉一根铁丝，继续之前的动作，用原本被掐掉的地方与另外一根铁电线连接，再套上橡皮圈，之后再把连接的地方焊接好。虽然只需要焊接三个地方，但对我来说已经很难了。拿起焊机，上面冒出丝丝热气，手有点抖，这是什么玩意儿啊，从来没有见过啊，肯定会很烫吧。小心翼翼地把焊头处触碰焊接处，但是只冒出丝丝热气，却没有其他反应。过了一会儿仍然没有反应。于是，我就把焊头像小鸡啄米似的不停地在焊接处点来点去，仍是没有用。旁边的金叶说，把焊头靠在焊接处就可以了。可是我试了一下，还是没有用，正想要把笔插回去的时候，笔尖触到自己的大拇指，突然一下觉得自己的手指特别疼。仔细一看，被烫到的地方已经开始发红，看来要起泡了，没想到温度都这么烫了，却焊接不了。这到底是怎么回事？于是我又接二连三地焊了两节课，虽然两根手指都受伤了，但好歹三个焊接处是焊好了。接下来就是要把它与之前的按钮连在一起。把铁丝轻轻穿过小孔绕一圈再焊，这个地方好像好焊些，但是过一会儿发现又有问题了。我以为焊好了，就轻轻扯了扯，没想到，"啪"的一声断掉了。正好这个时候下课铃响了，我只好第二天继续焊。就这样又连续焊了两节课，终于马马虎虎算是焊好了，给老师检查，却被一口否决。他给我们做了个示范，让我们明天再继续。

　　第二天，金叶拿着老师给我们的锡丝，先把锡丝融化了然后再把上面的锡水沾到自己的焊接处，这样就行了。我被烫过两次了，对这个东西有了深深的恐惧感，于是金叶就帮我把电线焊好了。然后用热吹风机让橡胶圈收紧，这样就不容易脱落了。这一次，焊接得很成功，这个花费了我两个多星期的焊接工程终于告一段落了。看来，掌握正确的方法很重要啊。

### 刻钢管

　　焊完了电线，并且电路连通成功，我十分高兴。带着好心情去做钢管了，这个钢管就是插在原先钻的小孔上的，并且可以让之前连接好的灯泡穿过去。

排在我们前面有一个男孩子，也要做这个东西，可是我们都不知道怎么做，于是叫来了老师，老师在我们三人面前演示了一遍。那个男孩子切好以后，因为不小心将钢管掉在了下面的废墟堆中，找不到了。于是，他就错把一个之前人家做了不要的钢管当成自己的了，呵呵，倒也聪明的。

金叶做的时候，我发现有一节钢管掉在了旁边，打算拾起来，却发现上面温度很高，差点烫到自己的手。突然想到，这肯定是刚才那个男孩子落下的钢管。正犹豫着要不要还给他的时候，发现他已经把钢管装上去了，于是就想着把这节钢管给自己当个示范也好。

做这个钢管，程序不是很多，但需要换几次零件。因为要钻不同的孔，先要做一个漏斗型的，然后再做一个螺旋形的。帮金叶做完后她反过来帮我，但做完后却没有得到老师的认同，说是孔太小了。老师说下一节课他再帮我们指导，正打算回去问茹云衣的时候，她说她们只更换了两次零件，还有一次零件没有装上去。想了想，当时老师给我们示范的时候，也只说要装两次啊！有些灰心丧气。

茹云衣又鼓励我们说，不用重做，下一节课她帮我们就行了。第二节课，她暂时放下自己的任务帮我们做，真是感动，这才是好朋友啊，同甘共苦！我先去把做好的钢管给老师看，茹云衣在那边帮金叶。

等老师批准后，让我过去用胶枪把这些电线粘起来。我正疑惑金叶为什么还不过来的时候，发现了一个问题，先是胶枪的插座插不上去，于是就让老师帮我，然后又发现不知道胶枪是怎么开的，是不是身后的那个开关？小心翼翼地试着摁了下去。唉！不错，胶枪有反应了。因为开了电源，胶水是很烫的，加好以后就要把木块斜着放，以防胶水漏到别的地方去。

之后，老师给了我一个钢片。好不容易切好钢片，这个时候下课铃响了，下一节课就要磨钢片了。磨钢片好像不是一件容易的事，茹云衣磨了一节课都没磨好，看来我肯定也要花不少的时间。

## 磨钢片

今天是周三，上午最后一节课是木工课，我的主要目的就是把钢片的四个棱角都磨平，再把边磨好。

随着上课铃的敲响，我们走进了木工课的教室。我先让茹云衣示范一下，正好她现在也在磨钢片的环节。先要找一张桌子，再挑一个桌角上的任意一个固定架。把它打开，然后把钢片夹进去，再用力旋紧。一定要旋紧哦，要不然打磨的时候，钢片会脱落的。固定好钢片以后，要找一个磨钢片的锉刀。锉刀分为两种，一种是上面有网格形花纹的，而另一种上面是斜杠。打磨也分两次，第一次使用网格形花纹的锉刀，第二次则是用斜杠花纹的，第一次负责把它整体打磨，第二次则是精细打磨。

打磨需要掌握一定的技巧。第一次打磨是拉锯式的，上下都要用力，把四个角和两条边打磨好就行了。第二次打磨则要按一定方向，从上而下，还要有节奏感。打磨的时候要稍稍用劲，要有金属粉末掉下来，这样的话才会有效果。打磨完了，你会发现固定架上都是一些银亮亮的金属粉末，看着这些粉，就觉得好有成就感。

首次打磨比较复杂，一下就花了我半节课，老师检查认可后就开始精细打磨。这一次精细打磨需要选择斜杠花纹的锉刀，这样的锉刀只有两把，正好我和金叶每人一把，也不用把固定架松开，直接在上面磨就好了。锉刀的花纹是斜杠形的，所以经常会发出一些刺耳的声音，我有些受不了，但旁边的茹云衣对我说："这声音很好啊，如果你受不了的话，可以磨得轻一点！"然后她还亲自示范了一遍给我看。我用了她的方法，果然声音减少了很多，并且速度也加快了。打磨好了角，正打算松开固定器的时候，老师叫我们过去集体上课了。因为我们做完了这个手电筒，还要做一辆木制的小汽车。老师先把要求告诉我们。我们中间有一些人已经做好了手电筒，已经开始准备做小汽车了，所以老师要教他们怎样制作木块和画草图。我们三个没有做好的，就在旁边看，也算是为以后做些准备吧，先学会再说。其实就是把画好的草图贴在木板上，再用白胶粘住，但是白胶干得很慢，需要一个小时。

木制小汽车的临时教程很快就结束了，我继续回到房间里磨钢片。等到我磨到边的时候，金叶也过来磨了，我们两个继续奋发努力。看看手表，还剩5分钟了，肯定是磨不好的，但还是加快了速度。下课铃声响了，我们仍然在磨，一直到老师过来叫我们才肯罢休。唉！只好下节课再做了，有一些遗憾，低头看了看自己的手，发现上面全是银亮亮的粉，肯定是刚才磨钢片的时候沾在手上的。明天还要继续磨，希望明天可以磨完，然后进入下一步用砂纸磨。最后在木块里面安放上电池，用小钉子固定好钢片就大功告成了。

经历了几周，自制手电筒终于完工了，我忍不住朝有阴影的地方照照，出乎意料的亮！我给住家爸爸和妈妈看了我的作品，他们都给予了很好的评价，夸我能干！我还拍了照片用微信发给老爸老妈看我的第一件手工作品。其间所有的辛苦都一扫而光，心里满是喜悦和满足！

蓝天和美丽的街景

5月9日，星期五

# 连续受伤的我

加拿大图腾小镇樱花树下

  上周三，下午最后一节是体育课，老师告诉我们要学习跨栏！我当时整个就惊呆了。还没等我回过神来，老师已经拿出六个跨栏摆在草地上，然后还专门请了个老师过来教我们怎样跨栏。先是把一条腿抬起来，然后跨过栏杆的那一瞬间，再把另一条腿也抬起来。

  那个老师好像有急事，示范了一遍后就走了，接着由另一个老师组织我们跨栏。先是几个男生打头阵，然后是女生，我排在最后一个。看着他们一个一个都顺利过关，感觉心中压力很大。和金叶交换了位置，马上就要轮到我跳了，心里"砰、砰、砰"，好紧张啊！看前面几个人最多也就掉了两个，我肯定会掉更多吧？！

鼓起勇气，跑到第一个栏杆面前，突然，我情不自禁地停了下来，但还是跨了过去，栏杆不出意外地倒了。好吧，继续向第二个冲刺，第二个很顺利地过了，有一些小激动，正跑向第三个的时候，突然觉得脚底阵痛，又跑了一步，疼痛感又瞬间消失。正打算跨第三个的时候，不知怎的，我停下来不敢往前跨。于是旁边的老师对我说跨下一个吧，跳过这个跑向下一个，继续顺利过关。这样还有两个，一个跨过了，但是最后一个依然没有跨过，反而让跨栏给敲到了背，一阵疼痛。左脚之前的那种疼痛感又降临了，我一瘸一拐地走到草坪上，坐了下来，很痛。同学们马上过来，看我摔得怎么样？其实就是一块骨头被碰到了，没有什么大碍，只是稍微肿了点，在旁边碰碰它就会痛。背上也有块伤，她们给我轻轻捶了捶，似乎好多了。

　　第二天上学的时候，背已经好了，一点都不痛了，脚却还有一些隐隐作痛。记得中午那一节课是磨钢板。回忆有些凌乱，总而言之就是磨得三根手指都没了知觉，下午几节课拿书都拿不了，握拳也握不了。以至于有的时候，手指弯不了，突然咔嚓一声，就弯下去了，有点恐怖唉。就好像自己的手不是自己的一样，不听使唤了，只好使劲地将手指伸缩，再弯曲。心想，昨天才受伤呢，今天又受伤了，怎么搞的呀？心中充满怨气，慢悠悠地晃回家里。回家的路比较远，又都是一些有坡度的路，走得脚腕很痛。我走得很慢，到家的时候，那种疼痛感已经消失得无影无踪了。我以为我的脚好了，便坐到床边把袜子脱掉，发现脚上多了一小块淡淡的青色，按摩了一下还是感觉很痛。

　　第三天上学的时候，因为跟同学约好要早点到学校，所以走得快了些。没想到走的时候正好踩到一块石头，恰巧踩到石头的那只脚是前天扭到的那只，顿时感到一阵疼痛。想想还是慢点走吧，她们乘公交车应该也不会很快吧！终于到了学校，我赶紧找了个位子"扑通"坐下来，按摩着脚踝。疼痛慢慢散去，心中想着，怎么会这样呢？昨天不是已经快好了吗？为什么这几天我的手脚总是如此受罪呢？为什么这几天我总是受伤呢？哎！

　　吃一堑长一智，看来以后在加拿大生活，要加倍小心啊！特别是要注意体育课，我在体育课上受的伤已经不少了，当然我的朋友金叶也同样是。她昨天被球重重地砸了两下，砸得眼睛都红了，最后给老师看了一下，才确定没出什么问题。阿弥陀佛，安全第一！

布查德花园一景

5月10日,星期六

# 在Downtown的自助午餐

"和记"自助餐

  今天是周六,想要放松一下,就和茹云衣相约到Downtown玩,约好9:30出发,乘巴士去。我们先去了一个文具店,里面有很多小礼品,但价格都很贵。举个例子,一个本子,要14块加元,虽然做工精美,但也不至于这么贵吧?在中国14块人民币就可以买到一本很好的本子了。我们还去了书店。书店很大,就像苏州工业园区的凤凰书城一样,但书并不多。

  这一个书店我们就逛了一上午,然后商量着到哪去吃饭。我向茹云衣推荐了张涛之前去过的一个自助餐厅,一个人只要十块钱。其实她想去吃汉堡王,但最后还是采纳了我的建议去找那家自助餐厅。我记得张涛告诉我那家自助餐厅是在一个公交车站的后面，但是Downtown的公交车站很多，不下十来个，怎么找呢？我们一路向前走，后来发现有点不对，怎么走了这么远还没有看到那家店呢？于是我们就只好往回走，打算去吃汉堡王。不过我依然边走边四处张望，突然发现对面就是那家自助餐厅。原来我们刚才走反了。

  这家店的名字叫"和记"，是几个广东人开的自助中餐厅。现在变成一个人十三块，但还是走了进去。主人十分好客，发现我们是中国人，就用中文跟我们对话，给了我们一个很好的位置，还有沙发呢！店主十分热情，给我们介绍每一样菜。这里的菜很丰富，有玉米汤、饺子、寿司、鸡腿、炸鸡块、沙拉，还有春卷和麻婆豆腐，主食有白米饭、炒饭和炒面，还有很多甜点。种类虽不如中国的大型自助餐厅多，但是，在这个西餐的世界能够吃到如此这般的中餐已经很幸福了。

  盛了满满一盆，女店主微笑着把我们带到座位，给了我们几瓶不同种类的"老干妈"，还帮我们摆好筷子，真是好热情！看着满满一盆食物，肚子"咕咕"叫了起来，立马开吃！熟悉的味道溢满口腔。玉米汤的甜，饺子汤的鲜，鸡腿的脆，春卷的酥，真是太爽了，很快就吃完了第一盆。这时店主来了，给我们两小杯西瓜汁，还是鲜榨的，凉凉的，甜甜的，特别爽口。她见我们吃完了一盆，于是又叫我们快去取第二盆，希望我们吃得饱饱的。感觉这个店主真的好亲切啊！照顾好我们后又看到她去照顾外国客人了。虽然她的英文水平不是很好，但还是用自己断断续续的英文，满脸笑容、热情洋溢。

  我又去盛了一点东西，这一次我发现了麻婆豆腐和刚煮的白米饭，于是就把它们搅在一起，特别好吃。麻婆豆腐应该是辣的，但是我吃出了一股甜味，带着一些淡淡的辣味，很好吃。都说广东人吃甜的，一点也不比苏州人差，果然今天吃的很多菜都是带甜味的。

  饭后我还吃了一杯果冻，饱餐后躺在沙发上休息。女主人看我们吃饱了，于是又给了我们一个造型奇特的小饼干，做我们的饭后甜点。随后，她就愉快地和我们聊天，问我们吃得饱不饱、好不好,还问一些关于我们为什么过来,在这里学习生活如何,等等。我还是第一次遇见这么热情的店主。我和茹云衣躺在沙发上又休息了一会儿后,打算走了。主人很热情地送我们,还送给我们记次卡,邀请我们下次再来。

从餐厅出来,我们来到了刘老师的咖啡店。我向刘老师换了一些纪念币,打算回去送好朋友或者做纪念收藏起来。

晚上住在张涛的住家,因为我的住家这个周末很忙。

美丽的街景

5月11日，星期日

# 加拿大游行活动

盛大的游行方阵

今天早上8:00，带好了相机、帽子、水杯、手机、太阳眼镜等所有需要的东西，涂好防晒霜就和住家一起出发了，这是要干什么呢？

原来今天是庆祝加拿大日的游行活动。加拿大日是加拿大的国庆日，每年的7月1日，全国公众假日。此假日是庆祝1867年7月1日加拿大自治领籍《英属北美条约》将英国在北美的三块领地合并为一个联邦，包括加拿大省（今安大略和魁北克省南部）、新斯科舍省和新不伦瑞克省。此节日原称"自治领日"（英语：Dominion Day；法语：Le Jour de la Confédération），1982年10月27日改名为加拿大日。

今天的游行规模空前盛大。住家打算早上带我们去看这场游行活动，游行将在9:00开始，出发地点是之前逛过的四大购物中心之一Mayfair。住家妈妈载着我们三个女孩先出发了，而住家爸爸则准备好了一些椅子给我们用，在后面开着卡车摇摇晃晃地也跟上来了。

8:10我们到达了Mayfair前面的一条街。仰头望去，房墙上插满了加拿大国旗，街道两旁已经摆满了椅子，人们随意地坐在地上或坐在带来的椅子上，或铺一条毯子坐下，互相聊天，热情地讨论着这个盛大的游行。此时，马路上已经没有了车辆，小朋友们在马路中间玩耍，大人们在马路之间穿梭，还有的人在马路中央骑自行车。再看看马路两旁等候的人们吧，有的人坐在刻有枫叶图案的椅子上，有的人躺在枫叶毯子上，有的人围坐在铺着加拿大国旗的桌子边，还有的人则穿着画有加拿大国旗的T恤。节日的气氛多么浓烈啊！

9:00，盛大的游行准时开始。第一个映入我们眼帘的像是皇室人员，穿着很夸张的长裙，头戴很多精美发饰，牵着一条精致可爱的小狗，举着一把羽毛扇子。在她的身旁还有一个男人，穿的十分挺拔。他和那位女士在我们面前慢慢走过，后面还跟着一辆马车。一位车夫手上拿着一根皮鞭，赶着三匹马。这三匹马长得几乎一样，身上都有一些斑点花纹，由深到浅。马车很白、很精致，上面刻着各种花纹装饰。在他们的后面是一个士兵方阵。大概有百来个士兵，身高几乎一样，在我们面前，一边喊着口号，一边踏着整齐的军步走过。从侧面看过去，就好像是一个人在我们面前走过，可见他们排得是多么整齐啊，看来为了这个方阵花费了很多心血。

接下来还有一些车队，有很多车上都是人，这些车像是"二战"留下来的。有警车、救护车、挖掘机、消防车，还有坦克，我觉得这应该是在展示代表"二战"的历史篇章。车辆鸣着喇叭在我们面前缓缓地开过，里面的司机还不住地朝两边招手。这些军官都长得和蔼可亲，胖胖的，八撇胡，有点像动画片里的角色，这更增加了节日的气氛。

在接下来的两个小时内，又有好多个游行队伍在我们面前

创意复古独轮车表演

漂亮的裙摆

走过,而且没有重复的,其中还包括一些高中部的学生走的方阵。虽然每个学校的高中生穿着都不一样,但风格都差不多,一般打头阵的两个人都拿着一个牌子,上面写着这个学校的名称,后面一个则是特色表演,再后面才是真正的方阵部分,都是鼓号队,前面是吹管弦乐的,后面是击鼓的。每个学校的人数也不一样,少的只有近50人,最多的有近200人。我最喜欢人最多的那一支队伍,当他们向我们走来时,那气势是相当壮观啊!200多个人,清一色红色制服,敲着锣、打着鼓,踏着步伐,十分整齐有序。除了学校的方阵以外还有个军队的方阵。虽然都是方阵，但大不相同。相对于学校的方阵来说，军队的方阵更有气势，虽然人不多，但是步伐整齐，气势上确实大大超出了学校的方阵。后面还有一些军用的卡车，这更增加了军队方阵的威严。还有一个特别的苏格兰裙的方阵。这个方阵比较有趣，男人们都穿着苏格兰裙，他们踏着整齐的步伐，吹着乐器。我离得很近，甚至还能看到他们的苏格兰裙下的腿毛。

方阵之后就是其他国家的一些队伍，其中就包括中国的。中国的队伍主要是由当地唐人街的华人组成的，大部分内容以舞龙、武术为主，中国的队伍比其他国家的队伍都要庞大，很长一段呢，显得气势浩大。

方阵游行结束后，是一些关于品牌的推销，有牛奶、太阳眼镜、饭馆等，各色各样，并且在游行的时候还会派发礼物。

一直到中午12:00，持续3个小时的游行终于结束了。我因为坐了一个多小时，椅子又不习惯，腰酸背痛，弄得腰都直不起来了。

回家后，简单地用了一下午饭，就睡了一会儿。住家打算下午去采购一些晚上"沙滩BBQ"的材料。晚上6:00，住家妈妈带着我们来到沙滩，住家爸爸则是拿了椅子和烧烤箱。今天天气很好，来沙滩烧烤的人挺多，烤烟味也很浓。除了烧烤，还有很多人到沙滩玩。我看到一些年轻男女纷纷穿上泳衣跑到湖里去游泳，湖水很清澈，他们在水里嬉戏。而旁边的狗狗们也没有闲着，主人们总是随地捡起一根树枝就往湖里扔，然后它们就冲进湖里把树枝捡回来。还有一些人则在沙滩上打起了沙滩排球。这样的场景，听爸爸说起过，在他们小的时候乡下也是这样的，特别是暑假。

加拿大日，小小的沙滩上洋溢着快乐和笑声。突然间，我很想念五星红旗。在国内，每当国庆来临，爸爸就会把五星红旗绑在阳台上，随风飘扬！祖国啊，我有些牵挂你。还有远在故乡的爸爸和妈妈，你们好吗？

5月12日，星期一

# 愉快的饭后游湖时光

今天，晚饭吃的是BBQ，非常丰盛，有沙拉、火腿肠、热狗、土豆、沙拉、薯条等。晚饭后，我和Lusia（住家新来的一个女孩）帮住家洗了碗。打扫完厨房，住家就让我们准备一下，我们要带着库柏去湖边散步。一听到要去湖边就立马兴奋起来，库柏也围着我们兴奋地转圈。

很快来到目的地，就是原来我去过的那个湖，周围都有树木包围着，林中还有几个湖。我们在林间小道中行走着，不一会儿就到了第一个湖。这个湖面积比较大，旁边的沙滩也很大，住家爸爸像往常一样，随手捡了一根树枝，然后远远地抛出去。库柏就飞快地冲到水里，迅速把树枝叼起来，含在嘴里。上岸以后，它嘴里依然叼着那根树枝，晃晃身子，把身上的水珠甩掉。住家爸爸想要拿回树枝，可是以它的脾气，肯定是不会给的。于是住家爸爸只好捡旁边地上的一根，库柏立马松了口，去抢地上的那根，真是贪心啊！住家爸爸和住家妈妈在沙滩旁逗狗，而我和Lusia则发现了一群鸭子，3只大鸭子和4只小鸭子。大鸭子摇摇晃晃，小鸭子就像一个毛绒绒的球一样，浮在水面上。大鸭子羽毛丰满，而小鸭子全身上下都是灰黑色的绒毛，羽毛还没有长好。它们一家人，就在离我们不远处的湖面上，慢悠悠地游着，好像也是在"散步"，欣赏这美丽的湖景，我们似乎也成了他们眼中的风景。我和Lusia走到另一面，想要更仔细地观察鸭子。鸭子依然没有注意到我们的存在，仍是悠哉游哉地游着。我和Lusia爬到一个小山丘上，坐在石头上欣赏这美丽的景色。这时候，太阳快落山了，把丝

金门大桥，与住家爸爸的合影

丝金线铺在湖面上，还带着一丝暖气。暖洋洋的，很舒服。

  大概在这里待了20分钟吧，我们去了第二个湖。这时，太阳渐渐收敛了，将橙色的余辉撒在树林之上，又借着树叶将这一大片橙色分割成一小块、一小块，让它们洒落在土地上，一如绽放着的美丽花朵。第二个沙滩是专门给狗狗游玩儿的，远处的湖面上还有人在划船，浆随意地摆放在船身，人们微笑着坐在船中，享受着落日的沐浴，呼吸着新鲜的空气，看着都觉得很惬意。

  刚到第二个沙滩，住家爸爸就弯起腰，拿起手中的树枝用刚才同样的速度和姿势甩到湖中。库柏见状立马踏进水中，溅起朵朵水花，漾起层层涟漪，不一会儿它就将树枝叼了回来。不过，这一次它学聪明了，并没有将树枝放到岸上，而是放到了离岸边比较近的水中，这样我们就拿不到了。才过了一会儿，河边的水上就浮起一根根树枝了。这时候，住家爸爸让库柏到岸上来，要给它洗澡，他先将一些沐浴露倒在手中，然后搓出泡沫，涂抹在库柏的身上，全身上下都涂了个遍。库柏瞬间成了一只名副其实的泡沫狗。趁这个时候，住家爸爸从旁边拿了一根树枝，然后远远地甩出去。库柏立刻"呼"的一声潜入水中，等库柏回来身上的泡沫都被冲洗干净了。原来是为了让它把身上的泡沫洗干净啊！我和Lusia也尝试着帮库柏弄了一回泡沫狗，几次下来，库柏又变回了原来那只神骏的拉布拉多，被毛乌黑发亮，眼睛炯炯有神。这里的湖水都很干净，清澈见底，一眼就可以望到湖底里的水草。

库柏洗好澡，我们就沿着原路走回去。路上，住家妈妈还给我们介绍了几种植物，正好这几种植物我都认识，因为之前去森林的时候，那个老伯伯就跟我们讲过。回到家时，已经是20:50了。等Lusia洗好澡后，我也冲洗了一下，然后和妈妈视频聊了一会儿，就休息了。

这次游湖比以前要好玩多了，我感觉已经融入这个家庭里了，自己的喜怒哀乐都与这个家庭息息相关。

清山绿水间神骏的库柏

5月14日,星期三

# 练习羽毛球

练习羽毛球的我

　　这两天,我们开始了羽毛球课程。昨天是第一次,今天下午的体育课又是羽毛球课程,我对羽毛球是很感兴趣的,也很想看看国外的小朋友们是怎么打的。

　　上课铃响了,我们几个跑去教室集合,然后再和大队伍一起来到室内体育馆。Allen已经在那边等我们了,但是他并没有一开始就让我们打羽毛球,而是先让我们坐在地上,他则静静地站在旁边等我们安静下来。在国内上体育课的时候,大家也会很不安分,互相讲话,后来都是在老师的呵斥下停止的。而这里有点不一样,大家也不用集合,只要坐在室内体育馆的中心就可以了。刚开始你在那边讲话老师也不管你,但过了10分钟左右老师会提醒我们,如果还不够安静,他就会再等一会儿。实在还不能安静下来,就会不厌其烦地再提醒一遍,一直提醒到大家都安静下来为止。虽然这种方法效率不高,但是比我们原来学校的吆喝式方法似乎更容易接受,那些特别能讲话的同学会在大家的监督下停止。这一个环节,足足花掉了我们10分钟。然后Allen叫了一些男孩子把羽毛球网搭起来,我们四个人也跑过去帮忙。

一切准备就绪后，老师开始给我们做示范。他给我们介绍了两种发球方式，都是我所知道的，虽然我没有接受过正规的羽毛球培训，但是一些基本的发球和接球方式还是知道的，因为在国内爸爸有时会带我去威克多羽毛球馆打球。老师让我们每个人找一个队友，然后给每个队安排了羽毛球拍、球和训练的位置。

我和茹云衣一组，站好位置后我们就开始打了。我先发球，第一个球很顺利，而且还是用一种我不常用的发球方式，有一些小小的成就感。她接到了，但是她回过来的球擦到网了，导致我没有接到。第二个球仍然是我发，还是很漂亮，但是不知咋搞的只能来回一两个回合，要再接到第二个球的可能性几乎为零。不一小会儿，老师过来了，他指导了一下茹云衣，因为她的发球方式不是很标准。好不容易正确地打过来一个球，老师却不让我接！我和茹云衣此时才搞清楚，这堂课是练习发球的，我们俩却在死命地接对方发过来的球，哈哈！于是我调整好姿势，发过去了一个很漂亮的球，得到了老师的称赞，心里喜洋洋的，因为之前羽毛球打得不是很好，能得到别人的称赞，感觉很有成就感。

打了一会儿，老师就让我们休息了。大概5分钟后，换了一种方式。我们所有的人被分成两队，每一队再分成两组，然后，由第一个组的人发球过去，第二组的第一个人把球拍过来，然后再由第一组的第二个人接，再由第二组的第二个人拍回来，以此类推。昨天也玩过这个游戏，但我总是接不到，心中有了一些阴影。果然，今天刚开始时几个球又没有接到，不是擦到拍子，就是拍空了，有些垂头丧气。但接下来的几个球都接到了，真是一阵欢喜一阵忧，不过今天比昨天进步多了，很开心。

大概又打了几分钟，下课铃就响了，突然感觉这一节课过得好快啊！我似乎对羽毛球又增加了一些好感。

5月16日，星期五

# 重游Beacon Hill Park

　　今天是周五，是加拿大日假期的第一天，学校放假。我约了金叶和茹云衣一起去Beacon Hill Park，里面有一个儿童农场，之前住家妈妈也带我去过，真的很好玩，印象深刻。能够和同学再一次去这个公园，不知道会不会有新的意外收获？

　　我们约好10:00在学校门口见面，9:40的时候我出了家门。9:55我提前到达了。在学校附近四处张望了一下，却发现没有人。又在这里等了10分钟左右，发现有一辆14路公交从学校门口经过，以为是她们来了，但是没有人下车。于是我就直接走到学校门口，发现金叶已经坐在旁边的石凳上了。原来她已经在这儿等了15分钟了。我们继续等茹云衣。但是，连续开过两辆14路，她还没有来。我们有些心急，电话又打不通。于是决定直接跑到14路下车的那个站台等她。时间一分一秒地流逝，已经是10:15了。我跟金叶打算等到10:30，如果她还不来就不等她了。这时又一辆14路来了，我们满怀欣喜的等待，还是没有人下车。失落了一阵，10:22的时候，又有一辆14路开过来了，茹云衣正好在这辆车上，只见她不紧不慢地下来和我们打招呼。原来她把时间搞错了，当成是10:30集合。

　　我们先乘公交车到Downtown，然后再转车去Beacon Hill Park。到了那里，我们看好了回去的站台后决定先去公园喂鸟，然后吃午饭，下午再去儿童农场玩。住家给我特意准备了一包鸟食。喂鸟这件事让我感觉既熟悉又陌生，之前和住家一起喂鸟的时候，也是这个场景，也是这些鸟，但是今天却有些不同，因为这次是和同学。当鸟食还剩一半的时候，我们打算留一些等从儿童农场出来后再去喂。就这样，上午的时光就在愉快地喂鸟中度过了。12:15，我们去洗手间洗了一下手，打算开始吃午饭。

　　她们商议午餐在草坪上吃，却遭到了我的反对，理由是在草坪上蹲着吃午饭，有点不太文明，况且我们也没有塑料纸，午餐后的垃圾处理也是问题。于是我们就选择了在树荫底下的长椅上吃。今天的午饭是我自己准备的，因为早上住家急于上班，所以就没有时间帮我准备。我的主食是肉丸意大利面，肉丸很大，面酱也很足，很好吃！因为早上放进微波炉里转了一下，现在还有一点点温热。一杯果酱加上一碗意大利面，还有两块芝士面包，就是绝佳的搭档。可能量太足了，吃得我特别撑，以至于我吃不下带过来的饮料和饼干了，打算留着下午吃。吃好了午饭把垃圾收拾好，我们就去儿童农场玩了。

　　刚走进儿童农场就出现了一个问题，就是我们怎么买门票。买门票的那个窗口上没有人，只是旁边有个箱子，像是要把钱放在里面一样，可是我们又不确定。于是就开始查字典，但是字典上查出来的意思，都是迷迷糊糊的根本对不上号。在门口纠结了好久，终于鼓起勇气，把两块五加币投进那个箱子，就走进去了。

　　像上次一样，我们先看到一个鸟窝。里面的小鸟特别可爱，"唧唧啾啾"的在里面唱歌，不同的声音，混在一起就是一首最美妙的歌。欣赏完了"歌曲"，我们来到孔雀的地盘。正好有一只在开屏，它慢悠悠地转动身子，好让我们把它美丽的羽毛看个遍。拍了几张照，我们就到后面孔雀栖息的地方看了一下。又碰见一只孔雀打算开屏，它先是叫了几声，那叫声很清脆、很尖细，然后颤动尾部的羽毛，慢慢将羽毛打开。等到完全打开后，又开始抖动它的羽毛，特别好看，仿佛穿了一件华丽的旗袍。

　　告别孔雀，我们又去看兔子。这里的兔子比以前多了好几只，还有长毛的兔子，差点以为那是只小狗。兔子的邻居是羊驼，羊驼的样子很萌，一下子就把我们吸引过去了。我发现羊驼比上一次来更加呆萌可爱了。虽然不太喜欢把脸露给我们

小羊"欺负"小孩

看,但是却乐意摆出很多可爱的动作,先是把脚翘在屁股上,挠一挠,再把头埋在腿里,蹭一蹭,然后又慢悠悠地走到草堆里用小舌头卷着吃草。吃了草,它又想吃树叶了,走到旁边的一棵不高不矮的树,因为它够不着上面的树叶,于是就把脖子挺了起来,活像一只长颈鹿在吃树叶,真是太可爱了。过了一会儿,它又坐在地上,就像人一样,大屁股对着我们,又增添了一份可爱,呆呆的样子让人百看不厌。它那双铜铃大眼尤显可爱,头上两只耳朵竖起来,再把眼睛瞪大,那呆萌的气质显现得淋漓尽致。

接下来讨人喜欢的地方就是小羊游乐场。里面有很多品种的小羊,还可以进去抚摸它们、喂它们或者抱它们在身上,这次还多了一项活动,可以拿刷子给羊刷毛。茹云衣找了一只小羊,可是小羊有些不听话,总是喜欢乱跑。金叶则很兴奋,似乎是想把所有的小羊都摸个遍。她们两个因为第一次来这里,对所有事物都很新鲜,对小羊就更不用说了。这里的小羊千姿百态,有的躲在妈妈的肚子底下吃奶,有的躲在妈妈旁边晒太阳,有的则是和其他的小伙伴打架,还有的则干脆躲在树荫下睡觉。

在这里泡了很久,大概13:00的时候,我们打算出去一下,把手洗干净然后再回来。回来时小羊明显对我们好感大增,都跑到我们身边。有一只小羊直接跳到我身上,用牙齿咬住我的衣服不放,看来是喜欢上我这件衣服了,衣服被它咬了个遍。我回头看金叶,也不知怎么的,有一只羊死死地咬住她的书包带子就是不放。而茹云衣则是被两面夹击,一只羊咬她的衣服,另一只羊咬她的书包带子。努力摆脱了这些黏人的小羊,走出了羊圈,我们打算回去了。

正回来时,前面不远处有几个人在爬一棵大树。那棵大树树枝很粗壮,很光滑,于是我们几个兴趣大发,打算等他们拍完照以后也上去爬一爬。先是茹云衣,她很轻松地上去了,我也试了两下上去了,金叶也很轻松地上来了。我们坐在树枝上,感觉很新奇、很特别,之前从来没有做过这么调皮的事情,这种事情以前似乎都是调皮捣蛋的男同学的专利。在树枝上待了一会儿,正好这时有人过来,于是就请他帮我们拍了个照。留下这美好的回忆,以后怕是再爬不了树了吧!

16:00的时候,我们乘着公交车回到Downtown,去了刘老师的咖啡店。点了一碗小馄饨,充充饥。吃着小馄饨,我想到了之前爷爷包的小馄饨,味道不一样,但是样子很像。爷爷包的小馄饨菜多,而刘老师的馄饨则是肉多,味道各有千秋,但我还是比较喜欢爷爷包的,从小吃到大,现在也没有吃腻。越想越心酸,突然有些牵挂爷爷了,我还要等上几个月才能吃到爷爷包的馄饨啊!

坐在大树上,好有安全感!

5月17日，星期六

# 维多利亚购物中心
# ——Hill Side

　　今天早上，和同学约好10:30在教育局的转换车站见面。我邀金叶、茹云衣一起去Hill Side逛街。那是维多利亚四大购物中心之一，每次去教育局上学的时候就会看到它，其他购物中心我都已经去看过了，就剩这一个，所以心中很期待。

　　9:50，我按原计划出门。正好赶上10:00的那一班车。去转换车站时会路过金叶和茹云衣的家，但汽车一直往前开却没有看到她们的身影，也许她们早到了吧。10:15的时候，我到达见面地点，但是没有看到她们。于是就过去看了一下14路公交车什么时候会开过来（在维多利亚公交车站台大多数都会有一个牌子，上面有标注每个公交车到这个车站的时间），在10:22和10:37各有一班，我想这两班车都有可能赶到，于是就在车站里等她们。10:30的时候，她们还是没有出现。心想，如果她们10:37的时候还没有来，我就决定先回去。因为维多利亚的天气很古怪，早上还是晴空万里，太阳高挂着散发出丝丝暖气，现在天空却变成了阴天，有一点冷，而且我穿的又很单薄。

　　终于在10:42的时候，看见茹云衣来了，却没有看到金叶下车，又是一阵失望，但是好歹看见一个人了，给我增添了一点信心。好在太阳又从云层里出来了，于是我们俩就在太阳底下等。直到对面又过了两辆14路，才看见金叶的身影。只见她连头发都没梳好，可见她是匆匆赶过来的，她立马向我们解释，原来她以为今天不用出去，之前商量的地点也不是很清楚。又等了15分钟，第二辆14路终于来了，我们一起上车，顺

Hill Side购物中心

利到达Hill Side。

　　用"石头剪刀布"的方法我们决定先去书店。茹云衣介绍说这里有一家很大的书店，但是价格很贵，不过进去看一个上午的书是没有问题的。一走进这家书店，就有一种走进古堡的感觉，灯光很昏暗，里面的装饰很古典，虽然人不少，但是安静得很，这才是书店嘛。看书要静得下心，在这个氛围下看书是再好不过了。在每个书架旁边都会有一两把椅子，供大家坐着读书。书店分为三个部分，第一部分就是各个年龄段各种类别的书，第二部分就是小朋友们玩的益智游戏，第三部分则是收银台。这里的书很丰富，有关于小说、名著、历史、文化、餐饮、旅游、穿着的。小朋友的书也有很多风格，有的书中间会穿一个洞里面放上一个手指玩偶，可以边讲故事边用手指控制玩偶。

　　走进购物中心，发现这里非常安静，顾客也不多。Hill side和我之前去过的商场有些不一样，之前的都是地上有三、四层的，而这里则是地上地下各一层，除了这边的主楼，旁边还有一个商场。这里最有特色的就是服装打折非常厉害，每个店都有很大折扣的衣服展示在门口用来吸引顾客，不过在我看来好像款式都差不多。这里的服务员很热情，无论你买不买都很周到地为你提供服务。我们逛了一圈，好像没有感兴趣的，于是就早早回去了。

5月20日，星期二

# 100天修学日中的平常一天

伴着早晨明媚的阳光，我踏上上学的路途。小鸟像往常一样唱歌，花儿像往常一样微笑。学校操场上的鸭子们懒洋洋地晒着太阳，悠闲地吃着青草。今天是这周上学的第一天。四天的加拿大日假期终于过去了，这一周我们只上四天课，很满足。在这里，如果放假的话，下一个周六、周日也不用补课。

今天木工课上，我用一节课的时间画了八辆车，手都酸了，之前张涛可是用两节课才画了八辆车呢，感觉有一些隐隐的自豪感。下一节课也就是明天，我就要正式开始做小汽车了，很兴奋。手电筒已经大功告成，希望小汽车一切顺利。

下午的第一节课，我们又是去划龙舟。记得上一次去的时候可是走了很久呢，今天虽然还是去同一个地方，同一条路，却觉得走得很快，或许是我和茹云衣一路上聊着自己小学时趣事的原因吧。

她小学在沧浪小学，而我是在宝带小学。想到之前小学的朋友，大家都各奔东西，而我现在居然来到加拿大修学，这是多么不可思议的事情啊！想当初，我告诉爸爸有出国修学机会的时候，还是漫不经心的，根本不相信爸爸会支持我来修学。因为一方面我蛮胆小的，从没有离开爸爸妈妈独立生活过，另一方面我觉得毕竟功课会落下来，国内的课程会跟不上，还有语言关，我在马路上看见外国人都不敢搭理，更不用说要住在外国家庭了。没想到爸爸极力支持，而我则是心不甘、情不愿地经过轮轮考试，却奇迹般地通过了。虽然当时不是特别愿意出来，但是现在想一想，在国外的生活真是精彩啊，划龙舟，去野营，去沙滩，去BBQ，做手电筒，做洋娃娃，做小汽车，和住家一起种花，和一群外国朋友一起上课、交流……这都是我在国内所不敢想的事情，而现在却成为生活中的平常事。看来，这次听从爸爸的建议来到加拿大，的确是一个不错的选择，一来可以放松自己，二来可以增长见识，最重要的是我慢慢学会了如何把握自己的时间，掌控自己。

不知不觉来到了海边，像上次一样，穿好了救生衣，拿着船桨，然后把船推到水中。这一次我坐在中间，前后都是男生，旁边是金叶。掌握了技巧后，这一次划船比上次好多了，但仍然被前面的男生泼了一身水。有的时候他突然用力，加快划桨速度，这样我就被甩了一脸水，有的时候是转弯，他又把水泼到了我身上，一处也没放过，头上、身上、脚上、鞋子上，就像到河里游过泳一样，身上还有一股淡淡的海腥味！今天，我们的船速度很快，虽然是最后一个划的，却与第一名几乎同时到达岸边。上岸后，我发现我右腿有一块全湿透了，裤子都变颜色了。于是就跑到太阳底下晒。又帮着他们，像上次一样把船推进船架子里，费了我好大力呀！

打算回去的时候，发现自己脚酸软得都走不动路了，摇摇晃晃地经过差不多1小时，终于走到离学校最近的那个公交车站。

大概在太阳底下等了15分钟，裤子晒干了公交车也来了，心满意足地上了车。回到了家，拿出木工课的作业，又画了一辆汽车，然后开始做数学作业。过了一会，Lusia也回来了，她问我要不要去参加丹妮卡晚上的跳舞比赛。对此我挺感兴趣的，听说丹妮卡付出了不少努力，于是就答应了。当我数学作业做到一半的时候，住家爸爸叫我们吃晚饭了。饭后，正当我想提笔的时候，住家爸爸说住家妈妈马上回来接我们过去，他先把丹妮卡送到学校，让我们准备一下。于是我就只好停下手中的笔。15分钟以后，住家妈妈还是没有来。当我考虑要不要继续做作业的时候，住家妈妈回来了。她说要换一下衣服，然后就带我们去。于是我又放下了做作业的念头。

这个舞蹈演出是在丹妮卡的学校里举行的，从19:30到

21:30。知道要那么晚回来,我吃了一惊,但是又不好意思拒绝住家,就陪他们看演出。演出很好看、很精彩,创意很多,每一个演出都有自己的特点。我觉得丹妮卡表演得很好看。她穿着银色的上衣,搭配银色的短裙,很酷。她们在舞台上跳来跳去,非常灵活。舞台上的灯光变幻莫测,当舞台上的灯光变暗时,就好像有许多黑色的影子在跳动,小裙不停地摆动着,把全场的气氛都调动起来了。观众们情不自禁地鼓掌、叫好!

22:30到家的时候,我整个人都要累虚脱了,澡也没洗,就直接睡觉了。

划龙舟的"湖"

5月23日，星期五

# 手工课程介绍

### 汽车模型制作

这个星期都是一些很有趣的课程，比如木工课。

木工课是周二到周四，每天午饭前的一节课。上一次我们做了手电筒，而这一次是做小汽车，将画好的图纸给老师，老师确定后就把图纸贴在木头上，静静等待木头干。

第二天早早来到木工教室，过去一看，木头果然干了而且粘得很牢，美中不足的就是有一点缝隙。老师给了我一根大头钉，让我把之前他确认的稿纸拿出来。再让我按照稿纸上画的轮廓，用钉子在木头上钉出一辆汽车来。用钉子钉简单，10分钟后，一个车子的轮廓就已经钉出来了。但是因为当时画得小，所以我做出来的车子也将会很小，记得老师还惊讶地说了一句"So small"！我的车模是按照爸爸的那辆途观的外型回忆出来的，不知道爸爸看了会有啥想法。

老师让张涛陪我去钻孔。首先，在车轮的地方钻一个小孔，这样就可以把车轱辘塞进去。然后，在车轮中心那四个小圆孔旁边分别钻一个大孔，但是这个孔不用钻到底，只要一厘米就行了。钻完了孔给老师看，这时候还有20分钟才下课，之后老师让我去做一个大孔，这回是在车尾上的。他帮我画好了十字架，用来定位。我们回到钻孔机边上操作。我搞定之后，还需要等张涛完成她的车子，于是我就等啊等，10分钟后她才跑过来，还说要给老师看。我只能继续等，等到马上要做了她又说木头不平，让我跑去另外一个机器上打磨。于是我走到打磨机边上，旁边一个男生热心地帮我开了机器，并且教了我方

我的木头小车

法。结果张涛一来，说不是这样的，给我调换到另外一个机器，唉，又白费了我一番折腾。她再帮我切割木头，总算是切平了，但由于时间关系，钻孔这个事又要等到下节课了，这节课始终都没有把车子弄好。哎，这节课就能完成的非要拖到下节课，真可惜！

### 英语课

英语课每周只有两堂，而且英语课做的东西都很奇怪，就像不是在上英语课一样。上课不是在玩就是在讨论，要么就是在看书，总是能令人提起兴趣。这一阶段，我们用学校的iPad看了几个故事。接下来的英语课，老师就让我们挑选出其中的五个故事，然后给这五个故事分别设计一个封面，不要求画得有多好看，但是一定要用心投入。

第一节课，我将第一个故事的封面草稿和勾线完成了，打算下节课再做修改并完成第二幅画的初稿。回头看看茹云衣的，画得简直是太美了，就像一本书上的真实拷贝一样。茹云衣的画并没有上色，却比我的好看多了，看上去没有任何瑕疵，线条很优美，虽然断断续续但有一种凌乱的美感，整个画面很有质感,让人觉得身临其境。再看看我的,简直就是一个垃圾。唉!叹了一口气,本以为自己的画画水平还挺好的,没想到山外有山、人外有人。

第二节课,我和茹云衣一起来到英语教室,我先去拿彩笔,茹云衣则继续画她的第二幅画,她说她不想上色,或者等所有的画都画好了再上色。学校里的彩铅质量很好,但是毕竟是彩铅颜色很淡,所以画不出什么。我又没有带水彩笔过来,所以只能加重力量。好不容易涂完颜色,觉得自己还满意,有深有浅,并且眼睛也看得出来。回头看看茹云衣,她的第二幅画的线稿已经完成,很漂亮:一个小姑娘站在一块石头上,旁边是一片海,对岸有一棵大树,还有海鸥、鸽子和野鸭,简直是比上一幅画还要美。我佩服得五体投地,她不仅画得快,而且画得好。

我不敢怠慢,开始我的第二幅画。这一次我的画风好像被她传染了一样,画得和她差不多,这也给我增添了一些信心。当茹云衣画到第三幅画的时候我第二幅画才画了一半,信心又被无情地打压下去。她画得那么快,而我慢腾腾的,唉,还是不能跟她比呀!毕竟她是学过素描的,回国后我一定要去学素描,一定要学好它。下课铃响了,我的初稿顺利完成,而茹云衣的第三幅画,也已经完成了草稿。忽然之间,我觉得这好像不是英语课,倒像是美术课。

## 袜子猴(Sock Monkey)

好不容易等到周五。上周五因为放假,所以做不了袜子猴,好可惜。今天,我终于又可以去做袜子猴了,好兴奋哪!刚到那儿,就拿起自己的针线,把袜子猴的尾巴和两只耳朵都缝好了,并且填上棉花,虽然没来得及将它缝在身体上,但已经很满足了。我心想,下一节课一定要把这些都做完,再下一节课,就要做脑袋和嘴巴了,真期待啊!

袜子猴是我做的第一个布娃娃,当初报名的时候,我还不知道这个项目是做布娃娃的呢,现在想来一点都不后悔,还可以带一个布娃娃回去,多有意义啊!

懒洋洋的Sock Monkey

6月3日,星期二

# 在加拿大生病的日子

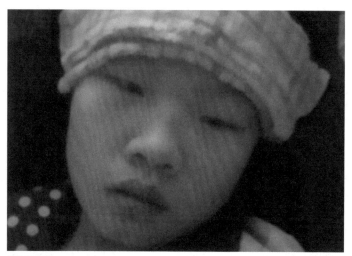

病快快的我

上周因为身体原因,没有写日记,耽搁了很多。今天是生病后的第一天写日记,让我来阐述一下前几天发生的事情吧!

上上个周日,我跟金叶出去逛一圈后,觉得腿酸脚酸,而且头有点晕,便赶紧回家躺在床上休息,连晚饭也没有怎么吃。想到第二天就要上学了,8点多就睡了,打算明天保持良好的身体状态去学校。但晚上,觉得被子很热,就开始折腾,一直折腾了将近一个多小时,才慢慢安定下来。

睡前,我在床头柜留了一杯水,已经变冷了,本来打算倒掉的,但没想到后来有了用处,大概第二天早上三四点的样子,又被热醒了,浑身上下都很不舒服,口干舌燥,嘴唇已经裂开来了。正好看到旁边有一杯水,于是"咕嘟咕嘟"喝了两口，看了一下时间，还早，继续睡觉。没睡几分钟，嘴巴又干了，又去喝了两口水，再继续睡觉，这样的动作重复了好几次。

早上6:00，我又一次起来喝水，这一次我坐在床上，突然感觉头一阵眩晕，喝了水依然没有好转。于是我就跟住家说，今天想在家里休息一天，有些头晕。她一口就答应了，并且还问了一些我的身体状况。

住家爸爸妈妈都出去上班了，我一个人在家继续睡觉，一觉睡到了9:30。醒来后头依然是晕乎乎的，起来走动了几圈，倒了一杯水，三口两口就把那杯水喝掉了。整个上午我就不停地喝水。中午，住家爸爸回来一趟，给我做了一点点午饭，很简单的午饭，但是我没有胃口，吃了几口就放下了。

晚上没有洗澡睡得很早，因为周三的时候，学校老师集体罢工不上课，于是，我觉得既然周三可以在家休息一天，那么周二就可以去上学呀。所以今天打算养好精神，明天看看病情有没有好转，好的话就去上学。

晚上和昨天一样备了一杯水在床头。大概在凌晨三四点的时候又爬起来喝水，然后继续睡觉。早晨起来感觉好多了，虽然还是头痛，没有胃口，但是觉得还是可以去上学的。住家开车送我去学校，早锻炼我没有参加，原本想试一下的，但是没想到跑几步就胸闷。同样，体育课也是站在旁边没有参加。这一天觉得很难受，但是想到明天可以在家休息一天，就好多了，但愿明天能把这些失去的精力都补回来吧！

熬到周三，是那个来自阿根廷的住家女孩——Lusia离开的日子，我早上6:00就被叫起来，她说要拍照留念，稍微理了下发型，还是披着头发出去的呢！我换了衣服，晕晕乎乎地出去了。

拍完照我立马回去睡觉，一直睡到将近10:00才醒来。醒来后看了一下微信，今天同学们都趁着这个阳光明媚的日子出去玩儿了，有的逛商场，有的看电影，还有的去吃粽子。下午我和爸爸妈妈视频聊天了一下，他们打算去海钓，感觉挺兴奋的，我也似乎好多了。

周四如约而至。早晨醒来，一个趔趄没有站稳，我摔倒在自己的房间里。踉踉跄跄爬起来后，觉得头晕乎乎的，恨不得继续回到床上睡觉，于是和住家说："今天身体不适。"

没想到住家对我说："学校和我们沟通了，让我们带你去看医生，你今天可以在家休息。"

我挺感动的，早上住家爸爸就带我去医院。在医院里等候，等着等着头又晕了，按摩了一下才稍微缓解点，就那样我一直坐在座位上等了一个多小时。这事烦透了，看看身边也就两个人，进去一个人真需要那么久吗？

好不容易被邀请进去，又坐在那里等了十几分钟医生才来。那个医生先问了一下我的身体状况然后又按了一下我的肚子，说没什么大碍。接下来又给我测了体温，虽然偏高一点点，但还是很ok的！又说了几样容易消化、对我好的食物，就是香蕉、苹果酱，还有烤面包。出医院后住家爸爸就去采购医生说的东西。

很自然，香蕉和苹果酱成了我的午饭，还有一块烤面包。我并不想吃东西，但想想医生的话，想想住家爸爸为我专门去购买，还是勉强吃了点。下午美美地睡了个午觉，然后和爸爸妈妈视频。爸爸妈妈很担心，很关心我，我也不想让他们过于担心，也就没有和他们谈论我的病情。周五本来想去学校的，但住家妈妈说我状态还不好，于是我又一次在家休息了，想到自己肯定落掉了很多功课，心里不免就有一些紧张。

整整一周时间，我就待在家休养，整天就是睡觉、上厕所、喝水、和爸爸妈妈视频、看电视。就连做作业、看书的精力都没有了，只是一味地躺在床上。我奇怪生病为何不去看病，老是在家里休息？

一周后，我似乎已经好多了，虽然头痛还是难免的，但是我的胃口好像好多了。不巧的是这周又出现一个新问题，老是咳嗽，停不下来，但是毕竟能去上学了。咳嗽的时候总是用手捂着，这样就不会传染了。

一个星期生病的经历让人难忘。这段时间其实挺难熬的，特别是这几天，挺想念家里的，住家再悉心照顾，也强不过爸爸妈妈的关心,而且同学们这几天正在快乐的过"六一"节,而我则病殃殃地躺在床上,什么事也没有做。

不过,来的时候爸爸就说了,在国外100天的时间里,会有很多快乐的时光,记得好好珍惜。当然,也会有许多不愉快的、懊糟的事情,要学会自己去体验和承受,经历过、努力过、认真过就不会遗憾!是啊,我会铭记这段生病的日子的,也会记住住家爸爸妈妈和同学对我的关心照顾的。阴霾已经过去,还有一个月的时间,我要用接下来的时间,好好感受,好好体验!我想,生病也是一种体验,它可以让我想起爸爸妈妈曾经在我生病时对我的悉心照料,这段时间也确实收益匪浅,病痛让我变得更坚强!

盛开的鲜花

6月5日，星期四

# 筹备回国的小礼物

今天是周四，但是学校老师又一次集体罢工，所以我们不用上学。我计划和同学一起约好了出去玩。

一大早起来准备了一杯果汁和几片饼干作为点心。9:55的时候，我检查好了一切东西和住家告别。到了车站，等了很久14路公交车才来。

一路晃晃悠悠来到张涛家门口的车站，原本我以为会在过去的路上遇见金叶，但是迟迟没有看见她的身影。于是我就只好在车站默默地等待下一班14路。下一班14路是10:27。10:30是我们约好集合的时间，但是10:27的那班车到了，仍然还没有茹云衣和金叶的身影。

于是我想，这个车站离张涛家很近，要么我就先到她家，看她有没有准备好。到了她家正好10:30，在门口的时候突然遇见金叶从里面开门出来。哎，搞了半天原来她不在车站，在张涛的家里呀！

我们等张涛准备好以后一起结伴去车站。结果我们三个在车站看到了曹雨，她是另一个学校的，但是离我们都很近。于是也加入了我们的队伍，很快我们四个就来到了Downtown。

先定好了中饭地点，就是上次去的那家自助餐厅。金叶和曹雨买了一些水果，然后我们就去吃午饭了。午饭吃得特别饱，自助餐的老板娘依旧很热情。上次我来吃过一次，这次的菜明显全变了，除了自己喜欢吃的馄饨没有变。

很开心地吃完了午饭，我们四个就躺在沙发上玩手机，老板娘也没有说什么，还跟我们聊了几句。后来，实在是无聊

在"白马王子"旁留下回忆

了,打算出去呼吸新鲜空气,于是就付了账,老板娘却还留我们到楼上沙发厅坐一会儿,那边有一把吉他,两个老虎和狮子的玩偶和三文鱼。于是我们童心大发,玩了起来,大概半个小时后,我实在熬不住了,就和张涛先出发去礼品店。

这一次主要目的就是买礼品,因为还有近一个月的时间就要回国了,需要准备一些小礼品。但是我们走了很久也没有看到金叶她们,于是就打算先自己逛的。

先逛了几家店,这一次我一改之前的风格。之前我总是想着要省钱,虽然现在还是很节约,但明显没有原来那样吝啬。我先买了两罐糖浆,听说这边的糖浆很有名,打算带回国内,给爸爸妈妈尝一尝。然后又买了一个小鹿模样的小钱包,这个钱包可是我很早就看中的,只不过不舍得买而已。还买了四个回形针,挺别致又很便宜,打算回国送给同学。

花了不少钱，有一些隐隐的心痛，正好也走累了，于是就和张涛在街上逛，路过一家冰沙店，就进去选冰沙。这里的冰沙有各种口味，只要拿一个杯子，然后每个冰沙都可以选一点，组合成自己喜欢的口味。我是第一次吃这样的冰沙，没有什么经验，结果搞的很难看，而张涛则是吃过几次，觉得她调的颜色很好看。

　　买好了冰沙，走出店门，发现马路两旁有空着的长椅，于是我们俩就坐了过去。才吃几口就有一个老伯伯走过来，他穿得很单薄，头发有些许蓬松，裤子很脏，他向我们伸出手，问我们能不能给他一些零钱，让他买一杯咖啡，我开始有一些犹豫，说我没有多少硬币，但是后来看着他那渴望的眼睛，我还是情不自禁地拿出背包，从里面掏了一个1块钱硬币和4个25分的，因为没有另外的一块钱了，张涛也掏出了一块多。突然感觉帮助别人很好，这点钱显然还不够一杯咖啡，但是我们心中暖洋洋的。

　　帮助别人真的是件很愉快的事。在加拿大，哪怕是在路边要钱的人都是很有尊严的，他们并不会坐在地上向你眼巴巴地乞求，要么就是拿着乐器，弹奏一曲音乐，要么就是像我们刚刚碰到的那位一样，不给钱就走人，并不会可怜巴巴地缠着你不放。

　　吃了冰沙，我跟张涛又去购物中心逛了一圈，没有什么喜欢的，于是就回去了。今天一天过得虽然累，但是很充实，吃了自助餐，买了东西，并且还帮助了别人，真是好开心呢！

6月6日，星期五

# 家庭和朋友是快乐生活的源泉

今天，用完简单的早餐，就踏着清晨明媚的阳光上学去了。今天是学校的CC Day，只要你做完作业，那么10:35就可以回家，也就是说只要上一堂课就行了。

到家的时候，已经11:00了，想想要不要买些午饭，因为实在不想吃住家准备的三明治了，但是旁边的饭馆没有开门，就打算回家自己烧点饭。

到家后，发现住家妈妈竟然在家，跟她说了一声，就开始亲自动手做午饭。食材很有限，只有半个西兰花，四个鸡蛋和一点点米。我先拿了两个鸡蛋，用叉子把蛋调好，撒了点盐，然后开始煮饭，在煮饭的同时把西兰花洗干净并且切好，又拿了一点蒜切成蒜末，我尝试着做蒜炒西兰花和蛋包饭。

趁着还在煮饭，我倒了点油把锅烧开，把蒜末倒入锅里爆一爆香，等到油"滋滋"响的时候，再把西兰花放进去。先放一会儿，然后开始翻炒，觉得差不多了，就开始撒盐，然后再把盐拌匀。尝了下味道，根本没有什么味道嘛，这个盐好淡啊，而且西兰花也很硬，看来还要继续烧。我又加了点盐，炒了一下，又用碗盛了一点点水。"滋啦"一声，水倒了进去，感觉锅像是沸腾一般。这个时候我又尝了一下，还是很淡，只能撒了一堆盐上去，味道适中后，我才盛出来。

把锅子和铲子洗了洗，继续热锅——倒油，接下来我要做蛋包饭了。先把油锅烧好，然后把鸡蛋全部倒入。因为锅子不大，又很圆，也不粘锅，所以鸡蛋一倒进去就形成一个圆形。等鸡蛋稍微凝固一些，我就用铲子想把它翻个身，没想到中途

住家爸爸BBQ

失误了一下，蛋皮变成了一个半圆形，有些许失望，但还是翻了过去。蛋皮做得还算成功，虽然有一点瑕疵，但很嫩，就像之前在中国吃的一样。然后我拿出一个盘子，把已经煮好的米饭堆成球形，然后再把蛋皮包上去，一个蛋包饭就完成了，还要加一些番茄酱，这回色香味都有了。

　　午饭做好了，自豪感油然而生。我拿去端给住家妈妈看，得到她的大肆表扬，说我做得非常不错。午饭吃得很香，是自己做的饭，这可是我第一次做蛋包饭，成就感爆棚！

　　今天晚饭住家邀请了他的朋友一起来家里吃烧烤。有几个叔叔之前见过，虽然他们很热情，但仍很面生有些压抑。知道我是从中国来的，他们对中国很好奇，问了好多关于中国的问题，又问我到这边来想不想家，我说住家爸爸妈妈对我很照顾，但是时间长了还是很想念家人和家乡啊。有一个阿姨说，她也是后来读书的时候到加拿大这边来的，之后就在这儿生活了，她身边也没有家人只有朋友，但是她在这边生活得很愉快。她最擅长讲法语，英文不是很好，但是和她的朋友交流得很好，基本上无障碍。

晚饭是住家的一个朋友做的，他是一个很搞笑的人，穿得大大咧咧的，总是喜欢做一些搞怪的表情或动作，或者在饭桌上讲笑话，逗大家笑。总之晚饭吃得很开心，我觉得那个怪叔叔就像一个老顽童，他和我的住家爸爸一样，看上去年纪都挺大了，住家爸爸已经是满头白发，他倒还有几根黑丝。两个老顽童聚在一起，就充满了开心和快乐，根本没有满头白发的忧虑。我坐在旁边没有怎么说话，只是静静地听他们聊天，说身边的故事，谈论自己的想法。

晚饭是在18:45开始的。大家边吃边聊，基本上没有一刻沉默的时间。有的人和旁边的人窃窃丝语，有的人则招呼着整个桌上的人一起聊天，大声宣布自己身边有趣的事情。大家都哈哈大笑，这顿晚饭，满肚子的话语盖过了肚子里的饥饿，笑声盖过了食物的香味。

饭后住家妈妈拿来冰激凌让我们品尝。我对这些冰激凌不是很感兴趣，所以就没有吃。而对面那个做晚餐的怪叔叔，吃了一根五颜六色的大冰棒，还炫耀着对我说："看这是彩虹的颜色哦，多漂亮啊，你要吃吗？要吃吗？！我可不给你吃。"搞得大家都哈哈大笑。他大口大口地咬着冰棒，看着我有些惊呆，他又含糊地说："好冷啊，好冷啊！"而他旁边一位女士则是拿着勺子优雅的吃着水果冰淇淋，两者反差巨大。当他吃完最后一口的时候，捂着肚子说"哦，我的肚子被冻住了"，又一次引得大家哄笑。

这位老顽童引来的笑声远不止这些。他对我说："你在这边一定要好好吃东西哦，把自己吃成一个大胖子，这样回国坐飞机的时候，你就可以坐两个位置啦！"我对他说："好啊，我会努力的，你要常来住家做客哦，要来帮助和辅导我哦，否则我长不胖就要怪你啦！"

时间慢慢过去，太阳落山了，温度变得有些冷，那位老顽童只穿着一件T恤，还是短袖，于是就哆嗦着说："好冷啊"，还对我说，"把你的外套给我，快给我。"

我坚决地对他说了一句："No! I also feel very cold！"

他假装有些不开心，哭丧着脸，居然还把桌布掀起来盖在自己的身上，说："Oh, I'm much warmer, more comfortable!"他又向住家妈妈问道："Can you give me two hairpin? I want tablecloth caught, so it will not out."

大伙一片哄笑，住家妈妈进屋里给他拿了一件夹克。结果他又故意把夹克穿反了，又一次引得我们哈哈大笑。大概20:45的时候，我觉得很冷，于是就对住家妈妈说要先回房间了。

今天在住家自己独立做了午餐，还认识了一个老顽童和住家的一帮朋友，享受了她的朋友带来的家庭聚会的快乐和温馨。人是需要朋友的，我为自己能够融入住家的生活感到开心。

6月7日，星期六

# 嘉年华的盛大场面

今天12:00，我和张涛、茹云衣、金叶在当Downtown集合，打算一起去参加Oka Bay的嘉年华。

刚到那儿，就被一片热闹的气氛和一大股涌动的人流给吸引住了。这里就像一个大型游乐场，有小型过山车、海盗船、碰碰车等。每一小块游乐场中人都很多，可以算得上是人头攒动了。

我们四个在门口站了一会儿，简直被这场景给惊呆了。好一会儿才反应过来，挤进人流之中，因为已经将近中午，所以我们决定先吃午饭，下午再玩。在大树底下吃饭就像野餐一样，心情愉悦。美味的午餐后，我们往游乐场进发，但是纠结于怎样买票？

我和金叶因为胆子小怕晕，所以就选择坐迷你摩天轮，一个人5张票，那两个人就是10张票。张涛和茹云衣则选择了一个比较刺激的游戏，同样也是10张票。我和金叶决定先去买票，然后再排队。票还是挺贵的，10张票要12.5加元。买好票我们就匆匆去排队，排队的队伍好长好长，都排到旁边一支队伍去了。只能说我们两个的眼光不错，将近排了25分钟，张涛她们都玩完了，我们两个还没排到。好不容易排到，却没想到我们正好停在下去的位置上，开始上去因为还要等上面的人下来，所以转得很慢，把我吓了一跳，就像被吊在空中一样。后来转得快了，反而让我觉得轻松了很多，和金叶拿着相机疯狂地拍照，把整个嘉年华的全景都拍了下来。

玩好了游戏满足了好奇心，我们决定去买棉花糖。我很少

Oka Bay嘉年华全景

买棉花糖,也很少吃到,好像印象中也就吃过两次吧,这算是第三次。我们买了一包混合味的,但是觉得太甜了,没有怎么吃,坐着等张涛她们买冰激凌回来。休息了一会,我们打算去玩一些付费的小游戏,但是我们先被旁边一个不用付钱的环保游戏给吸引住了。游戏方式各不同,还能得到不同的礼物,很高兴。

随后,我和金叶去看旁边的付费小游戏,就是付一些钱,玩游戏后还可以拿到一些洋娃娃。但看到那些洋娃娃长得都不怎么好看,我们就提前放弃了。后来看到有一个游戏,其中一个奖品是一条毛茸茸的尾巴,而且有很多种颜色的搭配。游戏也很简单,于是我们就打算玩这个。这个游戏的价格各有不同,有2个球5块钱的,有5个球10块钱的,有12个球20块钱的。开始,我们打算玩5个球10块钱的,但后来经理说,每个人都要出10块钱,我原本以为是两个人一起出的,于是我们就选了最贵的那种，12个球20块钱。游戏规则很简单，只要把球投到对面的篓子里就可以了，而且距离很短，基本上是百发百中。但是有一个球因为太重了被弹出来了，不过最后我们两个如愿以偿地拿到了尾巴。

  游玩的过程中我们碰到了曹雨她们，原来她们也是来参加嘉年华的。我又跑到沙滩去陪茹云衣，她一个人在那边玩石子有些寂寞。我还带了两个气球过去，结果在堆沙子的时候被沙子磨破了一个，不过没事，反正也不想带上公交车，有一个气球用来装饰就够了。

  下午4:30的时候，我们打算回去了。我拿着气球领着自己的礼物，背着背包，和金叶、茹云衣踏上了回家的路程。经过好一番波折，我们才回到家。

  回家后，感觉整个人还是很有活力，并没有像前几个礼拜一样觉得累，不知是身体的原因还是开心的缘故。这个嘉年华，很让我难忘，这是我在国外参加的第一个嘉年华，也是我单独一人唯一参加过的一个嘉年华。去年和爸爸妈妈去新加坡和香港，玩过环球影城、迪斯尼乐园，那里有很多高科技的东西，这里却有些不同，都是适合我们这个年龄段的游玩项目，而且还在海边，能和大自然亲近，更有意义。

6月9日，星期一

# 维多利亚的公共巴士

每天清晨上学，都会看到3辆14路公交车飞驰而过。说到公交车，在维多利亚修学的这段时间里，我接触很多了，加拿大的公交车和国内的相比，可是大有不同呢！

先来说说公交车的种类。这里的公交车有两种，一种是普通公交车，还有一种就是双层公交车，也叫双层巴士。如果你有幸能够坐上双层巴士，并且是在第二层第一排的位置，那么你就会享受一场3D盛宴。面对一块又大又亮的玻璃窗，你就可以饱览维多利亚美丽的街景，街边两排樱花树会时不时地被风吹下几片叶子和花瓣，让人觉得很浪漫。因为车是靠右行驶的，所以那些树枝有时会擦着车窗一掠而过，给你留下一片花瓣。这样的感受会让你觉得身临其境，仿佛真的有一根树枝从你面前划过，甚至还能闻到树的清香呢！听说我们苏州园区和太湖边也有双层观光巴士，但是我没坐过。

下面重点介绍维多利亚公交车的特殊设计。上车时，不同的人会有不同的待遇。走路比较缓慢的乘客，如一些老年人或者孕妇，公交车司机会特意把车身压低，这样他们就可以轻松自如地上车了，不用费力地抬腿。如果是一些坐轮椅的或者行动不便的人，那么司机不仅会把车身压低，还会放下一块板。这块板是嵌在车身里面的，按下一个按钮，这个板就会弹出来，然后搭在马路上或者车站上，这样那些坐轮椅的老人就可以通过这块板顺利上车了。上车后，坐轮椅的老爷爷老奶奶们会有特殊位置，就是车厢两旁的一排座椅。这些座椅是可以伸缩的，一旦有坐轮椅的老人上来，坐在那些可伸缩座位上的人

造型独特的公交车

就会自行让座,把位子缩进去。这样,就腾出一块区域把轮椅停在那里。还有一些婴儿车,也是如此。但要把轮椅或者婴儿车放进那个位置也不是件容易的事,所以司机会耐心地等待,大家也会主动热情地帮助,而且每当有这些情况出现时,司机起步会很慢很稳。下车时,司机同样会放下那块板,等坐轮椅的老人下车后,后面的人才有序地排队下车。由此看出,在加拿大生活的老人们是多么幸福啊!其实我觉得帮助别人和被别人帮助都是件愉悦的事情。

如果你下一站要下车的话,就可以摁一下车厢中的一个按钮。车厢的不同位置,不同区域旁边都会有这样的按钮。如果没有人下车,车站上也没有人,司机就不会在这个站台停留,这样可以节约时间。如果你不知道下一站是不是自己要下的那一站,你可以直接去问司机,司机会耐心地跟你讲解。这里的公交车司机非常熟悉线路,就像一张活地图,他们很了解维多利亚的情况,所以如果不认识路,只要问他们就可以了,他们会很热心并且耐心地回答你的问题。

　　接下来，再聊聊维多利亚的公交车站。这里的车站都有让人看着很清爽的玻璃窗，而不是像国内的车站贴满了各种各样的广告。车站旁边会有一根杆子，杆子有一张表格，上面标明了首末班车和各个时间段的班车到站时间，工作日和双休日的时间都是不一样的，这样的话在这边等车的人会心里有数，只要看好了时间就不会错过公交车。这里的公交车一般都很准时。不过偶尔有误差也是很正常的，基本上不会超过3分钟。有一次我坐公交车的时候，司机因为到了第二个站台发现时间早了，于是就停在那个站台上，大概停了两三分钟吧，然后才继续开车，目的就是为了不让时间表乱掉，导致后面的人不能准时上车。这里的车站并没有标注几路车会在下面的哪几站到达，因此如果你不知道要乘哪路公交车，只要有一辆公交车来了你就可以上去问公交车司机，司机会停在马路边上，然后告诉你应该乘哪一路车，大概会在几点来。这边的司机都很和蔼可亲，说话也不会急躁，让人听着很舒服。当你上了车，却不知道在哪一站下车的时候，司机也会特意告诉你。想想在国内这种事情是不可能的，我们乘公交的人实在太多了，而且很拥挤，司机要回答乘客很多问题的话，估计一天下来会累得够呛。这里毕竟人比较少，看来真是环境影响人啊。

　　还有一个情况值得介绍一下，就是上车和下车的礼貌问题。没错，上公交车也要注意自己的礼貌，上车拿出公交卡的时候，要对司机微笑一下，他也会回报你一个微笑的。下车的时候要说一句"Thank you"，司机通常会回一句"You are welcome"。现在我每次下车的时候都会说一句"Thank you"，然后怀着美好的心情下车。感谢别人或对别人微笑的时候，就会觉得心里暖洋洋的，特别舒服。我想我回到国内也要在上车的时候送给司机一个微笑，在下车的时候说一句"谢谢"，把好心情带给更多的人。

6月10日，星期二

# 我难忘的住家

住家爸爸&住家妈妈

住家漂亮的花园

今天的晚饭是住家在我们旁边的一家中餐馆买好了以后打包回家的，好不容易吃上中餐了，挺高兴的。

在加拿大，所谓的中餐和在国内吃的食物是完全不同的，这里的中餐指的就是春卷、炒饭或是炒面之类的。而且口味都是偏甜的，殊不知中国有那么多菜系，川菜、粤菜、徽菜、苏帮菜……不过能够在外国吃到中餐，已经是一件很幸福的事了。

上一次住家买中餐回来给我们吃也是在那家店，今天的菜和上次的差不多。有干锅包菜、炒饭、炒面、炸鸡块、咕老肉、春卷，我每个都夹了一点，晚饭吃得很满足。晚餐是在花园里吃的，夕阳还没有全部落下，一边沐浴着金色的阳光，一边品尝着加拿大式的中餐，真是一件很享受的事情。唯一的缺点也许就是，这些菜都不是特别符合我的口味，虽然冠着中国菜的名字，但是实际上没有一点家乡的味道。一顿晚饭就让我勾起了对家乡苏州的想念，此时此刻的我，坐在花园里，优哉游哉地吃着晚饭，而同学们则是在为期末考试而奋战。还有，我在这边享受着国外的美食，而爸爸妈妈则是在享受着美味的中餐。

我的住家妈妈非常勤劳，除了一个主要的工作外还兼职好几个工作，其中有一些工作还是没有报酬的。住家爸爸是搞建筑的，负责刷油漆项目和修理机器，平常他一般都会在家，有电话来的时候才出去工作，似乎没有固定的工作时间。我的住家虽然不是很富裕，但是他们很会生活，很阳光温馨。住家妈妈在花园里种了很多花，有时候还能看到小蜂鸟来光顾花园。

我的住家都很喜欢户外运动，他们每年都会去野营两次，一次在复活节，一次在感恩节。丹妮卡姐姐和她爸爸非常喜欢曲棍球运动，我们曾经去温哥华观看过丹妮卡的曲棍球比赛，她穿上球衣带上球帽全副武装的样子好酷。我的住家有时候还会去海钓或野营，他们买了房车和游艇。除了享受自己的家庭生活以外，还有很多亲密的朋友。他们非常好客，经常会带朋友来家里聚餐，一起聊天、烧烤，有时候还邀请朋友们住在他们家里。

来加拿大以后，晚饭我没有一次是在外面吃的，都是回家和住家一起享用。住家做的晚餐也很好吃，通常都是需要准备1~2个小时。住家爸爸的手艺也特别好，他做的三明治很好吃，他最喜欢做烤鸡，而且每次都不会重复，起码我来的这2个多月里，他做烤鸡的次数也有好多次了，但是我没有吃到过一次重复的。在我之前生病的时候，住家体贴入微，把我照顾得特别好。我生病的时候整天躺在自己的房间里，无论是早饭、午饭还是晚饭，住家妈妈都会亲自送到房间，嘘寒问暖，倍加关心。住家爸爸还亲自带我去医院，工作日的时候，甚至不惜舍弃自己的午休时间回来看我。他们还带我尝试各种新的东西，在来加拿大修学的整个团队里，我是唯一一个去野营、去海钓过的，并且也是第一个去温哥华、第一个坐上大海轮的。细数那么多的第一次，对于这样的住家，我满怀的就是无限的感激之情，感谢他们对我这2个多月的照顾，剩下的1个月不到的时间，我也要为他们多做一些自己力所能及的事情。

这个星期六，一起来加拿大的这批中国学生就要去温哥华了，我却不与他们同行，因为我的住家也要带我去温哥华。周五的中午我就要回家，然后周五、周六都会在温哥华过夜，住家会带我参观温哥华一些有名的地方。相对来说我的时间会比和老师一起去充裕很多，毕竟他们只去一天，而且早上5点多就要集合，9点多才能到温哥华，下午5点又要坐轮渡，也就只能玩一会儿，还要去掉车程和吃午饭的时间。虽然还是有一些遗憾不能和朋友们一起去温哥华，但是能够和住家一起，共同度过这段在温哥华的时光，还是很美好的。

晚饭后，和丹妮卡一起把碗都洗了。在这里他们都是会把碗累积了几天后，再一起洗的，所以量会很多，但我还是很珍惜这样的机会。还有不到1个月的时间就要回祖国了，有些兴奋又有些不舍，能够遇到这样好的住家也是一种缘分。所以现在趁还有机会，我要多帮他们做一些自己能够做的事情，有付出有回报才是美好。

这里的蓝天、绿树、鲜花，还有形形色色的人，我也只有不到1个月的时间与他们相处了，所以我会格外珍惜接下来不多的时光，为自己的加拿大之旅画上一个圆满的句号。

和住家海湾合照

6月12日,星期四

# 放暑假前奏

Shoreline中学海湾一景

今天已经是6月12号,周四,上学的时候老师说这周将会是我们本学期的最后一周,也就是说明天上完学,后天我们就要放暑假了。虽然说放暑假是一件让人很期盼的事情,但我还是希望能够晚点放暑假,真不知道放了暑假之后该做什么?而且这么快就要和国外的同学告别了,还没有做好准备呢!于是我与茹云衣商量着,明天把礼物都送掉,还要和同学们分别合影。

最后一节木工课了,我们的汽车还没有做好,于是我们临时决定,先把轮胎做好,颜料来不及可以回国后再上色,况且我的颜料已经上得差不多了。老师帮我做好了钢管,另外一位辅导老师指导我把车轴做好了,然后我去拿了轮胎,把它顺利安装上了。下面只要把车顶和车身连在一起,就大功告成了。彻底完成的人就我一个,张涛她们还没有做完,于是我就在旁边帮金叶调颜料。下课后,她们三个仍然没有做好,接下来要吃午饭了,于是她们就告诉我箱子的密码,让我去把她们的午饭拿来,然后在食堂会合。

到了食堂正好有一张空桌子，我搬了四把椅子（一直都是要自己去搬的），真是累得够呛，看她们还没来就自顾自地吃了起来。等我吃完了，她们还没有来，这时候还有15分钟就要上下午的第一节课了，我开始收拾东西。见她们还没来，有些着急。大概还有12分钟时，终于见她们三个狂奔过来，然后狼吞虎咽。还好，我们没有错过下午的第一节课。

我和茹云衣是一个班的，下午的第一节课是社会课。其实我不是特别喜欢社会课，因为社会课读的内容很多，有很多生单词都不认识。今天这节课老师让我们自由活动，于是我就和茹云衣开始画画。一开始我描述她画，后来她描述我画，结果简直千奇百怪。就这样，一节课我们画了好多画。

这里的学校是没有课间的，一定要说有的话，课间就是用来拿书本跑到自己要上课的那个班级。下一节课是体育课，但是上课了却没有同学跑到楼下的体育馆去，大家都在楼上整理自己的柜子，我和茹云衣也开始整理这学期做的一些作业还有一些纸。虽然带回国内也很重，还不如在这里丢掉，但还是要把一些比较特殊的留下来。剩下的时间，我们请木工老师帮我们的车"精装修"一下。我车子后面的轮胎不是很灵活，但是也没有什么办法可以补救，只好就让它那样了，反正今后也不会这样一直滑着玩，就把它当成摆设吧！心里虽然有些遗憾，但是看到自己做了大概一个月的车子终于完工了，有一股说不出的喜悦感和成就感。

明天就是学期的最后一天了，我好舍不得在国外的这些同学，还有老师，还有这所学校。记得往常每天上学的时候，平常走路比较多，上学途中总会遇见一两只毛毛虫，把我吓得胆战心惊，虽然现在看到还是有些害怕，但是已经比往常冷静多了。有时候我也乘公交车上学，坐在双层巴士上一路看着风景。真的好难忘，接下来就很少会有这样的感受了吧。还有，拐角处每天上学要等的那个漫长的红绿灯，有时候等得心中很焦急，但是现在留下的都是怀念与不舍。

即将告别自己在国外的同学、老师以及学校了，我一定要珍惜明天与他们在一起的最后时光。

6月13日，星期五

# 我们毕业啦！

送给老师的书法作品

　　今天是最后一天，过完今天，就要放暑假了。我们都有一些激动，但是心中更多的是不舍。这三个月过得好快呀，眨眼间就没了，和这些同学朝夕相处了两个多月，现在想想马上就要分别，心中满满的都是不舍之情。这里的老师是那样的和蔼可亲，这里的同学像小联合国一样，各种肤色、不同性格，我们快乐相处，难道就这样要与他们告别了？

　　今天早上我特意早早地来到学校，因为过了今天就要和这所学校说再见了，也许再也见不到了，所以要倍加珍惜在这里的分分秒秒。今天老师说取消早上的ABL，就是早间锻炼。然后老师会在教室里讲一些东西。

　　今天茹云衣像往常一样，没有及时到校，让我很着急，因为我们说好今天要带礼物送给同学的，不过还好，她在我即将崩溃的时候赶到了学校。一上午就是看电影，但是我和茹云衣没有看，因为我们还有另外一件事要做，就是要把之前没有完成的袜子猴做完。袜子猴是我从小到大做的第一个玩偶，并且这个袜子猴除了老师口头上的帮助外，从头到尾都是我亲手完成的，所以我一定要尽全力把它做好。一个上午，把四肢和两只耳朵都缝好了，就差一个尾巴和嘴了。

上午11:00的时候，老师带领我们去楼下的体育馆，那里现在成为了一个临时的大会厅。今天不仅是六年级和七年级暑假前的最后一天，还是八年级的毕业典礼。

在这里，九年级就是高一，所以初中是在八年级毕业的。今天很多八年级的女生都穿了很漂亮的裙子，她们将在大会厅唱歌、跳舞，还有一些颁奖活动。老师把一些图片作为纪念，放在PPT上，给我们一张一张地看，这些都是学校师生一年中所有的活动，包括上学期的。老师和同学们看到这一张张充满汗水和欢笑的照片，都开心地笑了。从照片中就可以看出，学校里的活动很丰富，有划龙舟，有万圣节的时候扮鬼，有野餐，有观测天象，有搭帐篷，各式各样、层出不穷。在这些照片中，大部分都充满了微笑和喜悦，但背后更多的是实践和汗水。从这些照片中可以看出，在一个学期中，老师和同学相处得是多么快乐啊，老师们玩得捧腹大笑，学生们扮鬼脸躺在草地上更是多得数不清。这些照片满载着老师和同学这一个学年来的美好回忆，也是最珍贵的记录。

今天八年级就要毕业了，身为在八一班的七年级学生（因为开学的时候，一个班级没有那么多的柜子，所以就被分配到了八年级），我为他们感到高兴，他们先是在"司令台"上一一走过，然后下台和在旁边站成一排的老师互相握手拥抱，并且接过老师手里的红帽子戴在头上。虽然并不是很了解红帽子的意义（会不会是象征着中学毕业呢），但肯定是希望学生们能够在高中有美好的生活，天天开心快乐。这次的毕业典礼，不少老师都流下了眼泪，可见这里的老师与学生感情是多么深厚。午饭我们四个小伙伴是在学校操场的草坪上吃的，坐在山坡上，晒着太阳，躺在松软的草坪上，我们享受着这顿"最后的午餐",心情满是美好与不舍!

　　下午我们看了一会儿电影。电影还是《Frozen》，虽然之前看过两遍了，但还是很希望看第三遍，因为自己本身就很喜欢这部电影。电影没有字幕，是纯英文版，但是我觉得没有字幕比有字幕更好，也许是因为看过两遍的原因吧，基本上都能懂。看完电影，我和茹云衣就趁这短暂的时间把准备好的礼物都送掉了。在送礼物的同时我觉得特别开心，就好像是在送祝福一样。看到同学们收到礼物时开心的笑容，自己也很满足，但是同时又觉得很惋惜，今天是最后一天了，也不知道以后还能不能再见到他们，能够在一起朝夕相处2个多月，也是一种缘分。

　　今天就要放暑假了，他们毕业了，我们也算是毕业了。这让我想起曾经我小学毕业，踏上初中的殿堂。当时面对小学的同学、老师也是多么不舍，而现在这种感觉又一次出现在我的脑海里。虽然只是2个多月，而且和他们的交流也不是很多，但一种深深的不舍感仍萦绕着我。

　　今天，我们在Shoreline毕业了。我和茹云衣、金叶、张涛一起在校门口合了几张影。我将会把在Shoreline的这段美好记忆深深地珍藏在心中。

教育局合影

Shoreline中学同学照

加拿大维多利亚
海岸线社区中学
八年级毕业留影

加拿大维多利亚
海岸线社区中学
我的班级合影

加拿大维多利亚海岸线社区中学我的修学毕业证书

离开维多利亚时的合影

和老师、同学们告别

和住家妈妈告别

整装待发

6月21日，星期六
# 出海观鲸鱼

出海观鲸鱼

　　今天，教育局又一次组织我们出去户外活动，这次的集体活动就是出海赏鲸。只不过今天的活动只安排上午，中午之后就是自由活动。

　　在来维多利亚之前，听爸爸说学校会安排我们到大海上去赏鲸，来这里快三个月了，终于期待要变成现实了！除了在电视上或者照片里看到图片，我还没有见过真正的鲸鱼，今天的活动让我充满了向往。

　　因为兴奋，集合地点又不怎么熟悉，于是就和金叶提前约在她家公交车站门口集合，我正好赶上8:37的那班车，金叶正好上来，居然没有浪费一分钟。集合时间是9:30，而我和金叶在9:00还不到的时候就已经到达了集合地点。由于时间还早，我们就在一家礼品店里逛了一圈。离9:30还有15分钟的时候，我们跑去集合地点，没想到我们两个是第一批到达的人。

集合、点名、买票、上船，我们开始了奇妙的赏鲸之旅。我们乘的是观赏游艇，挺大的，有两层。上面一层是露天的，下面一层有座位和窗，船头和船尾都有一个小平台可以让我们观赏海景。本来是想坐在上面的，这样可以全方位地观赏景色，但因为我们排队排得比较后，就只能坐在下面。船上的待遇很好，还会提供热巧克力和咖啡，讲解员姐姐也很热情，指导我们做了一些逃生技巧和一些门的开关方法。

大概10:00的时候，船终于开出了海湾，我们面前，就是一片广袤无垠的大海！我有些激动，跑到船头的小平台拍了几张照，但是照片也无法诠释这美丽的景色。蓝天碧海，此刻已经融为一体。海风激起层层海浪，阳光洒在海面上，点缀出一闪一闪的亮片。远处时不时响起海鸥的叫声，周围还有很多海鸟在海上游泳，它们潜进海里，再冒出头，让人觉得很可爱、很机灵。欣赏了一会儿美景，这时船停了，原来船长发现有一批海豚正在船的不远处，因为一下子冲到平台上的人太多，所以我被挤到了边上，没有看到海豚的全身，只看到一群海豚打了个滚儿就游走了，觉得很可惜。回到了船舱顿时感觉手脚冰凉，在外面被海风吹了很久，手都没有什么感觉了。正想着怎么取暖的时候，看到周围有很多人都在喝热巧克力，于是也取了一杯用来焐手。即使是在船舱，我也不忘把头靠在窗户上，这美丽的海景实在是太漂亮、太诱人了。这样的美景，在我的印象中还是第一次。

今天天气特别好，明媚的阳光让这大海的风景变得更加美丽，让我的心情也变得更加舒畅。我忍不住又跑到船头上，看见几只海狮在打滚，那胖乎乎的身子实在是太可爱了。在海上看海狮，是那么和谐，那么神奇，他们那灵动的小身体和海水、蓝天交相融合，有一种说不出的美妙。不一会船经过了一个海岛，那里是鸟儿的天堂。这是由几块巨大的礁石组成的小岛，很多很多的海鸟都在这里安家。有一块大礁石上全是海鸟，基本上座无虚席。在岛的周围还有很多海鸟在海上游泳、嬉戏，不远处还有更多的海鸟不断地飞向这里，加入这个鸟儿的大本营。

终于，船在小岛前停下了。讲解员姐姐跑过来兴奋地对我们说，一群鲸鱼正在向我们游来，这是一个鲸鱼大家族，大概有20多只。因为不能让鲸鱼受到惊吓，所以我们必须和他们保持1000米以上的距离。当大家都还没看到这一群鲸鱼时，还是眼尖的我最先发现了！看——它们正在远处的海面上不停地喷水，还有一些鲸鱼很高兴地在翻滚，露出他们的鱼鳍。等离得近一些，就能够隐隐约约地看清楚它们那个三角形的鱼鳍，黑色的很漂亮，在太阳照射下一闪一闪的，特别神气。因为是一群鲸鱼在集体活动，所以很壮观，很引人注目。它们在海上不停地翻滚着，不停地游弋着，我们的船也跟着他们的方向前行。再向周围看看，有好多像我们这样的船和游艇，都在观察着这一个鲸鱼家族。虽然和它们离得很远，但它们翻滚时的动作深深吸引着我，从一开始冒出一个尖尖的鱼鳍，然后慢慢变成完美的三角形，再慢慢沉入海中，过一段时间再慢慢浮起来，再慢慢沉下去。就这样鲸鱼家族一直沿着那个小岛，游了好久好久，游得好远好远，我们的船也跟着它们，就好像和这一群鲸鱼在一起嬉戏。虽然离得很远但幸运的是还能偶尔看到它们翻起来的样子，看到它们露出的白肚皮和眼睛那一圈的白斑！看来这一群鲸鱼家族应该是虎鲸，那漂亮的黑色背脊，眼睛那边漂亮完美的椭圆形白斑，和雪白的肚皮，在大海上，形成了一道美轮美奂的风景线。我被深深震撼了，一直站在船头。直到后来，实在受不了海风，才依依不舍地回到船舱里。

一直等到这一群鲸鱼家族游走，我们的船才回去。在回去的路上，船长还亲自捞了一根海草，这根海草或许就是海带，头是圆柱形的很光滑，切开来是空心的，白白的，然后有一个圆球，圆球下面就是一大片海带。讲解员姐姐给了我一片海带，告诉我可以生吃。我放到嘴里细细品味了一下，感觉挺好吃的，带着一股淡淡的咸味，脆脆的。船长还把那圆柱形海带切成一小段一小段，然后戴在手指上当戒指。

伴着满足和收获，我们回到了原来的那个码头。我和小伙伴们自行解决了午饭，然后就回家了。晚饭后，还和住家爸爸一起到家门口的那棵樱桃树下摘樱桃，樱桃在夕阳下显得更加红艳、润泽，更加诱人。更让我留恋的是和住家爸爸一起摘樱桃时的幸福时光。

在这100天的时间里我感受了很多，收获了很多。感谢住家、感谢海岸线社区中学的老师和同学。在我来加拿大的这段时间里，你们关心我、鼓励我、支持我、照顾我，我真心的谢谢你们！

漂亮的虎鲸，难得的回忆

6月29日，星期日

# 第一次海钓

住家爸爸把游艇开进海湾

下海喽

  今天是周日，平常周日我都是一个人在家的，马上就要回国了，打算整理一下东西。但是这个周日不同寻常，因为住家要带我出海钓鱼，这使我非常兴奋，因为我从来没有出海钓鱼过，之前唯一一次出海还是看鲸鱼那次，一想到那亮闪闪的波浪和蓝天碧海，心里充满兴奋。

  11:30的时候我们出发了，今天的早餐和午餐是在一起吃的，因为住家起晚了。这次住家妈妈让我带上防晒霜，一双袜子和一块毛巾。防晒霜当然是因为海上的太阳可能比较烈，袜子是怕鞋子湿掉，然后我还特意穿了一双防水的鞋子，毛巾则是因为座位可能会被淋湿，这样就可以擦一下。

  住家有一艘四个人座位的小游艇，船上还备有两个蟹笼、几捆麻绳和四根海钓鱼竿。我们这次钓鱼的地点是在

Downken，之前住家妈妈也带我来过。住家爸爸在后面用卡车拉游艇，所以比较慢，于是丹妮卡就带着我在港口逛了一圈。

　　这周围的景色可谓是有山有水有佳人。远处望去两座高山耸立形成一个峡谷，山不是很高但种满了树，山上依稀坐落着几栋别墅，这可是海景房啊。别墅很大，但是数量不多，有的时候一座山上只有两三栋别墅。我们驻足的地方是一个渔船码头，有很多船都停靠在这里，有小游艇，有帆船，还有一些大游艇，各式各样的船，还有小木船和龙舟呢！再看看水下，海水很清澈，一眼望下去就可以把底下的景色尽收眼底。这里有紫红色的海星，红壳的和灰壳的螃蟹，而且很大个呢，有三个拳头那么大。还有很多很多的水母和海胆，成片成片地长在水下。这么多的海底生物，在中国我可只有在水族馆里才能看见呢，而且水族馆里的和在这里看到的完全不同。这里的海星长得很大、很肥，慵懒地趴在水里的沙子上，晒着阳光。螃蟹们也是纷纷爬到岸边晒太阳，或是躲在水里一动不动。这里的水母呢，数量多得出奇，有大有小。啊！这里的水母和在水族馆里看到的完全不同，虽然品种一样，但是它们更健康、更活泼、更自由。它们看上去更像一个打碎的鸡蛋，中间有一个黄黄的东西，边上则是透明得像蛋清一样的，底下的须还很长，随着海水的飘动自由地摆动着，很漂亮、很美丽。

水母

萌萌的小海狮

等住家爸爸来了以后，住家妈妈和住家爸爸就开始布置蟹笼了，我和丹妮卡就到旁边去钓鱼。我以前从来没有在海里钓过鱼，所以这一次感觉很兴奋。旁边的丹妮卡都钓了四条了，我却一条也没有钓到，不免有些失落。这时住家爸爸和住家妈妈又叫我们上船了，真是可惜。

游艇的轰隆声随着游艇不停地前进而不停地扩大，而我们也离岸边越来越远了，向着大海的深处进发！

天公不作美，不时飘下一点点小雨，随后又变成了大雨，就这样下了半天，雨终于停了。这时，我们的船也停在了一个海狮小岛旁边，这个小岛是由两三块礁石组合而成的，不是很大，几十头海狮都栖息在这个小岛上，它们或是慵懒地睡觉，或是盯着海底，或是打着哈欠。我们的船固定好后，有几头海狮就把头转向我们，忽闪着小眼睛打量我们。每次我在海上看到海狮都会觉得异常兴奋，而且这一次我看到了这么多海狮，还是不同品种的呢。有黑白斑点的，有白色的，有黑灰色的，有黑色的，还有白黄色的。它们都有着一双水汪汪的眼睛，好可爱好可爱呢！小嘴旁边的六根胡须，长长的，隐隐的好像还在抖动。看到我们的船停了，有一些海狮就回去睡觉了，但是依然有两只海狮盯着我们，眼睛一眨也不眨，真是执着得可爱。

等住家爸爸抛了锚，我们就开始钓鱼了。海狮在旁边看着我们，海风吹过我们的面颊，我感觉在海上钓鱼真是太好了。虽然海上会很冷，但抵不住我的兴奋劲，唯一让人扫兴的就是大雨又回来了。于是我们只好边淋雨边钓鱼，但是没有一点收获。本来是可以钓到一条的，但是由于我没有经验让那条鱼给跑了，真是太可惜了。几头海狮看到我们没有钓到鱼，就把头转了回去，看来他们和我们一样也很失望。因为天气的缘故，看来今天钓鱼不是时机，我们和海狮们说了一声拜拜后便起锚回航了。

这一次出海钓鱼，虽然没有如愿以偿地钓到海鱼，但是巧遇了憨态可掬的海狮们，感受了海风海雨的洗礼，见识了海边盎然生机的海底生物。这是我与住家爸爸妈妈和丹妮卡的最后一次户外运动，让人感到难忘和兴奋，收获颇多。

令人兴奋的海钓

丹妮卡和我

# 致　谢

　　没有想到，我会非常荣幸地成为星海实验中学的一员；没有想到，我会远渡重洋去加拿大修学；没有想到，我会把修学的所见所闻记录并付梓出版；更没有想到，我这段短暂的经历给我、给我的家人、给我的老师和朋友们带来了如此美妙的变化……

　　要感谢许多给我关心帮助的人。

　　我要感谢星海实验中学。如果学校没有给我这个出国修学的机会，我就不可能去加拿大维多利亚这个美丽的城市，结交那么多陌生人，也更加不可能写成我人生中的第一本书。

　　除了学校给我的机会，我还要感谢最最重要的人——爸爸妈妈。回想当初学校发给我们出国修学通知书时，都是自愿申请的。当时我甚至看都没有看一眼，就塞进了桌肚，因为那时的我从来没有想过我能够出国修学，而且出国这么长一段时间也是不大可能的，因为功课会刷刷地掉下去，因为我从没有离开过爸爸妈妈独自去旅行过，因为那可能要花掉一大笔钱，因为……回家后我漫不经心地跟妈妈讲一声，并且表明我自己不想去，妈妈也同意我的选择。但是第二天吃早饭的时候，无意间跟爸爸谈起这件事，他却异常欣喜地一定要让我去，还说这是一次不可多得的机会。也是因为爸爸的鼓励、支持和强烈要求，我才会去到那美丽的国度，写下这一本对我来说很重要的书。从决定开始，到顺利归来，爸爸妈妈给了我很多无微不至的关爱，决策时他们反复推敲，临行时他们依依不舍，在他乡生活，快乐时他们比我快乐，病痛时他们比我着急……除此以外我还要感谢我其他的家人，不管外婆还是爷爷奶奶，他们一开始都不支持我一个人去国外修学三个半月，爷爷甚至提出要自己出钱陪我去加拿大。临走时奶奶给我的行囊中装了一袋家乡的泥土，说是防止我"水土不服"，回来后我也装了一袋加拿大维多利亚的沙土，为的是留下"美好回忆"。

我要感谢星海中学的老师。为了能够让我们这些出国修学的同学功课不落下，学校特意安排了两位老师——一位数学老师和一位语文老师来辅导我们初一下学期的功课。数学老师就是带我们出去的杨蕴菊老师，语文老师是一个很有经验的老师，谢佳老师。是她们在出国前的一个月对我们进行全面辅导，做习题，划字词，背古诗等，才让我们回国后能够跟上大家的脚步。不过因为每天下午都要参加这样的课程，有很多副科，包括历史、生物、地理等，也都安排在下午，所以这些课我通常都上不了。在这里，也要感谢各科老师的体谅。

　　那么，我为什么会写成这本书呢？其实是因为廖江龙（一个以前去过加拿大修学并成功写成一本书的大哥哥）写了一本书叫《加拿大的邂逅》，使我深受启迪。读了他的书后，我对加拿大充满了期待。于是我也决心要写这样一本书。我决定把我每一天的所见、所闻、所感写成日记。在这途中，我也曾经想过放弃，但是每当我想放弃的时候，我心里总会对自己说，廖江龙初一时能写成这样一本书，为什么我同样也是一名初一的学生，却不能坚持呢！所以在这里，我要谢谢这位没有见过面的陌生人，是他激励了我，我才能有今天的收获。

　　当然，我还要感谢初一（10）班的同学们，谢谢你们给我的留言册。我每次在加拿大想念学校、老师、同学的时候都会翻开这本小册子，它使我不再孤独。除了初一（10）班的同学们，我还要感谢陪我一起去加拿大修学的同学，特别是张涛、茹云衣、金叶。是你们陪我度过了一个又一个美妙的周末时光，使我在陌生的加拿大收获了美好真挚的友谊。回头再看一遍，这里面一篇篇日志中，大部分都出现了你们的名字，每当我一遍又一遍翻看日记的时候，我的脑海里总会回忆出与你们在一起度过的欢乐时光。虽然回国后我几乎没有和你们再见过面，但是我们Shoreline群还在，我们在一起度过的回忆还在。

　　在加拿大维多利亚的这段时光，除了与朋友们聚会，快乐地学习生活，还有和住家在一起尝试的各种不同体验。从和张涛住家体验遛狗，到自己住家的野营、烧烤、聚餐、海钓等等，都使我的修学生活充满了乐趣。当然，除了住家给我带来的不同体验，我还要感谢他们对我的体谅。每次我邀请朋友们到我的住家Sleep Over，住家都是欣然同意的。同样我去朋友家做客，他们也从不多说什么。在我生病难受的时候，他们常常陪伴在我身边，精心地照料我。每次我把自己独自关在房间里时，他们都会叫我出来和他们一起享受家庭时光。我真的要好好感谢我的住家，这样一个无微不至、细心难得的住家。还有拉布拉多库柏，我原来很害怕动物，尤其是大型的狗，在维多利亚的时间里，我和库柏不可思议地成了好朋友，这种美妙感觉真是无法形容。

在加拿大更多的是美好的校园时光。在这里要感谢Shoreline Middle School，感谢Shoreline的每一位老师和同学。是他们新奇有趣的教学模式使我每天怀着快乐的心情上学，快乐地放学。是他们每次举办的新奇活动让我对这个学校充满好奇和欢喜，还有课间时同学与老师和我的交谈使我满足。此外，在加拿大还要感谢一个人，那就是在加拿大对我们这个项目负责的刘老师，他关注着每一个学生在学校里和与住家之间的生活。他温雅、友善、和蔼，让我们在维多利亚度过了安全、快乐、充实的时光。

从加拿大回来后，我忙着补习，参加各种补习班。而爸爸总是抽时间辅导我修改日记、编辑图片等。他甚至还找了小马叔叔帮我的文章润色，还找了翻译把这本书的部分翻译成英文，送给我的住家。我的修学经历能够出版，离不开爸爸和周围关心关注我的人对我的帮助，这种帮助让我感受到写完一本书的快乐和满足。其实它已经不是一本书了，它是一份浓浓的亲情。我还要感谢小顾阿姨，她送我相机让我完美地记录了加拿大的风土人情。我还要感谢伯父、姐姐、舅舅……他们给了我很多信心，让我觉得虽然远在他乡，但并不寂寞。

最后还要感谢苏州大学出版社，是他们愿意为我出版这本书。如果没有他们的帮助，那么我的书只能在认识的人之间口口相传，我的这些快乐的生活经历也不能与更多人分享。

秦艺雯
2014年10月于苏州

# 生活
## 是无声的教育

—— 班主任邱玉立老师寄语

席慕蓉说"青春是本太仓促的书",而雯雯把自己青春中短暂却难忘的游学经历变成了书,留下的不再是仓促,而是永远的回忆。想来她以后每每翻开都能够看到往事如此鲜活地跳跃在纸上,该是一件多么幸福的事啊。

记得当时雯雯爸爸在QQ上第一次发雯雯日记给我看的时候,我只当成是一个孩子报平安的方式,一个帮助班上其他孩子了解加拿大学习生活的资源,一个出国游学的初中女生图文并茂但是心血来潮的随笔。但是雯雯爸爸告诉我说,这是雯雯出国前夕和爸爸商量后给自己定下的要求:去了加拿大之后,把每天的学习生活变成日记记录下来。而这一去三个月还真被这个苏州"小娘鱼"给坚持下来了。看着教师节姑娘放在办公桌上厚厚的大信封我心中就有数了,然后就是拿着这初稿在办公室到处显摆,引来办公室老师们声声赞叹和羡慕,这真是今年收到的最温馨的礼物。刚接10班的时候,我对自己说,陪他们一路走,一个都不能少,而这礼物让我弥补了我缺席班级两名孩子(同时赴加的还有一名男生)三个月的成长的缺憾。

100天的修学生活,100页的白纸黑字,一旦读了起来就停不下来,和孩子一起体会在异国他乡对祖国更加深沉的爱,对父母更加真切的感恩,对伙伴更加深挚的友谊,还有对生活深深浅浅的领悟。

看着夕阳中的温哥华,忍不住地赞叹道"别提有多美丽了",小姑娘却不由自主地想起了家乡的三山岛;享受着加拿大的蓝天白云,小姑娘却仍想着家乡苏州的雾霾天有没有消散;写下"加拿大学生与中国学生的玩与作业",没有意气用事的抱怨和没来由的妄自菲薄,而小姑娘一句"这又算是国外和中国的不同之处吧"留足了思考的余地……"爱国"是个让人容易热血沸腾的名词,在这个小娘鱼这里却体现在每天鲜活的生活中,成了最朴素的感情。

雯家是非常幸福的三口之家。爸爸妈妈的爱也让雯雯健康快乐地成长为了一名优秀的中学生。孩子在国内的时候就总是在家校本中时不时地夸夸老爸、"晒晒"

幸福，这出了国更是时常怀着一颗感念的心对住家爸爸和住家妈妈的悉心照顾表示感激，而在享受天伦之乐的时候也不忘惦记着家中的父母。记得刚接10班的时候，要确立班级班风，我就把"感恩"二字放在了首位，让学生用感恩之心去体味世间的亲情、友情和恩情，懂得尊重，懂得负责。而我相信一个常怀感恩之心、懂尊重且有责任心的人无论走到哪儿最后都会顺顺利利。

看着小姑娘的日记总是忍不住笑出声来，无论是各种迷路还是各种找手机，这种事儿，对于"糊涂虫"来说，出门在外总都遇到过，也包括我自己。而小姑娘总是很幸运，朋友的帮助总能"化险为夷"，也正应了"出门靠朋友"这句话。但是不论"吃香喝辣"还是"受苦遭难"，姑娘心中总是想着国内的同学们此时此刻在干嘛，彼时彼刻是否都好，对待朋友的帮助也总是充满感激，深深地领悟到"人是需要朋友的"。

为了是否该让雯雯出国，秦爸爸特地打过电话征求我这个班主任的意见。当时我们觉得孩子什么都好，就是有点儿内向，有点儿怯生，所以想着能够让孩子多一些历练，那这肯定是一次很好的机会，但是又有些担心。好在孩子对于大人的考虑都非常的理解，所以出去之前做了充分的准备，最后带着爸爸的六字鼓励——自主、自立、自信踏上了修学的道路，当时也许忐忑多于坚定。三个月后，用小姑娘自己的话说，就是学会了"控制自己"，明白了"吃一堑长一智"，敢于做些"不敢想象的事情"，变得"更坚强了"，是一次"蜕变之旅"。看到这些字眼，我为她高兴。想来以后的路她都可以走得更加坚定。

就算青春真是一本太仓促的书，可也喜怒哀乐俱全。每天的生活就是写书的素材，而生活本身就是无声的教育。希望我的学生们都可以像雯雯这样，能认真生活、体验生活。

The book is presented to the homestay families, my dear parents, other family members, my teachers and friends who care about my growth.

March 19, Wednesday

# Last Night before Going to Canada

Arriving at the Shanghai Pudong International Airport

A picture with my parents

Today is the last day before I go to Canada for a study trip. I am lying in my little cozy bed, with a lot of emotions. I am inevitably excited at thinking about the time of three months in Canada, but more unwilling to leave my parents, teachers and friends and also worried about this trip. I grow up happily under the care of my parents without worries, which makes me feel reluctant to leave home. However, my father hopes the study trip to Canada this time can make me more self-contained, independent and self-confident so that I can obtain practice and improvement in all aspects.

On the morning of March 19, I stayed at home packing the luggage. At noon my mom took me to my grandparent's home to have lunch. In the evening when receiving a message book of my class from Chen Jinyi (my good friend in middle school), I could not check my tears that were held for one day. It was a message book from my classmates. I carefully and seriously read those goodbye messages and

A picture of all the team members during the trip of further studies in Canada, 2014

A picture of members of Suzhou Industrial Park Xinghai Experimental Middle School

blessings: "Bring your camera and take pictures", "Don't starve yourself in Canada", "Enjoy yourself", "Expecting a new you", "Xiaomi, go for it!"

I felt a little bit sorrow. I will not see my dear teachers and friends for one semester. The only thing I could do is to keep their wishes with me and bring them to Canada.

My mom made all that I like for the dinner. In the coming three months or more, I will not have the opportunity to have the dinner made by my parents. I slowly tasted and chewed, and felt very sad, controlling my tears not to drop.

I am going to Canada, shaking off school, heavy homework and wordy parents, which seemed to be great for many people. But for me it is very sad. I have to say goodbye to Xinghai School, teachers and

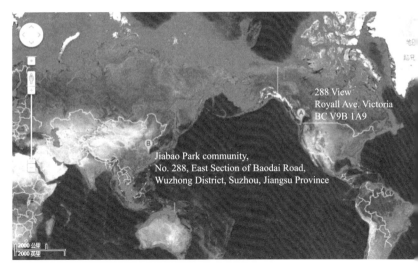

A screenshot of Google map

friends. What's more, I would be away from my parents, studying and living in a place far away. I cannot eat the nutritious breakfast made by them, or talk with them about the things happening at school, and they will not instruct me on my homework. I will have to eat bread and sandwich, speak in English and live a life that I am not used to.

However, I still have a lot of expectation on this trip because I will be able to learn their culture, go to supermarket with my homestay family, communicate with foreign students in the school in Canada and celebrate festivals with the Canadians. In general, I have a mixed feeling. Everything, whether expected or feared, I should confront them. Thinking that I will take the plane to go to the faraway Canada, I am full of hope. I think that I am ready for a brand new life there. Canada, I am coming!

March 20, Thursday

# On the Way to Canada

Information of the flight to Canada

Today, the students going to Canada for further study gathered in front of Xinghai School and we took a bus to go to Pudong International Airport. After two and half hours, we, 21 students, happily arrived at Shanghai Pudong Airport under the leadership of Teacher Yang. We checked in and went through the Customs, and then to the boarding gate, waiting in a seat. Soon we boarded on time. I found that I was sitting with two students also from Xinghai and felt lucky. Then I started a long trip on the plane over ten hours.

On the plane I did not feel bored at the beginning. I was talking with my schoolmates. When it was time for dinner (chicken rice), I started to feel a little bit sleepy, and then unawares took a nap. When I woke up, I found very few people were walking around, and my friend beside was watching TV quietly. Then I started my writing. However, I felt nothing to write. The plane encountered turbulence, so I closed the computer. I picked up the air cushion pillow to sleep again.

I woke up again after a while. It was only one third of the trip, but 4 hours had passed unconsciously. I wanted to get spirited. I asked the air hostess for a glass of icy water and continued with my journal. The plane encountered turbulence again soon after I started writing. It was

The rising sun outside the plane

shaking, which made me feel worried. Even the toilet was closed.

Suddenly I began to miss my parents when I was writing. It was my first time to go so far alone, and I was in nostalgia. However, I knew that the purpose of my parents this time was not only to broaden my views and make me learn some foreign culture, but also want me to learn how to take care of myself instead of relying on parents like a little kid.

I finally arrived in Vancouver after more than ten hours' flight, 37 minutes later than expected. We went to take the luggage, and then transferred to Victoria. Unfortunately Zhang Xinyue and I were left behind, neglected by Teacher Yang, the leader of the team. We wandered in the place with the luggage like ants on the hot pan, anxious to look for our teacher. When wandering in the airport with another 2 students from Xingwan, we suddenly found Teacher Yang in yellow jacket. We four ran toward her, but she did not notice us, focusing on picking up the luggage. It seemed she did not notice that someone was missing until we appeared in front of her. She was surprised.

When waiting to transfer in Vancouver Airport, we took out mobile phones to call parents. But I could not find my mobile phone. I turned to Miss Yang and she helped me search in the bag, but failed. I had to look around, and ran across a foreigner at the information desk who talked with us in English but we did not understand. After looking around again, I still failed to find my mobile phone. I had to go back to the previous seat. When I was so frustrated, I surprisingly found that the mobile phone was just beneath my bag. It was more a scare than hurt. I should be more careful in the future.

After we successfully arrived in Victoria, we came to the Education Bureau and got arranged on the homestay families. I was going to live with Zhang Tao for a few days because my homestay family went to Mexico for holidays and would come back in a few days. I will temporarily live in Zhang Tao's homestay family, a young couple with a 2-year-old daughter named Julie. Julie was very cute, and was after us all the time. She also let us enter her room to play games, but threw toys all over on the ground. We had our dinner at 21:00. It was a pizza made by the homestay mother, very delicious.

MARCH 22, SATURDAY

# A Day of the Naughty Girl

Today I woke up at around 6:30 in the morning, and felt a little bit dizzy, which might be the result of jet lag. Zhang Tao and I went upstairs to eat breakfast, which was a little bread in blueberry flavor, half of the fist size. It was good but I did not get full, so I went back to my room to eat a Big Rabbit candy (brought from China).

After a while the homestay father said that he would bring us to walk the dog in the morning. We were very happy to hear that, as we also wanted to get familiar with the surrounding environment right after arriving in Canada. We happily went out.

The morning in Victoria was very cold. Both the ground and the glass of the cars had a thin layer of frost, white and beautiful. We kept moving, and breathed the fresh air on the lawn. We came to the gulf of Victoria, where we together with other people were walking their dogs.

The Julie family

Julie, "the little devil", is quite lively and lovable

Maggie (the dog of the homestay family) started to bark a lot as if finding other dogs bigger than her. Some dogs ignored her and some barked back. The mother of the homestay family pointed to Maggie's nose to stop the conflict among dogs.

On the way back, Julie saw several slides and swings. She cried and dragged us to the mini slide, and insisted that we both climbed up. But that slide was really too small and very naïve. Under Julie's request over and over again, we had to get onto the slide, but it was too small, so we did not want to slide. It was rather like squeezing booth paste than sliding down. Julie did not agree, and cried a lot, very spoiled. Finally her mother asked her to come down, and persuaded her a lot. She was really good, crying and stopping at the same time. After a little while, she happily ran toward the swing. At first her mother helped her push, but later she insisted that we two help her. Then Zhang Tao accepted the challenge and went to push her. Julie did not want to stop at all, which made Zhang Tao exhausted.

Soon we were going home, but she still did not want to stop. Eventually she got a "roar" from the father: "Julie, back home now!" She then reluctantly followed us home.

I got another challenge after arriving home. She drew me to the refrigerator, and picked all the refrigerator magnets one by one and put them in my hands, and then took these magnets one by one and wandered around me. After a while, their dog Maggie came around me. When I was nervous, Zhang Tao came and drew Julie's attention. She put the magnets on Zhang Tao's head. Soon she felt bored, and put back the magnets onto the refrigerator. Zhang Tao and I slipped back to the bedroom.

We had two sandwiches and a bowl of strange tomato soup for lunch. In the afternoon, the homestay father sent us to a shopping mall to buy stationary. But we did not find any stationary store there, so we asked a Chinese shopping girl and found a store. After we bought the stationary, we came to the bus stop as we wanted to go uptown by bus, where we met an Asian guy. We thought he was a foreigner and we asked him a lot of questions with poor English. Unfortunately, he did not understand, but suddenly he said some Mandarin, which made us speechless. We got on bus with him and came uptown under his guidance. We inexplicably entered a supermarket and bought a bunch of very expensive pens. At last we actually missed the bus, so we had to go back to the place where we were apart from the homestay father, waiting for him to come to pick us up.

After I arrived home, I felt very tired, so I directly went back to the room for rest. In the afternoon the family went out for errands, so we had dinner at 19:00. The dinner was very simple, with a bowl of butter rice. Please let me explain. It was rice mixed with butter, very greasy and very bad. I randomly took some rice. After a shower, I finished my journal in the bed.

The Victoria Bay

March 24, Monday

# Be a Member of Shoreline

The screenshot of the Shoreline Community Middle School on the Google map

　　Today in the morning I found that my mobile phone was switched off, so the alarm did not ring. That made me get up at 7:00. I hurried up cleaning myself and had a glass of oatmeal, and ran to the school with the lunch prepared by the family.

　　Zhang Tao and I walked to the nearby bus stop, very excited. Today is our first day to school, full of expectations. We came to the bus stop and saw some foreign students waiting for buses. We were quite surprised to see how they were dressed. The girls all left their hair loose, dressed in long sleeve T-shirts and a pair of canvas sneakers without socks, while the boys were all in T-shirts, pirate shorts and sneakers. The bus arrived five minutes later.

　　Two girls went to the bus shoulder by shoulder. The door of the bus suddenly had a harsh trumpet, so one girl had to go back to the queue. It was quite normal in China to jump a queue, and nobody would care. This might be one of the differences between China and Canada.

　　We ran across Ru Yunyi and Jin Ye (they are students from

Xingwan Middle School, going to the same school as me in Canada during this trip), who were also taking bus to school. After a while, we arrived at school. The classmates were all very nice. As soon as we arrived, they surrounded us and made self-introductions, and someone took us to the Principal's Room. The Principal ardently met us and gave each of us a pen bag, in which there was a national flag of Canada.

Later, the Principal asked a girl to show us around the school. The girl speaks very fluent English. Both the speed and tone and the expression method were very good, easy to understand. After the visit and introduction, we started the class. The first class was Mr. Kronker's English course, which gave me a lot of thinking. It is so relaxing to study here. Students did not care about the teacher, some stretched the legs, some lied on the table sleeping, some watched TV on the phone and some listened to music with earphones. Anyway, except the Chinese students, almost nobody was seriously listening to the teacher.

The bell rang and the students left. No one stayed in the classroom. The teacher tried to ask them to stay but nobody listened. They ran out without the permission of the teacher. The next class was biology? I thought so. Anyway I did not understand at all. In every sentence of the teacher, I could always understand several words, haha! I thought that I had to practice my oral English because I was not clear about what the teachers were talking about on class.

After that we had a 20-minute rest. The girl with great eloquence continued to show us around her school. We came to the day room to rest for 20 minutes, ate some bread and had a glass of juice. When we were about to throw the trash, she introduced all the information about trash cans to us. She asked us to classify the trash. The trash that can be recycled includes: paper board, plastic, bottles and newspaper; the trash that cannot be recycled comprises: fruit peels, leftovers and household garbage. Then we went to different rooms including music room, computer room and kitchen, and visited all kinds of appliances.

In the afternoon we had geography and sports, in which sports left me deep impression. At the beginning the teacher gave us 8 minutes to warm up, to run around the room. Then the formal class started, which was playing games. The teacher took out many balls and asked us to throw. I was not familiar with the rules at the very beginning and was hit very often. I moved around aimlessly, and eventually the sports class was over.

After school my homestay family came to pick me up. The mother had a nice name called Christina D. Lloyd-Jones, and the father's name was Randy Stuart. The mother took me home, where there was a sister 2 years older than me, called Dannika Pauline. They had a dog. It was only 2 years old, but it was as tall as to my breast if it stands up. The new homestay family was much better than the previous one. The dinner was great, plus dessert after dinner. Moreover, they did not bother me at all. Around 21:30 they went to bed.

  I had a good time today, expecting to see my new classmates tomorrow.

The Shoreline Community Middle School

March 25, Tuesday

# One Day in Shoreline Community Middle School

The panoramic view of the Shoreline Community Middle School classroom

Today, Ru Yunyi and I came to a new class and got a cabinet. Mr. B told us the password and told us how to unlock it. It was very difficult to open this kind of lock. First it should be turned two rounds and then enter the password in the clockwise and anti-clockwise sequence. Ru Yunyi and I got confused at the very beginning, and the teacher repeated three or four times. Then the teacher asked us to try. I tried but failed. I did not give up, and tried to unlock it again. It was opened! Right after that Ru Yunyi's cabinet was also successfully opened. The teacher went back to class after seeing us know how to do it. We took out our books and began the first class of science.

The lesson of science today was about the internal structure of the earth. The book was full of so many technical terms about the earth that I did not understand at all. So was what the teacher was talking about. I had to guess wildly the meanings meanwhile consulting the mobile phone for the pronunciations and meanings of the key words. After a while the teacher took out several rolls of plasticine asking us to make a model of the internal structure of the earth. This was what I know, so I wrapped the plasticine according to the color sequence of the shell of the earth, and formed an "earth". After it was done, the teacher cut the "earth" into two parts, which was the model of the internal structure of the earth. I cooperated with Ru Yunyi and succeeded very soon. The teacher's cut made our model flat immediately. It was a pity, but the earth in fact is an ellipse. Finally the teacher arranged the homework and the class was over in our exploration. There was another class of mathematics in the morning. I went back to open the cabinet and failed again. I had to stay there studying the lock, but could not succeed after trying over and over again. At that time Mr. B came. He easily helped me open the cabinet, and I said a lot of thanks to him.

It was a mathematics class. I came to the classroom (we do not have a fixed classroom. The school would give us a paper of the arrangement of classrooms one week in advance, and we would come to the appointed classroom to attend class. We call this "walking studying"). The teacher gave me an exercise book and asked us four to go to the library for registration. We came back quickly. The teacher arranged my seat beside a girl, who ardently helped me with many things to be done. Then the class started. I found it was very easy because the lesson was reviewing the contents of the previous lesson. After doing the exercises, the teacher distributed number cards to me and to the girl beside me in order to check our multiplications. I found that the girl was not good at arithmetic abilities, using fingers a lot when doing multiplications. Basically I could get the answers by a glimpse.

It was not allowed to have lunch in the classroom but there were several choices: one little room beside the teachers' office, the library (where you can eat and read) and the lawn on the ground. I chose the library. The lunch was very good—a sandwich prepared by the homestay mother. It tasted like a hamburger. She also prepared various fruits and snacks, etc.

The class in the afternoon was fine arts. Before class we met the boy who always said "Ni Hao" to us. He stopped us and said a lot of things that we could not understand. We suddenly got speechless. The teacher of fine arts asked us to draw a painting about one's hometown and hobbies. We discussed a lot and got the summary. I drew a fluttering Chinese national flag on the upper left of the paper, and a pen beside. Under the flag, I drew a lot of figures, including me doing homework, mother watching TV, father running, aunt going shopping, grandma planting vegetables and grandpa reading newspaper, etc. When the teacher saw my draft, he praised me: "Perfect!" However, I liked Ru Yunyi's painting. She made a horizontal picture, with a Chinese flag, homes along the river, an ancient village in the south of the Yangtze River and the silhouette of parents riding bikes. The class of fine arts was over unconsciously. The last class was sports. We kept skipping rope basically. I had a lot of exercises and sweated a lot, but felt very comfortable.

After class my homestay mother picked me up and went to her working unit to do something, and then we went back home together. I had some noodles and rice for dinner. Today was fulfilling.

A picture with classmates during the break

The schedule of Grade 8

March 27, Thursday

# A Brand New Schooling Experience

In China the morning is busy. My father gets up early to prepare breakfast (of course abundant, nutritive and delicious) like a battle. Because I have to arrive at school at 7:00, I usually dress myself, wash up and eat breakfast like in a war. My father or the father of Chen Jinyi drives us to school everyday, so in the car we usually talk about the homework of yesterday or some private talks of girls.

Today is the fourth day in Shoreline Community Middle School. I go to school every day on foot. On the way I would run across some friends, and worms and big ants that make me scared. (Certainly I can take a bus, but the homestay mother advises me to walk, which is good for health and gives me chances to see the views on the way.) Today I went out for school after a simple breakfast.

The way to the school takes around 15 minutes, but in fact it takes me longer because my homestay family is beside the sea. The way to school is a basically steep slope, the same as climbing the mountain, full of ups and downs. If I walk faster I will be out of breath. However, the view along the way is great. The cherry trees are blossoming; the vague mountains are horizontal at faraway; different big birds are flying tweeting in the sky, enjoying the morning sun…Before I came here, I found from the Baidu's results that Victoria is a beautiful garden-like city with a mild climate. I did not expect that I could live in such a city. I thought on the way to school that the homestay mother's suggestions are not bad at all!

I arrived at school at 8:00 on time. It is not advocated to arrive in advance because the school gate does not open!

The first class today was reading. The English teacher brought his pet dog Lucy. This is what you can never imagine in China. Lucy was a lovely black dog. The whole reading class was playing with it, and nobody was reading. We threw a green ball here and there. Lucy

Class break

seemed to love this ball a lot, so she followed the ball. We passed the time of the reading class by playing with the dog. The other classes in the afternoon were boring: in mathematics, I knew everything, so nothing was fresh; in the science class, there were a lot of technical terms, I could not understand them at all.

I chose to go to the playground for lunch. The ground was very big and there were many local Canadian geese (you can find our playground on Google map; a lot of black spots on the green, which are in fact the geese). They were enjoying the sunlight on the lawn, relaxed and friendly. Surrounding the playground were dandelions and blossoming daisies, which attracted everyone's attention. The vision on the playground was broad. The match of the blue sky, the white cloud and the green lawn was harmonious. I had a good appetite on the ground.

The first class in the afternoon was society. The teacher asked us to make a mask for the Easter. This class was for us to search for information and the class next week is making the mask. When I tried to use my mobile phone to get online to search for information, I suddenly found that my phone was missing. I was worried. The teacher provided some basic reference books when finding that I had no phone. Relying on the reference books I preliminarily decided my topic of mask-the mask of the minority in Guizhou China. Ru Yunyi decided to make a mask of Sanxingdui, and Zhang Tao and Jin Ye decided to make a mask of Peking Opera. Having lost my mobile phone, I felt upset. After the class I ran to my cabinet to look for my phone. I found it in my lunch box. It was a false alarm!

We had another class of fine arts, which might be our last class in the classroom. The fine arts class next week will be changed to a carpenter's workshop. Today I should continue with our painting of hometown and hobbies. The teacher asked us to do it at home and then hand it in to him. I wanted to escape but it seemed to be in vain. I had to finish the painting. Before the class was over, the teacher gave us each a piece of chocolate. The teacher gave us a candy almost every class. I did not understand why. This might also be another difference between foreign and Chinese educations. (When we were in the kindergarten or elementary school, the teachers usually gave red flowers to the students with good performance. Now I think candies are much better, haha!)

It was worthwhile mentioning that we had a thin female teacher temporarily for the sports class. In fact she was also a mathematics teacher and had given us a science lesson. She asked us to run around the room right after the class began. A girl called Annie was running beside me, followed by a foreign boy. When we were running, the circle became smaller and smaller. I felt a little dizzy. When I was about to run outward, I heard a noise. The boy behind me suddenly fell in front of me. I was astonished, and drew back several steps. Obviously Annie was also shocked. Instead of withdrawing, she fell forward. The result was horrible! She fell onto the boy directly. In fact she did not completely fell on the boy, but she pushed the ground with her hands and pushed against the boy onto the ground. We were all shocked! Such gesture lasted several seconds and they stood up one by one. The boy had no problem and went to play, but Annie looked pale with shock. We made fun of her beside, "Why are you shocked like this? The one that was impacted felt nothing. You have to record this in the journal." She rolled her eyes. After a while, she still seemed to care about this. In order to attract her attention, we started skipping rope until we were tired. Several minutes before the class was over, the teacher let us practice leapfrog, high leg lifts and push-ups. I was so tired that I was out of breath. The sports class was challenging, consuming all the calories that I took during the lunch. I did not want to move anymore.

After school I told the homestay mother that I wanted to buy crayons on the weekend because I have to finish the homework of fine arts. She agreed. At around 20:00 the homestay father brought a box of crayons home and told me "5 Canadian Dollars". My god, it was RMB 30, so expensive! I had a video talk with my mom and took a shower, wrote the journal and went to bed. Let's wait for the brand new tomorrow!

March 30, Sunday

# A Wonderful Day

The homestay family and I

    Today is Saturday. In the morning the homestay family brought us to walk the dog at 9:00. We drove to a forest beach (a small beach in the forest beside the sea). Cooper, the dog of the family, sat with me on the back seat of the car. He is a Labrador, covered by a black "jacket". Although he is only two years old, he is very tall. The mother said that Labradors are all mild and active, not aggressive and very smart. It is a local dog of Canada, called as the three non-aggressive dogs together with Husky and Golden Retriever. She told us not to be afraid of him.

    The homestay mother told me that Cooper was found during camping. At that time Cooper was small and thin, so they adopted it and took good care of him. They even put Cooper's picture in front of the gate, reading "Labrador Cooper lives here!" Now he is already a member of the family. Cooper rarely barks but he is very ardent, and likes to follow people. On the way he put its head out of the window, as if he knew the way very well and loved that place the most. He was singing.

Soon we got to the destination. The view was great, and there were many dogs. We walked along a mountain road and came to a little beach where there was a clear lake. The homestay father picked up a short tree branch and threw it into the lake. Cooper saw the branch, so he ran into the water and swam toward the branch. Soon he picked up the branch, put it beside him and dried his hair, full of pride. When the homestay father took the opportunity to pick up the tree branch beside Cooper, Cooper suddenly got upset, wanting to take back the brand. However, the father raised his hand high and Cooper could not get it. He jumped over and over again, but in vain, so he had to sit down. Suddenly the father pretended to throw the branch. Cooper thought that the branch was already in the lake, so he dashed into the water, which made us laugh because the branch was still in the father's hand. After a while, more and more dogs came to walk, and Copper played with them happily. There was another Labrador called Chocolate. They played in the water. The owner of Chocolate also threw a branch. Cooper thought that the father threw it, so he dashed toward the branch again. Chocolate also followed to the water. The two dogs played in the water.

After some time, we came to the second beach. Then, It was lunchtime, so we left the beautiful forest beach. We had lunch in McDonald's. I found that the foreign restaurants were very clean and there were many things for self-service, such as ketchup, straw and cups, etc. After lunch we went to the supermarket to do some shopping and went back home to pick up Dannika from school.

We and Cooper walked around her school and then went to climb the mountain. The mountains in Canada are original without stairs, so we had to climb. It was not very steep but I got tired. Eventually we arrived at the top. We took a group photo on the top. Suddenly I found that my camera was out of battery, so I had to use the mobile phone (It seemed that I was not very well prepared!). We appreciated the panorama of the whole Victoria, which was really fascinating. Most of faraway Victoria was ocean, decorated with some islands. The whole city was covered with green trees, and houses in all colors could be seen. The sky was as blue as the ocean, dotted with white clouds. It reminded me of a poem by Wang Bo, "The autumn river shares a scenic hue with the vast sky; the evening glow parallels with a lonely duck to

The seaside, the forest and the beach

fly", which shows the same scene.

At around 3:00 pm, we picked up Dannika and bought some food in a Japanese restaurant, and went back home. In the evening I wanted to show my Chinese cuisine, so I made fried rice with eggs for the homestay parents. I thought it was bad, not as good as at home, but they liked it a lot and had several bowls. I was surprised and very happy. After dinner we watched "Finding Nimo", which is the favorite movie of the homestay father. However, I was not very interested because I had already watched it when I was young.

I went to bed at 22:00. This weekend I watched 6 movies. I thought that maybe the homestay parents wanted me to get familiar with the language environment as soon as possible. It is a shocking number. Tomorrow is Monday, and I really hope to go back to school.

April 3, Thursday

# Happy Time with Homestay Mother

Today after the last crazy sports class, I went back home, very tired. I saw the parents watching TV in sofa. The homestay mother told me that she had made a sandwich for me in the refrigerator. I said "thanks" to her and rushed to the refrigerator, took out the sandwich and heated it. Then I got a glass of juice and started to shovel. The sandwich made by the homestay mother was so delicious. It had the flavor of both hamburger and sandwich.

After eating I started to do homework. After a while the mother came to ask me if I would like to go to the supermarket with her. I happily agreed. Cooper also wanted to go but the mother asked him to stay at home. He was not happy, but pretended to be obedient, sitting on the ground. When I opened the door and was about to go out, he suddenly rushed to the car of the mother, waving his tail to her, as if to ask her to take him to the supermarket. She had no remedy and said, "You can only stay in the car." Cooper understood her and went to sit down in the back seat.

We got to the supermarket very soon. The mother left Cooper in the car and took me into the supermarket. After choosing, she bought some snacks and beverage, and asked if I needed anything. I saw the prices plus the exchange rates and immediately shook my head.

When we got home with fruitful results, the homestay mother asked me if I wanted to go with her to plant flowers. What? I had never planted flowers before. So I nodded and happily agreed. I followed her to the backyard and saw Dannika there too. The mother helped us with small pots, shovels, mud and some seeds. Then we started. I picked here and there and eventually took one that was quite beautiful. When I poured half of the seeds into the pot, I suddenly realized that was there too many seeds? I asked the mother and she said only two or three would be enough. I suddenly felt dull! "Oh, my God!" I sowed at least twenty or thirty seeds! It seemed that I was really a green hand to plant flowers, so I had to take back the seeds into the bags, and made three pots. The homestay mother gave me another four flowerpots, so I started working hard again. When I filled the fourth pot, the father came to ask us to go for dinner. The dinner today was great! Vegetable salad, lettuce, roasted chicken legs and rice, especially the chicken legs were so aromatic and tender, in rich flavor, much better than those bought outside. The father said that it took one hour to roast the chicken legs, and today he put some barbecue source on the legs. He knows a lot about cooking, same as my father. He cooks well, and I like it.

After dinner they started watching movie and I started my journal. Tomorrow is another day.

The backyard of the homestay

The dinning hall of the homestay

April 4, Friday

# Sports Class on the Beach

In the sports class this afternoon, the teacher took students of the 7th Grade and the 8th Grade to the beach. Our school is right near the sea. After around 15 minutes of walking, we got to a dense forest, through which we saw the beach. There were many tall and big dark rocks, and bizarre shells on the beach. The ocean was as blue as the sky. There was a small island in the sea, on top of which stood a lot of trees. The beach was surrounded by a dense forest, which protects the great land. The seagulls were flying and singing in between blue sky and ocean, very relaxed.

When we got to the beach, the students spread out. Some took off the shoes to walk on the spindrift; some took a little wood stick trying to catch crabs in the seams of the rocks; some climbed up the tree to feel the wind; and some lied down on the rock to take sunbath. I was also touched by the beauty of the sky and ocean, and ran toward the beach. I stepped on the shells and came to the water against the sound of ocean. A lot of shells in different colors and shapes were lying here. I picked up a white shell and put it into the water, seeing that the water slowly rinsed off the sand in it. The water was so clear! Even looked from a tall rock, algae and shells in water could be seen clearly.

After playing for a while, I came back to the beach, sitting on the rock and looking at the beautiful view. I started to think: is China at the end of the ocean? If I throw a drift bottle, will it drift to Shanghai? I also found many bubbles and some unknown algae that looked like a green "love heart". When I was in the mood to study these plants, a yellow worm crept beside me, which astonished me because I am very sensitive to worms. I dragged Jin Ye down from the rock. Because I put too much strength when jumping down, I got a lot of mud on the feet. We used tree branches to clean the shoes and then went to look for Zhang Tao and others. We found that they were writing on the beach

A view of the PE class on the beach

using branches and stones, so we joined them, and wrote "Canada" in Chinese on the beach, and what they wrote was "Suzhou", and then added "Victoria" and a plane, which meant that we came all the way to Victoria by plane. This could be a "footprint" of us in Victoria. Before leaving, I picked up several beautiful pebbles as souvenir.

After a little time, the teacher asked us to go back. The short time on the beach was over like that. We walked through the forest and went back to school. On the way we were very puzzled. Was this a class? In China this might be absenteeism.

After getting home, I rested for a little bit. The homestay father brought Dannika and me to her school. The plan was to send her to learn hockey, but Dannika's foot had not recovered, so we had to cancel the plan and went to buy some discs so as to go back home to watch movies.

April 5, Saturday

# Visiting Teacher Liu's Café in Downtown

Mr. Liu and his Café

Today is Saturday. I went to downtown with Jin Ye. Yesterday we decided to meet in front of the school at 9:00. We got to the school at 8:45 by coincidence. A bus arrived and we successfully got to downtown.

We were not familiar with the place, so we wandered along the main road. In the beginning we thought that we would not get lost if we followed this road. But unconsciously we turned. Although it was a little turn, it was hard for us to go back to the original place, the "top-level" road nerd. Then we started to turn left and then right, and finally came back to the main road. It took us more than half an hour. It was already 10:30, and we felt hungry. We decided to have lunch in McDonald's. Jin Ye brought her lunch but I did not, so I had to order a Hot Cake. Then we wanted to look for the café of Teacher Liu (who is the liaison and responsible person for our schooling trip in Canada). We heard that his dumplings are very good, and free for the first time.

After walking for more than ten minutes, it started to rain. Jin Ye wanted to buy an umbrella, so we walked into the nearest supermarket, which was big, clean and quiet. We went to the shelf of umbrellas. Jin Ye liked one but then she saw the price: 14.00, which is around RMB 85, plus tax over RMB 90. How could we afford an umbrella with RMB 90? But Jin Ye said that her umbrella was broken, while the umbrella of the homestay family was too big and strong, plus Canada is the country with a lot of rains, so a quality umbrella is very necessary. Moreover, things here are usually of good quality, and can be used even after going back to China. So she made up her mind, took 20 Canadian Dollars and went to the cashier.

At that time, an old man was going out with a cart. His wheel knocked over a plastic bucket by mistake. The bucket had several little hooks on it, and thus fell onto the ground by such a knock, and many hooks got under this cart. It was obvious that he could not move very well, but only stay beside the cart, and cannot reach the bottom of the cart. I saw his situation, so I squatted down to pick up all the hooks beneath his cart as a favor. The old man smiled and said "thank you" to me gently. I suddenly felt very warm.

After buying the umbrella, we continued looking for Liu's café. We took his name card and asked people for the way. The people were all warmhearted, patiently pointing the way for us. We ran across an old lady, who did not know how to go there but took a map for us in a department store. We continued asking with the map…

In the wind and rain, two "road nerds" shared one small umbrella, using their poor English to ask for the way. I don't remember how many roads we crossed and how many circles we turned, but when we were exhausted, we found the sign of Teacher Liu's café at one intersection. We eventually arrived! We screamed and rushed to the door of the café, and took several pictures in front of the café to show how difficult it was to find the place.

Teacher Liu did not recognize us. We had to make self-introduction again and told him about our hard journey. When he heard that we looked for his café from 9:30 to 12:00, he could not believe it. He saw that we were exhausted, so he gave each of us a bowl of free wontons, double in quantity. We were hungry again after wandering for the whole morning. The wontons were hot and delicious. After such a long time abroad, it was our first time eating such good wontons. I was so moved. I did not even finish the first one, Jin Ye turned and asked me, "How many have you eaten?" Every time I answered: "I did not count, why you care?" She said, "If you are still eating when I am done,

I will be jealous." OK, what a strange idea it was.

When we were talking, I heard someone from the door saying in Chinese "hello, Mr. Liu". I looked carefully and found they were our tutors, Teacher Yang and Teacher Pan. Seeing us eating wontons, they also asked for some, and asked Mr. Liu to recommend them places with good food. After eating, we talked for a while and went out.

We asked Mr. Liu about the chocolate shop, and he showed us the closest way. However, we suddenly found us lost. We looked at the map and returned to Mr. Liu, feeling very embarrassed, "We are lost again, Mr. Liu!"

The three teachers suddenly got speechless. Mr. Liu explained again to us patiently. We set out again and eventually found the chocolate shop. We were moved and took pictures in front of it again before entering. So many chocolates in the shop made us astonished. The waiter let us taste the flavors of different chocolates. They were so good! But when I saw the price label, I got shocked, 9.99 CAD, which was RMB 60. Who would buy such a piece of chocolate of gist size with RMB 60? Why was it so expensive? Wasn't it just some chocolate cream frozen? Jin Ye's eyes were shining. she asked me, "Which one should I buy?" I reminded her of the price converted into RMB plus tax, and complained why it was so expensive here. But even like this, she did not change her mind, and bought a piece of cheaper chocolate, which was still expensive for me.

We planned to go back to Mr. Liu's. I asked her if she knew the way back. She shook her head. We experienced another half-hour time missing. When we saw Liu's café, we were so excited that we screamed. But we still adjusted our mood before entering the café.

When we told the three teachers about our experience, they said that we should go out more often, and asked us to go out to play instead of staying in the café. So we decided to go to the China Town. We went to the corridor. Jin Ye saw a duck and asked me if that was real. I saw that the duck did not move at all, so I said randomly, "For sure it is fake". When we came back, we saw an old lady playing with that duck and I realized that the duck was real. So we took the chips given by the old lady to feed the duck as she did. Seeing the duck eating happily, I suddenly had a strange idea: the ducks abroad are so happy. They even have chips to eat. In China, they would just wait to be served on the table.

At around 14:30, we were so tired that we decided to go back. The day in downtown was tiring, but we got familiar with the environment and the routes. Next time I think I will not get lost.

The wonton made by Mr. Liu

Downtown view

A picture at the chocolate shop

April 8, Tuesday

# Mr. Kronker Learning Chinese

Mr. Kronker at work

The sports class in the afternoon was cancelled because of the rain. Several of us chose to do homework in the classroom of Mr. Kronker's (the English teacher).

At the beginning, Mr. Kronker was surfing the Internet beside us and we were doing our homework. After a while, when he heard us whispering in Chinese, he was very curious, and asked us what type of Chinese it was. Because we did not know the English expression for "Mandarin", we told him that we were talking in Suzhou dialect. He was very interested and asked us to teach him some.

He said that he wanted to learn Suzhou dialect of "hello". In this school almost everyone could say "ni hao", which is as popular as "hello" in English. So Ru Yunyi said "ni hao" in Suzhou dialect. Mr. Kronker listened and imitated with distorted face, we could barely understand. The pronunciation of "ni" was good, but "hao" was hard to say because he made a wrong accent. Ru Yunyi repeated, and he followed, but the result was the same. Ru Yunyi had to repeat patiently.

This time Mr. Kronker seriously repeated three times. After practising, he seriously said: "Chinese is so difficult!"

But he insisted on learning. We wanted to teach him "thank you" in Suzhou dialect. Again Ru Yunyi taught him and he followed. After a few times, I found that Ru Yunyi said "thank you" in a strange way. It was not authentic Suzhou dialect. I taught him once and he frowned to repeat. In fact this time he made it. But he said that he did not want to learn Suzhou dialect any more because it is too difficult. I said that we can teach him something more interesting in Suzhou dialect, such as "you are my teacher, and we the girls invite you to come to Suzhou for a visit", which would be much more difficult to learn.

Mr. Kronker shrank back from the difficulties and he turned his interest to the names of cities. The first one was Qingdao, which he pronounced very skillfully and sounded standard. The next one was Beijing. "Bei" was OK, but he could not say "Jing" correctly, instead he pronounced as "chiong". We laughed, but I admired him. Although it was very difficult for him, he persisted in speaking several times.

After making a lot of efforts, he found some pictures online and showed them to us, all about Suzhou. He said that Suzhou was so beautiful, with so many green trees, lakes and gardens. But Jin Ye said in Chinese that how they could make the sky so blue, trees so green and view so beautiful by PS! We all agreed. It was impossible to combine the pictures with the reality in Suzhou. In Canada, the pictures and the view match, and sometimes even the pictures are less beautiful. However, our sky is very different from the real environment. Before I came to Canada, Suzhou had serious haze, and there was even a record of serious pollution for one week continuously. This is the consequence of damaging environment!

Today I got a strong sense of satisfaction after teaching Mr. Kronker Chinese. At least I am better than others in Chinese.

April 10, Thursday

# Vancouver Impression I

On the ship to Vancouver

Today is Thursday. After I got home after school, the homestay mother told me to pack the luggage, and said that we were going to Vancouver to attend Dannika's hockey match. I was very excited and finished the luggage right away. My mother came to tell me only to take a bag instead of the suitcase, so I packed again.

At around 5 o'clock, we had instant pasta for dinner. We did not want to eat because we were not hungry, but the homestay father said that we would not sleep until 10 at night, and would not get anything to eat during those hours, so we had to make ourselves full, haha!

We left on time at 17:45. The homestay parents sat in front, Dannika, Cooper and I behind. Cooper was more excited than us. He opened his mouth, looked out of the window and pressed me so hard that I could not move. Dannika dragged to get Cooper toward her. As a result, Cooper's saliva dropped on Dannika's mobile phone. She shouted and Cooper looked at her with eyes open. Then he turned to appreciate the view. Dannika took the mobile phone and rubbed on his back. She said, "Get it back, now my phone is clean." I was surprised.

Soon we arrived at the port. The homestay mother pointed to the boat that we were going to take, which was big and awesome. The boat was blue and white, windows reflecting hilarious light under the reflection of the sun. The mother drove the car to the boat, which meant that the car would follow us to Vancouver. I was still surprised. Everything here was new to me, including the big boat, super big parking and the metropolitan Vancouver, etc.

We entered the cabin. The first floor was a large shopping space and a buffet area. The second floor is for seats, including desks, sofas, small round tables and TVs. Outside the cabin was a place for seeing the ocean view. The steam-whistle rang, and the boat slowly moved. The homestay mother took me to the cabin to appreciate the view.

She patiently introduced those small and big islands to me as well as the continuous snow mountain in front. There was a tiny island of the size of three to four buildings, extremely beautiful. That little land, was full of trees and flowers, also a paradise for the sea birds. Around 50 birds were staying, and some were swimming beside. I moved my eyes to another rock beside, where a fat sea lion was taking the sunbath, and several little birds singing for him around. He was enjoying himself.

The boat moved between two big islands. The sun was setting, making the sky red. Both mountains were like having red gown, on top of which a fire ball was adding glamor to the gown. The seagulls were singing and flying, like in the painting. I have seen a great sunset in Sanshan Island of my hometown Suzhou, but this was my first time to enjoy the sunset on a seat boat. Against the mild sea wind, breathing the fresh air and having the sunset behind, I made a very nice picture, and left a great memory in my mind.

At 21:00, we arrived in Vancouver. The homestay father bought some snacks for us at a gas station. Then the homestay mother took us to a vacant house of her friend's. Because it was left unused, so we could stay here for two nights. As soon as we entered, Cooper glared at the ceramic dog beside the fireplace, which made all of us laugh. During the night I slept on the same bed with Dannika. It was already 22:30. She was lazy to take a shower and directly went to bed, and I took a quick shower. Tomorrow we are going to get up early to watch Dannika's match. Today both my feet and eyes are tired, but it has been a beautiful day.

April 12, Saturday

# Vancouver Impression II

Chinatown in Vancouver

The match of Dannika today was quite early, so we hurried to the site to watch their fierce competition. We planned to go out together, but Dannika wanted to go to her friend's place and I went to have lunch with the parents. After lunch, the homestay mother bought many donuts and cakes for the athletes in the afternoon to encourage them.

At noon the homestay mother drove me to the place where she grew up. It was a beautiful, rich and prosperous mountain, which she described as a big park named Stanley Park. We drove in and saw a street, splendid and full of Chinese atmosphere like China Town. Many shops were written in Chinese, supported by small English letters. It suddenly made us feel very friendly to see Chinese. We passed by a temple. She had never seen those types of Chinese religious places, and she thought it was a supermarket.

After crossing the street there was the residential area. The houses were obviously different from those in Victoria. All buildings were high, with more than 10 floors, or 20 floors and even 50 to 60 floors,

The burning torch tube

like in Suzhou Industrial Park. The colors of the glass were different, including transparent, white, blue, purple, yellow and green. There was a new building that the glass of each floor written with a series of English letters. Compared with those here, houses in Victoria City were all like villas, scattered or gathered.

Our car arrived at a port after passing a lot of high-rises. The homestay mother stopped the car on purpose to show me the torch on the port, which was a landmark of the 2010 Vancouver Winter Olympics. It was assembled by four thick iron tubes, on top of which the fire was on as if it would never go out. Many people were surrounding it, taking pictures. The homestay mother even slowed down to let me take a picture. Surpassing the torch were mountain and ocean. I told the mother that I wanted to take pictures of the mountain and the sea, so she drove me to the hillside.

As expected, the view here was more beautiful. Trees were tall, a lot of beautiful flowers were blossoming under the trees to contribute their smile to the beautiful weather. On top of the remote mountains, there were white clouds and snow, fusing with each other. The blue sky and the ocean reflected each other. What a nice picture it was! Seeing far toward the sea, there was submarine making dome of water; boats making whistles; and seagulls hovering and singing… Over the sea there was an elegant iron bridge, painted all in green, perfectly matching the surrounding green trees and the snow mountains. The bridge had a nice arc. From far it seemed like the background of meteor, adding nice element to the sea. The homestay mother told me that the name of the bridge is Lions' Gate Bridge, the longest bridge in Canada. How magnificent!

Down from the mountain, the homestay father took me to a park

Lion's Gate Bridge

The bird mask totem

The hockey game

inside Stanley Park. He told me that this park was to the west of the English Bay, being the largest city park in the whole North America. There very few artificial landscapes. The virgin forest with coniferous trees such as redwood was the most famous scene of the park. As soon as we entered the soft lawn, I saw six wood columns standing in front of me. Each wood was painted with several masks connected to one another. They like birds or beasts. In general, I called these woods mask bird woods. The homestay mother introduced that these were totems, left by Indians, the original residents of Canada. Each totem column represented one family. The key chain that I bought also had one of these patterns. After saying goodbye to the totem columns, the homestay father took me to a small souvenir store. I had a glimpse and saw many small gifts such as postcards and key chains, etc. Many toys had totems painted. I guess that these totems am like the facial masks in Peking Opera, possessing special meanings and long history.

Due to limited time, we did not enjoy the big park but only had a tour. But only by such a tour, I had a deep impression of the park. The streets, mansions, the ocean, trees, flowers, snow mountains, marks birds and souvenir stores had all been printed with the most beautiful bookmark of the memory about Canada.

Coming out from Stanley Park, we drove to watch Dannika's hockey match. After the match, because Dannika would have a match tomorrow, and the homestay parents had other things to do, they would bring me back to Victoria first, and leave Dannika to her friends to take care. However the homestay mother was reluctant to leave her daughter. When I saw them hugging and saying goodbye, I remembered my departure in Pudong International Airport on the day when I left China. I hugged my parents like this, and kissed their faces. I was a little sad, missing my parents in China. Although I talk to them by video everyday, we can only talk and see each other, but not touch. There is a good saying that people should cherish what they have but not to think about what will have in the future. When I was in China, I often lost temper with my parents and acted as a spoiled child. Now I think I was too naïve. What parents do is all for the children, just as the homestay mother spent a lot of money buying helmet and amour of a goalkeeper for Dannika. It is top priority to cherish what we have. We should cherish the parents' love and care. As what I could see now, even the mother did not buy new helmet and amour for Dannika, she could still finish this match. However, in order to help her confront the competition comfortably, they bought her the new helmet and amour.

April 14, Monday

# Play and Homework of Canadian Students and Chinese Students

Sitting on a wooden chair

It is said that Chinese students are good at remembering and doing examinations, while foreign students are good at creation and invention. However, they are not born like that.

Today when I got home after school, the homestay mother was there. She prepared a plate of vegetables and fruit and two yogurt bars. Then she invited me to the garden to talk with her.

She asked me if I wanted to go to see Dannika play hockey that night. I realized that I had to make up the journals that I missed because of the visit to Vancouver, and had to do some mathematics homework arranged by Teacher Yang, and also to recite the words of Unit 4 of English. Then I thought that the hockey match should start at 17:00, and I would come back around 21:00. I refused her, thinking that I might not have enough time.

She did not understand that the reason I did not want to go was for doing homework. She asked, "Do you have a lot of homework? Shoreline should not have a lot!"

So I told her the homework and the journals that I planned to finish tonight. I also told her that if it were in China, this time we would still be at school, only 16:00.

She was shocked, and asked, "What do you do after school?"

I said, "Homework, usually do it until dinner, and after dinner I will continue with homework."

She asked, "Do you have homework every day?"

In order to make her understand, I gave her an example of everyday homework, and it was a quite easy day.

She was astonished. She said, "When Dannika was in Grade 7 and Grade 8, she never had homework."

This time it was I that got shocked. When could I have no homework? Maybe in kindergarten, even in the first year of elementary school I had some homework.

Now I am studying in Grade 7 in Shoreline. Almost 20 days have passed. I have only done homework twice by far (only homework, not including the work on class of mathematics): the first one was a French menu for three weeks; and the second one was to simply rinse a milk box. In particular the first one, although it said three weeks, cooperation was accepted. Under the cooperation with classmates, it only took me three hours, including complicated procedures of transacting English into Chinese, Chinese into French, and French into English. The second homework only took me a few minutes. In China, I usually spend 2-3 hours on homework every day. This is equal to 20 days' homework in Shoreline!

Then the homestay mother asked me how we had spent the weekends. I told her that besides a lot of homework, we had to go to some extra classes. For example, I had an English class after school on the evening of Friday. Sometimes I could only have dinner on a bus. On the morning of Saturday I had to prepare for the 3-hour mathematics class in the afternoon. Because we had too much homework, I had to digest it, otherwise it would be difficult for me to take the class in the afternoon. Then I rested for a while before going to the class. After coming home, I would relax a little bit. Then I spent the whole day of Sunday finishing the homework of the school, or did part of homework on the evening of Saturday.

She was so surprised at my introduction, and asked, "Are you not tired?"

"Of course I am, but I have to, only like this we can learn knowledge!"

"Oh yes! In my mind, Chinese are studying well, working hard, and are good at anything that uses brain!" She signed with emotions: "They are trained like this. In Canada the kids only play. After they come back home for weekends, it is family time. The whole family will play together, eat a good dinner, or watch TV, spend a nice night. The second day is for sleeping, and after getting up, you can go shopping with family or friends, do whatever you want to relax. The evening will still be family time. The morning of Sunday is for entertainment. You can do whatever you want or invite friends to come home. In the afternoon you can watch TV or chat with family members. In the evening you can do homework if you have or spend it as your private time."

I was very attracted by what she said. Comparing the time of weekends of the kids in the two countries, you can easily find the differences. When I was in Suzhou, the good time of weekends for me is for homework or extra classes. Now in Canada, I dedicate my weekends to family time and entertainment.

The homestay mother asked me about the arrangement on Canadian Day, and I said that I had no plan. Then she gave me two choices: one is to take a boat with them to see fireworks, and the other is to invite my friends and their homestay families to come to my homestay family to eat Barbecue. I was afraid that my friends would only speak in Chinese when they come and thus make the homestay family embarrassed, so I chose to watch the firework.

When we were still chatting, she pointed to a hammock under a big tree, asking me to lie down on it for a rest and enjoy such a nice day. I failed to climb onto it and even fell down. At last the mother helped me climb onto it. I lay in the hammock and let the flower pedals drop onto my face, thinking about my days in China, when it should be the last class for self-studying, or doing homework or listening to the teacher. Anyway I would not lie on a hammock like this. The spring wind gently flew on my face, flowers fell and little hummingbirds sang beside me. The big tree above kept out the dazzling sun, but only let warmth cover me. I closed my eyes to enjoy the slow life in Canada, the beautiful scene, the precious blue sky, the fresh air and the leisure time…

In the hammock under a tree

April 19, Saturday

# The First Day of Camping

The homestay parents are preparing the caravan

Today I got up very early in the morning because the homestay mother said that we were going camping after breakfast. I was very happy to think that I could sit beside bonfire, surrounded by the forest, with birds and squirrels jumping on the branches. I was looking forward to this camping, my first camping experience.

This time besides my homestay family and Cooper, Tylie, the boyfriend of the homestay sister also went to the camping. The westerners were so open. She is only two years older than me and already has a boyfriend, and they were very intimate. She can also invited her boyfriend to camp and the parents agreed. It was incredible!

After having a delicious breakfast, the homestay mother started to pack. Although she packed for a day yesterday, she still had many things to prepare for two days of camping, including food, kitchenware, household appliances, pillows and quilts, tent and cloth for preventing rain. I basically had nothing to prepare because the mother told me the day before yesterday and asked me to organize things. Therefore, I made a small suitcase and a small bag pack the day before yesterday.

At around 10:00 we set out. The homestay father drove a caravan, which seemed to be very heavy, and the mother took Dannika, Tylie, Cooper and me by her roadster. After half an hour or so, we arrived at the site of camping. It was formed by mountains, with planted trees. A road connected it with the forest, green here and there. Between trees we could see blue sky and bright sunshine. Birds were singing and jumping between trees, and several squirrels running in the grass faraway. Sometimes they jumped to the tree roots. Smoke from kitchen chimneys went up from the forest, which was made by the camping people cooking breakfast. The whole picture was fresh and natural, making me intoxicated.

We choose a place and then divided the work. Firstly the homestay mother made the bed for Cooper. Then she took out the suitcases organized with the father, including suitcases for flashlights, for pots and pans, for clothes, trash, tents and chairs. In general there were more than ten suitcases of different sizes. On the other side, Dannika and her boyfriend were setting up the tent for Tylie. Because the caravan was not big inside, only three beds, her boyfriend has to sleep outside. Even so, his tent was twice bigger than any bed inside the caravan. It was a hexagon tent, several square meters big, inside of which many things could be put.

I looked to the sky. It started to rain. The father immediately took off some blue plastic cloth from the caravan to cover things with the mother. I saw they were very busy, so I went to help. It was not easy to put on the rainproof plastic cloth (I don't know how to say, so let me use this name to substitute). Everyone was almost done. The mother asked me to get familiar with the surrounding environment with the sister, so the sister took me to a very important place—our bathroom. It was a small wood house, not far, but we had to walk there to use it. The caravan had a toilet as well but it was small and simple, without water, so we could not use it.

When we came back, Tylie was chopping the wood. Dannika and I were very curious and ran toward him. He was tired, and sometimes missed the wood or did not make the chops even. Therefore, the homestay sister went to help. She rolled up her sleeves and chose a relatively smaller axe to chop, but she failed in the middle. Tylie laughed beside her, and took the axe to set an example to the sister. Although she failed again the first time, the second time she chopped the wood into two halves perfectly, very even. When the homestay

Tylie is chopping the wood

sister saw him working very easily like that, she asked to let her try again. This time she made a lot of efforts, but did not make it. We got speechless because the wood was really difficult to chop. Tylie tried again and still failed half way. He tried vertically and then horizontally, but could not split it due to the texture of the wood. The homestay father came and chopped it into two halves.

The wood was ready, so we started to make the bonfire. It was cold in the forest, and the fire made us warm. After a while, the homestay mother let us play cards. Tylie recommended two ways. Although it was recommended in English, I understood more or less the rules. Then we had some noddle soup for lunch. I felt a bit tired, so the mother asked me to rest in the caravan.

In the evening we went all the way to wash and then all the way back. The homestay mother let me go to bed first. However, the bed was too small, only 20cm tall and 40cm wide, similar to capsule hotel that I heard before. I climbed up the ladder, but almost sprained my waist and hurt my feet. The mother had to let Dannika try to see if she could climb onto the bed. She made great efforts to go to the bed. When she turned, she almost fell. She complained how could she sleep on such a bed! So the mother let us sleep on the same small bed. During the night she took half of the quilt and I only got a little bit, very cold. In the morning when I woke up, my legs were numb. I did not sleep well for the whole night!

April 20, Sunday

# The Second Day of Camping

Tylie's big tent

This morning after we got up, both the homestay sister and I complained that we felt cold last night, so her mother let Dannika and I sleep on their bed, and Tylie on the small bed that we slept on last night. The parents moved to Tylie's tent.

After breakfast, we stayed beside the bonfire to warm ourselves. The homestay mother said, "we will go to attend a game around 10:30." I was quite excited that I would play games with foreign friends!

Time flied very fast in the morning and it was 10:30. We arrived at the game site on time. Dannika and Tylie were divided into the same group, and the mother and I into another group. We gave strange names to the groups. Ours was called Amazing Team, and the one of Dannika and Tylie was called Drink Water because on the back of Tylie's jacket these two words were written.

The first game we played was to shoot a small plastic ball into the glass of the opposite party. There were six balls in total. If one was shot, the glass will be put aside. The team that shot the glasses of the other team first would win. I have learned table tennis, so I hit four glasses, while the homestay mother only hit one. When there was only one left, they shot all, so we lost the game.

The second game was to throw a rope that was fixed with a small ball on each end to a random point on the three columns faraway. By hitting each column, relevant score would be obtained. Our competitors were Dannika and Tylie. I did not get used to it at the beginning, but soon things improved. The homestay mother played very well already, but young Dannika and Tylie played even better. We had the opportunity to win them 3 points, but a ball was hit back after several circles even though it hitched up the column. The mother was upset and she blamed Tylie jokingly: "You must win? I don't let you marry Dannika." The winner was innocent and the loser was righteous, very funny! Then we played another three games and all lost. Oh, my God!

With some regret, the homestay mother brought me back to eat snacks and soup. On the way I saw a lot of chocolate eggs in the forest and I asked the mother about their sources. She told me that these were Easter's gifts to children. If I saw chocolate eggs I could pick them up, so I grabbed all the chocolate eggs around our place, more than twenty! I was so happy that I went to tell the mother, holding all the chocolate eggs in my arms. She was surprised to see that I got all the chocolate eggs. In fact they were placed very obviously, with elegant packages outside, shining. Plus there was not a lot of grass to cover them, so they were naturally exposed on the ground. After picking up so many chocolate eggs, I was in a very good mood and forgot the loss in the games. After having the delicious soup, I went to take gift with the mother. I picked up one and drew a card of popcorn, although I did not know what it was. She told me that this card was useful and she would bring me there to eat, where the popcorns are golden but in brown, blue, yellow, pink and purple, representing all kinds of fruits, so we happily went back. The homestay mother started to prepare lunch, which was a small hotdog of the size of half palm.

The dinner was rich. All the camping teams and each family provided one or two special dishes to share with everyone. The desert after dinner included apple pies, blueberry cakes and small balls that I did not know the names.

We came back to the campsite, very satisfied. We made the bonfire and talked about it. It became dark. Although it was only 19:00, the forest was already dark, and the sky was still. The trees covered the

The bonfire at dusk

Dannika and I beside the bonfire

light, so it was dark. The whole forest became dark at 20:00 or could even be said as pitch dark. The homestay mother took the florescent rods and let me carry. I put two on the wrist, the mother hung it on the buckle of clothes and Dannika put it on the hair as hair band. Then the father brought sausages to let us make BBQ. He borrowed my flashlight to move some branches, and broke the branches to make the BBQ fire. We cleaned the branches with fire, and insert the sausages on them, very primitive. After some time, we started to feel bored, so the mother took out the speakers to play music. We sang and danced beside the bonfire, happily.

I slept very well and comfortably. Today was a great day!

April 21, Monday

# The Third Day of Camping

On the way home

The homestay mother started to prepare things after getting up on the morning of the third day. Today we would leave the beautiful forest. However, my stomach was not feeling well and I even felt dizzy. I sat on the bench to rest. The mother realized my problem after organizing all the things, and then arranged me to rest in the caravan.

After getting home, I still felt bad with my stomach and got dizzier. I did not have the appetite for lunch, and directly went to bed. I guess maybe I was not used to the BBQ or something was not clean enough. I decided to clean my stomach and not to have dinner, but sleep.

Today was a school day. I felt better when I woke up, so I decided to go to school. But as soon as I left the door, I found myself still not well. My stomach was fine, but I did not breathe well, and felt dizzy. I went to tell the homestay mother and asked her to ask for leave for me.

She agreed, but felt guilty about my sickness. She was afraid that I had eaten something wrong, and asked me to take some medicine. I was moved. I planned to have a good rest in bed, and the mother stayed at home today as well because she did not need go to work today. In order not to bother me, she stayed in the living room watching TV. She kept the volume down and I was sleeping very well.

    I had a small bowl of noodles for lunch, and then I felt bad again with my stomach. So I decided not to have dinner because I might feel bad again. The mid-term examination is coming; I want to make use of the time to review. I took out the book to recite words, did some mathematics exercises, but I felt as dizzy as before. The third day was a bad day of suffering. At night I felt much better. Tomorrow I can go to work, expecting…

A view on the way home

April 23, Wednesday

# Let's Go Picking Up Rubbish!

The first class in the afternoon today was Mr. Allen's as usual. The routine was to read and study on our own in the first half of the class, and then an inferential subject in the next half of the class, very difficult. I don't know how to do them until now. However, today Mr. Allen (class director) called us to the classroom and cryptically took a big bag with several long clamps in hand, which seemed to be for picking up rubbish. When he took out the environmental protection clothes from the big bag, people rushed toward him to grab, and also the column for picking up rubbish. Although Ru Yunyi and I were the closest to him, we did not get anything because the foreign classmates that herded up grabbed everything. Mr. Allen distributed a plastic glove to each of us, which was very solid, like the one worn by the doctor for surgery. Then he announced: "Today we are going to pick up trash." I thought it was going to pick up trash in school. In my mind, it was easy, and so was it inside the school.

People organized the team and set out in formidable array, around 20 people plus 3 teachers. Our team passed by the playground. Ru Yunyi and I looked at each other, and paused. Were we going out of the school? Were we going to pick up trash in the streets? When I was in Xinghai School, I had never gone to the streets to pick up trash. Although I picked up trash on the ground when I saw, it would never be something organized like this.

As expected, we went out of the school from the side gate and came to the sidewalk. Ru Yunyi and I started to hesitate. Should we pick up while walking or should we start when we got to the destination? At that moment we saw a paper ball on the road, hidden in the grass, not matching the beautiful scenery. We picked it up. Although we did not know the situation, the nice view should not be damaged. Maybe the people in front treated indifferently, but we not only represented us, but

The view of Vancouver street

our school, and even our country. We should win honor for our country! Haha, I am exaggerating.

We walked all the way. It was quite far, with all ups and downs. Ru Yunyi and I did not feel well and the whole way was ups and downs, which made us bump. At last we made a turn and had an even way, and felt much better. We chose a piece of grass and sat down to rest. Our trash bag was not satisfactory, but there were various things inside: tissue, small paper balls, cans and cigarette ends …We looked at the blue sky and the white clouds, big green trees and tulips beyond; in the sky all kinds of birds were flying, and fat bees were taking sunbath in the flowers, very lazy. Maybe because of us picking up such a little rubbish, the beautiful environment would be even nicer. Suddenly I felt that this activity was very meaningful, and gave us much sense of satisfaction!

After some rest, we went on to pick up trash. We saw a lot of people talking and laughing in front, followed by only two boys and three teachers. Suddenly Mr. Allen saw a beer bottle and two paper cups in the bush. The two boys behind us rushed into the bush to pick up those paper cups and the bottle. It took them some efforts to take out the things and they put them into the trash bag because there were only three bags, and the nearest one was at ours. The two boys almost vomited after they threw the paper cups because they were almost rotten.

Nearly two hours later we went back to the classroom. No one wanted to move, feeling very exhausted. I felt quite satisfied, as I not only picked up a lot of trash, but protected the environment in Victoria. This is the education abroad, to experience in studying and to study in experience, which is very good.

April 26, Saturday

# A Pleasant Excursion

At the brook

    At 9:00 in the morning, we gathered in the Education Bureau of Victoria to set out for an excursion.

    I thought I arrived early, but seven or eight students were already there talking. I ran to join them. Between 8:35 and 9:00 people came successively, but still a few were left. The teachers called them over and over. The plan was that four students would be together, but only three arrived at 9:20. Teacher Liu and Teacher Pan decided to drive to pick up the other one directly. We got to the place that we fixed at the beginning, but someone opposed it. After thinking, Teacher Liu drove to the place that they mentioned. As expected, the person was there. It was already 10:10. It would still take half an hour to drive to our destination—Golden Creek Park. We had less time to play. What if everybody had respected time!

## Golden Creek Park

We reached Golden Creek Park by the school bus. It was a forest full of trees and some wood tables and chairs. At the beginning it seemed like our campsite last time, but in fact it was not, but the same mountain range.

We walked across a wooden bridge and got to a stone platform, beside which there was a clear creek. The water was shallow and clear, with pebbles in the bottom, very colorful. A lot of trees were beside it, offering a nice view. Teacher Liu said that it was the cradle of salmon and also the tomb. In every July and August, salmons flow upstream from this creek until where the water is shallow and they have no strength, and finally die here. After they are dead, many brown bears that have been waiting for long beside or other wild animals will come to eat the salmons. Therefore, this place is full of fishy smell in July and August. It was a pity that we stopped only half way of the creek and went toward another spot.

## Wall Painting Town

We slept on the bus and got to the Wall Painting Town. As the name indicated, the walls of the whole town were paintings. I even saw ancient Chinese wall paintings, and paintings about slaves conveying woods and royal families having tea...After a tour, we started to eat lunch. Mr. Liu bought bananas and cupcakes for us. Then he recommended an ice-cream store to us. I followed them even though I did not want to buy any. The ice-cream store was in a very beautiful yard, where there are many bears, of course fake. Some bears were fishing, some were playing swings, some acting as guards at the gate,

The wall painting

The wall painting inside a room

some playing and some climbing columns, very funny. After they bought ice cream, we went out of the yard. I saw a wooden bench along the street, on which there were several bear paws, super cute.

### Totem Town

Our next target was the Totem Town. According to Mr. Liu's introduction, all the totems in the town were created by the aboriginal people in Canada, representing special significance. According to Jin Ye, each totem represents one family. In order to seek different families, we separated to explore. We crossed the road and came to a market, where people were selling things but we did not join in the fun. As we walked around, we ran across a lady pushing an iron ball, which seemed to be made of bicycle tires of different sizes. She saw us looking at it, so she asked: "Do you want to take pictures?" We agreed happily. We took a picture three together. She said that we could enter to take pictures, so I took the lead to span into the big tire, and then moved slowly my body into it, then drew another leg in. It was quite interesting but difficult to control the gravity. We said goodbye to the lady after we played enough, and moved toward the next destination.

We found a café to rest. Two dogs were having sunbath in front of the door, of which one was black and white, dressed in bright yellow skirt, sleeping on a big pillow and drinking water, so funny! Another one was brown and white, dressed in orange miniskirt. Its tail was shaking, very cute. I could not help to touch their heads, and they showed me their tongues, so lovely!

After a little rest in the café, we came to a gift store. There were a lot of cute things in the store, and quite cheap. We looked at the colorful things for quite a long time, and I bought some gifts for my friends in China.

After we reunited, Mr. Liu took us to a shopping center. It is said that the big chicken leg here is very delicious. I bought one and it turned out to be good.

A view of the Totem Town

April 27, Sunday

# Beacon Hill Children's Farm

Jin Ye is feeding the goose

Today is Sunday and I woke up very late. After having the delicious breakfast, the homestay family took Zhang Tao and me to Beacon Hill Children's Farm.

It is a children's farm. Our school will organize us to come here in the future. But I thought it was also good to get familiar with the environment. In order to go to Beacon Hill Children's Farm, we had to go through a big garden and a lawn, where a creek passing through. On both banks of the creek there were willows and some unknown trees alike peach trees. Many lazy ducks were taking sunbath on the lawn, looking very relaxed. Some ducks were sleeping in couples in the shadow of trees. Most of the ducks were green-headed ducks, and some were grey. They were like Mandarin ducks. Some were swimming in the creek in groups, sometimes shaking their wings, sometimes pecking the neck of other's, sometimes waving the tail and sometimes merging into water. It was a harmonious view.

The homestay family took us to Beacon Hill Children's Farm. It was not big in size but there were many interesting things. We first entered a well-decorated wooden house decorated well. On the lake there was a little tree branch hung with a lot of paper cranes, and some elegant bird houses with colorful birds. Some were blue, some had yellow bodies, some had orange mouths like chicken, and some were white and brown. There were a lot of species and the bird houses were full of bird tweets.

After visiting the bird house, we came to a peacock activity site where a male peacock was displaying its tail feathers. It showed the feathers in a fan shape. The peacock slowly turned to let us appreciate its beautiful feathers. At the same time, it was flirting with the female peacocks beside. Several grey peacocks were sitting and shaking the feathers, as if being deeply attracted by it. The domain of peacocks was not only this one, but another two nearby. The piece of site beside us was special for the love of male peacocks. A male peacock was opening its tail feathers, and two female peacocks were looking. It shook its feathers as if to show how beautiful its feathers were. However, only one peacock was in love with it and surrounded it. Seeing another female peacock coming out, another male peacock went up quickly to open its tail. It was as brilliant as the other. You could see two male peacocks slowly opened their tail feathers, and two female peacocks were beside them. When in Shanghai Zoo before I seldom saw this kind of scene, male peacock slightly opened its feathers and drew back immediately. "We are what we eat." The peacocks of the two countries

A peacock in his pride

are so different!

After watching peacocks, we went to the rabbit nest. There was strange odor. Rabbits were cute. Their lunch was rich, including carrot salad, lettuce salad and water. Some rabbits dared not come out from their wooden home. Maybe they were taking a nap!

We went to visit pacos and small horses after seeing the rabbits. There were black and white pacos, which we also call "grass mud horse", dumb and lovely. There were three small horses, one white, one brown and one cream. They were very elegant. The breeder used a comb to comb their hair.

The homestay sister took me into the goat "space" after seeing the horses. There were little goat just born and female goats. Maybe people were afraid that they would fight there, so they cut their horns. What a pity it was! The little goats were the cutest here. They jumped here and there like kids, played with their friends, lied on the other's body, or competed who jumped the higher, or chased after one another. I saw many adults and kids were closely contacting with the goats, touching them and hugging them. I couldn't help touching a little brown goat beside me. It looked up and saw me and then ran away to play with other goats. I also saw two little goats like twins competing who jumped the higher, or lied down on the head or the back of the other, very cute. They were playing like dogs, and sometimes bleated. When I was looking with my mind wandering, a female goat came to draw my clothes, and put her head against my hot chocolate cup in my hand. It seemed that it was attracted by the aroma of chocolate, so it always wanted to move close. But every time it was touching the cup, I withdrew the cup behind to let it work in vain. It did not seem to be too disappointing, but tried harder to press its head onto my cup. Of course eventually it did not get the hot chocolate. Then Zhang Tao and I went to the goat house, where most of the goats were big and were sleeping. Some occasionally came out to eat something, and then went back. Zhang Tao and I randomly "caught" a goat to take some pictures. When we came out, we found that the homestay mother and the sister were teasing a goat, so Zhang Tao and I moved close. We saw a little goat in the color of a cow, very cute and vigorous. The homestay sister made some strength to hug it, but it tried to escape.

The homestay mother told me a method. She asked me to sit on the rock beside, and the goat would come. As was expected, a yellow female goat slowly walked toward me. She saw my hot chocolate and showed a little bit gluttonous. However, she saw that I would not give it

A lovely goat　　　　　　　　　　　　　　　　Dannika and a goat

to her, so she left as if knowing the situation. I took the chance to finish my chocolate. After a while, the female goat that smelt the chocolate came again, running toward me when she saw my cup. I pretended not to give it to her, and let her lick a little bit and moved the cup away. She started to fawn, rubbed my jeans with her head, and used her body to rub my jeans. After trying a lot in all the ways which did not work out, she left. Then a little brown goat came from behind. When it saw my hot pink jacket, it bit my jacket firmly. In fact, it liked this color. We said that it was bad, but it just did not want to let me go. Suddenly it fell on the ground, and then stood up. It went to the feet of Zhang Tao's and mine, and easily jumped onto my leg. Therefore, I was pressed by a goat. Its feet were stepping and pedaled on my leg, very interesting. Due to the limited time, we soon had to go to the next place to "feed the birds", so we said goodbye to the little goat.

　　We rushed to the lawn to feed birds. The homestay mother gave us a bag of birds' food each and let me go to feed the birds. This place was very big. There're many different types of birds, including crow, seagull, big bird similar to vulture, duck and peacock. Some ducks were on the bank, taking sunbath, and some were swimming in water. Peacocks were walking beneath the peach trees in an elegant attitude, and crows flied disorderly.

It was not easy to feed the birds. First I had to get a bird or duck that was quite outgoing. Usually ducks are easy to get along well with, but you have to find one because there were so many ducks and they ran away when seeing people. It took me some time to find a duck, so I pour some food in front of them. They ate with their flat mouths, and made "gu gu" sound. I saw how they ate, and it was funny. Then I changed my target and decided to feed two pigeons. I followed the pigeons, and threw some food in front of them to let them taste the sweetness. As expected, the pigeons that had eaten the food slowed down, so I threw a handful of food again. They immediately tried hard to peck, and later even turned toward me to eat. But they did not look at me at all. I grabbed the chance and took a picture of them eating. Later I decided to feed the peacocks, which were really picky! They did not even look at those yellow rice-like things. So I took a handful of sunflower seeds. They got spirited when they saw the seeds. The mouth of peacock was sharp, and it was quite painful when they pecked me. I loosened my hand immediately. I realized that I did not have a lot of birds' food, so I returned to feed the ducks. I grasped some in hand, and they came immediately to peck with their flat mouths. It was fine at the beginning, but later they almost pecked my hand.

After feeding the birds, we asked the homestay family to send us to a restaurant in downtown recommended by a teacher to try fish and chips. It tasted OK. After lunch we went to visit a supermarket and shopping mall, and came back home very satisfied.

Today was very fulfilling.

This weekend was substantial.

These days in Canada are very rich!

April 29, Tuesday

# Rowing Dragon Boat in Shoreline Community Middle School

Rowing Dragon Boat

At 13:00 we gathered in the classroom of Mr. Allen's because we were going to row dragon boats. We started off after everyone was there on time.

We had to walk to the place. We had to cross a big bridge, a long boulevard and half lake before arriving at the destination. Because many people were going to row the boat and we were in two grades—Grade 7 and Grade 8, I found there were arrows drawn by chalk at intersections, indicating the way for us. I felt very warm seeing these straight arrows. It took us around half an hour to get to the right place. My legs were tired when I arrived. I felt tired. It was because that I did not do enough exercise usually.

Then we divided the groups, one for Grade 7 and one for Grade 8. The group of Grade 8 used a big boat and Grade 7 used three small boats. Ru Yunyi and I are in Mr. Allen's class, so in fact we are in Grade 8. However, we have mathematics classes with Grade 7 because at the school starting time we were divided into the team of Grade 7, and then transferred to Grade 8 as there were no more cabinets left for Grade 7.

Our first mathematics class was in Grade 7. Later it was not made clear, so we followed the mathematics of Grade 7. Therefore, we are still in Grade 7, while our class director is the teacher of Grade 8.

It was not easy to make things clear and divide the group. We rested beside. Seeing others busy taking off shoes and socks and running on the cement, we also took off our shoes. Zhang Tao said, "There must be a reason why they do so. What if later our feet are wet? Let's take off the shoes!" So we four took off our shoes and socks. The cement ground was cold and not comfortable to step on, not very smooth. Later we followed the tutor entering the warehouse. The warehouse was dark and cold without sunlight, and we walked on the ground as if walking on thin ice, smooth but very cold. After changing the life jacket, we came out to take the paddles.

Everything was ready. We gathered on the beach. As soon as Jin Ye and I walked onto the beach, our feet were like cuts by the knife. The beach was not made of fine sand but big debris. Walking on it was like walking on a sharp knife. These stones were angular, which made us not dare move the feet. When seeing our faces, the tutor told us to put on the shoes. We ran toward the shoes as if we got any great treasure. It was not difficult to walk on the cement. We changed our shoes but Zhang Tao and others did not. They still were walking on the gravels with a lot of difficulties. I did not know if her skin was thicker or she had a strong mind.

I was divided into the same group with Jin Ye. It was so good hat we could take care of each other. We first pushed the boat into the water. The boat was made of wood. It was not big, but very heavy, just like a rock of iron. It took us a lot of efforts to push it into water. Then we had to get onto the boat one by one. We were the last two. There was another student fixing the boat. He waited for us to get onto the boat, and to push the boat into water. After pushing, he jumped up very skillfully. After regulating the direction, we started to row the boat. I had never rowed a boat, so I did not know how to hold the paddle. After some guidance from Mr. Allen, I gradually understood. The one sitting in front of us was a main strength controlling the direction and speed of the boat. So I followed his movement to row the boat. Because he was the main force, the ones behind could rest but he could not. He had to use a lot of efforts to row without a stop. I was following his speed, so I used all my energy to row without a stop. My arms had lost consciousness and I still rowed. I never imaged that rowing a boat was so hard!

When we rowed the boat, the heavy paddle should be correctly grasped in hand, with the right hand holding the center of the paddle and the left hand on the handle of the paddle. Then insert the paddle into water to push backward. Besides realizing one's own actions and skills, the person in front must keep the speed and maintain the same rhythm of actions. Only with such a method can rowing a boat be fast and stable. Although I kept a consistent speed as the one in front, the one behind me always hit my paddle. It was because that we did not have the same rhythm.

The river was not deep but the water was very clear. We could see aquatic plants in the water. It gave some salty smell as ocean. Along the water, one side was a boulevard. A lot of green trees had their branches hanging. Below the trees, benches were set for people to rest. In general, tiredness was nothing when rowing the dragon boat in such a beautiful environment.

We slowly rowed one circle, and the situation suddenly became tense. The three dragon boats surrounded were competing with one another. We were ranking the second, and the third one was left far behind. The one in front of us was the one that Zhang Tao took, only one boat head distance, but it just prevented us passing. Finally we got beside them. A teacher behind pushed our boat and used the force to push their boat ahead. How bad he was!! All the members screamed to protest. But the people on their boat poured us with water. I was sitting in the front, so I kept off the water for the people behind. I got water splashed in my pants, sleeves, glasses and nose. I was so upset! So I accelerated the speed and forgot the aches, through efforts by all, the two boats arrived at the bank at the same time.

After we landed and took off the lift jackets, we pulled together the boat shoulder to shoulder to the land. Someone voluntarily went to the water to support. It seemed that he was totally soaked in water. It was easy to lift the boat to the bank, but we had to lift it to the rubber cushion, and then turn it, and lift to the shelf. The shelf was very tall, so we had to lift our hands like lifting dumbbells. Eventually we were made exhausted both in hands and legs, but there were still two boats waiting for us to move!

When everything was finished, it was already 15:30. We decided to go back home. Some people brought their bags so they could go directly home, but we four had to go back to school first and then go home. I had to walk 20 minutes to go home. It took half an hour from here to the school and I was very tired.

The rack of Dragon Boat

Finally we supported each other and got to the school. I immediately started my water supplementation mode: I finished the water in my cup and then had an apple that I left during the lunch time, very juicy. Then I had three strawberries offered by Jin Ye. At last I had two pieces of soda biscuits to supplement my energy. I felt not enough, so I had a glass of juice for lunch. When I got home, I had another glass of water. Eventually I had all the water lost and felt energetic again. I started to review my studies because the mid-term examination is coming soon. I am quite busy but have to review alone. Suddenly I miss the teachers and the students in school back in China. They surely are busier than me now.

May 2, Friday

# Visiting Primitive Forest

The school was organizing the five exchange students of us (four Chinese and one Thai) for hiking. This morning we four Chinese girls were sitting in the teacher's car, and the other one was in the car of another old man, who was the guide to bring us to hiking.

I was a little excited because we did not know where we were going for outing. I only knew more or less the direction, which was on the road beside my homestay family.

We got to the destination 15 minutes later. It was a forest. The guide brought us to enter, and picked some leaves and gave us one respectively. It was fresh like pine needle, but not that hard and long. It was soft, comfortable in hand, giving a special fragrance and a little bit sweet. I felt very relaxed with this fragrance. I held it in hand, and my palm smelt sweet and nice.

Entering the forest, we found the marvelousness of the forest. When I was in China, I rarely had the opportunity to go to such a big primitive forest. A creek was running quietly far, the sound of which we could hear. A lot of trees were as tall as into the sky. In our sight, we could see some stone bridges and hear silvery tweets. All kinds of grass blossomed flowers all over the ground. A wandering and long path had been made by the steps of people. In fact it was made by fallen trees and branches, maybe for hundreds of years and decades, so it was softer than carpet.

The old man guided us, introducing plants to us. Some trees were straight, some very solid but not tall. He said that different trees had different meanings. For example these thick, solid and tall trees, although the wood was not that strong, the primitive people found their uses. They took off the barks and twisted, and then bundled up for decoration or making clothes and hats. These tall trees were overspreading, which were very important for the primitive people. The

A big stump

leaves of such tree were medicine. Those hard but not tall trees were generally between 2 and 3 meters, not only solid but very straight, but they grow slowly. These wood is precious, usually only to be used to build ships or houses.

Then the old man introduced some different berries to us. They were in different shapes, but had something in common, such as similar sizes. However, these berries will only get mature in July, so they are very small now, like strawberries before mature. We walked and the old man found a lucid ganoderma, which was growing on a broken tree pile. It was as big as a human face. He introduced us quite excitedly, but did not get close to it. He told us not to damage it.

We continued walking along the creek. Suddenly we saw three dogs playing in the creek, splashing dome of water, very excited. The creek here was shallow and clean, with colorful pebbles on the bed. If you are well sighted, you could even see grey fish swimming below the pebbles. They were smart, and move very fast in between the seams of pebbles. After crossing a bridge, we saw something very big like lettuce planted at both sides of the bridge. One leaf was like a small banana leaf. The old man told us that this plant was used to cook before, having strong flavor. He picked up a little bit to let us smell. It was strong but had some fragrance as well, quite strange. After crossing the bridge, we saw more "lettuce" like this. I suddenly realized that the people were so intelligent that they could found so many things with unique values, and used for their survival. Then we saw several different wild berries, and also the type of trees that had fragrant leaves previously. However, the first one we saw was quite old, and the one we ran across now had tender branches, dotted with light green leaves. He picked up several leaves for us. We smelt and found that the tender leaves had better fragrance than the dark green ones.

We passed through the forest and saw an old castle in the front. According to the introduction of the old man, it was a film base and had been used to shoot a movie with the castle as the topic. It once belonged to a rich guy and his wife, and later he gave it to their son. It looked grand, with a forest on the back and facing the sea. In front of the castle there was a vast lawn, where the boarder between Canada and the U. S. could be seen. Over there were snow mountains supported by blue sky, very beautiful.

Walking on the soft lawn, the old man randomly picked up a grass and put it to the mouth, blowing different sounds, ups and downs. We also tried but failed. Suddenly I made some sound. I realized that I must straighten the leaf and tightly clamp with two hands, and then blow the part in between. The position must be correct, otherwise no sound will be made. The old man taught us another method, which was to keep it in the mouth and blow. It was quite difficult, and I was not able to make it, except occasionally several sounds.

With whistles and happiness, we entered another thick growth of grass. The old man picked up a flow, and arranged its pedals into a ring according to different directions, and then gave it to me. Some pedals dropped on my body. We learned in spirits. There was a lot for us to learn from the nature and it brings us great interests. We cannot learn all these in the class.

We walked closer, and he found some sharp stones and shell debris. He said that this place was used to roast clams. The sharp stones could be used to make tree branches into rod, and he showed us how to do it. As expected the barks could be easily peeled off.

We walked across the lawn and entered another forest. All we saw was the things like lettuce previously. We smelt something strong smell. We also found something sticky like glue on the trunks. The old man said that it was seeped from the trunk, which was edible. I did not resist the curiosity and picked up a little bit with clean wood rod, and dipped with my finger to dry. There was no flavor at the beginning, but after a while I found that my throat was very comfortable, and slightly bitter. The old man took out something that he made before. He poured this sticky thing onto a shell, and then ignited it as a candle. It can be used to hunt, to attract the attention of animals.

We passed a section of the forest and found a tree lying on the ground, chopped into halves. He said that this tree had a history of 700 years. I saw its growth ring, which made me get some intensive phobia. A lot of plants were growing on the trunk. Bypassing the trunk, we also found some blue debris of bird eggs. After crossing a bridge we found some fungi on the tree piles. Some were in grey with white edges, and some had a round of patterns in different colors, and some were like little umbrellas. We also found a small sticky animal, similar to snail without shell. It looked like a baby but I dared not put it on my hand. After a while the old man found one bigger in the trees, creeping like snail. Where it passed, some sticky liquid was left.

At noon, the old man led us to leave the beautiful virgin forest.

The last class in the afternoon was armature class. Ru Yunyi and I continued to do Sock Monkey. Today was a wonderful day.

A snail without the shell

May 3, Saturday

# Cooking Chinese Food in the Homestay Family

Today is Saturday. I invited Zhang Tao to my homestay family and planned to make a Chinese lunch for them. Early in the morning, I wandered a lot to meet Zhang Tao, and then we went to the supermarket to buy some food for lunch.

We got home at 11:20, and we started right away. The first dish was fried tomato with eggs. After taking all the necessary things, Zhang Tao was responsible for cutting tomato and I scrabbling the egg. Although we both knew how to cook, we had not done it for a long time. I almost forgot to heat the fry pan. After preparing, I started cooking. I first poured the egg into the pan. All the fry pans that the homestay family had were flat, and the scoop was soft, which I was not used to. This fry pan was not easy to get sticky, so I fried the egg very tender, and then poured the tomato into the pan. Soon tomato became soft, indicating that it was going to be done soon. I added a little bit of salt and turned down the fire. Because I was not used to the kitchen and afraid that the flavor of the dish would not be good, I tasted it and found it almost with no flavor. I added more salt but still no flavor. After adding three or four times, I found it to be the correct flavor. Maybe the salt here is different from that at home, or maybe I was too prudent with the quantity that I added.

The next dish was fried green pepper with sliced potato. I washed both the pan and the scoop, when Zhang Tao has already started to peel off the potato with knife because we did not find the thing for peeling off potato. On half way, the homestay mother came. She found something specially for peeling off potatoes for us. Soon we finished this. Then we had to cut the potatoes into pieces and then slices. We also had to soak them in water to get rid of some starch. When the potatoes were in water, Zhang Tao and I started to prepare green peppers. We cut the peppers into halves, and took out the things in the middle and cut them into slices. We turned and saw the bowl with potato slices covered with a layer of white thing. The potatoes abroad has really a lot of starch. We poured the water and started to fry. Because the potatoes were quite hard, we first fried them. Zhang Tao did this dish.

When she was frying potato slices and green peppers, I started to prepare the next dish: garlic broccoli. I decided not to cut the broccoli but to use hand to bend them. First I had to clean the broccoli well, so I carefully washed the outside, and then layer by layer to the inside until the whole broccoli was made into strips. The whole broccoli was not big. Then I had to cut the garlic. I peeled the garlic and used a machine to protrude the garlic. However I did not know how to use it well. I had to flatten the garlic and then use a knife to cut. After cutting, Zhang Tao had almost finished her potato slices. She put some salt and felt the flavor was light, so she added a bit more salt. However, nothing is perfect. Because she did not pay attention, a lot of potato slices were stuck to the pan and made the pan covered with a layer of dirt, difficult to remove. So she gave the heavy task of washing the fry pan to me, and went over to fry the broccoli. I had to use cold water to rinse the pan over and over again, and wipe it with a mop. It was not easy and eventually I used my nails to remove the dirt. Luckily Zhang Tao gave me a mop to make my work easier.

Garlic broccoli was made. Although it was not of big quantity, it was very nice. We counted that we had made three dishes, but our plan was to make four. What could we do? OK, let's make a cabbage. It was already 12:35. We had to hurry. Zhang Tao did not know how to make cabbage, so I started working alone. I peeled off the cabbage and cleaned with it water. Then tore them into small pieces. I took out a sausage from the refrigerator and asked Zhang Tao to cut into pieces for later use. Then I prepared half bowl of water. I heated the pan and put some oil into it, then fried the sausage first before putting the cabbage. When the cabbage was softer, I put some water on top and waited. When the cabbage was totally soft, I added some soy source to make some color and add more flavors. Then I added some salt. It was done.

It was already 12:45. The dishes made were cold. I heated them in the microwave and then served them onto the table. When Zhang Tao was serving the table, I filled the rice into the plates and took them out. The rice was well done. After the table was set, everyone sat down to eat lunch.

The homestay mother did not stop cheering when she saw the colorful vegetables, and said a lot of "thank you" to Zhang Tao and me.

At a popcorn shop

Dannika who disliked vegetable had a lot, but her boyfriend did not like eating vegetables. It seemed that he is allergic to vegetable, so he could not eat a lot. I felt guilty. Because I am not good at cooking meat, I cooked vegetables today, except ham and egg. I tasted every dish and found that I was pretty good at cooking. The dishes were cooked by Zhang Tao and me in one hour. The homestay mother happily said that she would like to have another meal like that. I felt so warm in heart. I did not expect that the foreigners liked Chinese food so much. In the afternoon I went to the shopping mall with Zhang Tao and went to the supermarket. I bought some popcorn because I won a coupon of popcorn in the camping on the Easters. I could spend 15CAD. So I used the money to buy a bag of popcorn, which was good. The store had different types of popcorns, with fruit or cream flavors and different colors. Zhang Tao and I ordered a caramel-flavored popcorn. We said that in China popcorn only has the original flavor, not like here, people had a lot creations and even made popcorn stores into chain.

Then we went to a clothes store where the sales were crazy: five dollars for three, or buy one and get two, or buy one and the second one 5 dollars. I did not care about the discount, but selected a sport pants without any discounting. The fabric was very comfortable and it was loose. When I went to pay, I found that it only cost 8 Canadian dollars. I thought it must be over 10. So the pants are less than RMB 50, incredible!

Later we went home. Today I walked a lot and my legs were tired. I lied down on bed right after coming home. However, I feel very satisfied, especially happy with the praise of the homestay family for my Chinese food. I did not expect Chinese food to be so welcomed. I have to work harder and make more Chinese dishes for my homestay family. Let them taste the flavors of Chinese food. In fact we have "A Bite of China".

May 4, Sunday

# Some Thinking and Feelings

Thinking at a wooden table

Today I had a lazy sleep in the morning and got up at 8:50. The mother went out early in the morning, and came back home after I finished shower. She asked if Dannika and I had breakfast. I said no and she asked Dannika to make some breakfast. After having some simple breakfast, I went back to my room for a rest. Then I reviewed some mathematics. The morning passed very fast.

I had lunch quite late, a sandwich and some celery. Although it was simple, I got quite full. After lunch I felt tired, maybe because yesterday I was too busy. I went back to the room to take a nap, and woke up after 15:00. When I got up, I realized that I had not done my homework of the foreign school, so I started doing it. The homework was only to answer one question. It might be easy for foreign students but very difficult for me. I had to read and collect all necessary answers to the question. It was social homework. I brought books back home because I did not understand very well at school, so I decided to consult the dictionary and understand all the contents before answering the question. I got shocked because I could barely understand the book, not even the general meaning. There were many names of places that I did not know at all, such as Euphrates, Tigris and Delta, etc. There were some special terms. Although I got the Chinese equivalents, I had to find out the meanings after a while.

There were not a lot of contents, but a lot of new words, nearly one page. I understood more or less the contents but still was a little bit confused. So I put the Chinese words into the book to compare and got the overall idea. The translation might not be correct. Eventually I made myself clear and found in fact the question was quite simple. I found six reasons and wrote them all. The answers were in the book. I was thinking that the homework for the weekend was only a question whose answer could be copied from the book. If I understood the book, it might only take me ten minutes to finish (including the reading time). If I were in China, homework usually took me three to four hours. This is another difference between Canada and China.

The homestay mother once told me that kids should be like kids. In childhood, kids should play and broaden the mind, accumulate knowledge from playing and travelling instead of reading a lot. It is true that there is a lot of knowledge in books, but the knowledge to be grasped by kids is not all in books. Instead some should be grasped through life experiences. For example, when we were learning things about plants in the primitive forest, although I could not totally understand the English that the old man said, I could basically know the general meanings. We did not know some edible plants at all, but I only learned after tried. Practice gives real knowledge. China has a legend of Shennong Tasting Hundred of Grasses. I guess it is the same meaning.

It reminded me also of the picking up trash in the streets organized by our school. I would not do so before even in my own community, and rarely picked up trash. I sometimes felt embarrassed. Everyone said that protecting environment is the responsibility of all. Who really picks up rubbish when seeing some? In Canada, the school organized us to pick up trash. People would pick up a cigarette end on street, or plastic bags and cans in grass. It is not really true that foreigners do not throw trash randomly because sometimes I see it in the street. However, people have the consciousness of protecting environment and are active in behavior. Naturally trash will not easily appear. The activity of organizing us to pick up trash was to educate us the importance of environmental protection. This gave us a deeper impression than simple teaching.

I also remembered the dragon boat race. In China I only saw this in books and on TV, but it is so popular here even though the dragon boat was invented in China. The boats are different. We made a joint effort to push the boat into the water. At that time the teacher called everyone to move the boat because it was quite big. When we moved the boat out of the storage room, we had to make a return, because the boat was long and it requested the cooperation of everyone. The ones behind should not be impatient, and should support the tail. The ones in front should not return too fast so that the ones behind could handle. After the head of the boat was out, the ones in front should not move, but wait for the ones behind to return to continue. To push the boat into water, more active cooperation of all was requested. The last person that pushed the boat was voluntary because he was not only pushing the boat into the water, but should jump onto the boat at the same time. He was also the main force of the rowing of boat, controlling direction and speed of the boat. When the boat was in water, everyone had to row in concerted efforts, otherwise the boat would not move forward if the paddles hit each other. Everyone's rowing speed was also important and both those in front and those behind should be cared. No one should stop due to fatigue or aching because other people would be affected and they would have to spend more time to compensate yours. On the other hand, those on the bank should not be idle, but help because the boat became very wet in water after a long time and the gravity of the boat itself would be increased. When the boat was turned upside down, we would be prudent and take care of our teammates to avoid the one at the opposite side be hit by the boat.

I have been in Canada some time and gradually realize the different education between the two countries. I cannot say that the education in China is not good, but it focuses more on grasping knowledge for the students, while in Canada they focus more on the overall development. They are weaker than us in military, but better than us in terms of environmental protection and coordination. This is what we should learn from them. Under the situation of not staying behind in studies, I should pay attention to education in other aspects to make myself develop. I have had many new attempts during these days in Canada. People might think they are good, but I have made a lot of efforts and adaptation. I am trying to fuse into the totally different studying environment. I hope that when I go back, people will see a well-developed student in many aspects instead of a student that only know studying, or only care about studying.

The trip to Canada not only provides me with the opportunity to study and to experience a foreign life, but it will become a trip of transformation in life as well.

May 6, Tuesday

# Carpenter Class (Process Writing)

### Sketching

We started the course of carpenter in the third week in Shoreline. The teacher was a very nice mid-aged guy. We called him Mr. Mark. Our first step was to sketch. In the first class, the teacher drew a sketch of flashlight on the blackboard and gave each of us a grid paper. After the sketch on the blackboard was drawn, we counted the grids to paint according to his specifications. It was quite difficult because the teacher was talking in English and many words were not very clear for me. What's more, our desks were too far from the blackboard. I could not see well the centimeters that he wrote, so I half guessed, and then discussed with the classmates beside me to draw. After class, I went to the blackboard to confirm. Such a sketch of flashlight took us two classes' time. The next classes were to practice 3D drawing, which was quite easy.

### Making proto

Because everyone had different progress, Mr. Mark gave each of those who had already finished a wood block, and took all of us to a workshop, where machines were placed. He took us to the front of the drilling machine and made a display. Because there were too many people in front, we did not see very well, and had to do it after seeing what the people in front of us was doing. The machine seemed to be terrible. When you turned it on, the horsepower became very strong, and an iron drill inserted on top of it started rotating at a high speed. You had to press the handle beside and push slowly, align well and push downward. The second push should be harder. I did three holes, and went to another machine to drill the fourth. This time the hole to be made was small, and it was not so terrible as the machine just now, as I was braver. But I did not know how to operate, so my friends helped me.

Making a flashlight in the carpenter class

After drilling the wood block and successfully passing the teacher's inspection, we started the next step: to cut off the excessive part of the block. It sounded simple, but it was very difficult to do. The thin place was easy to cut, but the thick part was difficult to cut. I could not use my strength, but had to knock the block (this was my own idea). After cutting the edge of the wood block, it was time to cut the angle. Because the big cutter was taken by Zhang Tao, I had to use the small cutter. However, after knocking for a long time, only a small crack was made. I turned to look at Zhang Tao and she had already cut off one angle. I saw her face and realized that even the big cutter was difficult. She was obviously "grinding her teeth". After she finished using the big cutter, I borrowed it immediately. The big cutter was heavy, but very useful. A piece could be easily cut off by one cut. But after some time, I was exhausted. I continued to use wood to knock. With the big cutter, the wood rock soon "surrendered".

The next class was to grind the wood block. It was to polish the block including its inside. It was not easy to polish, and it took us two classes. Then we changed a sand paper and then oiled it. Firstly I dipped some oil with brush to apply to the wood block. When the block is stuck with oil, I used another red sandpaper to grind the oil. Then I applied oil, and then ground. After repeating this seven or eight times, the wood would become super smooth as if waxed. No pains, No gains. In order to make the wood block bright, I spent almost two classes' time!

## Welding circuits

After we ground the wood block and submitted to the teacher for inspection, he gave me some wires and rubber rings, asking us to assemble them first and then weld. We came to the room for welding wood, which could only contain 4 people. So I stood outside the door, but found many people jump the queue, and some did not realize that it was full, and entered without worry. I waited like this until there were only three inside, and then I entered.

Firstly I used pliers to pinch off the rubber parts at both ends of the wire. I did not have a lot of strength, so I called the girl beside to help me. Then I connected the pinched off end with a piece of iron wire and then covered it with rubber ring. Then I pinched off an iron wire, and continued the previous procedure, connecting the place pinched off with another iron circuit, and covered it with rubber ring to weld the joint. Although only three places were to be welded, it was already difficult for me. I took the welding machine, which emitted a lot of heat.

I was trembling. What was this? I had never seen this before, which must be super hot. I carefully touched the welding end but only saw heat emitted out without other reaction. After a while still nothing happened. Therefore, I spotted the welding head on different welding places but failed. Jin Ye was beside me, and she said that it would be fine by putting the welding head at the place to be welded. I tried and it did not work out. When I decided to put back the pen, the pen point touched my thumb and suddenly I felt pain. I looked carefully and found the place burned red. It seemed that the thumb would have a scald. I did not expect that such a hot temperature could not weld. Why? I continued for two classes of welding, although got my two fingers hurt, I succeeded in welding three places. Then what I should do was to connect it with the button. I gently passed the iron wire to a small hole, rounded and then welded. It was easier to weld this place. But after a long time I did not see the effect. I thought it was done, so I gently pulled it. Out of my expectation, it got broken. The bell rang for class was over, so I decided to continue welding the second day. Like this I used two more classes to weld. Jin Ye and I did the welding, just so-so, and gave it to the teacher to check, but was rejected. He made an example and asked us to continue the next day.

On the second day, Jin Ye took the tin wire that the teacher gave us and melted it. Then she dipped the tin solution to her welding place and succeeded. I got burnt twice, so I had a deep fear for it. So Jin Ye helped me with the welding. Then I used dryer to make the rubber ring shrink so that it would not fall off. This time the welding was very successful. The welding project that took me more than two weeks eventually ended.

### Carving steel pipe

Finally I welded the circuit and connected it successfully, which made me very happy. So I went to make steel pipe with a good mood. This steel pipe was inserted in the previously drilled small hole, and could make the connected bulb pass through.

A boy in front of us was also going to make this, but none of us knew how to do it. So we called the teacher and he demonstrated it in front of us. After cutting, the steel pipe dropped in the wastes below and could not be found because of carelessness. Therefore he took an abandoned steel pipe like his, which was quite smart.

When it was Jin Ye's turn, I found a steel pipe fallen aside. I wanted to pick it up but found it was super hot, which almost burned me. I suddenly realized that it must be the steel pipe dropped by the boy just now. When I was hesitating if I should give him the pipe or not, I found that he had installed the steel pipe already. OK, I could take this as an example.

The procedure to make the pipe was not complicated, but several components were to be replaced. Because it was necessary to drill different holes, I had to make a funnel shape and then a spiral shape. After I helped Jin Ye, she came to help me. But I did not get the recognition from the teacher because he thought the hole was too small. He said that he would guide us next class. I went to ask Ru Yunyi, and she said that we only changed components twice and still left the expanded components. I thought over. When the teacher did the demonstration, he only said twice! I was frustrated.

But Ru Yunyi encouraged us, and said she would help us next class. On the second class, she put aside her task and came to help us. I was moved by her friendship. I showed the steel pipe done to the teacher, and Ru Yunyi went to help Jin Ye.

Upon approval of the teacher, I used glue to stick these wires. When I doubted why Jin Ye did not come, I found a problem. The socket of the glue gun could not be plugged. I asked the teacher for help. Later, I found that I did not know how to open the glue gun. Was that switch behind me? I carefully pressed it. It was correct, and the glue gun started to react. Because the power supply was turned on, the glue was very hot. After adding the glue, I had to lean the wood block to prevent the glue from leaking to other places.

After making the glue, the teacher gave me a piece of steel. Finally I cut the steel and the class was over. The next class was to grind the steel, which would not be easy. Ru Yunyi failed in one class, so for sure it would take me some time.

## Grinding sheet steel

Today is Wednesday. The last class in the morning was carpenter. My main purpose was to grind the four angles of the sheet steel, and grind the edge.

With the bell ringing, we entered the classroom. I asked Ru Yunyi to set an example for me as she was in the same progress of grinding sheet steel. I picked up a table and then a random fixing frame on the corner. I opened the frame and put the sheet steel into it and tightened it. It must be tightened, otherwise the steel would drop during grinding. After the sheet steel was fastened, I went to look for a filer to grind the steel pipe. There were two kinds of files, one of which had grid patterns and the other had oblique. Grinding also comprised two steps: the first time using the file with grid pattern, and the second time with the oblique. The first time was to do a general grinding, and the second time fine grinding.

Grinding requested certain skills. The first time was sawing type, when energy should be used both on top and on the bottom. For the second time, grinding should follow certain direction from up to bottom in rhythm. Firstly only the four corners and two edges were to be ground, and efforts should be made to make metal powder drop to achieve the effect. After grinding, you would find out the fastening frame with silver powder. I looked at the powder and felt very proud.

The first grinding was quite complicated, which took me half a class. After the teacher checked and approved, I came to fine grind. This time the file with oblique pattern was chosen. We only had two of these files, so Jin Ye and I got one respectively. It was not necessary to loosen the fastening frame but to directly grind on top. Because the file had oblique pattern, sometimes it gave harsh noise. I could not stand it, and I was afraid that the iron rod would not stand. Ru Yunyi said to me beside, "The sound is good. If you cannot stand it, you can grind more gently!" Then she set an example for me. I took her method and as expected the noise was reduced, and the speed was faster. After grinding the corners, when I was planning to loosen the fastener, the teacher called us to the class. We had just finished the flashlight, and were going to make a wooden car, so the teacher first told us the requirements because some of us had already finished the flashlight and were already preparing for the car. The teacher taught them how to make wood blocks and draw the sketch. We three hadn't finished and watched beside. Let's learn first. In fact it was just to adhere the drawn sketch onto the wood block, and then stick with glue. The glue would dry quite slow, taking around 1 hour.

Temporary course for wooden car finished very soon. I returned to the room to continue grinding the sheet steel. When I was grinding the edge, Jin Ye came to grind as well. We both continued working hard. There was only five minutes left, and for sure we could not finish, but we still accelerated. After the bell at the end of the lesson rang, we were still grinding until the teacher came to call us. We could only do it next class. I felt it a pity. I looked down to my hands and found them full of bright silver powder, which was for sure stained on my hands when I was grinding. The next day I had to continue grinding the steel.

Hopefully the next day I could finish grinding and then enter the next step—to use sand paper. The last process was to install battery into the wood block, and use small snails to fix the sheet steel.

After several weeks my self-made flashlight was done. I could not help using it in a place with shadow during daytime. I showed my homestay parents my work, and they praised me. I also took pictures and sent them to my parents by Wechat. It was my first handcraft. All the hardness has gone. I feel very happy!

Blue Sky and Nice Street

May 10, Saturday

# Buffet Lunch in Downtown

Buffet dinner at He Ji Restaurant

Today was Saturday and I wanted to relax myself, so I had an appointment with Ru Yunyi to go downtown at 9:30. We took the bus to downtown. First we went to a bookstore that also sells high-priced souvenirs. For example, a notebook cost 14 CAD. It was nice but too expensive. In China RMB 14 would be enough for a good notebook. Later we went to the bookstore and the stationary store. It was like Phoenix Book City in Suzhou SIP. The bookstore was big but there were not many books.

It took us the whole morning to look around in the bookstore. Then we discussed where to go for lunch. I recommended a buffet restaurant that Zhang Tao had been to, only 10 CAD per person. She wanted to eat Burger King, but finally accepted my suggestion to look for that buffet restaurant. I remembered that Zhang Tao told me that the restaurant was behind a bus stop, but there were so many—more than 10—stops in downtown. How could we find it? We went along the street until the end. We found it not correct. How could we walk so far without seeing that restaurant? We had to go back, and decided to eat Burger King. But I still looked around. Suddenly I found the buffet restaurant across the road. We walked in a wrong direction.

The name of the restaurant was "He Ji", a buffet restaurant opened by several Cantonese. Now it was 13 CAD per person, but we still entered. The owner was very warmhearted. She talked to us in Chinese after finding out that we were Chinese, and gave us a very good position with sofas. She introduced us all the dishes. They served a lot of dishes, including corn soup, dumplings, sushi, chicken leg, fried chicken, salad, spring roll and mapo doufu. The staple food included steamed rice, fried rice and noodles, and some desserts. There were not as many species as in big buffet restaurants in China. We felt very happy to eat such Chinese food in the world of the western cuisine.

We ordered a lot and the female owner ardently took us to the seats and gave us several bottles of different spicy source. She arranged the table for us. They were very enthusiastic. Seeing the full plate of food, my stomach started to protest. We started immediately and the familiar flavor came over to the mouth. Sweet corn soup, delicious dumplings, crispy chicken legs and tender spring rolls. They were so good. We quickly finished the first plate. Then the owner gave us two small glasses of watermelon juice, which was fresh, cold and refreshing. Seeing us finish the first plate, she told us to eat more, expecting to make us full. We thought that the owner was very friendly. After taking care of us, she went to look after the foreign customers. Although her English was not very good, she used her discontinuous English and smile to treat those foreigners.

I wanted to order some more food. This time I ordered mapo doufu and the steamed rice. I mixed them together, and it tasted super good. The mapo doufu should be spicy but here it tasted sweet, slightly spicy, very good. It is said that the food in Guangdong is more sweet than in Suzhou. It is true. Many dishes today were sweet.

After lunch I had a cup of jelly and then rested in sofa. The owner saw that we were full, so she gave us a specially formed biscuit as the desert. Then she happily talked with us, asking if we were full and if the food was good. She also asked why we came here and how our studying and life were, etc. It was my first time seeing such an ardent owner. I rested in sofa with Ru Yunyi for some time and decided to leave. The owner came to say goodbye to us, and gave us a point card, inviting us to come again.

  We came to Mr. Liu's café after coming out from the restaurant. I exchanged some commemorative coins with Mr. Liu, wanting to give my good friends or collect them. Tonight I would sleep in Zhang Tao's home because my homestay family was busy this weekend.

Nice Street

May 11, Sunday

# Canadian Parade

The grand parade

At 8:00 this morning, I set off with my homestay family, carrying the camera, hat, cup, mobile phone and sunglasses, applied with sun cream. What was this for?

In fact today is the Canada Day (National Day of Canada, on July 1 every year, public holiday of the country). This day is to celebrate that the British North America Act reunited the three territories of U. K. in North America to a commonwealth, including Canada (the current Ontario and the south of Quebec), Nova Scotia and New Brunswick. This holiday was called "Dominion Day" (in French: Le Jour de la Confédération) and was renamed the Canada Day on October 27, 1982.

The parade today was unprecedentedly grand. The homestay family decided to take us to see the parade in the morning, which would start at 9:00 from Mayfair, one of the four biggest shopping malls that I have been to. The homestay mother drove us three girls to set out first, while the father prepared some chairs for us and followed us in a truck.

We got to a street in front of Mayfair at 8:10. All the houses were full of national flags, and both sides of the streets with chairs. People were randomly sitting on the ground or the chairs that they brought with them, or laid with one carpet. They talked to each other, ardently discussing the grand festival. At that time, no vehicles were in the streets, with only the kids playing, and adults crossing, someone even riding bicycles in the middle of the street. I looked at the people waiting on both sides, some were sitting on chairs with maple pattern, some lying on maple carpet, some sitting around tables covered with national flags and some wearing T-shirts with the pattern of national flag of Canada. The festival atmosphere was everywhere!

At 9:00 the parade started on time. First appeared a woman dressed in exaggerating gown like a royal family member. She was wearing a lot of nice hair decorations and carrying a cute dog. She slowly walked by us with a feather fan in her hand. Beside her there was a man dressed very well. He and the lady walked past us slowly, followed by a horse-drawn carriage. A carter drove the three horses with a whip. The three horses looked almost the same, with dots on their bodies, from dark to light. The carriage was white and elegant, carved with all kinds of patterns. Following them was a soldiers' square formation comprising around 100 soldiers of the same height. They shouted slogans and marked with organized military steps. Seen from the side, it was like only one person walking in front of us. They were in such a good order. I was sure that they spent a lot of time and energy on this square formation.

Then some motorcades appeared with so many vehicles and people. There were police cars, ambulances, excavators, fireproof trucks and tanks. I guessed that should be a display of the historical chapter of the Second World War. They honked and slowly passed by us. The drivers inside were waving hands to both sides. The officers were all very nice and friendly, fat with beard, similar to the roles in the cartoons, which added more atmosphere to the festival.

In the next two hours, more parade teams passed by us, none of which was repeated, including square formations of some high school students. Although every school had different uniforms, they had the similar style, usually two students in the front holding a board with the name of the school, followed by special performance, and then the real formation. The formations were all drum teams, with orchestra in the

The creative monocycle show

The beautiful skirt

front, followed by drums. Each school had different number of students, 50 as minimum, and nearly 200 as maximum. I liked the one with the most people most. When they walked toward us, it was marvelous! 200 people in red uniform, accompanied with drums, walked toward us in order. Besides school formations, there were military square formations. Although they were both formations, they were greatly different. Compared to those of schools, the military square formations were more vigorous. There were not many people, but their steps were better those that of schools. Some military trucks followed, adding more seriousness to the formations. There was a special square formation dressed in Scottish kilt. It was quite interesting. Men were all dressed in the

Scottish kilts. They marched with the same steps and performed instruments. I was so close that I could even see their hairs on legs under the kilts.

After the square formations there were teams of other countries, including China. The Chinese team was made of the people in China Town here, comprising dragon dancing and martial arts. The Chinese team was longer and bigger than the teams of other countries, which was very dynamic.

After the parade of square formations, there were promotions of brands, including milk, sunglasses and restaurants, and they even distributed some gifts in the parade.

At 12:00, the three-hour long parade ended. After sitting in a chair that I was not used to for more than one hour, I felt aching all over my body.

After going home, I had an easy lunch and took a nap. The homestay family decided to purchase some materials for the "beach BBQ" tonight. At 6:00 in the afternoon, the mother took us to the beach, and the father carried chairs and BBQ rack. Today the weather was great, and many people came to the beach for BBQ. I was choked by the smoke, which made my belly ache. Besides BBQ, many people came to the beach to play. I saw some young people dressed in swimming suits go to the lake to swim. The water was very clean, and they played and swam in the lake. The dogs did not get bored as well. The owners randomly threw some tree branches into the water, and then they rushed into the lake to pick up the branches. Some people played beach volleyball. The scenery here reminded me of what my father told me about his childhood in the village, especially in summer holidays.

After the parade for celebrating the Canada Day, the little beach was full of happiness and laughter. Suddenly I missed my own national flag. Every time when the Chinese National Day came, my father would set up a national flag on our balcony and let it swing in the wind. I miss you, my country, and I miss you, my parents. How are you doing?

May 12, Monday

# Happy Time on Lake after Dinner

The dinner today was BBQ, which was very abundant, including salad, sausage, hot dog, potato and chips. After dinner, I washed dishes with Lusia (a girl who newly came to the homestay family). After cleaning the kitchen, the family asked us to take Cooper, their dog, to the lakeside for a walk. Cooper was so excited as soon as he heard that we were going for a walk beside the lake.

Soon we got to the destination. It was the lake that I had been to. There were several lakes surrounded by trees in the forest. We walked along the small path in the forest and soon arrived at the first lake. This lake was big and the beach beside was also big. Same as usual, the homestay father picked up a tree branch and threw far. Cooper immediately rushed into water and held the branch in the mouth. After he landed, he shook his body to get rid of the water. The father wanted to take back the branch, but according to Cooper's character, he would not give him for sure. So the father picked up another from the ground beside, and Cooper immediately opened his mouth to grab the one on the ground. He was greedy! When the homestay parents were playing with the dog on the beach, Lusia and I found some ducks, three big ones and four small ones. The big ducks were staggering, and the small ones were floating on the water like hairy balls. The big ducks had rich feathers, and the small ones only had grey and black fine hair. This duck family slowly floated on the lake not far from us, as if they were also walking and appreciating the nice lake view. Lusia and I went to the other side and wanted to observe the ducks more carefully, but they did not pay attention to us, still very relaxingly swimming. Later I climbed to a small hill with Lusia and sat on a rock to appreciate the great scene. The sun was setting, laying the golden rays on the lake with some heat, very cozy.

Around twenty minutes passed, and we went to the second lake.

The homestay father and I on the Golden Gate Bridge

The sun had drawn its light, leaving the warm orange color on the forest, while the forest cut the color into small pieces and let them drop on the ground as blossomed flowers. The second beach was especially for dogs. People were rowing boats on the lake. They put the paddles on the boats, and sat in the boats smiling and enjoying the bath of the sunset, breathing the fresh air. It was a pleasant picture.

    As soon as we got to the second beach, the father bent and threw the branch in his hand into the lake using the same speed and gesture as before. Cooper went to the lake right away, splashing a lot of water. Soon he got the branch. But this time he was so smarter that he did not put the branch on the bank but to a place in the water close to the bank so we could not get it. Soon the waterside was floated with many branches. Then the homestay father called Cooper back to give a bath for him. The father poured some shower gel and rubbed out some foam, applied onto Cooper's body all over. Suddenly Cooper became a real foam dog. Taking this opportunity, the homestay father picked up a tree branch and threw it far. Cooper immediately submerged into water.

When he came back, the foam on his body were totally rinsed. It was for him to clean off the foam! Lusia and I also tried to make Cooper a foam dog once. After several rounds, Cooper became the beautiful Labrador, with bright black hair and piercing eyes. The water at the bottom of the lake could be seen, as well as the aquatic plants under the lake could be seen.

After Cooper finished shower, we went back along the previous way. On the way the homestay mother introduced us several plants. By coincidence I knew them all because the old man told me when I went to the forest last time. We got home at 8:50 pm. After Lusia took a shower, I also took a shower, and talked with my mother on video, and then went to bed.

This time the lake I visited was much more fun than before. I feel that I am already a member of the family and all my happiness and sadness was related with them.

Cooper

May 20, Tuesday

# A Normal Day in 100-day Schooling Trip

Accompanied by the enchanting sunshine, I went to school. The birds were singing as usual, and the flowers smiled. Ducks on the playground of the school lazily took the sunbath or ate green grass. Today is the first day of this week. The four-day holidays of the Canada Day ended. This week we would only have four days of classes. I was very satisfied with that. In Canada, if holidays are encountered, students do not need to make up the classes next Saturday or Sunday.

On the carpenter class, I used a whole class time to draw eight vehicles, which made my hand very tired. It took Zhang Tao two classes to finish the eight vehicles, so I was slightly proud of myself. Next class is arranged tomorrow, when I will formally start making the car. I am very excited. The flashlight has been successful, and I hope the car will be successful as well.

In the first class in the afternoon we went to row the dragon boat. I remembered that I walked a lot last time. But today, although it is the same place and the same road, I felt it quite close. Ru Yunyi and I talked about our stories in elementary school on the way.

She studied in Canglang Elementary School and I was in Baodai Elementary School. All the friends in the elementary school are on a different way. Now I am studying in Canada. What an incredible thing! When I told my father about the opportunity of schooling trip abroad, I was not serious, and did not expect that my father would support me to come here. I was quite nerdy and had never left my parents to live independently. On the other hand, I felt that I would be left behind in study, and I would not catch up with the lessons in China. Due to the language issue, I dared not to talk to foreigners in the street, not to mention to stay in a foreign family. However, my father supported me a lot. While I was reluctant to take all the examinations, I passed the exams like a miracle. Although I was not very willing to come abroad, the life here is really fantastic. I row boat, go camping, go to beach, BBQ, make flashlight, toy and car, plant flowers with the homestay family and have classes and communicate with foreign friends and so on. All these are what I could not achieve in China, and become normal in life. It has been a good choice to come to Canada by following my father's suggestion. I have relaxed myself and broadened my horizons. The most important is that I have slowly learned how to allocate my time well.

Without noticing, we came to the sea. We put on the life jackets, took the paddles and pushed the boat into water. This time I was sitting in the middle, with boys in front and behind, and Jin Ye was beside me. After grasping the skills, we felt it much easier than before, but still got a lot of water by the one in the front. Sometimes he suddenly exerted more energy and accelerated with the paddle, so my face was splashed with water. Sometimes he splashed water by turning. I got wet all over, as I was swimming in the river, and I smelt like the sea. Today we rowed very fast. We started the last but arrived at the bank almost at the same time as the first one. After landing, I discovered that my right leg was all wet, and the pants had changed color. So I went to the sun to dry it. After a while, I helped them again to push the boat into the rack. It cost me a lot of strength!

When we were about to go back, I found that my legs were so tired that I could barely walk. After staggering for nearly 1 hour, I finally arrived at the closest bus stop to take the bus. I was exhausted.

After waiting for 15 minutes in the sun, my pants got dry and the bus arrived. I got onto the bus with a lot of satisfaction. When I got home, I took out the homework of the carpenter class, and drew a car. Then I started doing homework of mathematics. After some time Lusia came back. She asked me if I would go to Dannika's dancing competition. I was interested and agreed because I heard that she had made a lot of efforts. I hurried to do my homework. When it was half done, the homestay father called us for dinner. After dinner, when I took the pen, the father said that the mother would come back right away to pick us up, and he would send Dannika first to the school so that we could get ourselves ready. So I had to stop to prepare. 15 minutes later, the mother did not come. When I was considering if I should continue with my homework, she came back to change clothes, and then she would take us out. So I gave up the idea of doing homework.

The dancing performance was held in Dannika's school, from 7:30 to 9:30 in the evening. I was shocked to know that we would come back so late, but I was embarrassed to refuse the family, so I accompanied them watching the show. It was great with a lot of creation. Every performance had its own features. I think Dannika did a good job, and her silver jacket and miniskirt were very cool. They were active on the stage, jumping here and there. The lights on the stage changed. When it became dark, many black shadows were moving, and the skirts were swaying, enlivening the atmosphere of the whole site. The audience could not help applauding.

I felt exhausted when getting home at 10:30 at night. I went to bed directly without shower.

The lake for rowing Dragon Boat

June 3, Tuesday

# Sick Days in Canada

I'm sick

I did not write journals last week due to my health. Today is my first journal-writing day after the sickness. Let me talk about the things which happened a few days ago.

The Sunday before last, after going shopping with Jin Ye, I felt legs tired and dizzy, so I went back home to rest in bed, and did not eat dinner. I went to bed after 8, hoping that I could go to school in good conditions the next day. However, I felt that the quilt was super hot during the night. I turned from side to side for nearly one hour, and slowly calmed down.

I had kept a glass of water on the bedside table before I slept. It was already cold. I wanted to throw it away but it was useful. Around 3 or 4 in the morning, I woke up again because of heat, feeling quite bad all over, and thirsty. My lips were broken. I saw the glass of water and drank some water. I looked at the clock and it was still early, so I continued sleeping. After several minutes, I got thirsty again, so I went to drink water and then went to bed. I repeated this several times.

At 6:00 in the morning, I got up again to drink water. This time I suddenly felt dizzy when I was sitting in bed. After drinking water I still did not feel good. I told the homestay family that I wanted to rest one day at home, because I felt dizzy. She agreed and asked about my physical situation.

The parents went out to work, and I stayed at home sleeping until 9:30. After I woke up, I still felt dizzy. I got up and walked a little bit, took a glass of water and drank it all. The whole morning I was drinking water. At lunch time the homestay father came back to make a little lunch for me. But I did not have appetite, so I left it after trying it.

I went to bed very early without taking a shower. On Wednesday the teachers were on strike, so we would not have class that day. I thought that since I would have Wednesday for rest at home, I could go to school on Tuesday. So I decided to keep myself well and see if I felt better tomorrow. If I felt better, I would go to school.

I took a glass of water and put it on the bedside table. At around 3 or 4 o'clock, I got up again to drink. In the morning I felt much better although I still had headache and no appetite. I thought I could go to school. The homestay family sent me to school by car. I did not take part in the morning exercises. I wanted to try but felt chest distress after a few steps of running. Also I did not attend the P. E. class but only stood beside. The whole day at school I felt quite bad, but thinking that tomorrow I could rest one day at home, I felt better. I would get back all the lost energy tomorrow.

I endured until Wednesday, when the Argentinian homestay girl left. I was awakened at 6 in the morning. She wanted to take some pictures. I more or less combed my hair, left it loose and went out quite dizzily after changing clothes. Then we stood there and took pictures for half an hour. I got very tired.

After taking pictures I went back to bed immediately. I woke up at nearly 10 in the morning. I looked at Wechat after I woke up. It seemed that all the friends went out in such a nice day to play, some going shopping, some watching movie and some going to eat Zongzi (Chinese rice dumpling). In the afternoon I talked to my parents on video. They were going fishing on the sea, feeling quite excited. I also seemed to be much better.

Thursday came as expected. When I woke up in the morning, I staggered up and fell down on the ground of my bedroom. I staggered up and felt super dizzy, and must go back to bed. So I told my homestay family that I did not feel well.

Unexpectedly, they told me that the school had communicated with them, and asked them to take me to the doctor, and let me stay at home today for rest.

I was deeply moved. In the morning the father took me to the hospital. When I was waiting in hospital, I felt dizzy again, and released a little bit after a massage. I waited in the same seat for more than one hour, which made me impatient. I only saw two people nearby. Would it take so long for one person?

Finally I was called in, and waited again for more than 10 minutes for the doctor. I almost went into coma. The doctor asked me about my physical situation, and then messaged my belly, said there was no big problem. He measured my temperature, which was slightly high, but OK. He told me to have some food that was easy to digest and would do me good, including bananas, apple jam and roasted bread. Going out of the hospital the homestay father went to buy the things that the doctor recommended.

Naturally bananas and apple jam became my lunch, with a piece of roasted bread. I was not interested in eating, but thinking of what the doctor said. The father went on purpose to buy these things. I ate some, and took a good nap in the afternoon, and tell my parents by video. They were very worried about me. I did not want them to be worried, so I did not talk with them about my sickness. On Friday I stayed at home again. I wanted to go to school, but the homestay mother said that I was not in good condition, so I stayed to rest. I inevitably was a little nervous thinking that I must have missed some work.

I stayed at home the whole week resting, sleeping, going to toilet, drinking water, chatting with parents by video and watching TV. I had no interest in doing homework or reading, but only lying in bed. I was wondering why I did not go to the doctor but only stayed at home resting. I suffered a lot.

One week later I felt much better. Although I still had headache, my stomach was feeling better. But this week I started coughing without stop. I finally went to school. I closed my mouth when coughing so that I would not affect others.

The sickness experience of one week is unforgettable. It was difficult for me, especially during those days. I was missing home. No matter how well the homestay family treated me, it could not be better than the care from my own parents. Friends are happily spending the

"June 1st Children's Holiday", but I am lying in bed without doing anything. It was a pity for me.

However, before I came, my father already told me that during the 90 days aboard, I would have a lot of happy time, and should cherish it; and many unhappy things to experience and stand. I would not regret if I have tried hard. I will remember these days when I was sick, and will remember the cares from the homestay parents and my classmates. Now the shadow has disappeared. There is still one month left. I will use this one-month time to experience more. Being sick can also be an experience. It reminds me of how my parents were taking good care of me when I was sick, and how I should confront the sickness. I have learned a lot, and become stronger.

Fresh leaves pop up from under the soil

June 6, Friday

# Family and Friends Are the Sources of Happy Life

After a simple breakfast, I went to school in the bright sunshine. Today is CC Day of our school. As long as you did the homework, you could go back home at 10:35. That is to say, only one class to be done.

When I got home, it was already 11:00. I was thinking about buying some breakfast because I really did not like the sandwich that they prepared. However, I saw that the restaurant beside was not open, so I decided to cook myself.

I found that the homestay mother was at home. I told her that I would prepare lunch for myself, thus starting. The food material was limited, only half a broccoli, four eggs and some rice. I took two eggs and scrabbled by fork, added some salt and then started to cook the rice. At the same time I cleaned the broccoli and cut it well. I also took some garlic and cut into minces. I would try to make fried broccoli with garlic and rice wrapped in egg.

When the rice was being cooked, I put some oil and heated the pan, then poured the minced garlic into the pan to fry. When the oil was hot and gave some noise, I put broccoli into it, and waited for a while before frying. When I saw that it was almost done, I added salt, and mixed the salt evenly. I tasted and found it light. The salt was so light, and the broccoli was hard. I had to continue cooking. So I added some salt, fried and then poured some water into the pan, which seemed to be boiling. I tasted it again, and still felt it too light, so I added more salt until I thought the flavor was fine.

I washed the fry pan and the scoop, and continued to heat the oil. I was going to make the rice wrapped in eggs. First I heated the pan with oil, and then poured the egg. Because the pan was not big and it was round, and not sticky, the egg formed a round immediately, and moved on the oil without getting stuck to the pan. When the egg was solidified, I used the scoop to turn it. Unfortunately I made a mistake, and the egg

BBQ by the homestay father

skin became a moon shape, which made me a little bit disappointed. But I still turned it. The egg skin was quite successful, with some defects but very tender, the same as those I had in China. Then I took out a plate and made the rice into a ball wrapped with egg. The dish was made. I added some ketchup. Now it had color, aroma and taste.

After the lunch was done, I felt quite proud. I showed it to the homestay mother and she praised me a lot. I had a good lunch made by myself, and it was my first time to do rice wrapped by egg. I felt very satisfied.

Tonight the homestay family invited their friends to come home for BBQ dinner. I had met some of them before. They were very nice, but I felt depressed. Knowing that I am from China, they asked me many questions about China for curiosity, and asked me if I was missing home. I said that the homestay parents took good care of me, but I still missed my family and friends after a while. An aunt said that she came to Canada as a student, and then stayed, having no family but friends here. But she was happy here. She was good at French, not English, while she got along well with her friends without any obstacles.

The dinner was made by a friend of the homestay family. He was a funny person, dressed very casually, and liked to make some faces or movements, or tell funny stories to make us laugh. We had dinner happily. I thought that the uncle was like Peter Pan. He looked quite as old as the homestay father, but the latter has white hair, while he has black hair. The two Peter Pans gathered, full of happiness. They did not worry about their white hair. I quietly sat beside, listening to their chatting, talking about their stories and their ideas.

The dinner started from 6:45 pm. We ate while talking. There was basically no silent moment. Someone talked to the person beside, and someone called the whole table to talk, announcing funny things in life. Everyone laughed. During the dinner, the laughter covered the aroma of food, and the words won over the hunger.

After dinner the homestay mother brought some ice cream for us. I was not interested in ice cream, but the uncle that cooked dinner ate a colorful ice bar, and showed off to me: "This is the color of rainbow, very beautiful. Do you want to eat it? I will not give you." Everyone was laughing. He bit the ice bar in big pieces, which shocked me. He also said it was cold when he was eating. The lady beside him took a spoon to eat fruit ice cream slowly. They had a sharp contrast. After he finished the last bite, his hands flew to his belly, and said, "My stomach is frozen", which made us laugh again.

This Peter Pan caused more laughter than this. He said to me, "You must eat well here to make you fat, so that when you take plane to go home, you can occupy two seats!" I said, "OK, I will try my best. You should come here more often to help me and guide me, otherwise I will not be able to get fat!"

Time passed by slowly. The sun went down, and it became cold. Peter Pan only wore a short-sleeve T-Shirt. He trembled and said to me, "It is so cold. Give your jacket to me, quickly!"

I said to him firmly, "No, I also feel very cold!"

He pretended to be unhappy, and took the table cloth to cover his body, saying, "Oh, I am much warmer, more comfortable!"

He said to the homestay mother, "Can you give me hairpins? I want to catch the table cloth so it will not go out."

Everyone laughed. The mother went into the room to get a jacket for him. He put on the jacket inside out on purpose, and caused a lot of laughter. At 8:45 pm, I felt very cold, so I told the mother that I wanted to go back to my room.

Today I cooked lunch in the homestay family, got to know a Peter Pan and some friends of the family, and enjoyed the happiness and coziness brought by the family gathering. People all need friends. I feel happy that I can integrate into their life.

June 9, Monday

# Public Buses in Victoria

Every morning when I go to school, I see three No. 14 buses passing by. Talking about public buses, I have a lot of contacts during my studies in Victoria. There are great differences between the buses in Canada and those in China.

First let me talk about the types of the buses here. There are two types of buses here. One is normal pubic bus, which is similar to that in China; and the other one is double-decker bus. If you are lucky to take the double-decker bus, and sit in the first row on the second decker, you will have a chance to enjoy a 3D feast. Facing a big and bright glass window, you can enjoy the beautiful views of streets in Victoria. The trees on both sides of the street drop leaves and flower pedals from time to time, offering a lot of romance. The buses are driving on the right, so some tree branches will touch the window and leave you a pedal. The feeling is that if there was a branch scratching in front of your face, you could smell the fragrance. I heard that in my hometown in China, there are also double-decker buses in Suzhou Industrial Park and beside the Taihu Lake, but I have never tried.

Now let me introduce the special designs of the buses in Victoria. When getting onto the bus, different people have different treatment. For example, for the old people or pregnant women, or passengers that walk slowly, the driver will press the bus low on purpose so that they can get onto it easily. For the people in wheel-chairs or old people that are unable to move freely, the driver will press the bus and put down a step, which was inlaid inside the bus and will bump up by pressing one button. Then a step will ride on the road or the bus stop, and thus the wheel-chaired people can get onto the bus smoothly. After they get onto the bus, the wheel-chaired old people will have a special seat. On both sides of the compartment there are rows of chairs that are flexible. Once an aged person in wheel chair gets onto the bus, the person that sits on

The coach with a special frame

the telescopic seat will give the seat and make the seat shrink. This way a space will be provided for the wheel chair. Some infant carts receive the same treatment. It is not easy to put wheel chair or infant cart into that position, the bus driver will wait patiently, and people will voluntarily help. Moreover, when such event occurs, the driver starts very slowly and stably. When they are about to get off, the driver will let them get off first, and people behind will wait. Meanwhile, the driver will put down that step to make it easier for them to get off. Then the people waiting in queue behind will get off. It can be seen that the old people living in Canada are very happy. In fact, I think helping others and being helped are both happy things.

If you want to get off at the next stop, you can press a button in the compartment. This button will be available at different positions and different areas of the compartment. If nobody gets off and there is no person on the bus stop, the driver will not stop because it will waste time. If you don't know whether the next stop is where you want to get off, you can directly ask the driver, who will tell you patiently. The bus drivers here know the routes very well like a map. They are familiar with Victoria. If you don't know the way, just ask them. Anyway they will enthusiastically and patiently answer your questions.

Next, let me tell you about the bus stops in Victoria. The bus stops here are not like those in China, which are full of all kinds of advertisements. Here only clean glass windows are at bus stops. Beside the bus stop is a column on which a table is pasted, indicating the time of the first and the last bus as well as the arrival time of buses at different sections. The schedules during workdays and on weekends are different. This way the people waiting will have an idea and will not miss the bus. The buses in Canada are usually on time. Sometimes there might be errors, but basically not more than three minutes. Once I was sitting on the bus, the driver found that he arrived earlier on the second stop, so he stayed on that stop for two or three minutes before leaving, so that the schedule will not be disturbed and the people behind could get on the bus on time. The bus stops in Canada do not indicate which stops for which bus because if you don't know which bus you are going to take, as long as one arrives, you can ask the driver, and the driver will stop beside the road to tell you which bus to take and when it will arrive. The drivers are all very nice, talking in a smooth and patient way, which will make you feel comfortable. When you get onto the bus but don't know which stop to get off, the driver will also tell you. This is impossible in China. We have too many people taking buses. If the driver has to answer many questions, he will be exhausted. Canada has a smaller population. Different environment makes different people.

Another thing worth introducing is the manner when getting on and off the bus. It is true that you should pay attention to your manner on the bus. When using the bus card, you should smile to the driver and he will smile back. When you get off the bus, you should say "thank you", and usually the driver will reply "you are welcome". Now every time when I get off the bus, I say "thank you" and leave in a good mood. I feel very warm when saying thanks to others or smiling to others. I think when I go back to China, I will also say "thank you" when I get off the bus, and give a smile to the driver when I get on the bus so as to bring better attitude to more people.

June 10, Tuesday

# The Unforgettable Homestay Family

The homestay parents

The beautiful garden of the homestay

Today we asked for food from the Chinese restaurant nearby to go. I was happy to eat Chinese food.

The so-called Chinese food in Canada is totally different from the food in China. The Chinese food here refers to spring rolls, fried rice or noodles, and the taste is quite sweet. People here don't know that China has so many different styles of cuisine, such as Sichuan, Cantonese, Anhui and Jiangsu styles…However, I still feel happy to eat Chinese food abroad.

Last time the homestay family bought Chinese food from the same restaurant. Today we had more or less the same dishes, such as cabbage in dry pot, fried rice, fried noodles, deep fried chicken, sweet and sour pork and spring rolls. I had a little of everything, and was very satisfied. We had dinner in the garden when the sun hadn't set down. I enjoyed myself eating Canadian style Chinese food in the golden sunlight. The only pity was that the dishes were not to my taste. Although they had

Chinese names, in fact they were not of home flavor. The dinner reminded me of my hometown Suzhou. I am sitting in the garden and eating dinner easefully, while my classmates are fighting for the final examination of the semester. I heard that Jin Yi reviews lessons until very late everyday. Also I enjoy the foreign food here, and my parents are enjoying delicious Chinese food. I miss my parents very much, but now my homestay parents are in front of me. I appreciate their care a lot.

My homestay mother is very hardworking. She has several jobs, one main job and several part-time jobs, and some work is for free. The homestay father is engaged in construction, responsible for painting and repairing machines. Usually he stays at home, but goes out to work when somebody calls. He seems not to have a fixed schedule. Although my homestay family is not very rich, they enjoy life a lot, and they live a cozy life. The mother has planted a lot of flowers, sometimes we even see hummingbirds visiting the garden.

My homestay family like outdoor sports. They go camping twice a year, one on Easter and the other on the Thanks-giving Day. Sister Dannika and her father both like honkey a lot. We went to Vancouver to see Dannika's match. She looked very cool with her honkey outfits. Sometimes the family go sea fishing or camping as they bought caravan and boat. Besides enjoying the family life, they have many close friends that come often to chat and do BBQ. The family is very nice. Sometimes they invite friends to stay over night.

After I came to Canada, I have never had dinner outside, but always at home. My homesfay family do good dinners. Usually it takes them one to two hours to prepare. The homestay father cooks very well. The sandwich he does is very good. He also likes to make roast chicken, and dishes never repeat. At least during my stay here over two months, he did roasted chickens several times, and none of them were the same. When I was sick, the family took good care of me. I was lying in bed in my bedroom during those days, and the mother brought me breakfast, lunch and dinner, caring about me. The father took me to the hospital. In weekdays, they even came back to see me during their lunch breaks. They took me to try many new things. In the whole team that came to Canada for the schooling trip, I am the only one that has gone camping, sea fishing and am was the first one to go to Vancouver, and taking the big boat. So many firsts! I am full of appreciation to my homestay family, for their cares during these two months. In the remaining less than one month, I should do something that I can do for them.

The Chinese students that come to Canada together are going to Vancouver this Saturday, but I cannot join them because my family will take me to Vancouver as well. I will have to come home at noon of Friday, and stay over night in Vancouver on Friday and Saturday. They will take me to visit some famous places. Comparatively speaking, I will have more in this way than going with the teachers there because the teachers will be there for only one day, and they have to gather at 5 o'clock in the morning, and will arrive in Vancouver at about 9:00. Then at 5 pm they will take the ferry again, so they have limited time, minus the drive and the lunch time. Although I feel it a pity that I cannot go with my friends to Vancouver, it will be very nice to stay with my homestay family in Vancouver.

After dinner I washed dishes with Dannika. Here they accumulate the dishes several days and then wash, so the workload is heavy. But I cherish such opportunities. In less than one month I will go back to China. I am excited but also feel reluctant. It is my luck to meet such a nice family. Now I should use the time to help them do things that I can do. It is a beautiful thing to contribute and to get reward.

I only have less than one month to be together with the blue sky, green trees, beautiful flowers and all kinds of people here. I will extremely cherish this period of time to draw a perfect full stop for my trip to Canada.

The homestay parents and I at the bay

June 13, Friday

# We Have Graduated!

The calligraphy for my teacher

Today is the last day of this term; tomorrow will be the summer holiday. We are all quite excited, but feel more reluctant to go. Three months passed very quickly. I have been together with these students for more than two months, but now we are going to say goodbye. I feel very bad. The teachers here are so nice, and the students are like a little United Nations. We have different skin colors and different personalities, but we get along well. Now we will say goodbye.

This morning I came to school very early on purpose because today I had to say goodbye to the school and maybe I will never come back. I have to cherish every second here. The teacher told us that the morning ABL, the exercises were cancelled, and the teachers would say something in the classroom.

Ru Yunyi did not get to school on time as usual, which made me very worried. We said that we would bring gifts to our classmates.

Luckily she arrived before I got collapsed. The work this morning was to watch a movie, but Ru Yunyi and I did not because we had other things to do. We had to finish the sock monkey that had not finished before. Sock monkey is the first toy that I had done in my life. Except for the teacher's oral help, I did it all by myself, so I tried my best to finish it. During the whole morning, I sewed the four limbs and the two eyes, only the tail and the mouth left.

At 11:00 am, the teacher took us to the stadium downstairs, which became a temporary meeting hall. Today is not only the last day of school for Grade 6 and Grade 7 students before summer holidays, it is also the graduation ceremony for Grade 8.

Here Grade 9 is Senior 1, so middle school graduates from Grade 8. Many girls of Grade 8 were dressed in nice skirts. They would sing and dance in the hall, and there would be some award-receiving activities. The teachers made some pictures on PPT to show us all the activities of the school's teachers and students during the year and last semester. Everyone smiled happily seeing these pictures full of sweat and happiness. It could be seen from the pictures that the school had rich activities, such as rowing dragon boats, pretending ghosts on Halloween, camping, observing astronomical phenomena and setting up tents. Most of these pictures were filled with smiles, but more sweats and happiness. Everyone could see from the pictures that the teachers and the students got on very well during the semester. The teachers were laughing a lot, and the students made faces lying on the grass. This kind of pictures is enormous. The pictures were loaded with the beautiful memories of teachers, and students, of the year, being the most precious records.

Students of Grade 8 graduated today. As a student of Grade 7 in Class 1 of Grade 8 (I was divided into Grade 8 because there were not enough cabinets on the class when the school started), I was happy for them. They passed on the platform, and then shook hands with the teachers and hugged then standing in a row below the platform, and received the red hats from the teachers. I did not understand the meaning of red hats (maybe indicating graduation from middle school?). Certainly they expected that the students would have happy life in high school. Many teachers cried on the graduation ceremony, which indicated the good relationship between the teachers and the students. We four had lunch on the lawn of the school, sitting on the slope of a mountain, enjoying the sun. We were very happy to enjoy the "last lunch".

We watched a movie in the morning. It was "Frozen". Although I had watched it twice, I wanted to watch the third time because I like it a lot. The movie was in English without subtitles, but I felt it much better than with subtitles. I could understand it, maybe because I had watched it twice. After watching the movie, Ru Yunyi and I sent the gifts during the short time, and I was very happy as if I was sending greetings. I was satisfied with seeing their smile when receiving the gifts. But I felt it a pity at the same time. Today is the last day. I don't know if I would meet them ever again. The two more months together are also predestined.

Today the summer holidays started. They graduated and we graduated as well. It reminded me of my graduation from elementary school, when I felt so reluctant to leave my schoolmates and teachers. Now this feeling appeared in my mind again. Although I only stayed here for less than three months, and did not have too much communication with them, I had the same feeling.

We graduated from Shoreline today. Ru Yunyi, Jin Ye, Zhang Tao and I took some pictures together in front of the school gate. I will keep the beautiful memory of Shoreline deeply in my mind.

A picture in the Education Bureau

My Shoreline classmates and I

Graduation picture of Grade 8 of Shoreline Community Middle School

A photo of my class in Shoreline

My certificate of completion of the program in Shoreline

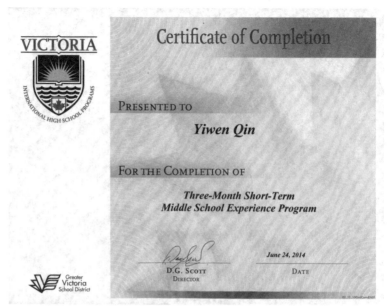

A photo before leaving Victoria

Farewell to my teachers and classmates

Farewell to the homestay mother

To start off

June 21, Saturday

# Going to Sea to Watch Whales

A view of the whale

The school organized an outdoor activity today, which was to go to the sea to watch whales. The activity was arranged only in the morning, and in the afternoon there were free activities.

Before coming to Victoria, my father told me that the school would organize us to go to the sea to watch whales. After almost three months passed, today the expectation came true. I had never seen real whales, except on TV or in the pictures. I was expecting the activity today.

Because of excitement and not being familiar with the place to gather in, I had appointment with Jin Ye to get together at the bus stop in front of her house. I caught the bus at 8:37, and she got on it without wasting even one minute. The gather time was 9:30, but we got to the place before 9:00. It was early so we went to a souvenir store first, then arrived at the gathering spot 15 minutes before 9:30. We did not expect that we were the first two to get here.

After gathering, calling the roll, buying tickets and getting onto the boat, we started our wonderful journey of watching whales. The boat we took was a sight-seeing yacht, quite big, with two decks. The top deck was outdoor and the lower one had seats and windows with a small platform on head and tail respectively for us to see the view. I wanted to sit on the upper deck to appreciate the scenery from all directions, but we were quite behind in the queue, so we had to sit downstairs. The reception on the boat was very nice. They provided hot chocolate and coffee. The guide girl was very enthusiastic. She even taught us some ways to escape and open/close the door.

    The boat left the gulf at around 10:00. The vast ocean appeared in front. I was excited and went to the small platform on the head of the boat to take pictures, but even the pictures could not explain such a beautiful scene. The blue sky and the ocean integrated. The wind turned waves, and the sun sprayed on the ocean, making a lot of flashing pieces. Seagulls were singing not far, and many sea birds were swimming on the sea. They even submerged into the water, and suddenly came out, cute and smart. After a while, the boat stopped. The captain found some dolphins were not far from the boat. Too many people rushed to the platform, and I was ridden off to the edge without seeing total dolphins, but I saw them swim away after a roll. I felt very pitiful. When I came back to the cabin, I suddenly found my hands and feet frozen. In the sea wind, my hands felt dumb. When I was thinking about how to get warm, I saw many people around me were drinking hot chocolate. So I took one cup to warm myself. Even in the cabin, I leaned my head onto the window because the view was wonderful. This is my first time to see such beautiful scenery.

    The weather was extremely good today. The bright sun made the ocean even more magnificent, which put me in a good mood. I could not help running to the bow again, and saw several sea lions rolling. Their fat bodies were very lovely. I felt it harmonious and mysterious to see sea lions on the sea. Their flexible bodies matched the water and the blue sky, offering a speechless wonder. Soon the boat passed by an island, which was paradise for birds. It was an island composed of several huge rocks. A lot of sea birds settled here. We could see that the rock was full of birds. Many were swimming and playing near the island. No far there were more birds flying toward this island to join the big base of birds.

    Finally the boat stopped in front of the island. The guide girl came to tell us excitedly that a group of whales were swimming toward us. It was a big family with more than 20 whales. However, we should not scare them, so we had to keep a distance of over 1,000 meters. At the beginning we could not see the whales, but I was the first one to find them. Look! They were spraying water on the faraway surface of the ocean, and some were happily rolling, showing their fins. When they got closer, I could see the faint triangle fins, black and beautiful, flashing under the radiation of the sun. Because a group of whales were moving together, it was very attractive. They kept rolling and swimming, and our boat followed them. There were many boats and yachts like us nearby, focusing on this whale family. Although we were far from them, their tumbling actions deeply attracted me. From showing a sharp fin to turning a perfect triangle slowly, they submerged into the sea. After some time, they came up again slowly, and then down. Like this the whale family swam a lot around that little island until very far. Our boat was following them, as if to play with them. Although there was a certain distance, luckily we could see how they looked when they turned up, their white belly and the white spots around the eyes. This whale family should be killer whales, with beautiful black ridges, perfect ellipse patches around the eyes and white belly. They formed a nice landscape on the ocean. I was deeply attracted by these whales and always stood on the bow until I could not bear the wind any more.

Our boat came back after the whale family left. On the way back the captain dragged a piece of seaweed, maybe kelp. The head was of cylinder shape, very smooth, and after cutting it was hollow. There was a round ball, beneath which there was a big piece of kelp. The guide girl gave me a piece of kelp and told me that it could be eaten like that. I put it into the mouth to taste carefully and found it was good, slightly salty and crispy. The captain cut the cylinder kelp into small sections and put them onto the finger as rings. It was hollow and white.

We returned to the port with satisfaction and harvest. I had lunch with my friends and then went back home. After dinner I went with the homestay father to pick up cherries under the cherry tree in front of our house. Cherries turned to be more beautiful, red, bright and attractive under the sunset. But what attracted me more was the happy time picking up cherries with the homestay father, the beautiful scenery and the killer whale family on the ocean. The most attractive is the wonderful time in Canada. During these 100 days, I experienced a lot and gained a lot. Thanks to my homestay family and my teachers and fellow students in Shoreline Community Middle School. You care, encourage and support me during these days. I sincerely appreciate it!

June 29, Sunday

# Sea Fishing for the First Time

The homestay father is driving the yacht to the bay

To the sea

Today is Sunday. Usually I stay at home alone on Sundays. I was leaving soon so I planned to pack the things. However, this Sunday was special because the homestay family took me to fish on the sea. I was very excited because I had never gone fishing on the sea. The only time that I went to the sea was to watch the whales. I could not control my excitement thinking of the bright waves on the ocean and the blue sky.

We set off at 11:30. We had a brunch today because they got up quite late. The homestay mother asked me to bring anti-UV cream, a pair of socks and a towel. The cream was certainly for the strong sun on the sea, and socks for the shoes in case they get wet. And I put on waterproof shoes today. The towel was for cleaning the wet seat.

The homestay family has a small boat with four seats. The boat was prepared with two crab cages, several linen ropes and four fishing poles. The place where we went for fishing this time is Downken, where I had been to with the homestay mother. The father was dragging the boat by his truck, quite slow, so the sister took me to take a tour around.

The scene was great with mountains, water and people. Looked from far, two tall mountains formed a valley. The mountains were not super tall, but were covered with trees all over, dotted with several villas facing the sea. The villas were all very big, but there weren't many. Some mountains only had two or three villas. The place where we stopped was a fishing port, where a lot of boats berthed, including small yachts, sailing boats and big yachts, even small wooden boats and dragon boats. The water was transparent, and you could see the bottom. There were purple sea stars, red and grey crabs as big as three fists. There were many jellyfish and sea urchins spreading under water. I could only see so many marine benthos in aquariums in China. Even in aquariums the benthos would be different. The sea stars here were big and flat, lazily lying on the sand to take the sunbath. Crabs went out to the shore to take sunbath or stayed in water. The quantity of jellyfish was incredible. They were very different from what was seen in the aquarium. Here they are healthier, more active and free. They looked like scrabbled eggs with something yellow in the middle, and the edges were like clear of eggs. They had very long feet swaying along the water, very beautiful.

After the homestay father came, the parents started to arrange the crab cage, and Dannika and I went to the side to fish. I had never tried fishing in the ocean, so I felt super excited. But when Dannika got four, I did not even get one. I felt frustrated. Then the homestay parents called us to get onto the boat. What a pity it was!

The yacht went forward with the sound of engine, expanded, and we were farther and farther away from the shore, marching toward the deep ocean.

The jellyfish

The lovely sealion

Unfortunately, it started to rain a little, and then heavily. After a heavy rain for a long time, it stopped. Our boat stopped beside a sea lion island, which was composed of three rocks, not very big, but full of sea lions. Tens of sea lions perched on the island, sleeping lazily, or looking at the bottom of the sea or yawning. After we fixed our boat, several sea lions turned to us and looked at us with their eyes shining. Every time I saw sea lions, I got excited and this time I saw so many of different species. There are black and white, all white, black and grey, black, and white and yellow. All of them had shining eyes, very cute. Beside the mother sea lion there were six very lovely babies, slightly shaking. When they saw our boat stop, some went back to sleep, but still two stared at us. So lovely!

After the homestay father anchored, we started fishing. The sea lions were beside looking at us. The wind touched my face, which made me feel very good. It was cold on the sea, but it did not win over my excitement. The only pity was that it rained heavily again, so we had to fish in the rain, and did not get any fish. I had the chance to get one, but it escaped because of my lack of experience. It was a pity. Later due to the bad weather, we decided to go back. We said goodbye to the sea lions and returned.

Although we failed in fishing this time as expected, we ran across the lovely sea lions, experienced the test of wind and rain on the sea, and saw vigorous marine benthos. This is my last outdoor sport with my homestay family. It was unforgettable. I have learned a lot.

The exciting fishing on the sea

Dannika and I

# Acknowledgments

I have never considered that I had the honor of being a member of Xinghai Experimental Middle School; I have never considered that I can travel far away across the sea and go to Canada for study; I have never considered that I would record and publish all that I saw and heard during my study; I have never considered that my short experience will make such a big difference to me, my family, my teachers and friends...

I would like to extend my sincere gratitude to all the people who care about me.

I would like to extend my gratitude to Xinghai Experimental Middle School. If my school hadn't given me such a chance to study abroad, I would never go to such a beautiful city Victoria, Canada and meet so many strangers, not to mention the completion of the first book in my life.

Besides the school, I would like to express my gratitude to the most important people in my life—my parents. I can still remember that when the school issued the notice of studying abroad for everybody to apply for voluntarily, I put it on the table drawer without even looking at it. I have never thought that I could study abroad, because it may be impossible for me to go abroad for so long a time, I would be left behind in study very soon, I have never traveled alone, the study may cost so much money and ...when I got home after school, I just told this to my mother casually; I said that I didn't want to go and my mother also agreed on my choice. However, when I talked about this with my father casually at breakfast on the second day, he was so delighted to say that I should go and grasp this valuable chance. Just because of the encouragement, support and urge from my father, I would go to that beautiful country and write this book, which is very important to me. From the day we made the decision to the day I returned, my parents gave me so much intensive care; they considered the decision again and again and were so worried before my leaving. When I lived in another country, I felt that they were always with me. They were happier when I was happy; they were more anxious when I was sick... I also want to express my gratitude to my other family members. Neither my maternal grandmother nor my grandfather and grandmother were against my studying abroad for three and a half months. My grandfather even proposed to accompany me studying in Canada at his own expenses. Before leaving, my grandmother packed a bag of native soil in my bag to prevent me from "climate sickness"; when I finished the study and came back, I also packed a bag of Victoria soil for reminding me of the "beautiful memory".

I would like to extend my gratitude to the teachers in Xinghai Experimental Middle School. Our school arranged two teachers specially—Teacher Yang of Math and Teacher Xie of Chinese to tutor the students to study abroad courses in Term 2, Junior 1, in case we would fall behind. The Math teacher Yang Yunju who led us study abroad and the Chinese teacher Teacher Xie, are very experienced teachers. They conducted a comprehensive tutoring to us, including doing exercises, highlighting the vocabularies and reciting the ancient poetry in the month before we went abroad, so that we can keep pace with everyone after we came back. Besides these courses, some other minor subjects, including History, Biology and Geography, were also arranged in the afternoon, thus I always couldn't attend all of the courses. I hereby would like to thank all the teachers for their understanding.

But why do I write this book? Just because Liao Jianglong (a senior student once went to study in Canada and wrote a book successfully) wrote a book called *Chance Meeting in Canada*. After reading his book, I was deeply inspired and full of expectation towards Canada. Thus, I was also determined to write a diary book about what I saw, heard and felt. Although I once thought of giving up, every time I wanted to give up, I would always remind myself that since Liao Jianglong could complete such a book in Junior 1, why I, another student of Xinghai Junior 1, cannot persist in this work! Thus, I would like to thank this stranger whom I have never met; he is the person inspiring me to get the achievements today finally.

Surely, I would also like to express my gratitude to my classmates in Class 10, Junior 1. Thank you for your message book. Every time I missed the school, teachers and you, I would open this book and feel no longer lonely. Besides the classmates in Class 10, Junior 1, I also want to extend my gratitude to the students studying in Canada together with me, especially Zhang Tao, Ru Yunyi and Jin Ye. They accompanied me on spending so many happy weekends that I could have such wonderful and sincere friendship in Canada. Your names appeared in most parts of my diaries. Evert time I read my diaries again and again, I could always recall the happy time with you in my mind. Although we have scarcely seen each other again after we came back, our Shoreline group is still there and the memory about the days we spent together is still there.

When I was in Victoria, Canada, besides the friends getting together and the happy studying life, I also tried to have different experience with my homestay family. Either the experience of walking the dog with Zhao Tao's homestay family or the camping, dinner party and fishing excursion, etc. with my homestay family make my studying full of happiness. I surely also want to thank the homestay family for their understanding, as well as the different experience they brought to me. Every time I wanted to invite the friends to sleep over, they all gladly assented; likewise, they never said too much when I visited my friends. When I got sick, they accompanied me and took care of me carefully. Every time I had myself in the room alone, they asked me to go out and enjoy the happy family time. I really should thank my considerate and careful homestay family. Oh, yes: the Labrador Cooper; I was scared of animals, especially big dogs, but it is amazing that I have been friend with Cooper in Victoria and I cannot have the words to express this wonderful feeling.

I had an enjoyable school life while studying in Canada. I want to show my gratitude to Shoreline Middle School, every teacher and classmate in this school. Their new and interesting teaching mode made me very happy in and after school every day. The new activities held by them made me full of curiosity and excitement towards the school; the chatting with classmates and teachers between classes also made me so satisfied. Besides that, I still want to express my gratitude to a person in Canada, Teacher Liu who is in charge of our project in Canada. He cared about every student's life in school and homestay family. He is gentle, friendly and affable. He is the person helping us enjoy a safe, happy and full time in Victoria.

After I returned from Canada, I am busy with taking part in various continuation classes for my lessons. My father often helped me revise my diaries and edit the pictures, etc. in his spare time. He even asked Uncle Xiaoma to polish my articles, found a translator to translate partial of the book into English and mailed to my homestay family. The publication of my studying experience cannot be realized without my father and all the people caring about me. This kind of help makes me feel so happy and satisfied to complete a book. It is more than a book; in fact, it is a deep sense of family love. I would also like to thank Auntie Xiaogu, who gave me a camera to record the local conditions and customs in Canada. I would still thank the uncle, sister, and maternal uncle… They gave me confidence not to feel lonely in the alien country.

At last, I would extend my gratitude to Soochow University Press, who is willing to publish my book. Without their help, my book would not come out and I could not share my happy life with more people.

Qin Yiwen
October 2014 in Suzhou

**Expression of unforgettable experience**

**Gratitude for my home stay family, my dear father and mother**

**For the teachers, classmates and friends caring and helping me…**